The Arena of Broken Soul's

Copyright © [2025] by D McCormick

All rights reserved.

No part of this publication may be reproduced, distributed, or transmitted in any form or by any means, including photocopying, recording, or other electronic or mechanical methods, without the prior written permission of the publisher, except as permitted by U.S. copyright law. For permission requests, contact DMcCormick-author@mail.com.

The story, all names, characters, and incidents portrayed in this production are fictitious. No identification with actual persons (living or deceased), places, buildings, and products is intended or should be inferred.

"Cover designed by Getcovers."

Paperback ISBN: 978-1-0686799-3-3
E-book ISBN: 978-1-0686799-8-8

To Chelsea Thanks for the help and support .

CHAPTER 1

Tension in the Control Room

My fingers dug into the armrest of my chair, each grip tightening progressively until my knuckles turned a ghostly white, as if all the blood had drained from them under the pressure. I anxiously scanned the wall of monitors in the dimly lit control room, where the soft glow emanating from the screens cast eerie, dancing shadows on the walls. It felt as if the room itself was alive, pulsing with the energy of the operation unfolding before me. Beads of sweat formed along my hairline despite the cool, filtered air humming from the vents above, and they trickled down my temples in tiny rivulets. The rhythmic thudding of my heart echoed in my ears, each beat resonating as forcefully as a bass drum, creating a relentless symphony of tension and anticipation. My focus was intensely trained on Lancaster and Keith below, their figures displayed in high definition on the screens before me. Their expressions were fierce and focused, eyes narrowed into slits and brows furrowed in concentration, as they navigated the maze-like training ground with precision and intent. This was their maiden exercise as a team, a pivotal moment of independence now that my constant supervision was no longer their safety net. This was their moment to showcase their skills, to demonstrate beyond doubt that they could operate in harmony and seamlessly without leaning on my directives or guidance.

The mission laid before them was clear-cut: Osaki and Danielle were their designated targets, two figures as elusive as shadows in the night, tasked to be neutralised with a single, precise taser shot. The stakes couldn't have been higher—failure was not an option, for it could spell a dire, potentially irreversible fate for them both.

The air was thick with tension, almost palpable, as Lancaster and Keith silently stalked their targets, every muscle in their bodies taut and ready, coiled like springs under pressure. Adrenaline surged through their veins, its fiery rush heightening their senses in preparation for the imminent showdown. It was a high-stakes game of cat and mouse, a strategic battle of wits and reflexes, where both hunters and hunted understood the gravity of the situation and that only one side would emerge victorious.

The first critical mistake they made was their decision to split up. Rather than moving as a cohesive force, they dispersed like a pack of ravenous wolves chasing down separate, elusive prey. Each team member broke away to follow their own path, abandoning any semblance of cooperative strategy. I could feel the tension surging within me; my fists clenched tightly as I fought the urge to bark orders over the comms system. The frustration built steadily as I witnessed their progress deteriorate—what once could have been a symphony of coordinated movement was now a disjointed scramble, reminiscent of an intricate puzzle with pieces that refused to align.

Slowly, almost imperceptibly, the scattered figures began to converge upon a single, focal area of the sprawling training ground. Their footsteps pounded relentlessly on the gravel pathway, creating a rhythmic thudding that resonated ominously in the charged atmosphere. Heavy breathing punctuated the silence at intervals, each exhale intensifying the palpable tension that hovered around them. It was as if we were witnessing the dramatic crescendo of an unfolding theatrical drama, where every element—the stakes, the setting, the pressure of the mission—heightened and interwove to amplify the gravity of our situation.

Then, in a sudden break from the mounting silence, Keith's voice erupted through the comms system, his words crackling with electrifying excitement. "Control, I have visual contact and am closing in for capture," he announced, his tone alive with a surge of adrenaline. It was immediately apparent that his communication was intended not just to relay information, but also to impress Lancaster, whose approval he so evidently sought. Further clarifying his intentions, he continued: "I confirm hostile presence, Danielle has been sighted in sector 5B, and I am currently in pursuit." No sooner had these words filled the air than the transmission abruptly cut off, leaving behind a sudden void and a lingering, tense atmosphere.

Instantly, my gaze darted to the array of monitoring equipment, frantically scanning the blurred, grainy images on the screen for any sign of Keith's whereabouts. Amid the static and shadowed visuals, I could discern the outline of his figure sprinting determinedly after a mysterious, elusive form. His resolute strides were narrowing the distance with every passing second, even as the quality of the image betrayed the urgency and chaos of our field situation. At that moment, Gudmundur's voice shattered the silence from the open doorway—a swift, commanding utterance that reverberated like the strike of a whip. "He isn't waiting for backup," he observed, his tone a mix of concern and resignation.

I found myself in reluctant agreement. "Doesn't look like it," I replied, my voice strained from the relentless intensity of our training exercise. The pressure of the mission was evident not just in my voice, but in the persistent trickle of sweat that dampened my forehead, mirrored by the continuous hum of electronic equipment and the heavy, laboured breathing that filled the room. "I think they're trying to prove themselves as individuals instead of working together as a team. It's a risky move."

Meanwhile, our attention remained fixated on the screens, which exhibited a labyrinth of corridors interwoven with simulated danger.

Through the labyrinthine digital mazes, we meticulously tracked our team as they navigated the complexities of the mission scenario, weaving through the intricacies with a practiced grace. In one of the intersecting corridors, I caught sight of Lancaster, crouched low and expertly blending into the shadows, his figure barely discernible. His presence served as a silent yet powerful reminder that at least one member of the team was listening intently to our communications, formulating and refining a tactical plan with every piece of information. Poised and prepared, much like a seasoned predator on the hunt, he tensed his muscles, ready to spring an ambush on his intended target—a skill perfected through numerous trials and tribulations. Just as I was about to share my observations with Gudmundur, he preempted me and spoke first. His deep, resonant voice sliced through the room's thick tension like a knife through butter. "Just as I suspected," he declared, a knowing smirk playing on his lips as he settled into the seat beside me. His fingers moved with practiced ease, deftly adjusting the controls. My curiosity was piqued, and I turned to him, one eyebrow elegantly raised in a silent inquiry. Anticipating my unspoken question, he continued with a hint of amusement, "Osaki is a master of trickery, after all."

Confusion began to cloud my mind at his words, much like a dense fog rolling in to obscure the clarity of my thoughts. Before I could articulate my need for clarification, he elaborated further, his tone patient and slightly conspiratorial. "She's a kitsune, remember? Illusions are her specialty." His words lingered in the air, taking a moment to register fully in my mind. As we continued to watch the blurred figure—a silhouette shimmering as if viewed through heat waves—turn the corner and slip stealthily down the dimly lit corridor where Lancaster lay in wait, everything suddenly clicked into place. The pieces of the puzzle, once scattered and fragmented, finally aligned to form a complete and coherent picture, revealing the intricate web of deception that Osaki wove with her mastery of illusions.

***

Keith's heart thundered in his chest, a rapid and erratic drumbeat that reverberated like a relentless storm, as he sprinted with all his might after Osaki's elusive shadow. The figure moved with an infuriating grace and speed, taunting him with every step, always remaining just out of his grasp, like a phantom engaged in a cruel game of cat and mouse. It was a chase that seemed eternal, a relentless pursuit through the dimly lit corridors, where shadows twisted and turned, mocking his every effort.

With a surge of determination fuelled by adrenaline, Keith pushed himself even harder, his breath escaping his lips in ragged, uneven gasps. Each inhale was like a fiery brand searing his lungs, fuelling his resolve as he strained to close the ever-narrowing gap between them. His legs pumped like relentless pistons, muscles straining with every stride, as he willed himself with sheer force of will to catch up to Osaki. But just as he was within reach, fingertips almost brushing the edge of a phantom coat, the figure vanished as if into thin air, leaving behind only the faint trace of musky cologne and the haunting echo of mocking laughter that reverberated through the hallway, seeming to emanate from all directions at once.

Confused and disoriented by the sudden disappearance, Keith slowed his pace, his footsteps faltering as he desperately tried to catch his breath, wiping the sweat from his brow with the back of his trembling hand. His mind was a whirlwind of thoughts, battling to regain composure, but before he could fully orient himself, a sudden, jarring shot pierced the air behind him with a loud pop, the sharp report reverberating off the walls like a thunderclap. The acrid smell of ozone assaulted his nostrils, a scent that clawed mercilessly at his senses, causing a visceral fear to grip his chest with the unyielding strength of a vice.

In an instinctive reaction driven by sheer survival instincts, Keith spun around with a rapid, almost desperate motion. His heart thundered violently within his chest, each beat echoing the surge of adrenaline that coursed through his veins with relentless intensity. This raw energy propelled him to raise his gun with a sense of urgency that bordered on panic. With a wild, uncontrolled flurry, he fired toward the direction from which the gunshot had reverberated, the sound still ringing in his ears. His hands, trembling with a volatile mix of fear and desperation, struggled to maintain their grip as each bullet left the chamber in a frantic bid to claw back some semblance of control over the chaos that was unfolding around him in a dizzying spiral.

Then, in a moment that seemed to stretch into eternity, Keith's eyes caught sight of Lancaster. The man was staggering forward, each step more unsteady than the last, as if he were a puppet with strings cut, before finally collapsing to the ground with a heavy thud. His hands clutched desperately at his side, and a grimace of pain was etched deeply across his features. It was a contorted, agonised expression that communicated more than words ever could—a silent scream of suffering and betrayal. It was then that the chilling realisation crashed over Keith like a tidal wave, cold and unrelenting—a brutal recognition that he had been ensnared in their cunning ruse. The truth, sharp and undeniable, pierced through his mind, bringing with it a flood of dread. His breath hitched in his throat, his lungs constricting as if bound by iron chains, the weight of his impulsive error pressing down upon him with a crushing, inescapable force. He was left to grapple with the enormity of what had just transpired, struggling to comprehend the layers of deception that had been skilfully woven around him. As the taser bullets that Lancaster had fired struck him, their impact was a cruel punctuation to the tragic mistake he had made, each jolt a biting reminder of his own hubris.

The trap had been deceptively simple, a mental illusion that should have been easily dismissed by two seasoned operatives who had seen and endured countless dangers before. Yet, instead of collaborating to vanquish their foes with the precision and unity expected of their training, they succumbed to the alluring yet treacherous path of rivalry. Isolating themselves in a misguided attempt to outshine each other, they had played right into the enemy's hands. Now, they lay writhing and jerking under the relentless assault of crackling taser rounds, each convulsion a testament to their shared failure. The air hummed with a charged energy, a constant, oppressive reminder of their dire predicament, as they struggled for liberation in vain. It was a grim tableau of human folly and the inescapable consequences of pride, a scene that would haunt their memories long after the pain had faded.

***

As I meticulously observed the chaotic scene unfolding on the array of monitors spread before me, my eyebrows knitted together in a mixture of frustration and disbelief. Each screen offered a different angle, yet all depicted the same inexplicable debacle.

Beside me, Gudmundur struggled unsuccessfully to contain his amusement at the extraordinary scene that was unfolding before our very eyes. Despite his best efforts to maintain a serious demeanour, I could clearly see the subtle tug at the corners of his lips, a silent giveaway of the amusement he was feeling. "This is not a joke," I said, my voice rising in intensity and a hint of frustration creeping in as my patience began to wear thin. "Both of them have accumulated years of experience working within team environments, thriving in collaborative settings, so why on earth did they fail this time? Am I missing something crucial here?" My voice was edged with a sharpness that matched the tension of the situation, as I tried to uphold a semblance of professionalism amidst the chaos and confusion that swirled around us—a chaos that seemed to defy all known logic and reason, leaving us grasping for explanations.

"Jess," Gudmundur began, his tone rich with a blend of genuine concern and a wry amusement that danced in the depths of his deep blue eyes. Those eyes, so penetrating and expressive, seemed to carry both an understanding of my internal turmoil and a hint of being mildly entertained by the unfolding events. His voice, calm and soothing as though specifically designed to mollify my fraying nerves, resonated with a deliberate gentleness as he continued, "It's going to take time for Lancaster to adjust to everything." He paused, allowing his words to hang in the air like a promise of eventual clarity, before elaborating on the monumental shift Lancaster had experienced. "You must remember," he said slowly, "that Lancaster transitioned from a world where he not only understood his place but also grasped how every little cog in the machine of his reality operated, to one where his entire worldview has been flipped upside down. Just weeks ago, he was blissfully unaware of anything beyond the mundane—unaware even of the existence of the paranormal." His explanation curled further into the surreal, "For Lancaster, vampires were nothing more than glittering creatures designed for fun in movies and dragons merely fantastical beings confined to the faded pages of fairy tale books. He grew up taught that magic was mere nonsense, the kind of absurdity relegated to fantasy and idle daydreams. And yet, here he is—not locked away in a mental facility, which in itself is nothing short of astounding—but instead, working with tireless determination, delving into realms he'd never even contemplated existed. His remarkable intuition, despite being nascent in this shadowed world, has made him a valuable asset on our team. Fresh eyes, a willingness to learn, and the hard-learned lessons from his recent upheaval—these qualities are exactly what we need."

I let his words settle over me, heavy and inescapable, as a growing frustration churned inside me. I could see where his reasoning was coming from, yet there was an undercurrent that still irked me deeply. "Fine," I replied, striving to keep my tone even despite the storm rising within, "I grasp the reasoning behind Lancaster's actions. However, Kieth should know better. He's been around long enough to not only understand the intricate workings of the agency but also to have accumulated ample experience dealing with the unpredictable paranormal community. Moreover, his personal connections with Danielle and Osaki should have served as a forewarning; he should have anticipated that something like this would eventually transpire." As I spoke these words, I felt my fingers clench into tight fists at my sides—a silent testament to the disbelief and anger bubbling beneath my calm façade. How could Kieth, with all his experience, have been so glaringly naive?

Before I could further mull over my discontent, Gudmundur's deep, resonant laughter suddenly filled the sterile control room. The sound reverberated off the walls, infusing the space with an energy that was at once both infectious and eerily unsettling. "Jess, I would have thought that you, of all people, would understand why he acted the way he did," he said, the timbre of his voice intensifying the perplexity swirling within me. The unexpected outburst left me caught between confusion and surprise.

My mind was a whirlwind of thoughts, desperately trying to untangle the web of confusion that surrounded this baffling situation. "Enlighten me then," I demanded, my voice now carrying a sharp edge of frustration that was quickly turning into a simmering anger, "because it's obvious I don't understand it at all." As I waited for his explanation, the atmosphere grew dense with tension, each passing second stretching into what felt like an eternity filled with unspoken questions and the undercurrent of burgeoning conflict.

"Keith is trying to prove himself," he began, his tone revealing a depth of understanding that I had not anticipated. "Both of them feel overwhelmed, like they're in way over their heads. But you have to remember, Keith has transitioned from a mere lab technician to taking on the role of a liaison with the human police force. And now, he's been entrusted with leading his own strike team for the raids targeting those facilities that are conducting unethical experiments. On top of all that, he's also a part of this high-profile task force that's been making significant strides and attracting a lot of attention. He's working hard to demonstrate that the faith you placed in him wasn't misplaced." The air seemed to vibrate with tension as his words lingered, shedding light on the deeper motivations driving Keith's actions.

I found myself at a loss for words, unsure how to process this new perspective. The enormity of the situation weighed heavily on my shoulders, but before I could articulate my concerns, he continued with unwavering determination. "Think about all of that," he urged me, his voice compelling me to consider the broader context. "You're setting them up against two highly skilled strike team leaders. It's no surprise they struggled to hold their ground. Kitsune are notoriously elusive and notoriously difficult to capture. Even I would find it challenging to go head-to-head with Osaki. So let's not be too harsh on Keith and Lancaster."

His words lingered heavily in the air, much like a dense fog that refuses to dissipate, serving as a palpable reminder of the formidable and daunting task looming ahead of our team. They underscored the intricate complexity of the challenges we were about to face, a reality that was becoming increasingly difficult to ignore. Despite my best efforts to maintain confidence, I couldn't shake the gnawing feeling that he was right, that perhaps my expectations were not only high but indeed unreasonable.

Every time I closed my eyes, I found myself involuntarily transported back to the ominous basement, the memory as vivid as if it were playing out before me once again. The stench of blood and sweat seemed to cling to my consciousness, an ever-present reminder of the harrowing events that had transpired. It was a haunting experience I was determined to never allow to happen again. With unwavering resolve, I knew I had to ensure that our team would be robust, resilient, and ready to face any situation that might arise, no matter how dire.

Just as my thoughts reached a crescendo, the door to the control room swung open with a decisive thud, abruptly pulling me back to the present.

"Why did you have to have all the fun?" Danielle's voice echoed through the room, carrying with it a subtle hint of frustration. Yet, beneath that lay a teasing undertone, suggesting she wasn't entirely serious. She entered the room with a lively bounce in her step, closely followed by Osaki. Both of them wore wide, mischievous grins that seemed to stretch from ear to ear, reminiscent of the Cheshire Cat from Alice in Wonderland. Their expressions suggested that they were in on some delightful secret that the rest of us were not privy to.

"You can't deny it was entertaining to watch," Osaki stated, her voice filled with a mischievous twinkle as she spoke. Her eyes sparkled with the kind of joy that comes from knowing something others don't. As they both settled into their seats, I couldn't help but ponder whether they truly grasped the seriousness of our mission and the potential dangers we faced. However, for the moment, I decided to push those heavy thoughts aside and immerse myself in their playful banter, which was as infectious as it was lighthearted.

"Your tactics were a bit ruthless," I said to Osaki with a smirk, doing my best to mask how genuinely impressed I was by her strategic skills. There was a fine line between admiration and intimidation, and I didn't want to tip my hand too soon.

she chuckled in response, a sound that was both warm and slightly wicked. "It's important to push them to their limits," she replied, her tone carrying a hint of wisdom. "That's the only way they'll improve and learn to work together as a cohesive team."

Danielle nodded in agreement, her expression turning serious for a brief moment, capturing the gravity of the discussion. "I have to side with Osaki on this one," she said with genuine earnestness, her voice carrying the weight of her conviction. "They had been struggling with teamwork, and it was absolutely crucial to drive the point home." Her eyes softened as she spoke, reflecting a deep understanding of the larger, more intricate picture, and I realised then that beneath their playful demeanour lay a profound commitment to our overarching goals.

As they turned to face me, a visible determination in their eyes burned with an unspoken challenge. In that moment, I felt the full weight of their expectations bearing down on me, along with the intensity of the rigorous training my team and I had undergone. However, I refused to back down or show any signs of weakness or hesitation.

I stood tall, my gaze meeting theirs with a determined energy that matched their intensity. These women demanded nothing less than complete dedication, and I was more than ready to deliver. "You're right," I stated with confidence, my voice ringing with resolve. "Their ability to function as a cohesive unit will be absolutely crucial for our future missions, and we cannot afford any lapses in teamwork."

Turning to each woman in turn, I hoped that their extensive experience and deep well of knowledge would provide valuable guidance and insight for my own team. Swallowing my pride, I mustered up the courage to ask, "Would you both be available for a few more drills with my team today?" My goal was clear: to tap into their expertise, harnessing it to enhance our own skills and improve our performance.

Danielle's initially rigid posture gradually softened as she mulled over my request with careful consideration. "Currently, I don't have any active assignments, so I was planning on conducting some intensive drills with my own team," she explained, her voice thoughtful and reflective. "However, collaborating with others could introduce new dynamics to our training sessions," she added, casting a glance towards Osaki, who nodded in agreement, acknowledging the potential benefits. "What do you think, Osaki? Perhaps we can demonstrate to this new team how we truly excel," she suggested with a hint of challenge. A palpable sense of camaraderie and mutual respect filled the room, as we all prepared to confront the upcoming challenges together, united by our shared ambition to succeed. Yet, as Osaki's eyes glittered with a mischievous sparkle, a sudden chill crept down my spine. What exactly had I just enlisted my team into? Only the unfolding of time would reveal the answer.

Gudmundur's sharp, observant gaze had been tracking the conversation in silence, but now he leaned forward, cutting through my wandering thoughts. "It appears we might need to consider relocating to a larger venue if our plan is to include three entire teams in the training," he suggested, his mind already working on the logistics. "What do you have in mind?" I asked, intrigued by what he might propose. "I envision a capture the flag battle Royale scenario, pitting team against team. The last team standing with all the flags will be crowned the victor!" Gudmundur announced with enthusiasm, his idea sparking excitement.

At that precise moment, Keith and Lancaster stumbled awkwardly into the bustling control room, each one leaning heavily on the other for much-needed support to maintain their shaky balance. Their evident exhaustion was unmistakable, with their clothes rumpled and their faces betraying the signs of a long, hard-fought day. However, despite their bedraggled appearance and apparent fatigue, I couldn't resist the golden opportunity to tease them about their recent and rather unfortunate defeat. "Do you think you two can pull yourselves together just enough to function as a cohesive and formidable team? Perhaps you can even show these two just how proficient we truly are," I challenged with a mischievous glint in my eye, my tone playful yet encouraging.

Lancaster's face immediately transformed into a mask of steely determination as he straightened his posture, his shoulders squared with resolve. "I won't allow us to face humiliation like that again. I made an error in judgment, but I vow not to let it happen a second time," he declared with a firm and unwavering resolve that seemed to burn brightly within him. His determination was infectious, quickly spreading through the room and infusing the air with an electrifying atmosphere of fierce competition and renewed energy.

The sting of the sudden loss appeared to ignite a fierce determination within him, evident in the way his jaw set resolutely and his eyes narrowed with focus. Keith, on his part, simply nodded in agreement with Lancaster's bold declaration of war, but his unwavering stance and the fire in his eyes spoke volumes more than words could convey. "Alright, let's split up and gather our respective teams. Gudmundur will send a message to all of you with the location, and we will reconvene there in exactly one hour," i instructed, voice authoritative and commanding.

As if propelled by an invisible force, everyone hurried out of the control room as if their very lives depended on it, leaving only me and Gudmundur behind, watching them go with mixed emotions. I couldn't help but feel a surge of excitement rising in my chest at the prospect of what lay ahead. "You sure know how to light a fire under their feet, dragon boy. This is going to be one wild ride," I mused aloud, a small chuckle escaping my lips as I finished speaking, the anticipation bubbling within me.

"I assure you, Jessica, they won't know what hit them," Gudmundur replied with a confidence that was both unwavering and reassuring, his voice carrying a steady, calming quality that seemed to dissolve any lingering doubts. "Now, if you don't mind, I have some arrangements to make. Meet me in the lobby in 30 minutes; I'll gather the rest of the team there as well," he added, his tone brooking no argument and leaving no room for doubt or hesitation. As he strode purposefully out of the room, his steps filled with determination and focus, I couldn't help but feel a tumultuous mix of nerves and anticipation for what was to come. The stakes were undeniably high, and the challenge ahead promised to test every one of us to our limits.

Gudmundur seemed to have everything in hand, so I shrugged and let him get on with it, trusting in his experience and the meticulous planning that helped bring us this far. With half an hour of free time on my hands, I made a beeline for my dorm room, eager to seize a moment of respite before the impending storm. The familiar hallway seemed to stretch on forever, each step echoing a sense of urgency as I hurriedly shuffled towards my destination. Once inside, I quickly shed my uncomfortable clothes, opting for something more suitable—something that would make me feel confident and ready for whatever lay ahead. As the scent of freshly brewed coffee filled the air, I took a moment to savour the aroma, the promise of its energising powers a comforting thought. I poured myself a cup of the dark, rich liquid, knowing I would need every ounce of its invigorating strength to bolster me for whatever Gudmundur had planned.

***

With adrenaline coursing through my veins at an exhilarating pace, I was the first to dramatically burst into the expansive lobby. My heart thudded rapidly in my chest as I braced myself to confront whatever formidable challenges awaited us in the day ahead. In anticipation of the potential physical demands that might be placed upon me, I had carefully chosen my attire: loose-fitting, lightweight jeans that allowed for ease of movement, a simple yet practical black tee, and a pair of tactical boots that were robust and sturdy, capable of enduring any terrain we might encounter. As I stood there, poised and waiting for my team members to join me, I took a deliberate sip from my steaming travel mug filled with rich, aromatic coffee. With the uncertainty of what the day held looming over us, I realised that I would need every ounce of caffeine I could consume to power through the tasks ahead. Just at that moment, the rest of my team began to saunter into the lobby, their energy almost tangible and electric as they geared up for our upcoming training exercise. As they approached,

I could distinctly hear Lancaster and Keith animatedly recounting their previous defeat at the hands of Osaki and Danielle. Their voices were filled with a determined resolve and a competitive spirit that seemed to electrify the air around them. The defeat clearly weighed heavily on their minds, and they were intent on ensuring they would not be outsmarted by the same tricks again. Their voices reverberated with an unwavering sense of determination and competitiveness as they mentally prepared themselves for whatever challenges lay ahead, ready to tackle any obstacle that might come our way.

"If you had worked as a team, you probably wouldn't have fallen for such an obvious trap," Abigail's voice rang out, a playful melody that danced on the edge of her words. Her tone was light and teasing, yet it carried a hint of wisdom earned through experience. She flashed them a toothy grin, her mischievous eyes sparkling with amusement at her own joke. Keith, ever the good sport, laughed easily at her comment, his laughter mingling with the atmosphere of camaraderie. Lancaster, however, was not as at ease. His face turned a shade paler, a response I couldn't blame him for. After all, it's not every day that you get a toothy smile from a vampire who could break you in half and drain you of blood before you even realised what was happening. After a nervous shudder, he managed to return her smile, though it was tinged with unease and a hint of dread at the thought of her true capabilities.

Suppressing a giggle, I took a moment to observe my team as they interacted with each other. Each one of them was so different, bringing their own set of unique experiences, perspectives, and quirks to the group. It was fascinating to watch the dynamic unfold, like a complex puzzle coming together in unexpected ways.

As the group moved closer together, Mini's vibrant voice rang out with her signature energy, always full of enthusiasm and an infectious zest for life that seemed to brighten the mood of everyone in her vicinity. Her words danced with excitement as she said, "So Jess, are you going to brief us on this training exercise?" Her eyes twinkled with a playful hint of amusement, reflecting her long-standing position on the team. Mini was not just any member; she was an empathic mage who had been with us since that fateful day when Lyn and I were rescued from the cave, and over the years, our shared experiences had forged a deep and meaningful friendship.

I paused for a moment, taking a deep, steadying breath, feeling the weight of the responsibility that lay upon my shoulders. "Yes," I responded with resolute firmness, "We are about to engage in a battle Royale contest of capture the flag, pitted against the teams led by Osaki and Danielle. Beyond that, I'm as much in the dark as all of you are." It was Gudmundur who had conceived the idea for this training exercise and was now in charge of orchestrating the entire setup.

Right on cue, the grand doors to the expansive, marble-floored lobby swung open with a decisive motion, as if propelled by an unseen force. Gudmundur entered, cutting a striking figure with an expression of intense focus and determination etched deeply into his features. The sharp contours of his jaw were set with unwavering resolve, and his piercing eyes intently scanned the room, methodically assessing each member of our assembled group.

"Excellent," he declared briskly, his voice imbued with a sense of urgency and authority that demanded immediate attention. "You're all present. We don't have the luxury of time on our side, so let's move swiftly." With a swift and commanding gesture, he beckoned us to follow him out into the sprawling parking lot. There, waiting in an impressive display of readiness, stood two massive Ballistic Armoured Tactical Transports (BATTs), their imposing presence heralding the adventure that was about to commence.

These vehicles were formidable, bristling with an array of weaponry and reinforced with thick layers of metal plating, prepared to withstand any potential threat that might arise. Their sleek, almost deceptive design belied their true purpose, as they appeared at first glance to be nothing more than everyday off-road vehicles. Yet, to the discerning eye, it was unmistakably clear that these were fully functioning tactical beasts—machines engineered to handle any perilous situation we might encounter.

My jaw dropped in disbelief as I stood rooted to the spot, staring at the sleek, black vehicles before us. The BATTs were unlike anything I had ever laid eyes on before. Gudmundur's sly smile only served to deepen my curiosity and intrigue. "Where did you get these?" I couldn't help but blurt out, my voice tinged with awe.

Gudmundur simply motioned towards the rear doors of both vehicles, his eyes twinkling with amusement and perhaps a hint of mischief. "Oh, these I just borrowed from an acquaintance," he replied, his tone casual yet enigmatic. "He also provided drivers for us so we can discuss strategies on our way to a training ground I've managed to secure." I nodded, still absorbing the marvel of the high-tech machines before me. As we split into groups and climbed into our designated transport, I was taken aback by the interior. On one side, a comfortable bench seat was thoughtfully arranged for us to sit on during the journey. However, what truly captured my attention was the wall of tactical equipment mounted on the opposite side. As we settled in, a large screen descended from above, seamlessly connecting us via video communication to the other transport.

I glanced over at Abigail, who had been assigned to ride alongside me for this intriguing journey. us, she let out a soft chuckle, her eyes twinkling with a mix of amusement and curiosity. With a playful shake of her head, she muttered under her breath, "Dragons and their toys," her tone filled with bemusement at the extravagant spectacle before us. It was evident from her expression that the journey ahead promised to be just as extraordinary and unpredictable as the fantastical vehicles that were set to carry us to our destination.

Abby and I took a moment to soak in the impressive array of advanced equipment surrounding us, each piece gleaming under the lights like treasures in a dragon's hoard. "Why would a dragon need all this?" I inquired, gesturing with curiosity towards the assortment of shiny gadgets and imposing weapons on display, each one more sophisticated than the last.

Abby chuckled again, her eyes sparkling with a mischievous glint that suggested she relished the mystery. "Dragons love to show off," she replied with a knowing smile. "If something is new or valuable, they just have to have it, as if to prove their superiority or indulge their whims."

Suppressing a giggle at her insight, I nodded in agreement, waiting patiently for everyone to settle into their seats. We were about to embark on an exercise with our team, an experience that promised to test both our skills and our nerves. As the engine roared to life with a powerful growl, I took a deep, steadying breath, focusing intently on projecting an image of seriousness and determination.

Once we were en route to our destination, the voice of Gudmundur crackled through the video communication system, demanding our full attention. "Listen up," he commanded, his tone firm and authoritative, ensuring that no one would miss his instructions. "The drill is fairly straightforward - it's a 3-team capture-the-flag exercise. The first team to successfully capture both other teams' flags while defending their own will be declared the winner." He proceeded to provide us with a quick but comprehensive rundown of the rules, ensuring everyone was on the same page before signing off.

My heart was pounding with anticipation, a relentless surge of adrenaline coursing through my veins as we sped towards our target destination. The engine's vibrations were like a living pulse, echoing through my body as our vehicle raced through the bustling city streets. Each passing moment brought us closer to the challenge that awaited, and though it took a mere 25 minutes to reach our goal, the journey stretched out like an eternity, every second laden with the weight of expectation and excitement that danced in the air.

As we finally came to a gradual halt, I eagerly surveyed our surroundings. We had arrived at an abandoned industrial area, an ideal setting for our training mission. Stepping out of the vehicle, I felt a thrill race through me at the prospect of what lay ahead. Gudmundur greeted me with an uncharacteristic toothy grin, his excitement practically tangible in the air.

"I've managed to secure access to this old industrial complex," he announced with pride, gesturing expansively towards the imposing structures that loomed around us. The massive buildings rose like ancient sentinels, casting long shadows over the desolate landscape. A dense wooded area surrounded the entire complex, adding an air of mystery and seclusion. Best of all, there wasn't a single soul in sight, ensuring that our operation would remain unnoticed and undisturbed.

Abby's earlier words kept echoing in my mind like a refrain from an unforgettable song—dragons, it turns out, have a natural flair for showmanship, and Gudmundur was the epitome of that trait. He radiated unabashed joy and excitement, reminiscent of a child unchained in an endless candy store, his enthusiasm spilling over in an infectious tide.

"Come with me, and we'll head over to the meeting point where I'll lay out the entire plan," Gudmundur announced with a commanding air, his tone both resolute and inspiring as he led us confidently through the winding passages of the labyrinthine complex. "Abby and Jess will hold down the fort, guarding our base and our flag, while Mini, Lancaster, and Keith team up with me to dismantle the opposition." His declaration was saturated with determination and conviction, an unmistakable signal of the challenges ahead.

Before the impressive dragon could conclude his grand speech, I found myself unable to remain silent any longer. "Wait just a second!" I nearly shouted, the intensity in my voice matching the steely fire in my eyes as I stared at the imposing figure before me.

"Let me get this right," I continued, frustration chiseling each word. "You're sending five of you on the offensive, leaving only the two of us to manage defence? That's utterly reckless and, frankly, idiotic." My words came out sharp and laced with exasperation as I tried to reason with him. "Give us at least one more person to even the odds." Deep down, I suspected my plea would fall on deaf ears, but I was determined to make him see the flaws in his plan—especially if it meant we suffered the consequences of his oversight.

Apparently sensing my inner turmoil, Gudmundur pressed on with his explanation as if he had read my thoughts. "Look, you two have formidable independent strength, and Abby's experience with those unaccustomed to coordinated combat makes it only logical to pair you up for this battle," he explained in measured tones. Although his reasoning was methodical, a nagging sense of unease crept over me. Perhaps it was the overwhelming responsibility we were being saddled with once again, or the unsettling notion that we were being thrust into unbalanced peril. "Besides," he added with a slight, conspiratorial smile, "I have a feeling the other teams will think twice before daring to attack such an intimidating duo." His words caught me off guard and rendered me momentarily speechless. I had never considered myself intimidating until now—before I could even muster a reply.

At that very moment, Mini stepped up with a presence that was both commanding and endearing, her voice laced with a mix of amusement and admiration that was impossible to miss. "Oh, come on, Jess," she chided gently, the awe in her tone unmistakably threading through each word. "You really can't be that shocked, can you? You're the one who single-handedly faced down a pack of Wendigo and lived to tell the tale. And let's not forget you unmasked Aldrich as the mole. it was nothing short of legendary. Plus, there's the small matter of you being officially dubbed the adopted daughter of a dragon queen. If that isn't both impressive and intimidating all at once, I honestly don't know what is."

In that extended pause filled with conflicting emotions and the weight of heavy responsibility, we found ourselves standing on the brink of what promised to be an extraordinarily intense training mission. Our hearts and minds were consumed by the daunting challenge that lay ahead, a challenge that loomed over us like a tidal wave threatening to crash. Her words lingered in the air like an unspoken dare, challenging me to deny the truth they contained.

I had never thought about it in that light before, but she was absolutely right. I had accomplished more than I ever imagined possible, even if I was hesitant to acknowledge those feats aloud. "Fine, if you really believe this plan will work," I replied with a heavy sigh, my frustration seeping into my tone despite my best efforts to contain it. "But what exactly will you five be doing while we're supposed to 'chill out' at the base?" My irritation was so palpable that it seemed to fill the space around us, as I spoke, unable to fully mask my feelings about the entire situation.

Gudmundur's eyes lit up with an undeniable excitement as he declared, "We will show Danielle and Osaki that we won't lose again." As we navigated our way through the sprawling industrial complex, he elaborated on the different tactics and weapons we would be employing.

The ammunition we carried into this exercise was exactly the same as what we had employed earlier in the day—a high-voltage shock mechanism designed with the purpose of rendering our opponents incapable of continuing the confrontation, and doing so both swiftly and effectively. In addition to this, we were allowed to use training bladed weapons, each of which had the capability of delivering an electric shock upon making contact with a target. However, the precise point of impact was crucial, as it would determine whether the shock would entirely incapacitate our opponent or merely stun them temporarily. This added an intricate strategic layer to our training that demanded both accuracy and skill.

After listening intently to Gudmundur's thorough explanation of the weapons, Abby and I began engaging in a detailed discussion about our own tactical approaches. Our feet eventually came to a complete stop, and we found ourselves standing directly face to face with the opposing teams. The tension in the air was almost tangible as our eyes locked onto theirs, each of us preparing mentally and physically for the battle that lay ahead. "Danielle, Osaki, I hope you are prepared for a hard-fought challenge," I declared, my voice brimming with determination, excitement, and a hint of competitive spirit. A wide grin spread across my face, barely contained, as I felt the adrenaline and energy of competition coursing through my veins.

Each of us had been provided with specific instructions for this exercise, which included infiltration, eradication, and retrieval. Gudmundur had meticulously arranged briefing packets for each team, ensuring that we were all thoroughly equipped with the necessary information and weapons for the task. As I glanced around at my teammates, I could see the same fiery intensity reflected in their eyes, a shared commitment to the mission ahead.

The terrain that lay before us was carefully marked out on a map, with each team having their own designated base of operations. It was time to put all of our training to the ultimate test. "At the sound of the clacks-on, we will commence the operation," I announced with unwavering confidence. "And it will conclude when one team successfully possesses all three flags and every member of the opposition has been neutralised." I scanned the faces of my opponents, fully aware that they were just as eager and driven to win as we were.

"Does anyone have any questions?" I inquired, standing confidently at the head of my team. I was poised and ready to lead them to victory in what promised to be the ultimate test of skill, strategy, and teamwork. The stakes were high, and the anticipation in the room was electric.

Osaki, ever the confident leader, spoke up with a voice that rang out clearly and assuredly, "Me and my team are more than ready for this." Her enthusiasm was nearly tangible, as she bounced on her heels with the kind of excitement you'd expect from a child who had consumed far too much sugar. She was brimming with energy and anticipation.

Danielle, never one to be outdone, added her voice to the mix with a determined tone. "I'm eager to prove that my unit is not to be underestimated," she declared. "We will give it our all to win this exercise." Her words carried a weight of conviction, and she punctuated them with a teasing smile, her forked tongue darting out like a serpent tasting the air, adding a playful yet competitive edge to her demeanour.

Her confident stride and determined expression were clear indicators that an intense competition lay ahead. With a mischievous wink, she sauntered away, leaving behind a challenge that lingered in the air: "Don't disappoint me." The words were both a taunt and a rallying cry, meant to spur us on to greater heights.

A deep, red blush crept up my cheeks at her words, but I fiercely pushed it back down. It was clear she was deliberately trying to infiltrate my thoughts and throw me off my game. I couldn't afford to let her get the better of me.

Abby's voice brought me back to the present, cutting through the haze of my thoughts. "Don't let her get into your head. She's definitely targeting you," she said with a sly grin, her eyes twinkling with amusement and understanding.

"How can you be so sure?" I asked, still feeling the heat radiating from my face, half-embarrassed by my reaction and half-curious about her certainty.

Her response was a breathy whisper in my ear, sending shivers down my spine. With a gentle touch, she leaned in closer, her warm breath tickling my skin. It was a sensation that was both comforting and exhilarating, grounding me in the moment while also heightening my senses.

"Gear up," she declared with unwavering determination, her voice carrying the weight of her resolve and echoing through the room. The excitement and tension in the air were palpable as we all methodically prepared for the intense competition that lay ahead. Our focus was singular and unwavering: protect our flag at all costs, no matter the obstacles we might encounter. The challenge was set, the teams were primed and ready, and the battle was about to commence with all its fervour and intensity.

With confident strides, she approached the weapons rack before us, her movements fluid and precise like those of a trained dancer executing a well-rehearsed routine. Her eyes, sharp and discerning, scanned the array of weapons with a practiced eye, and she selected an M4 carbine and a SIG Sauer P226 9mm with ease and familiarity. I followed suit, albeit with a bit more trepidation, carefully choosing my own weapons from the gleaming assortment laid out before me.

As she methodically loaded up her pack with ammunition, I couldn't help but marvel at the sheer amount of firepower she was carrying. It was an impressive arsenal, to say the least. But then again, considering the formidable adversaries we were bound to encounter and the high stakes of our mission, it seemed both necessary and thoroughly justified.

On my part, I was beset with uncertainty regarding which weapon would best suit my personal fighting style. I had always been more comfortable with close combat weapons; firearms felt too impersonal to me and made it alarmingly easy to take a life with the mere pull of a trigger. However, agency rules were non-negotiable and insisted that all agents must be proficient in firearms for the sake of preparedness and versatility. After much deliberation and careful consideration of my options,

I carefully selected a standard-issue Glock as my primary weapon, feeling its familiar weight in my hand, and then began the search for a suitable secondary option. I wandered among the racks, considering the submachine guns and shotguns that were on display. However, they didn't feel quite right in my hands; their weight and balance were unfamiliar and awkward, making me uncomfortable. I decided to turn my attention to the small section reserved for traditional weapons, hoping to find something more in line with my skills and comfort level, something that felt like a natural extension of myself.

As I scanned the selection, my gaze fell upon a set of spears, rigged at either end with metal enhancements that gave them a taser-like effect upon impact. They were intriguing, but not quite what I was looking for. Beside them were blades with similar modifications, gleaming under the dim lights of the armoury. And then I saw them—the Kbar tactical knives. They weren't the same as the sword whose hilt I had been absentmindedly stroking as I perused the rack of weapons, but they held a certain promise of reliability and effectiveness. With a heavy sigh, I reluctantly removed my sword and made the decision to temporarily replace it with two Kbar's, understanding the necessity of adapting to the situation at hand.

After securing the Kbar's onto my weapons rig, ensuring they were snug and easily accessible, I followed Abby's lead as we made our way towards Gudmundur and the rest of the team. They were already gathered and prepared, ready to embark on the dangerous mission that lay ahead. I quickened my pace, sprinting slightly to catch up with Abby just as Gudmundur's deep voice boomed out final instructions. His words resonated through the tense air, filling us with a heightened sense of urgency and the looming spectre of danger.

"Everyone, we need to maintain radio silence," Gudmundur declared, his voice resonating with authority, his commanding presence impossible to ignore. Standing tall, his demeanour was one of unwavering confidence and determination. "My team must stay focused and rely solely on non-verbal communication with your teammates." The small group gathered around him, absorbing his words with a mix of apprehension and resolve, all nodding in solemn understanding of the gravity of the situation. The air was thick with anticipation, each person acutely aware of the challenges that lay ahead.

"Jess, this applies to you and Abby as well," he continued, his gaze piercing as he addressed us directly, ensuring that his instructions were clear and understood by all. "We will have zero communication between us. If by chance you do hear from someone, assume it's a trap and act accordingly." His words were heavy with caution, and the weight of responsibility hung in the air, palpable and undeniable.

"Why do we have to remain completely silent?" I asked, my heart racing with anticipation, my mind already conjuring up images of a dangerous mission ahead, teetering on the edge of the unknown. The question hung in the air, echoing the unspoken concerns of the group.

Gudmundur's expression grew serious, his features hardening as he prepared to explain. "I'm not certain if the ancient legends are true," he began, his voice steady yet tinged with a hint of uncertainty, "but it is said that a powerful kitsune possesses the ability to mimic sound as well as create illusions." The words seemed to hang in the air, laden with the weight of myth and mystery. "If Osaki is capable of this, it means our usual forms of communication may not be secure." His explanation was met with widened eyes and exchanged glances, shock rippling through the team as the reality of the situation began to unfold.

My mind whirled with questions and concerns, the implications of his words sinking in. "What if we needed backup? How can we share important information with each other?" I asked, voicing the concerns that were likely echoing in the minds of my teammates as well.

"Jess, the point of these drills is to prepare us for all eventualities. As much as we might hate it, we may have more situations ahead of us when we don't have comms, and we need to trust in our teammates to do their mission while we do our own. Let's be happy that today, if we fail, it will only be our pride on the line and not our lives."

Gudmundur stood tall, puffing out his chest with a sense of pride and authority, as though he had just delivered a pre-battle speech that was powerful enough to rally an entire army to victory. His demeanour was so commanding that, if it hadn't visibly affected everyone around us, I might have jokingly remarked on how earnestly he was approaching this training session. Yet, as I glanced around, it was clear that our entire team was captivated, looking at him with a newfound sense of respect and admiration, as if seeing him in a new light.

Abby, sensing my contemplation, gently placed her hand on my shoulder. Her touch was meant to reassure, to convey in silence that everything was going to be alright, and that we were in capable hands. "Come on, Jess," she urged softly, her voice a soothing balm amidst the charged atmosphere. "We need to set up. Gudmundur can take it from here." Her words were both an acknowledgment of Gudmundur's leadership ability and a gentle nudge for us to continue with our part of the preparation, confident that he would guide the rest with his newfound vigour.

CHAPTER 2

Defending the Flag

Gudmundur had entrusted us with the significant responsibility of both placing and defending the flag, a task that left us with the decision of selecting the ideal location. After a period of careful and deliberate consideration, we finally settled on a modest, single-story reception area. Its strategic positioning was advantageous, as it made the area easily defensible, and its unobstructed 360-degree view provided us with the capability to vigilantly monitor every possible approach from all directions. As soon as the clacks-on signal echoed through the air, Gudmundur and his team vanished with impressive swiftness into the surrounding abandoned expanse. Observing Gudmundur's towering frame moving with such unexpected stealthiness left me feeling unsettled and slightly awestruck. It was akin to witnessing a mountain silently shift and transform right before my eyes, defying the natural order.

"Abby," I whispered, my voice barely audible as I attempted to draw her attention without disrupting the tense silence enveloping us. She paused her vigilant scanning of the area with her m4 rifle, her movements precise and practiced, and turned to look at me. Her piercing gaze met mine, seeming to penetrate right through to my core.

"Yes?" she responded, her voice unwavering and calm, as she continued her vigilant watch over our environment, her gaze never faltering. The air around us was thick with an oppressive silence, serving as a stark and unyielding reminder that the other teams had yet to make any noticeable moves or engage in any discernible activity. This quietude seemed to hang heavily in the atmosphere, intensifying the tension and anticipation that coursed through our veins, leaving us on edge and ready for whatever might unfold next.

I turned to her, my voice filled with a mix of curiosity and insecurity. "Why did you and Gudmundur sacrifice so much to join this team with me? And why did you both agree to have me lead it? Both of you have far more experience and know the ropes of leading a team. Honestly, I couldn't even manage to get two people to work together effectively on a good day. So why did you choose to follow me?"

Abby's expression gradually softened, her features transforming into a visage of unwavering support and steadfast faith. Her eyes, always sharp and vigilant, continued to meticulously scan our surroundings with an intense and unwavering focus, ensuring that nothing slipped past her notice. She leaned in closer to me, her voice firm yet imbued with an incredible depth of belief that resonated with every word she spoke. "We believe in you," she declared with conviction, placing a reassuring hand on my shoulder. The comforting warmth of her touch seemed to seep through my skin, dispelling the lingering shadows of doubt and filling me with a renewed sense of determination and purpose. I inhaled deeply, allowing the tranquil atmosphere of our surroundings to steady my racing thoughts and fortify my resolve.

Despite the calm, my thoughts couldn't help but drift back to the tumultuous recent events - the chaotic warehouse raids, Aldrich's unexpected and painful betrayal. Now, standing here as the leader of a team composed of influential individuals—some of whom held significant sway over the council—I felt the considerable weight of responsibility and doubt settling heavily upon my shoulders. But Abby's encouraging words provided me with the opportunity to voice my concerns, something that had been gnawing at me ever since I took on the mantle of leadership. "Thank you for your candour," I spoke honestly, my voice tinged with gratitude for this rare moment of vulnerability and openness between us. "I needed to understand...this is the first time I've been able to truly express my worries."

Abby's gaze held mine steadily, her eyes unwavering as she spoke, her words heavy with profound significance. "This isn't really the time to delve into this, Jess. We are in the midst of training and trying to demonstrate that your team possesses the necessary skills and fortitude. But I will give you a brief answer." Her tone was serious yet infused with an unshakeable faith in me. "We are at a pivotal tipping point of change, and your role will be instrumental in determining whether the changes we face will be for the collective good or if they will lead to our downfall. I believe the dragon shares this sentiment."

There was an ocean of words left unspoken, an entire universe of thoughts and emotions swirling within us, begging to be voiced. But as Abby's carefully chosen words resonated through the tense atmosphere, it became unmistakably clear that this moment was not the appropriate one for a deeper, more meaningful exchange. The time and place for such an open-hearted dialogue would come, perhaps when the dust had settled and our minds were less cluttered by the immediacy of the situation. For now, however, our focus had to be unwaveringly directed towards presenting a united front, a testament to our team's unparalleled strength and unyielding determination. "We will make them regret underestimating us," I declared with unwavering conviction, feeling the fire of determination blaze to life within me, brighter and more intense than ever before. It was a fire that fuelled my resolve as I prepared to lead our team into the uncertain future that awaited us. "They shouldn't mess with team Jess," Abby added, her words imbued with a commanding presence that demanded attention.

Her eyes, sharp and unyielding as steel, fixed unwaveringly on their distant target. Despite the subtlety of her voice, barely rising above a whisper, it carried an undeniable weight, a gravity that sent shivers cascading down my spine and caused the hairs on the back of my neck to stand on end. My gaze followed the trajectory of her unwavering eyes, landing on two figures in the distance—one a representative of Osaki's notoriously ruthless team, the other a member of Danielle's cunning, ever-strategic crew. A heavy feeling of dread settled in my stomach, a realisation washing over me like a cold wave as I understood the significance of this unexpected alliance. Our hopes had rested on the possibility that they would take each other, dismissing our team as the weaker link in this contest. But their shrewd union shattered that assumption, . The very air around us seemed to thicken, laden with tension and fraught with uncertainty.

The plan that Gudmundur had meticulously crafted was absolute in its precision and intent — absolutely no radio contact with the attack team. This was a strategy meticulously designed to maintain the vital element of surprise and ensure that our movements remained undetected by our adversaries. As we braced ourselves for the unfolding developments in this highly charged scenario, we were acutely aware that every decision, every action, would be pivotal, shaping the ultimate outcome of this intense training exercise. We knew we had to rely solely on our own skills, instincts, and stealth to navigate through this training mission, a task that demanded the utmost concentration.

As the enemy drew closer, closing the distance between us with each passing moment, Abby turned to me with a serious, almost grave expression on her face. Her eyes were filled with determination and readiness. "Jess, do you want me to open fire?" she whispered in a voice so low it was barely audible, yet it carried the weight of the decision we faced. I shook my head slowly, understanding that any premature gunfire would only serve to alert the entire compound to our presence and potentially jeopardise the success of our mission.

"No, not yet," I replied, my voice equally hushed.

"Let me see if I can take them down without being noticed," I whispered, my voice barely audible over the distant hum of the city. "But if things get too risky or it starts to look like a trap, then open fire immediately." Without waiting for further confirmation from her, I swiftly moved into action. I darted off like a shadow in the night, maintaining a low crouch as I navigated through the labyrinth of worn-out buildings and abandoned machinery. These remnants of a forgotten past served as makeshift cover, providing me with the concealment I desperately needed. Every step I took was measured and precise, each movement deliberate, as I kept my senses on high alert, scanning the environment for any hints of additional enemies lurking in the shadows nearby. The air was thick with tension, almost palpable, and the stakes had never felt higher in my life.

All I could initially see were the two scouts we had originally spotted, standing like sentinels, but experience had taught me to be wary, to never let my guard down too soon. This was going to be a challenging operation, one where every move had to be executed flawlessly, with the precision of a master chess player anticipating his opponent's every counter. Abby remained motionless in her position, her stillness a testament that our presence had not yet been detected by the enemy. With stealth and caution as my allies, I continued my approach, taking a circuitous route to remain unseen and unheard.

As I crept up behind the enemy scouts, the grip of the borrowed k-bar tactical knives felt reassuringly familiar in my hands, their weight a reminder of past encounters. I struck with precision and speed, my movements a blur, driving the blunted blade across the first scout's throat without a moment's hesitation. My past mistakes had been harsh tutors, teaching me the crucial importance of swift and decisive action in situations like this. There would be no room for mercy, no quarter given to my enemies.

The beat of my heart was like a frantic drum, echoing in my ears as the second scout raised his weapon, poised and ready to strike. My body tensed with the primal instinct, every muscle coiling tight like a spring loaded with potential energy, ready to unleash its force. Without a second thought, I swung my leg with all the might I could muster, delivering a swift and punishing kick to his groin. A deep, guttural groan erupted from his lips, reverberating through the air as he crumpled to his knees, his weapon slipping from his grasp and clattering to the ground in a symphony of defeat. He writhed on the dirt, his face twisted in agony, desperately clutching at his now injured manhood.

I stood there, panting heavily, my breath coming in ragged gasps as relief washed over me, knowing I had acted quickly enough to defend myself against my opponent. The atmosphere remained charged with tension, thick and heavy, as if holding its breath, waiting for the next move to be made in this high-stakes game.

The initial surge of adrenaline that had been flooding through my body began to ebb away, gradually being replaced by an overwhelming sense of guilt and deep remorse. It was as if the full weight of what I had just done crashed down upon me with the force of a ton of bricks. My heart pounded wildly in my chest, and I could feel my common sense finally catching up with the dire reality of the situation I found myself in.

The man lying prostrate at my feet was far from neutralised; he remained a determined combatant, his hand inching towards his weapon in a final, desperate bid to drag me down with him into the abyss. In a flash of instinctual reaction, I dropped to the ground with remarkable speed, delivering another powerful and decisive blow with my blunt k-bar knife.

The strike I delivered was swift, precise, and executed with such accuracy that it ensured the threat he posed was utterly neutralised. It was as if time had momentarily slowed down, allowing me to focus entirely on the task at hand. By the time I had finished, both men who had been opposing me were convulsing violently on the cold, hard ground. Their bodies were rendered utterly incapacitated, leaving them completely unable to continue their assault against us.

Pausing for a brief moment to catch my breath and regain my composure, I surveyed the area for any other potential threats that might be lurking in the shadows. My muscles tensed in anticipation of another attack, ready to spring into action at a moment's notice. However, after a thorough scan of the surroundings, it became clear that there was no one else in sight. The silence was almost deafening, and the absence of any other opponents brought a sense of temporary relief.

Feeling satisfied that we were indeed alone, I began the arduous task of dragging the two scouts back to our base, where Abby was waiting for our return. The path back seemed longer than it had before, each step heavy with the weight of the unconscious scouts. As I approached Abby, I could see a complex mix of emotions playing across her face—amusement, admiration, and perhaps a tinge of relief. She had just witnessed our first real encounter with the opposing team since we had begun this gruelling training exercise. Though we had emerged victorious, it was a stark reminder that we couldn't afford to let our guard down or become complacent in our abilities.

"Come on, Abby. Give me a hand with these," I said, reaching her side, my muscles straining from the weight of the two unconscious scouts in my arms. The exertion was taking its toll, and I could feel the burn in my muscles intensifying. "We have to move them inside and secure them," I added, gesturing towards our nearby base with a nod of my head.

With a determined look on her face and an eagerness that matched my own, Abby stepped forward to assist. Her toned arms flexed with strength and resolve as she lifted one end of each man, carrying them with surprising ease.

Together, we moved in perfect harmony, our steps precisely coordinated as we transported the captured scouts into our secured base. Every step was measured, each movement deliberate, ensuring that our mission was executed with the utmost precision. Once inside the confines of our stronghold, we gently laid the scouts down off to the side, taking care to restrain their limbs securely. This was a necessary precaution to prevent any potential escape attempts, as we were acutely aware that vigilance was the cornerstone of our strategy. Ensuring they remained contained was an integral part of maintaining the upper hand in this ongoing strategic exercise.

As we paused to catch our breath and take stock of our surroundings, Abby couldn't resist the urge to tease me about my takedown skills. Her eyes twinkled with mischief as she turned to me and said, "Jess, that was quite an intense move you pulled off back there. Even as a fellow woman, I could practically feel the pain you inflicted on that poor guy's family jewels. I'm honestly surprised he didn't pass out from the sheer agony," she chuckled, her laughter echoing softly in the otherwise tense atmosphere.

With a shared nod of acknowledgment, we swiftly resumed our positions, our senses heightened as we began scanning the perimeter for any signs of additional scouts approaching. The air was thick with anticipation, and the tense silence was only broken by the gentle rustling of leaves and the careful, measured sound of our own cautious movements.

After what felt like an interminable period of ten minutes, during which absolutely no activity took place, the environment around us continued to be enveloped in a profound and unsettling stillness. It was as though the world had paused, leaving only the gentle whispers of the wind to serve as a reminder of life beyond our immediate surroundings. The air carried a heavy silence that seemed to stretch infinitely, making the moment feel suspended in time. Sensing that the lull might be temporary, I made the decision that it was an opportune moment to check on our captives. I needed to ensure that their restraints remained secure and to assess their current condition, both physically and mentally.

With a purposeful stride, I entered the dimly lit room where the two figures sat restrained before me. The room was bathed in a muted glow, casting long shadows across their forms. My eyes carefully scanned their faces and bodies, noting that their earlier convulsions had finally subsided. Their breathing, which had been erratic before, seemed to have settled into a more regular and steady rhythm. "How are both of you feeling now?" I inquired cautiously, my voice tinged with a mix of concern and authority.

They exchanged glances, a silent communication passing between them, before bursting into unexpected laughter. The sound of their amusement filled the room, reverberating off the walls, but it was a brief reprieve. One of them suddenly groaned, his expression twisting into one of discomfort. "Oh Christ, please don't make me laugh, mama," he wheezed out in between laboured breaths. It was in that moment that I realised he was the one I had inadvertently kicked earlier during the struggle.

A wave of worry and guilt washed over me, compelling me to rush towards him with an urgency that surprised even myself. I was desperate to offer some form of comfort or assistance, anything to alleviate his pain. His face was contorted in agony, his once rosy cheeks now as pale as a ghost. Despite his obvious discomfort, he attempted to reassure me, gasping out, "It's okay. I'm fine, mama," though his voice lacked conviction.

Meanwhile, the other captive found himself unable to contain his mirth any longer. He was doubled over, consumed by a fit of laughter that seemed to emanate from deep within him. His boisterous glee echoed throughout the room, creating a stark contrast to the otherwise tense atmosphere. "Man, you should see your face. I have never seen someone look so terrified," he chortled, directing his amusement at the agent who was sprawled on the floor.

Gradually, a subtle hint of colour began to seep back into the face of the injured agent, as though the shared laughter possessed some kind of mysterious healing power. "You try letting her kick you in the nuts and see how you feel afterward," he managed to retort through clenched teeth, his words punctuated by sharp gasps of pain and discomfort. "I swear, I think she even managed to break my protective cup with that kick."

"That's enough!" I interjected firmly, striving to maintain a composed and serious demeanour despite the undeniable amusement their banter provided me. "Do either of you need a medic?" I inquired, my tone carefully crafted to blend sternness with genuine concern, as I glanced back and forth between the two, ready to offer whatever assistance was necessary to ensure their well-being.

The agent whom I had inadvertently injured replied with a hint of bravado, "We will be fine, mama." Yet, I could easily see the unmistakable pain etched deeply into his features, a clear indicator that he might indeed need medical attention. "Promise me you will get checked out once this training session comes to an end," I insisted, my voice firm with concern, before turning to make my exit. As I walked away from them, I could still hear their laughter echoing behind me, a lingering reminder of our peculiar encounter.

A calm, serene silence gradually enveloped me as i settled back into a defensive position. The silent atmosphere of my surroundings was only occasionally disrupted by the faint rustling of our clothing and the soft, rhythmic cadence of our breaths. With each passing minute, time seemed to stretch and elongate, making every second feel like an eternity. My nerves grew increasingly frayed, my mind racing with countless thoughts of the various ways in which this training exercise could potentially go awry.

"Do you think they have sent out a search party for their missing scouts?" I inquired of Abby, my voice slicing through the serene silence that had enveloped us, much like a thin, fragile layer of ice that could shatter at the slightest disturbance.

Before she could respond, the heavens above us suddenly detonated in a blinding explosion, casting an eerie glow across the landscape. The ground beneath us quaked violently as the concussive force reached us, sending debris flying in every conceivable direction. My heart pounded with a mixture of terror and uncertainty, a desperate plea forming within me that my team wasn't the cause of such destruction. Simultaneously, I hoped they hadn't been caught in the devastating blow of an attack like that. The air, once tranquil, was now thick with chaos and foreboding.

Abby's voice cut through the pandemonium like a fierce, piercing cry, demanding direction as she turned to face me, her eyes wide with a ferocious hunger for action. The air around us crackled and sizzled, reminiscent of a live wire ready to ignite at the slightest provocation. Each passing second felt like a precarious walk over a minefield, with tension and danger palpable in the thick, charged atmosphere that enveloped us.

We found ourselves standing at a metaphorical crossroads, confronted with a daunting decision: remain where we were, or venture out into the unknown dangers that surely awaited beyond our current position. The gravity of this choice pressed down on me like an immense boulder, suffocating me with waves of uncertainty. As Abby's gaze swept across the horizon, her body instinctively shifted into a predator's stance, poised to pounce at a moment's notice. I could see the glint of determination in her eyes, a burning desire to launch an attack and rescue our teammates. For an instant, I almost succumbed to my primal instincts, tempted to abandon our defensive position and charge forward to join my team in battle against our opponents.

However, with tremendous effort, I held myself back, maintaining my composure and steadfastly refusing to break radio silence. It required every ounce of self-control I possessed, but I understood that we couldn't afford to falter now.

My heart pounded in my chest as I meticulously surveyed the surrounding area, fully aware of the perilous exposure of our position in the aftermath of the thunderous explosion. "No, we hold our position," I commanded with unwavering determination, the adrenaline pumping through my veins like a relentless torrent. If Gudmundur's team had been eliminated, the opposition would soon be closing in on us, and we needed to be prepared to defend ourselves with every ounce of strength and resolve we could muster.

In the distance, I could still hear the echoes of minor explosions reverberating through the air, accompanied by the faint sound of debris cascading from the sky. Yet, strangely, there was an eerie absence of the familiar sounds of gunfire or combat. My senses were on high alert, every nerve in my body tingling with anticipation and heightened awareness. My trusty blades were gripped tightly in my hands as I meticulously scanned the area for any signs of movement or impending danger.

I was keenly aware that it was only a matter of time before the opposing teams launched a coordinated assault on our precariously exposed location. When that moment arrived, I was determined to be ready, to fight back with every ounce of strength and determination I possessed. Our pride as a cohesive unit depended heavily on how effectively we held our ground and defended our position against the oncoming storm. The tension in the air was almost tangible as we braced ourselves for the inevitable clash with the opposing forces.

Abby and I crouched down low, our ears finely attuned to the faint, almost imperceptible sound of approaching footsteps. We could just make out the low murmur of voices emanating from a cluster of buildings shrouded in shadows, their forms barely discernible in the dim light. Without a moment's hesitation, we adjusted our position, huddling closer together to present a smaller and less visible target while still maintaining a strategic vantage point to neutralise any potential threats.

As the voices in the distance grew louder and more distinct, my heart began to race with a potent mixture of nerves and excitement. The adrenaline once again surged through my veins, preparing me for the inevitable fight-or-flight reaction that my instincts demanded. Yet, I knew that I had to force myself to remain calm and focused; emotions alone could not be allowed to dictate my actions in this critical moment. Logic and strategic thinking were crucial if we were to emerge victorious in this confrontation that lay ahead.

I stood my ground, feeling my heart pounding relentlessly in my chest as I tried to steady my breathing through sheer willpower. From the shadows emerged a towering figure, an imposing presence that seemed more beast than human. My eyes were immediately drawn to the horns that protruded majestically from its temples, reminiscent of those found on a grand and regal stag. But this being wore its horns with an air of pride, as if they were a symbol of its immense power and unchallenged authority. Its movements exuded an effortless confidence and grace, akin to a member of high society who was accustomed to command and respect. However, it was its hands that truly captured my attention and sent a chill down my spine. Covered in a gleaming armour that resembled interlocking scales, its fingers ended in sharp, deadly claws, promising devastation upon any who dared to challenge its might.

As the creature approached with deliberate steps, I couldn't help but feel a profound sense of awe mixed with fear at the sight of this formidable being standing before me. The fearsome creature led my team into view, their steps sure and confident, showing no signs of injury or hesitation. As they drew closer, I could see the steely determination in their eyes and hear the excitement in their voices, a testament to their readiness for whatever lay ahead. "Abby, stay vigilant. This could be another trick by Osaki," I cautioned, my voice carrying the weight of my concerns. I didn't doubt my team's abilities, but I was also not willing to risk losing our precious flag to deceit.

We readied our weapons, every muscle in our bodies prepared for a potential battle that could erupt at any moment. "Is that creature with the impressive horns Gudmundur?" I asked, my voice laced with disbelief as I tried to process what I was seeing. "Yes," Abby confirmed with a hint of amusement in her voice, "that's our dragon. He has chosen to take on his warrior form for this training mission."

The vivid image of Gudmundur in his fierce, battle-ready form flooded my mind, evoking a complex blend of fear and admiration. The sheer force he commanded sent shivers racing down my spine as I pondered the incredible power he wielded. I could hardly fathom what it would be like to confront him as an adversary, for his very presence was enough to inspire a profound sense of dread and respect in equal measure. Yet, Abby seemed to possess some insight into this matter, so I resolved to make a mental note to seek her out for more detailed information later on.

Although my understanding of dragon culture had expanded somewhat through my acquaintance with Lyn and now Gudmundur, my actual knowledge remained quite limited. However, I was aware that dragons possessed the unique capability to transform into three distinct forms. They could assume the guise of a human or revert to their large, original dragon form. Yet, there existed a third form, one that few older dragons dared to employ. This particular transformation was viewed as a form of betrayal, combining what was perceived as the frailty of the human form with the might and superiority of their dragon form. This metamorphosis ignited controversy within the dragon community, rendering it a subject of considerable debate and speculation. To my mind, however, it only underscored the profound strength and adaptability of these mythical creatures. As I gazed upon the magnificent beasts before me, I couldn't help but wonder what other secrets lay concealed within each unique form, waiting to be discovered.

We stood back, taking in the scene as my team moved forward with a slow and deliberate approach. The precision of their steps was in stark contrast to the disorderly retreat of the two opposing teams, who trailed behind in a state of disarray. Their hands were securely bound behind their backs, and the unmistakable look of defeat was etched deeply onto their faces, as if carved there by the very battle they had just lost. A surge of triumph coursed through me, invigorating my senses and propelling me to my feet. With a sweeping gesture, I beckoned my team to join me, their faces flushed with a combination of relief and satisfaction, their bodies glistening with perspiration from the intense battle they had just endured. The atmosphere was electric, crackling with the energy of victory, and in that moment, I was filled with an overwhelming sense of pride in the achievement we had accomplished together as a unit.

"So, dare I assume you were responsible for that impressive explosion?" I asked, directing my question at Gudmundur, who stood tall and unyielding amidst his defeated opponents. His chest rose and fell with the exertion of the recent skirmish, but his lips curled into a sly grin, betraying his confidence.

"I had to create a diversion while the rest of our team snuck in and retrieved their flags," he replied, his voice carrying a note of self-assuredness.

"Ah, so they did form an alliance after all," I commented, my tone laced with a hint of admiration. It was a clever strategy, one that demonstrated not only their prowess as fighters but also their capabilities as strategic thinkers.

"Yeah, and they made the mistake of consolidating their forces in one location." Gudmundur's expression turned serious, a hint of gravity in his eyes. "When they didn't hear back from their scouts, they assumed something had gone wrong. So, they planned for a full-scale frontal assault, thinking we had focused solely on defence."

"Okay, that kind of makes sense," I nodded in understanding, appreciating the depth of their strategy. "But why the warrior form? It seems like overkill, considering you could probably defeat both the opposing teams in your human form."

Gudmundur nonchalantly shrugged his shoulders, the corners of his mouth curving into a sly grin as he spoke. "The element of surprise combined with intimidation," he said, his eyes glinting with a knowing look. "If you see me charging full speed at your base in this form, what would be your first reaction?"

A nervous chuckle slipped from my lips, and I swallowed hard to suppress the urge to admit to him that, if confronted with such a scenario, I would probably lose control of my bladder. Instead, maintaining a playful tone, I said, "Okay, mister intimidation, are we done with the training for today?"

With an air of casual authority, he replied, "Well, I have the facility available for the entire day, so ultimately, it's up to the unit leaders to decide what we do next."

Seizing this chance to maximise our training time, I raised my voice to call out to Osaki and Danielle, ensuring I had their full attention. "Let's see what they think about the idea of extending our training session a bit longer."

After a brief discussion, it was collectively agreed upon that taking advantage of the facility for additional training would be beneficial for everyone involved. However, rather than diving into a chaotic battle royal format, it was decided that we would take a more structured approach. Gudmundur, Abby, Osaki, and Danielle took the lead, each running specific drills that honed in on their unique areas of expertise. Abby took charge of overseeing hand-to-hand combat techniques, ensuring everyone sharpened their skills in close-quarters fighting. Meanwhile, Osaki focused on imparting her knowledge of advanced stealth and infiltration skills, teaching us how to move undetected and gather intelligence without being noticed. Gudmundur showcased his mastery in breach and clear tactics, guiding us through the intricacies of entering and securing hostile environments. Danielle, on the other hand, dazzled us with her impressive evasion techniques, demonstrating how to effectively manoeuvre and escape potential threats.

As for myself, I eagerly bounced between each of these specialised drills, enthusiastically participating in various roles. This allowed me to gain a deeper understanding of my team's strengths and weaknesses, while also picking up some valuable new skills that would enhance my own capabilities. I relished the opportunity to learn from each of my teammates, absorbing their knowledge and techniques to become a more well-rounded member of the team.

***

The sun cast its unyielding rays down upon us, creating an oppressive heat that seemed to seep into every pore. The sticky layers of sweat clung to my skin, drenching my shirt and leaving me feeling both weary and invigorated. Each step was a reminder of the intense and gruelling training session we had just endured, with my muscles protesting in soreness at every movement. Yet, amid this physical exhaustion, a deep sense of pride welled up within me. Our team had poured their very souls into the demanding drills and rigorous exercises, and it was evident in the way our coordination was starting to click, slowly but surely.

As we trudged back toward the agency's spacious lobby, our group gradually dispersed, each member drifting off to attend to their individual responsibilities. However, Abby and Gudmundur lingered at my side, their conversation focused on brainstorming potential improvements for the training session planned for the following week. Our determination was unshakable; we were resolute in our commitment to push our limits further, believing wholeheartedly that such dedication would only fortify us as a cohesive unit.

"Guys," I began, my voice brimming with an overwhelming sense of gratitude that matched the sincerity embedded in every word I uttered. "I am eternally grateful for all that you have contributed to our team and to me personally. Your unwavering support and tireless assistance have been nothing short of invaluable, and I find myself at a loss for words when it comes to expressing just how deeply thankful I am. Your dedication has not only fortified our team, making it more cohesive and resilient, but has also served as a tremendous source of inspiration for me, pushing me to continue striving for excellence in all our endeavours."

"It is indeed an honour to serve and support you in any way possible," replied Gudmundur, his face lighting up with a warm smile that reflected the genuine kindness he felt towards his colleagues. His voice, while carrying an unmistakable authority, was infused with a profound sense of camaraderie. "My resources are at your complete disposal, and I will do everything within my power to ensure that our team retains its status as the top-performing group within the agency. That is, of course, if such an arrangement meets with your approval," he added, his eyes scanning the room for any signs of dissent.

Abby, who had been listening intently to Gudmundur's statement, couldn't help but let a knowing smirk curl onto her lips. Her eyes rolled in amusement, clearly entertained by the unexpected turn of events.

"Wait, are you serious?" I asked incredulously, my disbelief unmistakable in the tone of my voice. "You want to be in charge of the team's training?" The question hung in the air, filled with both surprise and curiosity.

Gudmundur nodded confidently, a glint of enthusiasm in his eyes. "Yes, but only if it's acceptable to you," he replied, his voice steady and assured. "It has been quite some time since I've had the opportunity to train a group like we did today, and I must admit, I thoroughly enjoyed the experience," he continued, a satisfied smile playing on his lips as he recalled the day's events.

I took a moment to let his request fully resonate within me, carefully considering the potential implications. After a brief pause, I offered my response, nodding in agreement as I spoke. "It's fine by me," I said, conveying my consent. "However," I added with deliberate emphasis, "we must not lose sight of our top priority, which is to delve into the connection between Aldrich and Jeremiah and uncover the mastermind who is pulling their strings. The training can serve as a secondary focus, a side project if you will," I concluded, determined to keep our primary objectives at the forefront of our collective focus.

Gudmundur, upon receiving my approval, seemed to be positively brimming with joy. His face broke into a radiant smile as he bid us farewell, his departure marked by the same doorway through which we had entered only moments earlier. The atmosphere around him seemed to pulsate with an infectious energy, one that left us all feeling unexpectedly invigorated and filled with hope for the challenges that lay ahead.

Abby's voice cut through the room like a sharp blade, her words tumbling out with a sense of urgency and a hint of fear. "You have no idea what you have just agreed to," she said, her tone heavy with concern. Her warning was clear, and it hung in the air between us.

Despite her cautionary note, I found myself dismissing her worries with a casual shrug. My curiosity was a powerful force, outweighing any sense of apprehension that might have taken root. "He can't be that bad," I replied with a confidence that bordered on bravado. "Just consider what he accomplished with the team in a matter of mere hours. Imagine the possibilities if he is given the freedom to train them according to his own methods."

Yet, Abby's expression remained unchanged, her skepticism etched into every feature as she shook her head slowly.

Her apprehension was almost palpable, a heavy presence that seemed to cast a shadow over my own burgeoning confidence, causing it to waver ever so slightly. Could it truly be possible that Gudmundur was as intimidating and formidable as Abby seemed to fear? I knew that I would soon uncover the truth, whether it would correspond with her concerns or not.

Suddenly shifting the conversation, she leaned in closer, her movement abrupt yet fluid, and inquired, "So, what do you have planned for the evening?" Her breath was warm and gentle against my skin, creating an unexpected sense of intimacy as she spoke.

"I'm just heading back to my dorm room," I replied, envisioning the comfort awaiting me there. "I'm planning to take a long, relaxing shower and then collapse onto my criminally comfortable bed. How about you? Do you have any thrilling or exciting plans lined up for tonight?"

A mischievous spark ignited in her eyes, an enchanting gleam that seemed to dance with its own light, and she leaned in even closer. Her full lips curled into a devilish grin, one that was impossible to ignore, and I couldn't help but notice the sharp points of her fangs as they peeked out from behind her smile. "I'm off to the blood bank for a quick snack," she purred, her voice dripping with a seductive allure that was both captivating and unsettling. "And then I'll be making my rounds to gather some intel."

With an unexpected softness, she placed a gentle kiss on my cheek, a gesture that left me feeling both dizzy and breathless. As she sauntered away, I couldn't tear my gaze away from her, mesmerised by the effortless grace with which she glided through the exit. Her laughter echoed in the air, a musical sound that lingered long after she had vanished from sight. Vampires, I mused, were truly creatures of unparalleled grace and agility, moving through the world with an elegance that was impossible to replicate.

CHAPTER 3

Morning After Training

The morning following our intense group training session was a testament to the physical challenge we had undergone. I awoke to the sensation of every muscle in my body protesting with stiffness and soreness, a reminder of the exertion from the day before. With a reluctant groan, I slowly extricated myself from the warm cocoon of my bed, feeling the weight of exhaustion anchoring my legs as I stumbled groggily towards the kitchen. As I moved, the familiar and comforting scent of coffee began to drift through the air, gradually lifting my spirits and infusing a sense of anticipation into my weary morning routine.

I approached the counter with purpose, carefully measuring out the fresh coffee grounds with precision, ensuring they were packed tightly into the filter of my espresso machine. The ritual was one I had perfected over time, and it never failed to offer a sense of calm and order to my mornings. As I pressed the button to start the machine, I watched with quiet satisfaction as the dark, rich liquid began its slow, deliberate journey, dripping steadily into the small cup below. The colour was inviting, a deep hue that promised revival and energy, a liquid alchemy that would transform my sluggish state into one of alertness and vitality.

Closing my eyes, I allowed myself to savour the moment, inhaling deeply to let the warm, earthy aroma saturate my senses. It was a sensory embrace, akin to a gentle hug on a chilly morning, soothing and comforting in its simplicity. The steamy mug cradled in my hands radiated warmth, offering solace and a moment of peace amidst the inevitable rush of the day ahead. As I took that first, anticipated sip, the bold, bitter, yet immensely satisfying taste spread through my body like an invigorating wave, awakening every corner of my being with its potent essence.

In that solitary moment of quiet reflection, I found myself enveloped in a newfound clarity, understanding deeply why people often say that it's the little things in life that hold immense value and make existence truly worthwhile. It was as though a veil had been lifted, revealing the profound truth in the simple pleasure of a good cup of coffee. This was more than just a morning routine or a caffeine fix—it was an experience that transcended the ordinary, setting a comforting tone for the day and offering a gentle reminder of the small joys that enrich our lives, often overlooked in the hustle and bustle of daily existence. With each sip, I felt a growing sense of readiness to face the challenges of the day ahead, buoyed by this humble yet powerful ritual that marked the beginning of a new day. The warmth of the coffee cup in my hand was a symbol of the tranquility I so cherished, a momentary escape from the chaos that life often brings.

But just as I settled into the comfort of my ritual, embracing the calm it provided, there was an unexpected interruption—a light knock on my front door. It was so subtle yet intrusive, pulling me back from my moment of serene solitude. With a sigh of resignation, I opened my eyes, realising that in my irritation, I had unconsciously started to growl at being disturbed. "What could be so important that they would dare disturb a girl before she's had her morning coffee?" I grumbled to myself, my voice tinged with annoyance and curiosity mingling in equal measure.

With a heavy heart, I reluctantly left my cherished mug on the counter, feeling as if I were leaving behind the coziness and security it provided. I trudged to the door, each step a reminder of the peaceful morning I had hoped to enjoy uninterrupted. I couldn't help but wonder what could possibly be so urgent to disturb me this early. As I reached for the doorknob,

I braced myself for the inevitable disruption that was surely lurking beyond the front door, my mind a whirlwind of scenarios that might unfold. Would it be an unwelcome visitor, a delivery gone awry, or some unexpected calamity? The possibilities seemed endless as I prepared for whatever awaited me.

However, as I swung the door open with a mixture of trepidation and resolve, I found myself momentarily stunned. There was nothing, no one standing there to confront or surprise me. Instead, the space was occupied by something far more enigmatic—a small, unassuming envelope, strategically placed just beyond the threshold. It lay there with an air of quiet significance, as if it had been deliberately set down to catch my eye without making a sound, a silent herald of mystery.

The initial surge of annoyance I felt at the disruption was swiftly replaced by a burgeoning curiosity. What message did this unexpected visitor hold, and why had it appeared in such a peculiar manner? As I bent down to retrieve the envelope, the elegant, flowing handwriting immediately caught my eye. It was unmistakable—it belonged to Alexander. This method of communication was decidedly atypical for him; he usually preferred direct contact, whether through a summons or by appearing unannounced at my doorstep.

My curiosity piqued, I gingerly picked up the envelope, feeling its weight in my hand as I retreated back into the familiarity of my kitchen. Perhaps the comfort of a cup of coffee would cushion the impact of whatever news Alexander had chosen to impart through this unusual medium. I had always found that coffee possessed an almost magical ability to soothe and elevate my spirits.

Cradling a steaming mug of coffee in one hand and the mysterious envelope in the other, I made my way to the sanctuary of my bedroom. The soft blankets on my bed beckoned invitingly, promising warmth and comfort as I settled in. Nestled within their embrace, I took a long, satisfying sip of the hot brew, feeling its energising warmth spread through my body, momentarily lifting my spirits.

Yet, as the invigorating effects of the coffee took hold, the weight of the letter in my hand drew me back to the present moment, grounding me in reality. The sense of urgency that accompanied it was palpable.

With a deliberate and careful motion, I tore open the envelope, feeling the paper fibres give way under the pressure of my fingers, which trembled slightly with a mix of anticipation and anxiety. It was an emotion akin to opening a door to an unknown room, where anything could be waiting on the other side. Once the seal was broken, I extracted the neatly folded paper tucked within, its crisp edges whispering secrets that had yet to be revealed. What revelations awaited me in the lattice of Alexander's carefully chosen words, I wondered, my mind a flurry of curiosity and apprehension.

As I unfolded the paper with deliberate precision, the smooth, flowing letters on the note seemed to dance across the page in an elegant script, each curve and line meticulously crafted to convey the weight and importance of its message. It was immediately clear to me that this was no ordinary request; the very nature of the communication was imbued with a sense of urgency and significance. Alex, my superior, had summoned me to his office, after my morning team briefing. The gravity and seriousness in his tone, even in written form, could not be ignored or underestimated. I braced myself mentally for whatever news or mission awaited me, knowing full well that this was not a simple matter.

The instructions within the note were cryptic yet commanding, a testament to the high stakes involved: secrecy was of utmost importance, and not even my closest teammates could be privy to this meeting or its contents. As I made my way to Alexander's office, navigating through the corridors with a purposeful stride, my heart raced with a blend of anticipation and trepidation for what was to come. Each step seemed to echo with the weight of the unknown, amplifying my sense of urgency.

This was no ordinary assignment; it was of the utmost importance and classified as top secret, a mission enveloped in layers of mystery and intrigue that demanded the highest level of discretion, loyalty, and unwavering commitment. There was no room for error, no margin for compromise, as the stakes were higher than anything I had ever encountered before.

As I prepared myself mentally for the challenges that lay ahead, my mind raced with a dizzying array of possibilities and scenarios. I took a deep, calming breath, trying to steady my nerves and steel myself for the unknown that awaited me. The air around me felt charged with an electric potential, that indescribable energy that accompanies moments of great change or revelation, when the world seems to hold its breath in anticipation. Whatever awaited me in Alexander's office, I was resolute and determined to face it head-on, armed with the conviction that I was ready for whatever challenges might arise.

I quickly threw together an outfit that balanced professionalism with practicality, opting for a pair of well-fitted jeans and a plain t-shirt, which I topped with a tailored blouse and a sleek business jacket. As if by some miracle, the combination of these pieces came together to create an effortlessly chic and polished ensemble, the kind that exuded confidence and competence. Before slipping into the jacket, I took a moment to secure my gun and sword rig around my waist, feeling a sense of comfort and reassurance from the familiar weight of my weapons.

They were an extension of myself, symbols of my readiness and willingness to confront whatever challenges might arise on my path. With everything meticulously arranged and in its rightful place, I felt thoroughly prepared to embark on this journey into the unknown, equipped to tackle the enigmatic mission before me with unwavering resolve and steadfast determination.

As I marched toward my team's office, my nerves, initially jittery, gradually began to settle, soothed by the comforting, familiar weight of my gear pressing against me. My heart swelled with pride, still basking in the glow of yesterday's hard-earned victory, and I couldn't contain my excitement at the prospect of sharing that triumphant feeling with my teammates. I anticipated the joy of seeing their faces light up with smiles.

As I reached the office, my expectations were met. All my teammates were congregated around the coffee machine, their voices weaving together in an uplifting symphony of laughter and lively chatter. It was a scene of camaraderie and shared purpose, the chaos of our daily lives momentarily eclipsed by the warmth of connection. Yet, amid this delightful chaos, one particular sight captured my attention—a tray of doughnuts, left open and inviting. The sugary confections seemed to call out to me, serving as a beacon of comfort in a demanding landscape filled with tasks, deadlines, and the relentless pressure of our work.

Without a moment's hesitation, I charted a course directly toward the enticing box of doughnuts, my mind resolutely set on securing not just one, but perhaps two of those delectable delights. The moment was electric with purpose, as if the universe itself conspired to grant me access to this sugary bounty. It was almost as if the sea of people, sensing my single-minded focus and determination, instinctively parted before me, granting me an unobstructed path to my sweet reward. They seemed to understand that standing in my way was not an option, lest they inadvertently find themselves on their backsides, my fervour for confectionery rendering me an unstoppable force of nature.

A triumphant grin stretched across my face, revealing the faint indentations of my dimples, the smile a reflection of the childlike glee bubbling within. My eyes roamed over the array of doughnuts laid out like shiny glazed treasures, each one a small piece of heaven waiting to be devoured. The smell of freshly baked pastries enveloped me, making my mouth water in anticipation, the scent mingling with memories of past indulgences and promises of future ones. After much deliberation, weighing the merits of each tempting option, I finally settled on two: a raspberry jam-filled pastry with a creamy frosting that promised a burst of tartness and sweetness in every bite, and a chocolate-glazed treat with a luxurious ganache filling that spoke of decadence and delight.

As I turned to leave, my treasures secured, I couldn't help but feel a profound sense of gratitude for this small moment of indulgence amidst our often hectic and demanding lives. Abby stood nearby, sipping from a steaming cup of coffee, the aroma mingling with that of the doughnuts, and wearing a knowing smile as she watched me make my choices. Her understanding of my predictable love affair with sweets was evident in her eyes. The rest of our team stood around us, their expressions ranging from amusement to envy. Amused by my predictable love for sweets, envious of my ability to indulge without guilt, they watched with a mix of admiration and longing. But in that moment, all I felt was pure joy and contentment, surrounded by friends and enjoying every blissful bite of my doughnuts, each morsel a testament to the simple pleasures that life offers.

As my gaze scanned the room, taking in the familiar faces and the atmosphere of camaraderie and shared purpose, I couldn't help but feel a surge of hope bubble up inside me. My team, a remarkable group of determined and talented individuals, sat around the large wooden table with their heads bowed in concentration, the air humming with the quiet intensity of their efforts. "Any new leads or updates?" I asked eagerly, my heart racing with anticipation at the prospect of progress. I desperately hoped that one of them had made a breakthrough in our investigation, uncovering clues that might lead us to the people responsible for the unspeakable atrocities committed by Aldrich and Jeremiah's.

The room was charged with a palpable sense of urgency, an intense collective drive to ensure that justice would be served, and I was certain that together, we would not rest until we had uncovered every last shred of truth. Mini, who had been sitting quietly, slowly raised her hand. Her voice wavered ever so slightly as she began to speak, "I have a few updates, but I'm not sure if they're relevant." Despite her uncertainty, her eyes shone with determination, and her fingers fidgeted nervously on the edge of the table. "Jess, I've been working closely with Ogma to provide counselling and support to the victims we rescued from the facilities we raided." I was already aware of this information - Mini's powerful empathetic abilities had been crucial in establishing trust and gaining the cooperation of these deeply traumatised individuals. Nevertheless, hearing her speak about it filled me with pride.

I could see the inner turmoil reflected in her eyes, fully aware of how difficult it was for her to control and manage such intense emotions. Yet, with a nod and a determined look on her face, she continued to speak. "Some of the stories I have heard are truly terrible; the ones who put these kids through such horrors are truly monsters. But that's not what I wanted to say." Her voice trembled slightly, and she paused to take a steadying breath, gathering her thoughts before proceeding.

The weight of what she was about to share seemed to press down on her shoulders like an invisible burden, and I could sense the gravity of the moment as she gathered her thoughts, preparing to reveal something deeply significant, something that perhaps she had been holding back until now, choosing this moment to finally bring it into the light. Her eyes met mine, filled with a mixture of determination and apprehension.

"The survivors who have been there the longest are starting to open up about what they experienced," she began, her voice steady but tinged with the echo of the horrors she had witnessed. "It's horrifying, and I'm still trying to process everything they've told me, trying to make sense of the unimaginable. But what's even more disturbing, more chilling, is that some of the victims...if you can even call them that anymore...fully embraced what was being done to them. They weren't just passive recipients; they started encouraging others, convincing them to view the experiments as a good thing, something beneficial. And those with low self-esteem or similar vulnerable mindsets were taken away from the rest of the victims for long, isolating periods of time."

She paused, taking a deep breath to steady herself, her voice dropping to a whisper that seemed to carry the weight of the world. "When they returned, they were different. Changed in ways that were both subtle and profound. And all they would say is that they had been 'chosen'. That word, 'chosen', it haunts me. When I think about those individuals, I feel a cold fear creeping up my spine, an icy dread that won't let go." As she spoke, each word seemed to echo in the air around us, and I could feel my own fear rising, trying to imagine what those victims must have gone through, how it twisted and transformed them into something unrecognisable to their fellow survivors, their own humanity obscured by whatever they had endured.

I turned to Mini, my heart pounding, and asked, my voice low and urgent with the pressing need for answers. "Do we have any of the so-called chosen in our care at the moment?"

Mini's expression was solemn, her eyes reflecting the gravity of our predicament as she slowly shook her head, adding a layer of tension to the already charged atmosphere. "No and to be completely honest, I believe this situation might actually work in our favour, albeit in a rather unexpected way," she continued, her tone contemplative. "You see, our task would become infinitely more challenging, more intricate, if they were still being held alongside the other victims. The presence of even a single 'chosen' among them could shift the dynamics in ways we are currently unable to predict or control."

Hearing her reasoning, a faint sliver of relief washed over me, offering a small respite from the overwhelming uncertainty. "Well, that's a small consolation," I acknowledged, trying to find some solace in her words. "Do you think it could've been a case of Stockholm syndrome?" I asked, my curiosity piqued by the thought.

Mini's brow furrowed deeply as she pondered my question, her mind clearly sifting through the possibilities. "No," she finally responded, her voice firm with conviction. "From what I understand, they willingly embraced their role as chosen ones, seemingly without coercion or manipulation."

The thought twisted my stomach into knots, the implications unsettling. "Do we have any idea where they might be now?" I inquired, hopeful for any lead.

Once again, Mini shook her head, the motion conveying a mix of frustration and determination. "No, we don't have that information yet. However, I am committed to continuing my work with them, to see if I can uncover any additional information that might aid us in our efforts," she stated resolutely.

I nodded grimly, understanding the limitations we faced and acknowledging that there was little else we could do at the moment. "Are there any other updates or developments we should be aware of?" I asked, eager for any new information.

Mini's words lingered in the air, heavy with hesitation and tension. I could almost feel her inner turmoil as she braced herself to speak again.

"There are two things I must inform you of," she began, her voice quivering slightly, betraying a torrent of unspoken emotions that lay beneath her composed exterior. "The first is that once Ogma has successfully secured a safe site for the victims, I have made the difficult decision to transfer there. I strongly believe that my skills and expertise would be more effectively utilised in directly assisting the victims, rather than continuing to work on this case from afar," she elaborated, the firmness of her resolve unmistakable in every syllable she uttered.

Her words weighed heavily on my heart, sinking it like a stone being dragged to the depths of the ocean. Mini, my steadfast companion since I had first ventured out from the sanctuary of the cave, had stood by me unwaveringly through every gruelling step of my training at the agency facility and throughout the relentless challenges of this case. The thought of continuing without her presence by my side seemed impossible to fathom. Yet, deep within, I recognised the truth in her decision and found myself unable to contest it, however much I wished to do so.

As she spoke, her voice trembled with emotion, and I could feel my heart beating faster, its rhythm echoing in my ears. Her words lingered heavily in the air, each one striking me with the force of a physical blow, leaving an aching imprint on my chest. "And..." she faltered, taking a deep, shuddering breath before continuing with palpable hesitation, "some of the young victims we discovered are elves. They have described feeling powerful auras constantly surging through their beings, like relentless waves crashing against a rocky shore. And on one of the days when experiments were conducted, they witnessed a mysterious man observing them...someone they described as an imposing figure whose power reminded them of those belonging to the higher council ranks, perhaps even akin to the enigmatic watchers."

Her revelation added yet another intricate layer to an already overwhelmingly complex and daunting situation, leaving me with a cascade of questions that seemed to multiply endlessly, rather than providing any semblance of clarity or answers. A burgeoning sense of urgency gnawed at me, an insistent drive to fully comprehend the vast and intricate scope of what we were entangled with.

My mind was a tumultuous whirlpool, a chaotic spiral of dark and ominous figures that seemed to dance on its periphery, their sinister presence lurking ominously in the shadowy recesses of my thoughts. Their eyes, glowing like burning hot coals, were imbued with an otherworldly intensity that pierced through the gloom, sending relentless shivers cascading down my spine. The gravity of her revelation struck me with the force of a colossal tidal wave, a formidable wall of realisation threatening to engulf me entirely in an endless sea of fear and bewilderment. It dragged me under with an unyielding grip, pulling me down into the depths, leaving me gasping for air as I struggled desperately to keep my head above the chaotic, swirling waters.

My heart pounded furiously, each beat a thunderous drum within my chest, as though it would burst forth from its confines at any moment, overwhelmed by the sheer weight and enormity of our predicament. It felt as if the full force of an avalanche had come crashing down upon me, burying any flicker of hope or sense of safety beneath its immense, suffocating mass. Panic surged through my mind like a raging, tumultuous river, a relentless torrent that overwhelmed me with a flood of fear and disarray, as I frantically searched for any semblance of answers amidst the swirling chaos.

"Wait," I gasped, my voice catching as I struggled to form coherent thoughts amidst the storm raging in my head, "are you suggesting that one of the watchers could be responsible for all of this?" Her solemn, resolute nod confirmed my deepest and most terrifying fears, the implications of her words hanging heavily in the air like a foreboding death sentence. The fear that had gripped me tightened its unyielding hold, threatening to suffocate me with its paralysing, vice-like grip, as the reality of our situation settled over me like an oppressive shroud.

My heart was thundering in my chest, each beat echoing like a drum as I frantically asked if anyone else had any leads. My mind was a whirlwind of thoughts, teeming with the tantalising possibility that we might finally uncover the answers we had been relentlessly pursuing. I silently pleaded that no one else would have anything to add, yearning for a moment to fully digest the bombshell Mini had just dropped on us. The revelation was staggering, and I needed time to wrap my mind around it.

But my hopes crumbled like a fragile sandcastle as Abby's voice piped up. She spoke hesitantly, each word laced with a subtle undercurrent of fear and trouble, adding yet another layer to our already burgeoning list of complications. Anxiety twisted my stomach into tight, uncomfortable knots as I turned to face her, steeling myself for whatever information she was about to share. Perhaps, I thought with a flicker of desperate hope, it wouldn't be as catastrophic as the recent news that one of our trusted allies had committed an act of betrayal against us.

My heart felt impossibly heavy, like a leaden weight sinking ever deeper into the abyss of my chest, as I anxiously awaited Abby's revelation. Each second seemed to stretch into an eternity, the passage of time warping under the pressure of anticipation, and I found myself holding my breath, lungs aching for relief. Then, at last, Abby's words emerged, slicing through the oppressive silence like a lighthouse beacon piercing through the dense fog of night. It had been weeks—long, gruelling weeks—since we had stumbled upon any substantial leads concerning Aldrich, our elusive and cunning adversary. Could this be the breakthrough we had been yearning for with every fibre of our being?

"I might have something on Aldrich," Abby declared, her voice a hopeful chime in the otherwise somber and heavy atmosphere. Her statement cut through the tension like a sharp knife, sending a jolt of eager anticipation through me. My ears practically stood on end, straining to catch every possible nuance of her words, hungry for any scrap of information about our elusive target. We had been on Aldrich's trail for what felt like an eternity, our efforts yielding little to no success. But now, in Abby's hesitant yet promising words, there was a glimmer—a faint, delicate glimmer—of possibility, igniting a spark of hope that we might finally be on the verge of a breakthrough.

"Okay, I'm listening. What have you got for us?" I prompted eagerly, my curiosity piqued as I anticipated what she had uncovered. She hesitated momentarily, drawing in a deep breath to steady herself before finally speaking. "You're still relatively new to the inner workings of the paranormal society," she began, "so it's understandable that you might not have realised that within our community, drugs and other substances aren't regarded with the same level of taboo as they are in human society. You see, the effects of these substances don't linger for long, and there aren't any lasting side effects for supernaturals like us. Unlike humans, who can suffer from overdoses or have dangerous, harmful trips, we remain unaffected in the long term."

Her words hung in the air as she continued, "I've been hearing whispers about a new drug that's recently hit the market with quite an impact. Normally, this isn't something I would concern myself with, but it caught my attention when one of the technicians at the blood bank casually mentioned it to me. It's been spreading rapidly, making its way through the streets, but the unusual part is that they aren't selling it. Instead, they're distributing it without charge, giving it away for free."

My eyebrows knitted together in confusion, my mind grappling with the oddity of the situation. "Why would anyone do something like that?" I questioned, the perplexity evident in my voice.

"Apparently," Abby replied, her voice layered with tones of resignation interwoven with deep concern, "they believe in disseminating the experience of this magical high to as many people as possible, irrespective of the fallout." Her words trailed off as she exhaled a heavy sigh, the burden of the revelation hanging palpably between us.

I could feel the tension in the air thickening, pressing in on us from every side. With a tremor in my voice that betrayed both my resolve and inner disquiet, I ventured, "I've seen reports detailing scenarios where dealers dangle free samples in front of unsuspecting people only to later exploit them—squeezing them dry financially until they're forced into desperate acts like prostitution. Is that what we're confronting here?" I leaned forward slightly, eyes flitting among my colleagues, searching for any spark of confirmation or denial in their expressions that might quell my rising anxiety.

Abby's face remained inscrutable, her features a mask of stoic calm as she answered, "Our intelligence suggests otherwise. It appears that for paranormals, this substance does not trigger the typical addictive dependency associated with other drugs. In fact, it disperses from their systems within a few days. We haven't documented any surge in addiction within the paranormal community so far."

Taking a moment to digest her words, I tried to piece the puzzle together. "So here we have a hazardous drug being handed out like a free candy," I summarised, my tone a blend of incredulity and cautious curiosity. "But then you mentioned that it isn't actually classified as illegal in the eyes of most paranormals. So, why does it stir such alarm, and where does Aldrich fit into this tangled web?"

Abby's eyes darkened as she leaned closer, her voice lowering to an intense, almost ominous murmur. "The troubling aspect of this drug isn't just its availability; it seems to have the power to manipulate—a capability to bend someone's will while they drown in their dream-induced escape. Imagine being ensnared by an overpowering enchantment, trapped in a dreamscape where reality slips away—and think of the havoc that could ensue for those caught in its grip." The thought sent a cold shudder through me, the prospect of paranormals falling prey to such an influence is both chilling and deeply disturbing.

" I've met with several of my go-to informants—folks who always seem to possess insider information on major happenings in our world. They confirmed that Aldrich is not just another player; he's a major supplier of this drug. and Anything he touches seems destined to spell trouble for us." she paused, giving us time to think of the implications. "from what I can tell since he was unmasked as a traitor, he's been keeping a low profile, moving between secured locations, always shadowed by heavy security. Yet, despite this cautious behaviour, the whispers suggest he continues to pull strings for his mysterious superior behind the scenes." she continued

The mere mention of Aldrich sent waves of unease crashing over me, like relentless tides battering a fragile shore. The thought of him lurking in the murky shadows, orchestrating chaos and dissent from some hidden corner, filled me with an unsettling dread that curled around my spine. My mind spun wildly, reeling with the exhilaration of finally having a promising lead, yet this sensation mingled strangely with a profound sense of bafflement. Though we now possessed a crucial thread to follow, critical pieces didn't quite fit together seamlessly. Why would someone dare to risk capture by dispensing drugs with the nonchalance of handing out candy on a sunny afternoon? It struck me as an utterly reckless move—especially coming from a man already squarely on our agency's radar for immediate apprehension, a man who must have known the risks he was courting.

"Well, shit, this has been quite the briefing," I muttered under my breath, trying to process the influx of information swirling around me.

"Okay," I continued, gathering my thoughts and addressing my team. "That is a lot to take in for now. Keith, Milo, I want you to work closely with Mini and see if we can gather more information from the children. Let's try to get names and descriptions so we can locate the missing ones who identify themselves as 'the chosen.' And for now, no one should delve into investigating the watchers until I have spoken with Alexander. We don't want to step on any toes or risk jeopardising any part of this delicate operation." My instructions were met with affirming nods from my colleagues as they left the room, Mini trailing behind them. I could only assume they were heading straight to the hotel where Lyn had secured accommodations to assist in the recovery of the victims, a safe haven amidst the storm. This case was becoming more convoluted and knotted by the minute, and I couldn't shake off the feeling that there was something far bigger and more sinister at play here, lurking just beneath the surface.

Turning to face Lancaster, the former detective with years of experience etched into his features, I asked, "Lancaster, have you had any experience working in the narcotics units of the human police force?" His response was a confident nod, his eyes reflecting a history of collaboration and shared goals.

"A few of my cases have overlapped with theirs," he replied, "and I know some individuals within the department who owe me favours. I believe I can provide valuable insight into investigating this angle, offering a perspective that might prove crucial."

"Excellent," I responded, feeling a surge of determination. "Gudmundur, Abby, and Lancaster, I want our primary focus to be on dismantling this drug ring—if we can even call it that at this stage. Squeeze the dealers for every shred of information, gather intel on the whereabouts of Aldrich, and leave no stone unturned. As for myself, I will divide my time between both teams but for now I need to update Alexander on our progress."

As I exited the briefing room, each step felt heavier, my shoulders burdened as if carrying the weight of an entire world teetering on the brink of chaos. The situation was becoming increasingly convoluted with each passing minute. Survivors had courageously come forward, their testimonies pointing fingers at someone wielding immense power—possibly a figure seated among the esteemed council of the most influential beings in existence. The gravity of their accusations was staggering. Meanwhile, within our own ranks, a traitor was recklessly distributing dangerous drugs, treating them as if they were mere trifles. There had to be a link between these seemingly disparate events, but my mind was tangled in confusion, unable to unravel the web of connections. Perhaps Aldrich, in his desperation, was attempting to erase any incriminating evidence, opting for the swiftest and most ruthless path available. The more I pondered over these possibilities, the more my head throbbed with the relentless pounding of frustration. I realised I needed to compartmentalise, to shove these thoughts into the recesses of my mind and concentrate on the immediate tasks at hand. It was imperative to maintain my composure and keep my wits sharp. Yet, the mere thought of Alexander, with his imposing presence, requesting my company made my nerves flutter like anxious butterflies. I stood outside his door, my body tense and wracked with anticipation. He had summoned me, and I knew there was no refusing this call; I was already at his threshold. Taking a deep, steadying breath, I lifted my hand to knock, but froze in place as his authoritative voice resonated from within: "Yes, Jessica? Please come in."

With trembling hands, I pushed against the weighty wooden door, feeling its resistance before it creaked open, and I stepped into his opulent office. My heart pounded heavily in my chest, a rapid melody of anticipation and fear weaving through my veins. My gaze immediately landed on Alexander, his sharp, chiseled features set in a stoic expression as he sat regally behind his grandiose desk, like a king surveying his domain. Yet it was the sight of the sleazy man casually lounging on the plush leather sofa that made my stomach churn uneasily. He held a delicate, porcelain teacup in one hand, as if this was just another mundane meeting for him, an everyday occurrence in his world of shadows and secrets. My palms began to perspire as I cautiously approached, each step echoing my uncertainty about how this unexpected encounter would unfold. The atmosphere in the room felt thick, almost suffocating, with tension and unease, like the charged air before a brewing storm on the horizon.

"Jessica," Alexander's voice cut through the silence, usually warm and inviting, now imbued with a tone of control and unwavering authority. He gestured towards the man sitting in the chair next to him with a commanding sweep of his hand. "Allow me to introduce you to Mr. Rickson. He possesses valuable information that could greatly benefit us." I obediently took a seat across from Mr. Rickson, studying his appearance with a scrutinising gaze as he did the same with calculating eyes. His sharply tailored suit, likely costing a small fortune, exuded an air of power and command, a testament to his influence and wealth. Yet, there was something about him—a certain aura—that whispered of deceit and cunning lurking beneath his polished exterior.

A thin sheen of sweat glistened on his brow, betraying his discomfort and unease despite his attempt at maintaining a composed facade. As for myself, I couldn't shake off the feeling of apprehension and uncertainty that settled like a lead weight in my gut, an instinctive warning of the unknown paths ahead.

Alexander approached the table with a measured stride, presenting me with a substantial, weighty file, its contents almost spilling over the brim. "You will need this later," he stated with a seriousness that commanded attention, his voice imbued with an authoritative gravity that immediately captured the room's focus.

"But right now," he continued, "I'll explain why we need your help." The weight of his words intensified the atmosphere, casting an ominous shadow over the room, which seemed to grow darker with each passing moment.

As Alexander began to speak, the words that emerged from his mouth sent shivers cascading down my spine. "It has come to my attention," he declared, his tone steady yet laden with urgency, "that a new drug is circulating within the human population of the city." The gravity of his revelation caused my heart to race, pounding in my chest as the seriousness of the situation sank in. This couldn't be mere coincidence, I thought, as the pieces of a disturbing puzzle began to align.

His voice deepened with gravity as he continued, "Ordinarily, this isn't an issue we would entangle ourselves with, but we received a report from a laboratory that has been analysing the compound. The findings were alarming—it is concocted with magic and contains ingredients that should not be accessible to the human population." His words hung in the air, heavy with implication.

Overwhelmed by a rising tide of fear and suspicion, I couldn't help but interrupt. "Alex," I interjected, my voice tinged with urgency, "it might be a coincidence, but during the briefing I just held, Abigail mentioned something about a drug being distributed to the paranormal community. It might trace back to Aldrich." My mistrust of Mr. Rickson was palpable, and I was cautious about how much information I disclosed.

"This might be connected," Alexander replied with a calm assurance that somehow eased the tension. "I will speak to Abigail later to confirm the information." I simply nodded, feeling a wave of relief wash over me, reassured that Alexander was taking this matter with the seriousness it deserved.

Returning to his detailed briefing, his words struck me with the force of a ton of bricks. "The drug we are dealing with is called crimson," he began, his tone grave. "This particular compound appears to have certain similarities to the chemicals we discovered at the facilities you recently shut down. Based on the comprehensive information you provided, I'm convinced that whoever is behind the abductions, the murders, and the operation of those previous facilities is all interconnected in some nefarious way." He paused for a moment, allowing the heavy significance of his words to settle in before he continued with his analysis.

"The police first encountered traces of this dangerous substance in some of the city's most disreputable dive bars, which are infamous for their frequent brawls and violent incidents. It was also discovered in locations known for being frequented by addicts, but now, it has spread beyond those confines and has become the latest go-to drug in the club scene," Alex explained. His normally impassive face had taken on a somber expression as he described the situation.

"This lethal concoction is comprised of a disturbing mix of shapeshifter saliva and vampiric venom, combined with potent medicinal herbs, and is then cooked using dark magic," Alex continued, his voice carrying the weight of the grim reality. "The individual or group responsible for the creation of this drug has been enticing people with free samples, promising them an experience that will make them feel invincible and provide the most exhilarating high of their lives. Once these unsuspecting individuals are hooked, they are mercilessly exploited for everything they have. And that's if they are fortunate enough to avoid the peril of a bad trip, which could potentially transform them into homicidal maniacs."

Alex's explanation was meticulous and detailed, his typically stoic demeanour now replaced by a somber seriousness that highlighted the dire nature of the threat we were facing. His voice, usually calm and measured, carried an urgency that was hard to ignore. I leaned forward, my elbows resting on the table, hands clasped tightly in front of me, a sign of my intense focus and the gravity of the moment. I turned my attention to the guest seated next to Alex, a figure shrouded in an air of mystery.

The atmosphere in the room was almost suffocating with tension, a tangible force that seemed to press down on us, reminding us all of the critical situation at hand. The severity of our predicament was not lost on anyone present, and I could feel the weight of their collective gazes upon me, scrutinising my every move, analysing every word I was about to speak. It was as if they were searching for reassurance, a sign that there was a way out of the mess we found ourselves in.

"If this crimson substance and the drug Abigail informed me about are indeed the same," I began, my voice steady despite the underlying unease creeping up my spine, "they seem to have a completely opposite effect on humans compared to their impact on the paranormal community. This discrepancy is alarming and could be key to understanding the larger picture. Do we have any leads on who might be orchestrating this operation or where they could possibly be manufacturing it? Perhaps we could apply some pressure on the lower-level dealers, see if we can extract any useful information from them," I suggested, trying to maintain my composure and project confidence, despite the inner turmoil.

The guest's eyes widened with a hint of surprise, an involuntary reaction that spoke volumes, before they shared an uneasy glance with Alex. There was a moment of silence, heavy and expectant, before the guest finally spoke.

"Miss Dyer, Alexander has often praised your skills and capabilities," they admitted, their tone was a curious blend of respect and incredulity, as though they were trying to reconcile the reality before them with the tales they had heard. "However, I must confess, I didn't anticipate someone so young and, if you don't mind me saying, so delicate-looking to be at the forefront of such a serious operation."

I was momentarily taken aback by this comment, not entirely sure why my appearance should hold any significance in the matter at hand. It was a stark reminder of the biases that persistently lingered, even in high-stakes situations like this one. The focus should have been on my abilities and the task at hand, not on superficial appearances. Nonetheless, I chose to concentrate on what lay ahead, knowing deep down that appearances were irrelevant when it came to the substance of what truly mattered.

Mr. Rickson's intense gaze seemed to pierce through me, stripping away any facade of confidence I had managed to muster, as though he could see into the very depths of my soul and lay bare all my insecurities. I resisted the urge to shrink away from his penetrating stare, instead opting to meet his invasive gaze with a defiant lift of my chin. Before I could manage to inquire about the nature of this conversation or what it truly entailed, Rickson interrupted with a stern voice that echoed through the room.

"Alexander, I strongly advise against this plan," he declared with an air of authority. "This is an immensely risky situation, and placing this child in such grave danger is utter madness," he continued, gesturing emphatically as he spoke. "The fighters themselves are already highly trained and formidable enough, but when exposed to the effects of the drug... they become ferocious beasts. You would be signing this girl's death warrant by throwing her into the arena with these monsters. Miss Dyer seems more suited for strolling down the high street or sipping cocktails with friends," he added with a sneer of disdain. "But if you put her in there, the outcome will be me bringing back a battered and broken corpse. Is that what you want? Bring me a real fighter, and then we can have a serious discussion about this, but a little girl... you must be joking."

His words hit me like a punch to the gut, but I refused to show any weakness in front of this man. Whoever he was, he had no right to speak about me as if I wasn't even standing here, as if I were some invisible entity. A surge of anger boiled within me, and I could feel myself getting ready to snap. I clenched my fists, determined not to let his dismissive words affect me, and prepared to defend my position with every ounce of strength I possessed.

"Listen here," I growl through gritted teeth, locking eyes with Mr. Rickson, a man who seemed to thrive on intimidation. "I don't know who you think you are, but I won't tolerate you speaking about me as if I'm not even present in the room." My fists clench tightly at my sides, every muscle in my body tensing as I make it clear that I'll stand my ground, no matter the circumstances.

But before I can continue, the arrogant man interrupts me, cutting through the air with a smug smile plastered on his face. "A little girl like you? Against trained fighters under the influence of drugs?" His tone is dripping with condescension, each word carefully designed to belittle and provoke. It's all I can do to keep myself from lunging at him in a fit of anger and frustration.

My patience wears thin and finally snaps. "If you ever want to test your strength against mine," I retort, my voice laced with venom and a steely resolve, "meet me in the damn gym and I'll show you just how tough I am, you pompous asshole." With that final, fiery retort, I rise from my seat, preparing to storm out of Alex's office, my blood boiling with a mix of indignation and fury that threatens to overwhelm me.

"Jessica, please take a seat," Alex interjects, his voice calm yet firm as he gestures toward a leather armchair situated near his polished mahogany desk. "I apologise for our guest's rudeness." His jaw is tense, a visible manifestation of the effort it takes to maintain his composure. "But we have a lead that requires your immediate attention. Rickson will be serving as your inside contact."

Intrigued by this unexpected turn of events, I settled into my chair and crossed my legs, leaning forward slightly to show my keen interest in the conversation. "And what specific information or resources does he have that can aid our investigation?" I asked, choosing my words carefully to convey the importance of the matter.

Rickson mirrored my posture by leaning forward in his chair, a gesture that suggested he was about to share something significant. "I'm an event promoter who specialises in organising gladiator-style fights," he began, his tone carrying a hint of pride in his unique profession. "I organise these events by bringing together fighters, both human and paranormal, from various disciplines. These fighters engage in intense competitions, ranging from chaotic battle royals to intense one-on-one MMA matches."

"That's certainly an interesting line of work," I remarked, my voice carrying a mix of genuine curiosity and a hint of skepticism. I couldn't help but ponder the connection between his unusual career and the intricate web of our current investigation. As I mulled over his explanation, the enigma of how this peculiar profession could intersect with the case we were trying to unravel gnawed at me.

"Let me explain," he began, his voice taut with a palpable tension. "Recently, I've stumbled upon a rather disturbing discovery—a revelation that has shaken the very foundation of my work. Some of my top contestants, the ones who usually don't rise to the top but put a good show in these underground fights, have been using performance-enhancing drugs. Now, under normal circumstances, I turn a blind eye to most things—anything goes in these clandestine battles, except, of course, for firearms or explosives. But this situation is different." He paused briefly, drawing a deep, steadying breath before continuing to unfold his narrative. "The level of punishment they're enduring is beyond anything I've ever witnessed or imagined. It's as if their bodies are being pushed to limits that defy human capability." His eyes shifted toward Alexander, who stood beside him, a pillar of silent support and stoic resolve.

Alexander, exhaling a sigh so profound it seemed to embody the burdens of the entire universe, interrupted the ongoing discussion. "I've conducted a thorough series of tests on the blood samples provided by Rickson following his latest altercation," he began, his voice laden with gravity. "What I uncovered was deeply troubling—it's a significantly more potent and refined variant of crimson. Our analyst strongly suspects that it has been ingeniously laced with hallucinogenic compounds, transforming it into an even more perilous and unpredictable concoction." He fixed his gaze firmly on Rickson, and the silent exchange between them was thick with an unspoken understanding and a shared sense of urgent concern.

"So what does this mean for us?" I inquired, a knot of anxiety tightening in my stomach as I spoke.

"It signifies that attempting to trace this drug back to its origin will not lead us directly to our intended target," Alexander elucidated with a grave expression. "It's quite probable that this is merely a counterfeit version of the original substance that Rickson has brought to our attention."

I muttered a string of curses under my breath, feeling the frustration surge within me. "So what exactly is your plan? Do you expect us to infiltrate this operation and attempt to dismantle whoever is behind it?"

Alex nodded slowly, his eyes narrowing with resolve and determination. "In part, yes. I want you to infiltrate as a fighter and relay critical information back to me. I will then coordinate with your team, and together, we will dismantle the drug network responsible for this."

"How long do you anticipate this operation will last? And just how challenging will it be to infiltrate this network?" I asked, my voice barely rising above a whisper, laden with apprehension.

To my surprise, Rickson appeared uncertain, a flicker of doubt crossing his features. "Honestly, I don't have a clear answer," he admitted openly. "I've conducted some inquiries, but I keep encountering dead ends and insurmountable obstacles." His frustration was etched into his tone.

I couldn't help but snap back, feeling irritable and on edge. "Well, isn't that just fantastic? Our supposed inside man has no useful information for us."

Alex raised a hand to calm my rising agitation before turning his attention back to Rickson and gesturing for him to continue with whatever he had left to say.

"Look," he began, his voice laced with a hint of uncertainty, "all I know for sure is that a significant number of those who have been confirmed as drug users were underdogs. They fought with everything they had, with fierce determination and a sense of desperation, but despite their best efforts, they just couldn't manage to come out on top. So, in order to blend in with them and gain their trust, you'll need to adopt a strategy that makes you appear sloppy and unskilled in your fights." His voice wavered slightly as he concluded, his words hanging in the air.

My frustration quickly morphed into a confusing mix of bewilderment and anger. "What do you mean I have to lose most of my fights?" I demanded, a sense of disbelief colouring my tone. "Why can't I just fight to win?"

Alex's expression shifted, growing more serious and contemplative as he prepared to elaborate on his point. "Think about it," he said slowly, allowing the weight of his words to sink in. "Who would try to sell you enhancers if you were consistently winning every fight? We need them to perceive you as weak and easy to manipulate. Only then will they consider approaching you with their offers."

As I listened intently to Alex lay out his plan, a heavy, sinking feeling anchored itself deep in my stomach. He was right, this was indeed our only opportunity to dismantle the drug dealers' operations and halt the dangerous substance from spreading further. But did it have to be me who took on this perilous task? Was it really necessary for me to put myself in harm's way like this? I couldn't help but question if I was truly prepared to endure not only the physical but also the emotional toll of potentially being beaten on a regular basis.

Sensing my internal struggle, Alex spoke up, as if he had the ability to read my thoughts. "Jess, I know this is a monumental challenge for you," he acknowledged, his voice filled with empathy. "However, you're the sole person on our team capable of pulling this off. The rest of us are either too recognisable or lack the necessary training."

I paused, wrestling with my own hesitations, before finally conceding to the plan. "Alright, I'll do it," I agreed, albeit with great reluctance. "But just be aware that I'm far from thrilled about the prospect of constantly getting beat up."

Alex sought to reassure me. "We don't expect you to be a mere punching bag," he explained earnestly. "You need to fight back, to create the impression that you could actually win with minimal assistance." Despite his encouraging words, the fear and doubt continued to swirl within me, refusing to be silenced.

Suddenly, Rickson's deep, resonant voice cut through my swirling thoughts, pulling me back into the present moment. "I've obtained some video footage of previous fights involving individuals I suspect were using the compound," he announced, his dark eyes glinting with a captivating intensity. "You can study their techniques, observe how they fought, and note how their performance shifted after taking the compound." He leaned in closer, his eyes gleaming with a conspiratorial spark. "If you're willing to follow through with our plan, I can arrange a fight for you within the next four to six weeks."

The mere thought of stepping into the arena filled me with a profound sense of terror. The concept was daunting, an ominous shadow lurking at the edge of my thoughts. "But first," Rickson continued with a steady, determined voice, "we have to create a completely false identity for you. This will ensure your anonymity and safety as you infiltrate their complex and secretive world."

Rickson's words lingered in the room, each syllable adding to the heavy burden that seemed to press down on my shoulders with increasing intensity. "You will have to cut off all ties with anyone from the agency," he elaborated, his voice dropping to a low and urgent tone that demanded attention. "You'll live in shared accommodation under an assumed name, an alias that will become your new identity. Additionally, you will need to secure a job and register at a gym to maintain your cover. I have a few options lined up for you in that regard."

A thrill of excitement surged through me, mingling with a sharp undercurrent of danger that pulsated through my veins. It was an intoxicating mix that left me breathless, yet determined. I agreed to follow the intricate plan Rickson had laid out. "Okay," I responded, striving to maintain my composure despite the adrenaline rush that threatened to overwhelm me. "But I'll need some time with my team to ensure we tie up any loose ends before I plunge into this."

Understanding the gravity of the situation, Alex, who had been silently observing, interjected with a supportive nod, his dark eyes locking onto mine with unwavering resolve. "Of course," he affirmed, his voice a steady anchor in the tumult of emotions swirling around us. "I'll join you in briefing your team. But after that, it is imperative that you leave with Rickson to begin this crucial mission."

A wave of determination surged through me, affirming my resolve as I nodded in understanding of the task at hand. "Let's do it then," I proclaimed with conviction, ready to tackle whatever challenges awaited us in this risky yet exhilarating operation we were about to embark on.

With purposeful strides, I entered the expansive conference room, my presence drawing the attention of my team. They looked up from their computer screens like a pack of curious meerkats, their eyes tracking my movement as I approached the centre of the room.

"Attention everyone, we need an urgent team huddle," I announced, my voice carrying a stern and serious tone that sliced through the usual hum of the room. The abrupt change in atmosphere was palpable, and it immediately captured their full attention. Without hesitation, they gathered around me and Alexander, eager to hear the news.

"I have just been assigned an important undercover mission," I began, feeling a thrilling mix of excitement and anxiety at the prospect of going off the grid. "I will be completely disconnected for an unknown period of time," I continued, emphasising the gravity and unpredictability of the situation. "In my absence, Gudmundur will be taking point on all investigations and will serve as your main point of contact," I instructed, ensuring that the transition would be seamless and effective.

As I surveyed the room, I noticed that the determined expressions of my team members mirrored my own, their faces set with resolve and readiness. "Any objections?" I inquired, wanting to confirm that everyone was aligned with the plan before we embarked on this critical mission.

Abigail, known for her straightforward and no-nonsense demeanour, raised her hand with a characteristic air of confidence. "Why am I not surprised that you have something to say?" I quipped, a hint of humour lightening the tense atmosphere.

"I agree with the plan for the dragon to take over," she began, her words tinged with a sly smile that hinted at the mysterious nature of what she was about to reveal, "but I must request an urgent leave of absence. An unexpected emergency has arisen that will require my immediate attention," she continued, her words wrapped in an air of intrigue, leaving us all to wonder about the nature of her departure.

CHAPTER 4

Undercover Beginnings

After delivering an exhaustive and comprehensive briefing to my team, ensuring that every detail was meticulously covered, I made my way back to Alex's office, where I was poised to organise all the necessary components for the task at hand. The room soon became a hive of activity, alive with the bustling sounds that accompanied our focused efforts: the rustling of shuffling papers, the rhythmic tapping of keyboards echoing like a drumbeat, and the occasional murmur of concentrated conversation as we diligently sorted through the myriad details of the mission. My heart was a symphony of nervous excitement, each beat a reminder that this was my very first mission as an undercover agent. The weight of its significance was not lost on me, and I felt the enormity of the responsibility pressing heavily upon my shoulders.

Before me lay a vast array of extensive documents, each sheet an integral piece of the intricate puzzle I needed to assemble. There was everything from identification records and comprehensive banking history to a fully traceable work and educational background. The level of detail was staggering, and I understood that this was the kind of meticulous precision that could make or break the mission, determining its success or failure.

But then, amidst the focused chaos, a sudden and jarring realisation struck me like a bolt of lightning from a clear blue sky. It sent a shiver down my spine, and I felt a creeping sense of anxiety begin to take hold. If my role was to operate undercover, what exactly was my cover supposed to be? I found myself grappling with a profound uncertainty. I couldn't convincingly pass as entirely human anymore, not after the transformative changes I'd undergone, changes that had irrevocably altered my very essence. The anxiety threatened to overwhelm me, and I struggled to suppress the self-doubt that was now running rampant through my mind. "I don't know if I can pull this off," I confessed aloud, my voice tinged with a self-loathing I couldn't quite mask, despite my best efforts to sound composed.

It was Rickson who shattered the palpable tension in the room, his voice oozing with an unmistakable sense of superiority as he interjected with a certain smugness. "We've got you down as a hybrid," he announced, each word wrapped in an air of assured confidence that left little room for doubt. "Theoretically, it should work. The narrative we've constructed is that you possess a lineage steeped in the paranormal, though it has, over generations, been diluted through interbreeding with humans." His statement lingered in the air, heavy with implication, yet offering a faint glimmer of hope that this meticulously crafted identity might indeed prove sufficient for the daunting mission that lay ahead. I clung to that hope with all my might, recognising it as my sole lifeline in the turbulent and uncharted waters I was preparing to navigate.

As his words settled in, I felt a surge of anger rising within me — an instinctive reaction to his condescension — but I forced it down, suppressing it with the understanding that this was simply part of the job. I glanced down at my new identification, noting that everything remained unchanged except for my last name and place of birth. "Why did you only change my family name and place of birth?" I inquired of Alex, seeking clarity amidst the confusion.

"Smith is a common enough name that it shouldn't raise any flags or attract undue attention," he replied with a calm, measured demeanour. "And Essex is close enough geographically that you won't need to put on an accent or fabricate a backstory." Despite his logical explanation, I couldn't help but cast a wary eye upon Rickson, my instincts tingling with unease. There was something about him that set off alarm bells in my mind, a nagging suspicion that this mission was going to be more complex and challenging than I had initially anticipated.

With a sneer playing at the corners of his mouth, Rickson declared, "You will be staying at one of my properties in Uxbridge for the duration of your assignment. It may not boast the luxury of a hotel, but it functions as a halfway house for individuals hailing from other realms or for those whose presence might raise too many eyebrows in traditional lodging."

He leaned in closer, his voice dropping to a conspiratorial whisper tinged with an unmistakable contempt, as if he were sharing a dark secret that weighed heavily on his mind. "The two beings you will be residing with are a pixie and a tooth fairy," he began, his words laced with both caution and disdain. "Although they are renowned far and wide for their docile and submissive nature, I would still advise you to tread carefully around them." His harsh tone softened ever so slightly, as if a sliver of empathy had managed to pierce through his otherwise steely demeanour. His words carried a faint hint of warning wrapped in weary resignation, as though he had seen much and understood the complexities of dealing with such creatures.

"I have only briefly met them myself," he continued, his expression unreadable, "but they have been informed of your stay and will not interfere with your work." His voice was calm, but it did little to quell the unease stirring inside me. As he spoke, visions of tiny wings, shimmering in iridescent hues, and glittering magic danced through my mind, reminding me of the fantastical creatures that lived hidden within his world. A world that was at once enchanting and perilous.

A wave of frustration and discomfort washed over me as he casually dismissed my new housemates, reducing them to mere nuisances in his grand scheme of things. I longed to defend them, to speak up for these mystical beings with whom I would be sharing my living space, but I realised that I couldn't do so without knowing them first. So I chose to clamp my teeth down on my tongue, swallowing my words along with my pride. "They're aware that you'll be one of my new fighters and are unfamiliar with the area," he explained, his tone adopting a condescending edge, as though he were privy to all the secrets of the universe. "You have a strong dominant presence, so they will likely defer to you often." My shoulders slumped under the weight of his assumptions as he finished mansplaining everything to me.

"Just great," I muttered to myself, the irony of my situation sinking in. "I'm supposed to maintain a low profile, yet now I have submissive housemates. How am I expected to fly under the radar if they see me as some kind of leader?" The weight of this realisation settled heavily on my chest, already making me feel like I was in over my head, struggling to balance the demands of my mission with the unexpected responsibilities of being a reluctant leader.

"You don't need to change or pretend to be someone else; just stay true to yourself and try to avoid getting caught up in their issues," he advised, as if reading my thoughts and offering a glimmer of hope. "That sounds easy enough," I replied, skepticism dripping from my words, "but I have a feeling it won't be as simple as you make it sound." He released a deep, weary sigh, acknowledging the difficulty of the situation without uttering a single word in response to my comment. His silence spoke volumes about the complicated dynamics at play, leaving me to ponder the challenges that lay ahead in this strange new world.

*

The journey to Uxbridge unfolded in a thick, almost suffocating silence, a silence that was charged with tension as I mentally braced myself for the challenges that lay ahead. Each passing mile felt like stepping deeper into the unknown, and without the comforting presence of my team—my usual stalwart support system—I was left alone with my thoughts. The mere idea of confronting whatever awaited me without their backing sent involuntary shivers coursing down my spine, a chill that seemed to settle into my very bones. In an attempt to quell the anxiety bubbling within me, I closed my eyes, striving to calm my racing heart and focus intently on the task at hand.

However, my mind, ever restless, couldn't resist straying to thoughts of my elusive vampire ally. Her sudden disappearance had been abrupt and unexplained, leaving me to ponder what urgent matter could have possibly demanded her immediate attention. Was there a new, menacing threat lurking in the shadows? Or perhaps a personal emergency that required her immediate intervention? The sheer number of possibilities whirled around in my head, each more concerning than the last, and they only served to tighten the growing knot of apprehension in my stomach.

After what seemed like an eternity of introspective turmoil, Rickson—who had been silently navigating the journey—finally brought the car to a halt outside a dilapidated property. The sight that met my eyes was a building far past its prime; the paint was flaking off the walls in large patches, and the windows bore long, jagged cracks, casting an eerie aura over the entire scene. As if sensing the need for a change in tone, Rickson turned to me with a stern expression and stated,

"From this moment onward, I would like you to address me as Paul, not Rickson." His voice resonated with an unusual depth and gravity, a departure from the norm. "If you continue to call me by my surname like that, they will perceive it as rudeness on your part."

For the first time since our paths had unexpectedly intertwined, he seemed to be making a deliberate effort to be more personable, his previously rigid demeanour softening ever so slightly. As we stepped out of the vehicle, I couldn't help but observe a palpable transformation in his mannerisms—gone was the cold, distant man with whom I had been journeying all this time. Instead, there was a subtle warmth in his approach, a faint, yet perceptible shift that suggested an underlying willingness to bridge the gap between us, however minuscule it might have been.

"When we get inside, I'll guide you on a quick tour," he continued as we approached the entrance to the building. "Afterward, I'll leave you in their capable hands." He handed me a tattered, well-worn business card. "This is my direct line. We're in this together, so if any issues arise, let me know immediately."

I nodded, a mix of gratitude and unease swirling within me about our newfound partnership. Before I could articulate any further thoughts, he briskly strode towards the door, his demeanour shifting back to being all business. As I trailed behind him into the building, I couldn't shake off the persistent feeling that something ominous was lurking within these walls. Yet, for better or for worse, it seemed that Rickson—now Paul—was resolute in seeing it through alongside me.

With a smooth and effortless grace, he guided me through the house, showing me each room and introducing me to my new housemates in a swift and efficient manner. As we arrived at my designated room, he lingered just long enough to ensure that everything was in order before excusing himself, leaving me with promises that he would reach out to me in the days to come.

Upon entering my new room, I found myself awestruck by the meticulous organisation and thoughtful arrangement that greeted me. The bed was impeccably made, its sheets smooth and unwrinkled, adorned with a perfectly stacked assortment of plush pillows and a cozy, inviting comforter. It seemed to beckon me to relax as soon as I stepped inside. Against one wall stood a sturdy wooden cupboard and a chest of drawers, their contents neatly arranged with clothing that fit me as if they had been tailored just for me. On the opposite side of the room, I noticed a small, tidy desk, upon which rested a sleek, modern laptop that seemed poised and ready to spring to life at a moment's notice.

Before I could delve into my assigned duties, I was well aware that it was standard protocol to conduct a thorough sweep of the room for any hidden surveillance equipment. Yet, before I even had the chance to begin this task, a gentle, almost hesitant knock resonated at my door. From the tentative sound of it, I sensed that the person on the other side was probably timid and filled with a certain hesitancy.

As I turned the doorknob, a light breeze wafted in, bringing with it the sweet, intoxicating scent of jasmine mingled with the warmth of sunlight. Standing before me was Nixie, her coy smile illuminating her face like a soft, glowing lantern. Her honey-blonde curls danced playfully with each step she took toward me, and her eyes, brimming with a mischievous sparkle, seemed to hold their own secrets. "Well, hello there," she greeted me, her voice carrying a hint of shy charm that was both endearing and disarming. "I was wondering if you'd care to join Lunette and me for some tea," she offered, her fingers nervously tugging at the hem of her floral dress, as if she were unsure of how her invitation would be received. "But please don't feel obligated if you're busy," she added hastily, a rosy blush painting her cheeks as she spoke.

I found myself unable to resist the infectious warmth of her smile. "Thank you for the kind invitation. Tea sounds wonderful, and everything is already arranged here, so I would be delighted to join you both," I replied, my heart swelling with a comforting sense of warmth at the thought of spending time with my new housemates.

Nixie's grin broadened with sheer delight at my acceptance, and with an enthusiastic nod, she gracefully led me into the inviting warmth of the living room. The space was a snug sanctuary, thoughtfully embellished with an array of fluffy pillows and a soft, delicately woven blanket casually draped over the couch, inviting anyone to sink into its cozy embrace. The air was infused with the inviting aroma of freshly brewed tea, a scent that seemed to wrap around us like an invisible hug. This fragrance was beautifully complemented by the gentle, rhythmic clinking of porcelain cups that echoed softly in the background, creating an atmosphere of serene comfort. As we settled into our welcoming seats, Nixie and Lunette began to catch up on each other's lives, their voices intertwining into a melodious symphony of laughter and animated conversation, a harmonious duet that danced around the room.

I spent the rest of my afternoon in the delightful company of my new housemate, utterly engrossed in their enthralling stories and eager to learn more about their fascinating lives. As they opened up about their unique upbringings and the paths that had led them to make London their home, I found myself captivated by the vivid and intricate details of their childhoods, as well as the rich traditions and customs of their distinct cultures. The room seemed to come alive with their animated gestures and colourful anecdotes, each word painting a vivid picture that transported me to another world I had never experienced before. It made me profoundly grateful for the opportunity to connect with individuals who were so wonderfully different from myself.

Lunette, with an air of mystery and reverence, revealed to me the secrets of a tooth fairy's ancient and noble duty—a role that, despite the passage of time and changes in tradition, remained just as crucial as ever. Gone were the days when they transformed teeth into treasures; now, they replaced them with artificial ones. My evident confusion must have shown, for she patiently elaborated: "Tooth fairies are guardians, entrusted with the sacred task of safeguarding infants from malicious curses. In ancient times, malevolent magic users would acquire a child's discarded tooth and use it to cast a curse upon their entire bloodline. To prevent such horrors, an order of faeries was established, charged with the responsibility of watching over and protecting these precious little relics. And in exchange for the teeth, we bestow upon them a gift." As she spoke, her words conjured an image in my mind of a tiny yet powerful being, hovering protectively over a sleeping child, warding off unseen dangers with a determined vigilance. It gave new, profound meaning to the term "guardian angel."

"In today's world, parents often place gifts under their children's pillows, so we, the faeries, have adapted by leaving fake teeth in place of the real ones, thereby preserving an ancient tradition within a modern context. These teeth are far more significant than one might initially assume—they are transported to a secret village, where they are protected with the utmost care, much like one would safeguard a collection of invaluable jewels. My family has been involved in this revered duty for countless generations, and we take immense pride in our role. As Lunette completed her detailed explanation, her face lit up with a glow of pride and satisfaction. 'I had no idea about any of this,' I admitted, filled with wonder. 'I always believed the tooth fairy was just a fictional tale.' This newfound revelation seemed to cause Lunette to blush slightly. The notion of the hidden village and its devoted guardians suddenly appeared more mystical and fascinating than I had ever imagined."

"Nixie, why don't you tell Jess a little about yourself?" Lunette suggested, her voice a gentle attempt to redirect the focus away from herself and onto someone else. Lunette's words lingered in the air like a delicate mist, prompting Nixie to narrow her eyes in response.

Her glance held a subtle hint of disdain towards Lunette, a stark contrast to the playful and jovial demeanour she had exhibited up until that moment. The change in her attitude was so unexpected that I couldn't help but let out a light chuckle, the sound escaping before I could stop it. "Forgive me," I quickly interjected, aware that my laughter might have been perceived as impolite or even mocking. "I didn't mean to offend you in any way. Your sudden shift just caught me off guard." I paused for a moment, feeling the need to offer a more earnest apology.

"Please, I urge you not to feel any obligation to divulge anything about yourself that brings discomfort. I truly, sincerely, and wholeheartedly comprehend your position." Each word that escaped my lips was a meticulously crafted deception, a strategic dance of language designed to soothe and reassure them, while I skilfully masked my true intentions. Despite the complex web of motives hidden beneath my facade, I found myself unable to press these two individuals into disclosing their intimate stories if they were not naturally inclined to do so.

To my astonishment, Nixie began to speak, her voice a delicate blend of softness and hesitance. "No, it's alright," she said, her eyes reflecting a hint of determination. "One of the reasons I'm traveling is to truly discover who I am." There was a pause, a moment where she seemed to collect her thoughts like delicate petals before continuing her tale.

"My clan of pixies is renowned throughout all realms for our vibrant and gregarious nature. We are the masters of creating magnificent celebrations and lavish parties that leave an indelible impression on any who attend," she explained, her voice carrying the melody of pride interwoven with a touch of longing. As Nixie spoke of her people, a wistful smile graced her features, highlighting her deep connection to her heritage.

"The energy of my entire clan radiates with an infectious confidence and joy. It is ingrained in our very being to ease the worries and fears of those around us. This natural ability is a cherished trait among most, if not all, of my kind; however, I find myself as an exception," she confessed, her words tinged with a hint of vulnerability. "I am an extreme introvert, something unheard of among pixies according to the council of elders. I grapple with social anxiety and have been known to faint in large groups, much to my family's concern. In a heartfelt endeavour to help me conquer my fears, they sent me to the city to desensitise myself to the bustling throngs of people and overwhelming crowds."

Nixie blushed deeply, a rosy hue painting her cheeks, as she spoke about her personal circumstances, a mix of embarrassment and vulnerability colouring her words. Despite the guilt that gnawed at me for having laughed earlier, I felt a deep, genuine sympathy for her predicament. Her openness struck a chord within me. "Nixie, please forgive me for my earlier laughter," I implored, my voice filled with regret. "It was insensitive and thoughtless of me, and I truly apologise. If there's anything at all that I can do to assist you while I'm here, please do not hesitate to ask," I offered sincerely, hoping my words might provide some comfort. They seemed to wrap around her like a warm embrace, soothing her frayed nerves and encouraging her to open up even more about herself to us.

The melodic cadence of her voice hinted at a heritage rooted in the picturesque counties of Devon and Cornwall, her speech lilting with the distinct rhythms and musicality of those regions. "I have always felt a deep connection with nature," she explained, her lips curling into a soft, contented smile that spoke volumes about her love for the natural world. "If you ever can't find me, chances are I'll be somewhere barefoot, communing with Mother Nature," she added, a playful glint in her eyes as she gestured to the charm bracelet adorning her wrist. It was decorated with delicate leaves and feathers, each charm telling a story of her affinity with the earth. "I'm also gifted in the art of craft magic," she continued with a hint of pride. "If you ever need any charms or amulets, just let me know." A light, musical laugh escaped her as she added with a twinkle in her eye, "And don't be surprised if random animals show up around me. They seem to be drawn to my energy." Her eyes sparkled with warmth and sincerity as she went on, "But don't worry, they only come to me when they need something and then leave once their request is fulfilled. I wouldn't want you to think I'm some kind of crazy animal lady."

As soon as her words found their way into the air, my mind buzzed with a million questions and a rising tide of excitement.

"Oh my god, do you have any animals in the house?" I exclaimed, my voice bubbling over with excitement and enthusiasm that I could no longer keep locked inside. She cast a nervous glance at Lunette, her companion, before she responded with a slow, deliberate nod of her head, as though she was weighing each word carefully. "I have a cat in my room," she replied softly, her voice carrying a slight note of apology, as if she was already bracing herself for some sort of judgment or disapproval from me. Just the mention of a furry companion sent a thrill coursing through my heart, and the mere idea of meeting her little creature filled me with an overwhelming sense of joy and anticipation.

"His name is Argus, and he's a majestic Maine Coon," she continued, and immediately my eyes lit up with both joy and eager anticipation. "Could I possibly meet him sometime? Or is he not fond of strangers?" I asked nervously, my fingers fidgeting restlessly in anticipation of the opportunity. The thought of being able to shower love and affection on an animal, even if it was one that belonged to someone else, filled me with a warm, comforting feeling that spread through my whole being. Nixie paused for a moment, her bright blue eyes glinting with a hint of mischief and amusement. "I think he should be fine with you," she said with a playful grin. "I'll bring him down later and see how he takes to you. But fair warning, he can be quite judgy sometimes." A slight pang of nervousness shot through me at the thought of being judged by a cat, but despite that, I couldn't wait to meet sweet Argus.

As the afternoon began to slowly drift into the welcoming arms of evening and the sun began its gradual descent beyond the horizon, we decided it was time to call it a day. With lazy yawns and the gentle stretching of limbs, we each headed to our respective areas of the house.

Before I parted ways with Nixie, she enthusiastically asked if I would like to meet Argus, her cherished pet. Without a moment's hesitation, I eagerly accepted the invitation, my heart pounding with excitement at the thought of encountering such a magnificent creature.

As she opened the door to her private sanctuary, I was immediately captivated by the vibrant greenery that enveloped me. Every conceivable shade of green and brown seemed to blend seamlessly, creating a harmonious tapestry of plant life. The room was filled with plants of all shapes and sizes, each positioned with careful precision. Some nestled in ornate pots around the room's perimeter, while others hung gracefully from the ceiling, their tendrils cascading down like verdant waterfalls. With each step I took further into the room, I felt as though I had wandered into an ancient, untouched forest in an enchanting realm far from the mundane world. The intoxicating aroma of the assorted plants filled my senses, transporting me into a magical, dreamlike world.

Then, my attention was irresistibly drawn to a majestic figure reclined regally on the bed before me. It was Argus, the magnificent Maine coon, his fur as black as midnight, gradually lightening into a tapestry of greys and silvers. Without a moment's pause, I hurried over to him, settling his head comfortably onto my lap, eager to lavish him with affection. As I scratched behind his ears and heard the soothing melody of his contented purring, I was overcome with disbelief at my own audacity.

When I glanced up, I was met with Nixie's startled expression, a sudden realisation dawning upon me that I might have overstepped by assuming such familiarity with her beloved companion. Despite the wave of embarrassment that washed over me, I couldn't help but be in awe of the serene beauty and tranquility of this hidden oasis within Nixie's space.

Taking a deep, steadying breath to collect my thoughts and summon the necessary courage, I prepared myself to apologise sincerely. "I'm terribly sorry for any discomfort I may have caused. I truly didn't mean to be so forward, and I deeply apologise for any intrusion. I'll just leave you two to enjoy some peace and quiet," I expressed with genuine regret in my voice. Slowly and carefully, I began to rise from the bed, trying to gently extricate myself from

Argus's warm embrace. However, quite unexpectedly, I felt his sharp claws latch onto my leg like tiny, determined daggers, their grip causing a small gasp of surprise to escape my lips. Just as I was about to gently disentangle his claws from my leg, I felt the comforting presence of Nixie's hand on my shoulder. She gazed at me with a broad, reassuring smile that seemed to convey a multitude of unspoken words, instantly putting my mind at ease.

"Please, stay as you are. I must apologise for my initial reaction. I'm simply not accustomed to seeing him so friendly with someone new. It's his usual habit to hide away when he encounters unfamiliar faces. His current behaviour is quite unusual, but I choose to see it as an indication that you possess a kind-hearted nature. Argus doesn't approach anyone who harbours darkness in their hearts," she explained with a seriousness that caught my attention. As I absently stroked the cat, I couldn't help but inquire further, "Could you elaborate on what you mean? It seems like there's something weighing heavily on your mind."

Nixie gave a slight shake of her head, much like a dog trying to rid itself of water after a bath. "I'm sorry, it's really nothing significant. But should you ever find yourself in need of someone to talk to or simply desire the comfort of some kitty snuggles, Argus and I will always be more than happy to oblige," she offered warmly.

At that precise moment, Argus stretched his lithe and agile body with a languid grace, as if savouring every muscle's movement, before leaping elegantly from my lap. He wove his way around Nixie's legs, radiating an aura of deep contentment and serene peace, completely at ease and comfortable in his familiar surroundings.

With Argus no longer nestled on my lap, I found myself without the comfort of my feline companion and decided to make a hasty retreat to the sanctuary of my room. I needed to focus on the work that awaited me, stored on the USB drive. The tension that had earlier been hanging in the air had completely dissipated, replaced by a sense of warmth and comfort that came from the harmonious presence of Nixie and Argus.

As I turned the handle to my room and flicked on the light switch, a blood-curdling scream nearly tore from my throat. My eyes widened in sheer shock and disbelief as I saw her sitting in the darkened room, perched on my bed - a vampire, an unexpected and startling sight. She wore a smug smile, which displayed her signature toothy grin, as though she had just executed the most ingenious prank of all time. My heart pounded furiously within my chest as I tried to maintain my composure, not wanting to alert any of my unsuspecting housemates to her presence. "What the fuck are you doing here?" I half-shouted, half-whispered, while quickly and quietly shutting the door behind me. I approached her cautiously, demanding answers from this unwelcome and unexpected intruder. How on earth had she found me? What exactly did she want from me?

Abigail shifted slightly on the bed, making space for me with a sly grin that suggested she was thoroughly enjoying the situation. "Well," she began, "my little emergency was sorted out much quicker than I anticipated. So I thought it would be nice to check in on one of my favourite people while she's in the midst of a dangerous mission. Now, care to enlighten me on the finer details of your little adventure?"

Her eyes glinted with a mischievous sparkle, almost like tiny stars twinkling in a midnight sky, as she spoke. Yet, beneath her teasing tone, which danced lightly on the surface of her words like a gentle breeze, I could detect a subtle hint of genuine concern for my well-being that lay hidden beneath the layers of playful banter. It was as if her words were wrapped in a thin veil, disguising the true depth of her emotions.

I rolled my eyes in exasperation, feeling the weight of the situation pressing down on my shoulders, as I made my way over to the sleek black laptop that sat on the desk. Its screen was alive, flashing with neon green letters that seemed to pulsate with urgency. My fingers, well-acquainted with the layout of the keys, glided effortlessly over the keyboard, like a concert pianist playing a familiar tune, as I loaded the USB drive. I was trying, with little success, to shake off the irritation that the entire situation had stirred within me. "Fine," I muttered under my breath, the word barely audible, "I'm guessing you already know more than you should."

With a deep sigh that seemed to resonate through the room, I turned to face my colleague, raising an eyebrow in question, hoping for some reassurance in her response. "Can I assume you already swept the room for bugs?" I inquired, my voice tinged with a mix of hope and skepticism. Her response came quickly and confidently, her eyes never leaving mine, as if she was trying to convey both assurance and solidarity. "Yes, I did an in-depth search of the whole property," she replied, her tone steady and unwavering, "while you all sat having tea and got to know each other."

Her words painted a vivid picture in my mind of the gathering we had just left, a scene filled with laughter and casual conversation, all while she had been diligently working in the background. "The only odd thing I found was the cat," she continued, a small frown creasing her brow as she spoke, her expression betraying a hint of confusion, "there is something special about it, but I can't quite put my finger on it." The mystery of the cat seemed to linger in the air, adding an extra layer of intrigue to our already complicated situation. "Other than that," she concluded, "the place is clear." As she finished speaking, her words hung in the air between us, leaving me with a sense of both relief and curiosity about what lay ahead.

The next several minutes were consumed with the task of loading the USB drive onto the computer, my fingers flitting deftly across the keyboard as I meticulously opened each relevant file. Each click and scroll echoed in the quiet room, and I briefed Abigail on every detail I had gathered. Her expression grew increasingly grave with each new piece of information I shared. As I had anticipated, she was already quite familiar with much of the data I was presenting, nodding along with an air of somber understanding.

Once all the files were ready, we settled into our seats to watch the videos of previous fighters. The brutal nature of their matches was captured on film, each savage encounter replayed in excruciating slow motion. The sound of bones cracking and flesh being relentlessly pummelled reverberated through the room, casting a shadow of dread over me. I found it hard to comprehend that this was the world I had willingly entered.

As we continued to watch, I observed how some fighters seemed to transition from struggling against their opponents to overpowering them with an almost laughable ease. Their movements were ferocious, their combat techniques contorted into something almost monstrous. It was as though they had tapped into an ancient, primal instinct, unleashing a complete loss of control that allowed them to exert their full, unrestrained force upon their adversaries.

Seeking Abigail's perspective, I glanced over at her, noting the look of revulsion etched into her features. Any hint of humour had vanished, replaced by a steely and calculated hatred. When I inquired about her thoughts, her response was cautious, clearly influenced by the brutality we were witnessing.

"I wasn't expecting it to be that bad," she confessed, her voice tinged with disbelief and a hint of lingering shock. Her eyes widened slightly as she processed the brutality of what we had just witnessed. "Do you have any idea when your first match is scheduled to take place?" she inquired, her curiosity mixed with concern.

I could only shake my head in response, feeling a knot of anxiety tighten in my stomach, twisting with each passing moment. "No, I don't," I replied, my voice betraying my unease, a slight tremor revealing my inner turmoil. "I've been told that it might take anywhere from four to six weeks to get everything organised for the first match," I added, the uncertainty gnawing at me.

Abigail's expression grew serious, her features hardening with determination. "Well, we're going to have to train hard," she stated firmly, her voice carrying the weight of urgency. "These people want pain and bloodshed, they want it to be drawn out and brutal. The fights we just watched? They could have been over in seconds if you or I were in the ring. These fighters telegraph their weaknesses and focus on offence, not defence. We'll have to train you so you can take a few hits," she emphasised, her words leaving no room for doubt.

I shivered involuntarily at the mere thought of being struck in the ring. The idea sent an icy shiver coursing down my spine, yet beneath that layer of fear, I understood that it was an unavoidable necessity if I hoped to endure and perhaps even thrive in the cutthroat world of underground fighting. The haunting images that plagued my mind, scenes from various brutal videos I had watched, lingered like persistent phantoms. Every savage blow and each meticulously executed move were indelibly etched into my consciousness, serving as a relentless impetus driving my determination to train with unwavering intensity. I aspired to transform myself into a formidable force to be reckoned with. The journey ahead loomed intimidating and fraught with challenges, yet if I harboured any hope of standing victorious, I found myself with no alternative but to wholeheartedly accept the daunting challenge. I had to prepare myself for the violent reality that lay in wait, ready to test my mettle at every turn.

Abby stood beside me, her shoulders taut with tension, her entire body coiled like a spring wound tight and ready to snap. Her eyes were wide as saucers, a blend of fear and paranoia etched into her expression, as though the horrific scene we had just witnessed had infiltrated her very soul. She spoke in a hushed tone, her words tumbling out in a hurried, disjointed manner, each sentence a struggle against the trembling that seized her hands. The weight of her words hung heavily in the air, dense like an oppressive fog. Her gaze darted around with a frantic energy, as if searching for invisible threats, her fear palpable in her every movement. "It's not just about the fight," she said, her voice quivering with a mixture of rage and disgust that seemed to simmer just beneath the surface. "It's about what they symbolise—the twisted, dark underbelly of the paranormal world. It's a realm of violence, danger, and betrayal, always lurking just beneath the surface of our reality." Her eyes continued their nervous scan of our surroundings, vigilant for any signs of looming danger before she resumed speaking. "We don't hide it or dress it up with a veneer of respectability like some might. In fact, many within our community revel in the adrenaline rush of blood sports, Mixed Martial Arts matches, and other testosterone fuelled competitions. But what we just witnessed was a different beast entirely." She shivered at the recollection, her voice barely above a whisper.

"It was an unbearably cold, meticulously calculated, and heartlessly cruel approach, a strategic manoeuvre designed with precision to pit the mightiest fighters against those who had been stripped of any hope for victory, leaving them defenceless and vulnerable." They exploited every weakness and vulnerability, meticulously picking them apart until they were rendered broken and humiliated, only to dangle the tantalising promise of revenge and newfound strength before them like some twisted, sadistic game. A shiver coursed down my spine at the chilling reality of her words. "I've witnessed this behaviour before, back in the days when humans were still grasping the art of wielding power over one another. Whoever is orchestrating this is attempting to forge blind loyalty by systematically dismantling everything these fighters hold dear. It's twisted and sickening beyond belief, a grotesque perversion of power."

A heavy, tense silence drifted between us, settling like a thick, suffocating fog, each of us becoming lost in the labyrinth of our own thoughts as we processed this sudden, grim realisation. The weight of it pressed down on my chest like an invisible burden, making it increasingly difficult to breathe. "Abby," I finally managed to say, my voice sounding distant and hollow, as though it belonged to someone else. "I think we've seen enough for one evening." I glanced over at her, hoping my words might break the oppressive atmosphere that had enveloped us. "I have important job interviews scheduled for tomorrow, and I need to carefully consider which gym I should join to solidify my cover story." The words emerged weak and insincere, even to my own ears, but they achieved their intended effect. My vampire companion's expression immediately brightened at the mention of my job interviews. A spark of genuine excitement flared in her usually vacant eyes. "Oh, what positions are you interviewing for?" she asked, attempting to feign casual interest, yet failing miserably.

Her eagerness was almost tangible, a vibrant, electric energy that seemed to buzz through the air, clashing dramatically with the heavy, somber mood that had previously dominated the room like a thick fog. It always amused me how she could transform so effortlessly into a child in a candy store over the most mundane subjects; she had an uncanny ability to sleep right through high-stakes tactical operation meetings without so much as a twitch, but the mere mention of job interviews would have her perched eagerly on the edge of her seat, eyes bright with anticipation. It was a blend of endearing charm and mild exasperation. But in this particular moment, her enthusiasm was a welcome relief from the oppressive heaviness that had been weighing us down just moments before.

I knew her curiosity wouldn't rest until it was satisfied, so with a reluctant sigh, I showed her the few sheets of paper I had been given. Each page was filled with meticulously detailed information about various businesses, my fabricated backstory, and the schedule of my upcoming interviews. As she rifled through the papers with an air of focused concentration, her expression gradually shifted to something more serious and difficult to interpret. She read each word with the utmost care, her brows furrowing deeper in concentration with every paragraph. Finally, after what felt like an eternity of silence, she huffed in disapproval as she finished reading the last page.

"They aren't very creative or exciting with your fabricated backstory or the job options they have lined up for you," she complained, her tone tinged with disappointment. I could almost see the waves of discontent radiating off of her. "But there is one that could be suitable," she added, a hint of hope creeping back into her voice.

Rolling my eyes with a mixture of amusement and curiosity, I couldn't help but ask, "And which one would that be?"

She raised an eyebrow at me, her expression a mixture of challenge and amusement. "Isn't it obvious? The part-time barrister at the coffee shop. You'll have flexible work patterns, free coffee at your disposal, and people constantly coming and going. You never know what kind of information or clues you may stumble upon while working there."

"Well, that's certainly more insightful than I was expecting you to be," I responded, my voice carrying a hint of admiration despite the fatigue that was beginning to seep into my words. I couldn't help but let a small smile escape at her unexpected perceptiveness, which seemed to shine through even in my weary state. I turned to Abigail, my eyes heavy with the weight of the day. "But it's getting late, and it's been a relentlessly tiring day, so unless you're keen on watching me snore away the hours, I think it's time for you to head out."

"Okay, I can see you're getting cranky," she replied, her voice gently teasing but kind, her smile soft and understanding. She started to gather her things, her silhouette framed by the silvery moonlight streaming through the open window, casting a gentle glow over the room. "Please, Jess, be safe," she whispered, her voice carrying a note of genuine concern, before she turned and vanished into the night, leaving only the quiet rustle of leaves in her wake.

With Abigail's departure, I moved to close the window, the chill of the night air brushing against my skin as I shut and locked it securely. I felt a sense of urgency to ensure that my small sanctuary was a fortress against any threats lurking outside. After double-checking that my door was secured, I finally allowed myself to relax. I crawled under the soft, comforting embrace of my duvet and snuggled into my pillow, seeking solace in its warmth. The only thing that could make this moment more perfect would be the presence of Argus the cat. Closing my eyes, I willed myself to hope for a night untouched by dreams. Yet, deep down, I knew that hope was a fragile thing. The nightmares, persistent and relentless, would likely find me as they had every night since the harrowing facility raid. Despite my desperate attempts to banish them, the haunting images of innocent children being subjected to horrific torture and inhumane experiments continued to invade my thoughts, refusing to release their grip on my conscience.

CHAPTER 5

Captive Memories

The familiar cave, with its damp, musty air, once again held me captive in its cold, unyielding embrace. But this time, there was a haunting absence that made the darkness feel even more oppressive. There was no companion to share these stifling confines with me, no comforting presence of a dragon to ease the suffocating solitude as I found myself dragged back into the recesses of my memory—a memory where the cruel experiments they conducted on both Lyn and myself played out before me like a phantom theatre. I stood there, frozen in place, unable to escape the ghostly images unfolding before my eyes.

In this vivid memory, I watched as Jeremiah loomed menacingly over a younger, more vulnerable version of myself. We appeared as ghostlike figures, our bodies almost ethereal, translucent, and insubstantial, as if a single breath could disperse us into the shadows. His voice, dripping with malice and a chilling sense of control, echoed around us, resonating in the depths of the cave. "Come along, Jessica," he taunted, each syllable laced with a sinister promise, "or do I need to punish the dragon again to make you comply?"

It was a flashback to one of the earlier experiments, a time when he still relied on threats, wielding them like weapons, instead of resorting to the raw brutality of physical violence. But as the days turned into weeks and the weeks into months, his methods grew more sadistic, each action more calculated and cruel. He became willing to inflict harm upon Lyn, the dragon I cherished, just to elicit a reaction from me, to see how far he could push before I broke.

The younger version of myself, trapped in the confines of my own memories, was shivering as I recalled the chilling thoughts of Lyn's suffering. It was as if my entire being recoiled at the mere notion of the pain she might endure, and thus, I complied with his demands without hesitation. Deep in the recesses of my heart, I knew it was the sole way to shield her from any further harm that might come her way.

Jeremiah's voice, low and menacing, carried an edge that was impossible to ignore. His words were laced with a barely contained fury that seemed ready to erupt at any moment. "We have some very important guests coming to witness this today," he intoned ominously. "If you do not behave, it will not just be the dragon that suffers," he growled, his muscles visibly rippling beneath his skin as if they were coiled, ready to spring into action. Overwhelmed with fear, the younger version of myself stammered out a desperate plea, "Yes, I'll be good. I'll do whatever you say." As I observed this scene unfold in the vivid landscape of my dream, I found myself questioning whether it was all an elaborate fabrication. I had made every effort to block out most of my captivity, yet this particular memory seemed foreign to me. With a combination of trepidation and a burning curiosity, I followed the memory, unsure of what untold horrors I might uncover.

We navigated the familiar, winding path to the chamber where Jeremiah conducted his grim experiments. His muttering was a constant, unsettling drone, but the meaning of his words eluded me entirely. I could only discern that he appeared more agitated than I had ever seen him before. As we approached the entrance to his dimly lit laboratory, he suddenly reached out with a swift, brutal motion, seizing me by the throat and pinning me against the unforgiving cold of the concrete wall. The putrid stench of decay that clung to him was overpowering, making my stomach churn with nausea. Leaning in close, a malevolent gleam in his eyes, he growled with a voice that resonated with malice, "If you behave and impress our visitors, I will reward you. You'll have one day without being my personal toy. Would you like that, Jessica?" His voice reverberated through the cavernous passageway, sending icy shivers down my spine.

My response was nothing more than a mute nod, fear gripping me so tightly that it rendered me incapable of speech. My throat felt constricted as if an invisible hand was squeezing it, preventing any words from escaping. With his rough grip still firmly on my neck, he dragged me into the lab, his actions unrelenting and devoid of compassion as he began strapping my fragile body to the unyielding steel table. A sense of dread settled over me like a suffocating shroud, pressing down on my chest with an intensity that made breathing difficult.

Despite the constant spilling of blood in this place, it was the one area that remained immaculate, a bizarre juxtaposition of horror and cleanliness. The sterile scent of bleach hung heavily in the air, attempting to mask the gruesome events that occurred here, yet doing little to alleviate the sense of impending doom. My eyes scanned the pristine surfaces, searching for any sign, any hint of past treatments, but there was none to be found. The lab was a blank canvas, erasing the memories of those who came before me. As I stood there, taking in the familiar yet unsettling scene, I realised that no one else was present in the room. The absence of others heightened my isolation, amplifying the vulnerability I felt.

Suddenly, a soft, silky voice came through over a speaker, breaking the oppressive silence. Though it sounded distinctly feminine, I couldn't be sure of its origins. "Jeremiah," the voice purred with an unsettling allure, "how much longer until you begin? We don't have all day, and our absence will surely be noticed." The sound seemed to float on the air, both commanding and seductive at once, as if it was designed to both entice and intimidate. As the words echoed around me, a shiver ran down my spine, leaving a trail of cold fear in its wake. It was evident that whoever spoke held significant power and authority in this place, a puppeteer pulling strings from the shadows.

Jeremiah's cold, calculating voice echoed through the sterile laboratory as he meticulously prepared for the experiment. "Yes, we will be underway in just a few moments. I just need to administer the drug treatment," he stated with clinical precision, his tone devoid of emotion or empathy. As I lay on the table before him, restrained and in a state of panic, I couldn't escape the sensation of being an inconsequential object in his eyes, merely a subject for his twisted research.

"Very well, but are you sure she will survive the process and it won't traumatise her too severely?" A hesitant voice questioned, its tone laced with uncertainty and concern. The question hung in the air, a brief glimmer of hope that perhaps someone cared about my fate.

"It doesn't matter," Jeremiah replied with a dismissive wave of his hand, his voice carrying an air of indifference that chilled me to the bone. "I have learned quite a bit from this one, and if it proves that this is too much, I will dispose of it and start again with a new one." His words were callous, reducing me to a mere object, a tool to be used and discarded at his convenience.

There was a moment of silence before the voice responded, resigned and accepting of the grim reality. "Very well, continue and be quick about it." Jeremiah moved swiftly, preparing syringes and monitoring equipment with a determination that left no room for doubt. His focus was solely on carrying out his experiment, without regard for my welfare or the potential suffering I might endure.

The room felt as though it were closing in around me, the walls reverberating with the ominous echoes of my impending fate as I steeled myself for the inevitable events that were about to unfold. As I gazed upon the visage of my younger self, an overwhelming wave of anguish surged through my chest, threatening to engulf me in its relentless intensity. The terror reflected in my own eyes reverberated back to me, and I could feel the tears beginning to well up, unbidden. With resolutely gritted teeth, I waged an internal battle against them, fiercely determined not to surrender to any perceived weakness. Yet, my younger self was unable to suppress their fear as they recoiled from the needles piercing their delicate arms, injecting a toxic substance into their veins. In that harrowing moment, I was no longer a mere distant observer. Instead, I found myself trapped within the confines of my own body once more, reliving a nightmare I had long believed to be behind me. Each detail of the scene surged into my mind with an overpowering force, seizing me in its relentless grip. It was akin to being buried alive within the depths of my own memories, unable to escape the torment until it had run its full course. And even after its conclusion, the haunting spectre of it would remain with me indefinitely.

My gaze followed Jeremiah as he took his position before the array of mounted cameras, his voice projecting with confidence to the audience observing from afar. It was evident that he derived great pride from his creation. "Many of you have been receiving my detailed reports, so you are already aware of the remarkable durability of my creation," he commenced with a note of enthusiasm in his voice. "I have subjected her to an array of surface traumas, and yet she has not only recovered but has emerged even more resilient than before. Consider, for example, the time when I meticulously flayed the skin from her body. Methodically, I worked over every inch of her, section by section, including the soles of her feet, the palms of her hands, her scalp, and her lips. To my astonishment, I discovered that the most delicate areas healed faster and regenerated thicker and stronger than they had been previously. And, intriguingly, the more damage I inflicted upon her, the more rapidly she would heal."

He paused with a flourish, stooping down to drive home his point with added drama. Yet, as I watched him, my mind couldn't help but be flooded with memories of the gruesome tests he had subjected me to. He conveniently omitted the horrific details, like the time he didn't just cut away my skin but also poured acid over me, watching intently as it sizzled and devoured my flesh, then swiftly neutralised the acid to note how long it would take for new skin to regenerate. On another occasion, he branded me deeply, burning into my skin and mercilessly rubbing salt into the raw, inflamed wounds, simply to observe my reaction. He labeled these as "experiments," but to me, they were sheer torture, nothing less than plain, unadulterated agony.

After his dramatic pause, he launched back into his monologue with unrelenting precision. His voice was steady, each word carefully measured, the tone of someone who knew exactly how to manipulate his audience. "I have also conducted a series of experiments on her internal organs," he elaborated, "meticulously removing them at staggered intervals to assess how much stress her body can withstand before necessitating medical intervention. The comprehensive data derived from these experiments is meticulously documented in my reports, which have been prepared for your review in the packets distributed prior to this demonstration."

I observed Jeremiah closely; his excitement was palpable, building with each passing moment. The usually composed demeanour he wore like a second skin was slowly unraveling as he fidgeted with his hands, shifting restlessly from one foot to the other. Although I couldn't see his face, I was certain it would betray a feverish anticipation, a gleam of eagerness that he could scarcely contain.

Suddenly, a commanding female voice erupted over the speakers, slicing through the tension that had settled over the room like a thick fog.

"Yes, your work is undoubtedly impressive," she proclaimed, her exasperation seeping through every syllable, her voice rising above the murmurs of the gathered crowd. "But why have you summoned us all here? You promised us something truly groundbreaking, something that would revolutionise our understanding, so spare us the self-congratulatory speeches and present what we truly came for." Her words hung in the air, heavy and charged, a challenge daring him to substantiate his bold claims with action, to live up to the extraordinary promises that had brought us all here.

It seemed I was not alone in my perception of him as a sanctimonious pompous asshole.

"As you wish," he replied with a hint of defiance in his tone, his eyes narrowing slightly as if measuring the weight of his next words. "The only aspect of her that remains untouched by our experiments is her brain." A shiver ran down my spine at the mere thought of what those words implied, the sinister undertone that hinted at the horrors yet to be revealed.

Trapped in the restraints, I began to struggle against them, my heart pounding in my chest like a drumbeat of fear. Every movement only caused the cold, unyielding metal to dig deeper into my skin, a cruel reminder of my helplessness. Jeremiah stood beside me, an unsettling figure of calm amidst the chaos, holding a pair of clamps in his hand. His eyes gleamed with a sadistic delight that made my blood run cold.

"Jessica," he cooed, his voice dripping with mockery and malice, "this will hurt. So please, entertain our guest with your best screams." His words were a twisted invitation, a perverse anticipation of the pain to come.

I knew fighting was futile, yet my instincts screamed at me to resist. As he secured my head to the clamp, his movements methodical and deliberate, I could feel the inevitability of what was to come. He reached for a scalpel and bone saw, instruments of precision and terror, and the metallic scent of blood filled the air, mingling with the sterile odour of the laboratory. It was a scent that heralded the sealing of my fate, the moment when hope would be extinguished and horror would take its place.

***

My eyelids snapped open, and the room spun around me in a dizzying whirl. I struggled to sit up, my body racked with tremors as it rebelled against the violent churn in my stomach. Each movement sent waves of nausea through me, and I fought to keep the rising tide of bile at bay. With a desperate reach, my hand flailed blindly, grasping for anything that could contain the burning liquid threatening to surge forth. Just in the nick of time, my fingers found the waste paper bin, dragging it close with a frantic urgency. Bent over in sheer agony, my body heaved uncontrollably, tears cascading down my cheeks as I battled for control over the revolt within.

The pungent smell of vomit permeated the air, so overpowering it felt tangible, clinging to my senses like a thick fog. Clutching the bin tightly to my chest, I took a moment to absorb my surroundings. The room was small and sparsely decorated, with only a basic bed, a functional desk, and a solitary window offering a view of the bustling street below. My heart pounded in my chest, a frantic rhythm that matched the chaos in my mind as I struggled to piece together the fragments of memory. Gradually, they began to form a coherent picture - I was on an assignment, inhabiting this halfway house as part of my cover story. That realisation brought a fleeting sense of relief, yet the fear and panic refused to relinquish their grip on me.

As I wiped the tears from my face and concentrated on calming my erratic breathing, my gaze drifted toward the clock perched on the bedside table - 7:33 am. The day awaited, demanding my participation, but my body still trembled, a quivering vessel of adrenaline and lingering fear.

Sweat drenched my clothes, sticking to my skin and forming a stifling, uncomfortable second layer. I sat precariously on the edge of the bed, feeling utterly exposed, as though every nerve was raw and vulnerable to the world. The morning light streamed through the windows, casting harsh shadows that seemed to mirror the inner turmoil I was grappling with. My throat was raw and scratchy from the night's screams, a constant reminder that I needed to clean up before anyone else could witness or hear me in such a state. I hoped desperately that this room was warded and soundproofed, just as most safe houses were designed to be, offering me a semblance of privacy in my distress.

With a heavy heart and a body that trembled from the emotional toll, I managed to drag myself to the en-suite bathroom. The steam from the hot shower swirled around me, cocooning me in warmth and providing a much-needed sense of comfort and solace. As the water cascaded down, I scrubbed vigorously, determined to wash away the lingering remnants of the previous night's nightmare—the acrid taste of vomit that clung to me. With each lather of soap and generous dollop of toothpaste, I felt a piece of my humanity returning, slowly shedding the layers of fear and vulnerability.

Upon emerging from the bathroom, I inhaled deeply, hoping that the facade I had meticulously crafted would withstand the scrutiny of the day ahead. The crisp, minty scent of toothpaste lingered on my breath, effectively masking any residual traces of vomit. My outfit had been chosen with careful consideration for both professionalism and practicality—plain black trousers paired with a light blue blouse and topped with a tailored black blazer, all designed to convey competence and confidence. Practicality also guided my choice of footwear—sturdy everyday boots with reinforced toes, capable of inflicting damage if selfdefense became necessary.

After applying just the right amount of makeup to subtly enhance my features without appearing overdone, I meticulously styled my hair into a sleek bun. This hairstyle, like the rest of my appearance, was part of the carefully constructed disguise that I hoped would shield me from prying eyes. As I gathered my paperwork for the day's interviews, I caught a glimpse of myself in the mirror. The reflection was almost unrecognisable, a composed, polished exterior that starkly contrasted with the vulnerable little girl I had encountered in my nightmare. Yet, this was the image I needed to present to the world, a shield to hide the lingering fears that threatened to consume me.

I left my room with a sense of trepidation, feeling as if I were stepping onto a plank that led directly into a sea of ravenous sharks. My nerves were frayed, and my mind raced with anxious thoughts as I made a determined path toward the kitchen, seeking the solace that only a strong cup of coffee could provide. It was my shield, my armour, against the daunting prospect of facing a room packed with opinionated individuals who never hesitated to voice their thoughts. As I crossed the threshold into the kitchen, a wave of relief washed over me when I encountered the familiar and comforting sight of Nixie and Argus seated at the table. Nixie exuded a calming presence, sipping serenely from a cup that likely contained some soothing herbal tea, while Argus reclined with the ease of a majestic lion in his favourite sunlit spot near the window.

"Good morning, Nixie," I greeted, striving to project a casual demeanour despite the frantic pounding of my heart. "Is there any coffee, or should I just make a run to the coffee shop?"

"Oh, good morning, Jess," Nixie responded warmly, a genuine smile lighting up her face. "Why don't you take a seat and relax for a bit? I'll go ahead and prepare a cup for you." She paused, a playful twinkle in her eye, before adding with a mischievous chuckle, "How do you take it?"

I couldn't help but laugh, appreciating the double entendre in her question. "As strong as humanly possible, black, and with enough sugar to send me into a sugar coma," I replied, feeling some of the tension begin to melt away.

With that, Nixie sprang into action, moving around the kitchen with the boundless energy of an energiser bunny on overdrive. I settled into a chair at the table, content to watch as she expertly crafted my coffee with the precision of a seasoned barista. The rich, intoxicating aroma of freshly brewed coffee soon enveloped the room, and my mouth watered in eager anticipation. Within moments,

Nixie returned with a flourish, balancing a substantial travel mug filled to the brim with steaming hot coffee in one hand and a plate piled high with perfectly toasted tea cakes in the other. The cakes were a sight to behold, their golden-brown surfaces gleaming invitingly, almost as if they were whispering sweet nothings, enticing me to indulge in their deliciousness.

The aroma wafting from the coffee was intoxicating, instantly lifting my spirits and providing that much-needed boost of energy to help me tackle the daunting tasks of the day ahead. As I accepted the offerings with heartfelt gratitude, I took a sip of the rich, smooth coffee. It was heavenly, and I could almost feel my worries dissolving like sugar in hot liquid, leaving me in a state of serene readiness. This little ritual was exactly what I needed to help me navigate the morning's interviews with confidence.

"Jess, what do you have planned for today?" Nixie inquired, her voice casual yet curious, as I continued to savour the warmth of the coffee mug. Meanwhile, she absentmindedly scratched Argus behind the ears, eliciting a contented, rumbling purr from him that echoed through the room.

"I have a few interviews lined up," I replied, feeling the caffeine beginning to work its magic. "And if I have enough time afterward, I want to explore some of the local gyms to kickstart a daily training routine."

"It's great to see you settling in so quickly," Nixie remarked with a warm smile, showing genuine encouragement. "If you need anything, just let Lunette and me know. We're here to help in any way we can." With that, she gently scooped up Argus, who looked perfectly content to be in her arms, and made her way towards the garden. "I'm going outside for some fresh air. Make sure you have some tea cakes with your coffee. They'll give you that extra energy you need for your interviews." Without another word or a backward glance, she disappeared through the doorway, leaving behind the comforting aroma of coffee and tea cakes mingling in the air.

***

After an incredibly long and exhausting day filled with back-to-back interviews, I finally arrived at the house share, feeling a wave of relief wash over me. The weight of the day seemed to lift slightly as I fumbled with my keys and unlocked the front door. As soon as I stepped inside, I was greeted by the sound of laughter echoing through the rooms. Intrigued and a bit curious, I followed the cheerful noise that seemed to beckon me toward the kitchen. As I drew nearer, the inviting aroma of delicious food and wine wafted through the air, filling my nostrils and causing my stomach to grumble audibly with hunger.

When I finally walked into the kitchen, the sight before me was a heartwarming one. Abby, with her infectious laughter, was in the midst of carrying a tray laden with mouthwatering food over to the table. There, my two roommates, Nixie and Lunette, sat with tears of laughter in their eyes, clearly amused by something Abby had said or done. As soon as I entered, they all turned their heads and joyfully welcomed me with wide smiles. Abby, always the exuberant one, exclaimed, "Oh Jess, you're back!" Her words were filled with warmth and excitement.

Surprised to find such a lively scene and my roommates in such high spirits, I listened as Abby explained that she had taken the initiative to make dinner for everyone. Nixie and Lunette chimed in, expressing their surprise and delight at discovering Abby's hidden culinary talents.

They casually remarked that they hadn't realised I had such a talented partner in the kitchen. I was about to respond, but before I could form a suitable reply, Abby, always quick on her feet, interjected with a playful smile, "Well, Jess doesn't like to brag about me. She values her privacy."

Determined to maintain the playful charade and keep our little secret under wraps, I grinned broadly and said, "She's right; I just want to keep Abby all to myself. She's my radiant vampire." The room was filled with a sense of camaraderie and warmth, creating a cozy atmosphere that enveloped us all. Feeling an urge to address the situation and smooth over any rough edges, I added, "I apologise, ladies, for my abruptness. It's been an incredibly exhausting day, and I just need to change into something more comfortable. But rest assured, I'll be back in a few minutes to join you all." With those words hanging in the air, I excused myself and headed toward my bedroom, eager to shed the formal attire of the day and embrace the comfort of my personal sanctuary.

As soon as I closed the door behind me, I leaned back against the wall, allowing myself a precious moment of solitude. The cool surface supported me as I took a few deep breaths, trying to gather my thoughts. What was Abigail thinking? Her impulsive actions could have jeopardised everything before the mission even commenced. Just as I was lost in contemplation, there was a gentle knock on the door, followed by Abby's pleading voice, "Jess, please let me explain. Can I come in?" With a resigned sigh escaping my lips, I opened the door for my vampiric partner.

I let out a low, frustrated growl as Abby nervously closed the door behind her, the tension in the room becoming almost tangible, hanging thickly in the air like an ominous cloud as we both braced ourselves for the confrontation that was about to unfold. "Well, go ahead and say what you need to say. I'm listening, and this explanation better be good," I demanded, my tone sharp and impatient, as I prepared myself mentally to hear her justification for the earlier incident that had left us in this precarious situation.

With a deep breath, Abby began her explanation, her voice carrying the weight of the decision she had made. "After discussing and analysing the fight footage last night, I came to a decision. You need backup. And not just any backup - supernatural backup." She paused, allowing the gravity of her words to sink in, her eyes locking with mine for a moment before she continued, her determination evident. "I've cleared it with Alexander. He is the only one who knows about this plan."

My thoughts raced like wild horses, galloping unchecked as I processed this newfound information. It was a dangerous plan, fraught with risks and uncertainties, but I couldn't deny that having supernatural assistance would give us a much-needed advantage in our mission, potentially tipping the scales in our favour. "What do you have in mind?" I asked with caution, my eyes fixed intently on Abby's determined face, searching for any hint of hesitation or doubt.

She took a deep breath, her gaze steady and unwavering as she revealed her carefully crafted plan, a strategy born of necessity and ingenuity. "Everyone at the agency thinks I'm away on a personal business trip abroad," she began, her voice unwavering and resolute.

"No one will be on the lookout for me," she declared with a steely confidence, her voice unwavering as it cut through the charged atmosphere. "And to minimise the risk of being discovered by accident, I will employ a glamour specifically keyed to you. To everyone else, I will appear as a low-level vampire—an unremarkable presence that draws no attention or interest. Only you will be able to see through the facade, recognising me for who I truly am beneath the illusion."

Her words lingered heavily in the air, the audacity and complexity of the plan both exhilarating and terrifying. The gravity of the situation was not lost on me. Yet, as I met Abby's eyes, filled with unwavering resolve and a fierce determination to see this daring plan through to its conclusion, I knew that we were on the cusp of something monumental. The stakes were dizzyingly high, but with her by my side, I dared to believe that we could indeed succeed against seemingly insurmountable odds.

I couldn't help but feel a wave of admiration wash over me, impressed by Abby's meticulous preparations and her quick, nimble thinking. Her resourcefulness and adaptability were qualities that set her apart, truly remarkable traits that made her an invaluable ally. "And what about my housemates?" I inquired, my mind racing through potential scenarios and pitfalls.

"They think I'm your girlfriend," Abby replied smoothly, her tone infused with a confidence that seemed unshakeable. "But they won't suspect a thing since they can't see past the glamour I've crafted."

With a nod of understanding, I realised just how fortunate I was to have someone like Abby on my team. Her steadfast determination and ability to think on her feet were indispensable assets in our line of work, qualities that could very well tip the balance in our favour. Now, with her cleverly disguised as a low-level vampire by my side, we had a fighting chance—an opportunity to confront our enemies with a newfound advantage.

Despite the crystal-clear nature of the plan laid before us, an insidious doubt continued to gnaw at the edges of my mind. My voice dripped with a heavy layer of skepticism as I spoke, my eyes narrowing in a keen gaze of suspicion, as if trying to peel back the layers of her intentions. "What exactly is your game here, Abigail? Are you suggesting that I'm not capable of handling this mission on my own? Just because I have just recently stepped into this world doesn't mean I'm incapable of facing whatever challenges lie ahead—challenges that might, indeed, involve some inevitable losses along the way."

"Jess, I have complete faith in your abilities," Abigail replied, her voice infused with sincerity. Yet, for the very first time, she avoided meeting my gaze, her eyes shifting downward as if they held a secret burden. "But that doesn't mean you have to undertake this all by yourself. I worry about you," she added, her concern palpable.

Her words, despite their cautionary nature, washed over me like a soothing wave of gratitude. It was a comfort to know there was someone who cared enough to watch out for me, someone who had my back. "I appreciate your concern, Abigail. Truly, I do. Having you here is definitely a help." I paused, reflecting on my own vulnerabilities. "My fighting skills could use some improvement, admittedly. But next time, please, talk to me before making any decisions on my behalf."

"I'm sorry, Jess. You're absolutely right; I should have consulted with you first," she admitted, her tone filled with a gentle remorse. "But I just want to ensure that you have someone trustworthy by your side, apart from Paul."

I found it difficult to argue with her reasoning. Having Abby by my side offered a profound sense of relief, knowing she would always stand with me without hesitation or any hidden motives lurking beneath the surface.

"We're going to have to work on your fighting style," Abby declared with an emphatic determination in her voice, the kind that brooked no argument. Her eyes bore a fierce glint as she continued, "There's a place nearby that I'm preparing for our real training sessions. I'll be drilling you on everything I've learned about combat throughout the ages. I've engaged in battles that span the entirety of history, from the brutal clashes within the gladiator rings of ancient Rome to the raw intensity of bare-knuckle matches in back alleys. By the time we're finished, your fighting style will be transformed beyond recognition. Right now, it's too defensive and overly focused on subduing opponents. We need to shift our focus and concentrate on attacking, transforming your approach completely."

"Abby, I can't process all of this right now," I replied, feeling the weight of her words pressing heavily upon me, a sense of being overwhelmed washing over my senses. "Let's just get through tonight and we can deal with everything else tomorrow."

"Okay, I understand," she responded with a calm and soothing tone, as if she could sense the turmoil within me. Her hand reached out to squeeze mine reassuringly, an anchor in the storm of my thoughts. "We'll go over everything tomorrow once you've had some rest." Her voice was a comforting balm, a promise of clarity in the chaos. "Now let's head back downstairs and act like the loved-up couple we're supposed to be."

My body instinctively tensed as she reached for me, a sudden realisation dawning like a spotlight in a darkened room. "I don't even know what story you've told them about us," I whispered urgently, the words tumbling out in a rush. "I have no background knowledge for this role. I've never been in a relationship before and I have no idea how to act."

Abby threw her head back, laughter bursting forth like a joyous symphony, her eyes sparkling with an infectious mirth. "You really are unbelievably adorable, do you know that?" she managed to say between gasps for air, her laughter subsiding slowly as she struggled to regain her composure.

Confusion etched itself across my face, a puzzle I couldn't quite solve as I watched her laugh. "I don't understand what's so funny," I said, my voice tinged with genuine perplexity.

She delicately brushed away a tear that shimmered at the corner of her eye, her expression a mingling of mirth and mystery—a dance of light and shadow that seemed to capture the essence of our unusual connection. "You know," she began, her tone both teasing and sincere, "you rush headlong into perilous battles with barely a hesitation, charging bravely into danger with the paltry odds of survival that you confront with such fearless resolve, all in the name of saving a life. Yet when it comes to the softer realms of romance, love, and even the most uncomplicated emotional bonds, you suddenly become as timid as a little rabbit, frozen beneath the merciless glare of blazing headlights." As she leaned in, her warm breath mingled with mine, and her lips brushed against mine in a fleeting, electrifying kiss that sent ripples of sparkling electricity my way, igniting my nerves much like an exuberant array of fireworks bursting in the night sky. "I guess," she whispered playfully with a smile tugging at her lips, "that we are in desperate need of working on that little quirk." Her voice was a soft, velvety caress, a melodic murmur that lingered even as she pulled away, gracefully striding towards the door. At the very last moment before departing, she turned back, her gaze softening into a tender promise as her eyes kept a quiet vigil on me. "And don't you worry," she added with a conspiratorial lilt, "I'll handle all the talking."

Even as her words faded into the air, a mischievous glimmer played in her eyes, amplifying her already striking features with an extra spark. With a gentle, intimate closeness, she leaned in further, letting her warm whisper reach the delicate shell of my ear. "I will always protect you," she vowed, as though sharing an intimate secret meant only for the two of us. In that quiet moment, a swelling surge of warmth and deep affection blossomed within my chest, compelling me to squeeze her hand in reciprocation. Though I was well aware that the night promised a heady mix of excitement and inevitable trepidation, I felt a profound trust in her ability to lead and comfort me through every twist and turn the evening held.

As the hours meandered on, the night found Abigail drawing ever nearer to Lunette and Nixie, her presence weaving threads of camaraderie and connection among us. Argus, the steadfast feline companion, had finally chosen to settle himself on her lap, contentedly purring away as the tension of the day slipped into the background. In her warm, inviting manner, Abigail regaled us with vivid tales of her past adventures, her words painting rich pictures of daring escapades and humorous moments from our social escapades together. While she was careful to soften and alter certain details so as not to divulge the secret depths of our relationship, her narrative was enchanting enough to captivate every listener—each story gently binding us closer in the soft glow of camaraderie.

However, as the relentless hands of the clock inched ever closer to the later hours of the night, the comforting cocoon of our shared evening began to unravel, allowing the inevitable weight of reality to seep back into our consciousness. With a languid yawn that shattered the enchantment of our time together, I declared, "As much as I have cherished the delights of this wonderful evening, I must now bid you farewell and retire to my quarters. Without the rejuvenating balm of proper rest, I fear the dawn will greet me with nothing but a tempest of irritability and fatigue." With tender affection, I offered Argus a gentle scratch behind his ear, eliciting from him a soft symphony of purrs that served as a sweet, melodic farewell. I then slowly ambled toward the staircase, my pace unhurried and contemplative. As I reached the base of the stairs, I cast one final, lingering glance over my shoulder. In that moment, I noticed that Abigail, too, was preparing to make her graceful exit, quietly trailing in my wake. Her eyes, filled with a profound blend of quiet longing and tender protectiveness, remained fixed unwaveringly upon me—as though the very thought of my departure from her side, even for a brief moment, was something she could scarcely endure.

In a moment marked by gentle chivalry, I paused to hold the door open, allowing Abigail the opportunity to follow me into my room. She responded with a playful, mischievous grin that danced across her lips before she slipped inside with an air of impish delight. I found myself rolling my eyes at her playful antics, a gesture of affectionate exasperation. With the weight of the day pressing upon me, I undressed and slipped under the cool, inviting covers of my bed, choosing to ignore her soft giggles as I reached over to turn off the lights, plunging the room into a comforting shroud of darkness. Determined to clear my mind of any lingering thoughts of Abigail and her teasing presence, I surrendered to the embrace of sleep, my consciousness dissolving within moments of my head finding its familiar place upon the pillow.

CHAPTER 6

Drill of Despair

Agony coursed through every fibre of my being as a sharp, searing pain exploded within my skull. The overwhelming and relentless whirring noise of the drill pounded in my ears, drowning out any coherent thought and leaving my senses in disarray. My vision swam in a haze of red as blood cascaded down my face, mingling with the salty streams of sweat and tears that poured from my eyes. The acrid stench of burning flesh filled the air, turning my stomach and forcing bile to rise in my throat. The relentless grinding of the drill against my bone sent shockwaves of anguish through my head, intensifying the already unbearable throbbing that pulsed in time with my racing heartbeat.

It felt as though I was ensnared in a living nightmare, a hellish scene from which I could not awaken, as Jeremiah methodically continued his gruesome task. His gaze remained fixed and unyielding, cold and calculating, as he worked with a precision that belied the horror of his actions. With a sudden jolt that sent a fresh surge of pressure through my skull, he withdrew the drill, and a torrent of blood gushed from the newly created opening, painting the sterile room in a macabre tableau.

"That wasn't so bad now, was it?" he taunted, a cruel edge to his voice that cut deeper than any blade. His hand reached towards a metal tray, gleaming with a chilling array of instruments laid out for his twisted experiment. I watched in terror as he picked up a needle, its long, glinting form attached to one of the numerous IV bags swaying ominously above me. My heart galloped wildly, each beat a drum of impending doom as he approached once more.

"This is the last one to go in," he announced with a sadistic grin, the promise of further agony lurking in his words. And then, with a vicious, unrelenting thrust, he plunged the needle into the raw wound he had carved into my head. A tidal wave of excruciating pain surged through my body, consuming every thought, every breath, until all I could do was scream. My cries reverberated off the cold, unforgiving walls of the chamber, a desperate echo of my hopeless plight as I realised the terrifying truth: there was no escape from this chamber of horrors, no release from this unending torment.

My heart pounded violently against the confines of my ribcage, the relentless thudding echoing in my ears like a drumbeat as I jolted awake from a nightmare. My entire body was engulfed by a storm of panic, and my arms flailed wildly, desperately seeking any relief from the invisible needles that seemed to pierce my skin. The pain was excruciating, each prick feeling like a trail of fire coursing through my veins, threatening to consume me whole. In a frenzied attempt to end this torment, I clawed at my head, trying to tear out whatever was causing this unbearable agony. But just as I was on the brink of causing harm, strong and unyielding hands gripped me firmly, holding me still and preventing me from doing any damage. I felt trapped, caught in a vice of terror with no escape. My screams, raw and desperate, were muffled by the sobs that racked my body as I surrendered to the overwhelming fear that threatened to swallow me.

"Hush now, Jess. You're safe with me," came Abigail's soothing whisper, cutting through the lingering remnants of my nightmare like a gentle balm. Her voice, soft and comforting, was a lifeline amid the chaos, offering a beacon of hope. I struggled to regulate my breathing, my heart still racing wildly from the terror that had consumed me only moments ago. But as Abigail's reassuring words sank in, a sense of calm began to wash over me, like a soothing wave enveloping my soul. I realised I was safe, here in her arms, and I released a shaky breath, attempting to focus on my surroundings, to anchor myself in the reality of the present.

I was curled into Abigail's side like a frightened child seeking solace and protection from the demons that haunted my dreams.

My grip on her was tight, almost painfully so, yet she showed no signs of discomfort. She simply held me close, her presence radiating warmth and safety, as if she were a fortress shielding me from the darkness lurking within. Her steady heartbeat beneath my ear was a rhythmic reminder of the security she provided, grounding me in the here and now.

In this moment of profound gratitude, I felt an overwhelming appreciation for her unwavering presence and steadfast support. Her soft-spoken words and gentle, reassuring touch acted as a soothing balm on my troubled soul, easing the fear and anxiety that had consumed me just moments before. With each passing second, the terror that had gripped me began to recede, gradually replaced by a growing sense of peace and safety. In Abigail's comforting embrace, I found a refuge, a sanctuary where the relentless nightmares could not reach me. Despite this solace, I attempted to push away from her, overwhelmed with an intense feeling of guilt and shame for the pain I had caused my dear friend, and even more so for what she had been forced to witness. "I'm so sorry, Abby. I didn't mean to hurt you," I managed to say, my voice choked with emotion and regret.

Abigail simply shook her head, placing her fingers gently against my lips, silencing me with a tender gesture before I could utter another word. Her calm, steady gaze met mine as she posed the question I had been dreading: "How long has this been happening?" Her inquiry was gentle, yet it pierced through the layers of my defences.

I looked away, unable to sustain eye contact with her understanding gaze. The thought of revealing the truth about the endless nights spent tossing and turning, tormented by nightmares that felt all too real, was unbearable. I couldn't bear for her to think of me as weak or unstable, as someone who could not keep their fears at bay.

The air between us grew thick with a fog of tension, suffocating and heavy, clinging to my skin and making it difficult to breathe. My throat tightened as I struggled to maintain my composure, though I could feel the palpable fear radiating from my very being.

"Don't try to deceive me, Jess," Abby's voice cut through the silence like a sharp knife, both piercing and accusing. "I can still taste the remnants of your terror. This is not like you." Her tone was firm as she took a step closer, her eyes narrowing in search of the truth I was trying to hide. "How long has this been happening? How long have you been reliving those traumatic moments in the caves?"

A heavy lump formed in my throat, and despite my best efforts, I found myself unable to meet Abby's intense, probing gaze. The weight of my confession pressed upon me, and I spoke softly, my voice barely rising above a whisper. "Since the wendigo," I admitted, my words nearly swallowed by the oppressive silence of the room. "It all began that first night back in my dorm room. That's when it started, and since then, it's been happening almost every night. But now, it's only gotten worse." The gravity of my admission lingered in the air, charged with the unspoken fears that had haunted me and the stark realisation that I could no longer escape the truth that I had been trying so hard to deny.

Emotion thickened my voice as I continued, feeling the weight of my guilt pressing down on me with each word. "I didn't even realise you were still here," I confessed, a wave of remorse washing over me. "I thought you would have left through the window, just like the last time." Abby scoffed, shaking her head in disbelief, unable to comprehend my assumption. "What kind of backup would I be if I ran away every time you needed me?" she asked rhetorically, her voice tinged with a mixture of frustration and loyalty. She closed the distance between us with determined steps and knelt down to my level, her hands gently cupping my face with a tenderness that was both reassuring and grounding. "You have to trust me, Jess," she said with unwavering conviction. "We're in this together. You can rely on me. Please, just tell me what's going on." Her thumb brushed away a tear that had escaped from my eye as she pulled me into a comforting embrace. The warmth of her body enveloped mine, and for a fleeting moment, I felt safe, shielded from the haunting memories that plagued me relentlessly each night.

"I promised Lyn that I would safeguard you from anything and everything, so please let me at least try to shield you from this overwhelming darkness," Abby murmured softly, her voice a gentle caress that reached the depths of my troubled mind. Each word was imbued with such genuine sincerity that it wrapped around me like a warm, protective cloak, offering a fragile yet luminous hope that perhaps, with her unwavering presence by my side, I could finally face and overcome the encroaching shadows that threatened to devour my very soul.

Cradled in her comforting embrace, I drew a long, deliberate breath, attempting to steady the tumult of emotions swirling within me. The rich, inviting scent of warm cinnamon and nutmeg permeated the air, mingling with memories of homely comfort and causing an involuntary reaction—a delicious anticipation that made my mouth water. I found myself focusing intently on the soothing, rhythmic rise and fall of her chest as it met mine, each gentle movement grounding me further in the moment while smoothing away the jagged edges of my anxiety. Drawn in by the allure of this serene intimacy, I leaned closer still, absorbing more of the enchanting aroma she exuded—a fragrance that felt as though it were a tangible expression of her tender embrace, a sensory hug that combined familiarity with the promise of reassurance.

As the minutes passed, I could feel my racing heart gradually settling into a quieter, more even cadence, and the taut muscles that had held so much tension began to relax as if surrendering to the warmth of her care. When I eventually pulled away to regain a semblance of composure, I discovered that Abby remained completely at ease, holding me close with an understanding that radiated both warmth and safety from her very being.

With a reluctant blush of embarrassment tinging my cheeks, I confessed in a soft, hesitant tone, "I'm sorry, you're right. I should have spoken up, but I didn't want anyone—especially you—to think I'm weak." In response, Abby's eyes softened further, revealing a deep well of understanding as she gently replied, "Jess, there's no need for apologies. We're friends, after all, and true friends support each other through life's strangest and most unpredictable moments." With a playful gesture towards the damp spot between her breasts, she added with a light-hearted chuckle, "Though I must admit, when we head out today, I might have to pick up some new t-shirts!"

Her teasing comment blossomed into a wide grin that brightened the space between us, and she playfully chided, "I certainly wasn't expecting you to break down in such a dramatic fashion!" Perhaps realising the extent of my mortification, Abby's laughter soon filled the room, a sound filled with genuine mirth and affectionate teasing.

"Hey now, no hard feelings," she quickly reassured me as I prepared to part ways for a quick shower. Yet, still caught in a mix of defensiveness and reluctant humour, I retorted, "I can't be held accountable for my actions when I cry! And believe me, if you dare mention my pitiful, ugly crying to anyone, I'll hunt you down to the very ends of the earth!"

As I stepped away towards the shower, Abby's playful voice trailed after me, twinkling with mischief as she called, "No promises!" With the echo of her laughter still resonating in the corridor and the final traces of my tears left behind, we both felt a renewed sense of readiness to tackle the day ahead—starting with our plan to check out the gym Paul had mentioned, rumoured to have connections to those seedy underground fights.

*

The steam from my recent shower still clung to my skin, the warmth enveloping me like a gentle embrace as I hurriedly packed a bag. Inside, I placed my soft, well-worn gym sweats, their fabric exuding a faint, comforting scent of laundry detergent mixed with the nostalgic warmth of home. This small ritual brought a reassuring sense of familiarity to my jittery nerves. As I moved toward the kitchen, a flutter of anxious energy danced in my stomach, causing my fingers to fidget with anticipation and excitement.

Upon entering the kitchen, my swirling thoughts were immediately interrupted by a heartwarming sight: Abby was seated at the table, her attention focused on Argus, the sleek-furred cat comfortably perched on her lap. Her fingers glided gracefully through his fur, and the cat responded with contented purrs that filled the air, creating a soothing and serene backdrop to our impending conversation. Abby greeted me with a warm and welcoming smile, her expression radiating kindness. She informed me that the other girls had already departed for the day, but not without extending their wishes for a productive and successful day to us both.

A profound wave of relief surged through me as I absorbed this newfound information, feeling immensely grateful for the chance to have some privacy. It meant we could now delve into the intricate details of our plans without the looming threat of interruptions. "Have you had a chance to look at the list of gyms Paul provided?" I inquired, my voice carrying a hint of nervous anticipation, reflecting the gravity of our mission.

Abby's eyes lit up with enthusiasm, sparkling like stars in the night sky, as she nodded eagerly in response. "I most certainly have, and let me tell you, these are not your average gyms by any stretch of the imagination," she began, her voice brimming with excitement and intrigue. "Each one has a reputation for all the wrong reasons, a little notorious in their own right, but I can't help but agree with Paul's assessment. They will indeed be our best shot at infiltrating the underground cage fights. I think the last one on the list is going to be the most promising. It seems to be the main base of operation, but if you try the others first, it will help get your name out there, signalling that you're serious about participating in the fights," she explained in detail, her fingers never ceasing their gentle stroking of Argus's fur, which lay luxuriously across her lap.

"You know exactly what to look for when you're checking out these gyms," she continued, offering me a knowing smile that spoke volumes of her unshakeable confidence in my abilities. "So I am sure you don't need me there. Meanwhile, while you're busy visiting the gym locations, I have a few essential tasks of my own to take care of," she added, her tone imbued with determination and a clear sense of purpose, leaving no doubt that she had a plan of her own.

A mischievous glint danced in Abby's eyes as she leaned in closer, lowering her voice to a conspiratorial whisper.

"Oh, and before I forget, I took care of your employment situation," she revealed, a hint of satisfaction lacing her words. My heart skipped a beat, and a whirlwind of surprise and curiosity surged through me as I tried to comprehend the magnitude of what she had accomplished.

"During my glamour appointment, I made sure to create an exact replica of you," Abby elaborated with a mischievous smirk playing on her lips. "And, on top of that, I also recruited someone to take your place at work during the day so I can personally train you in private while ensuring that your cover remains intact." A torrent of disbelief and gratitude overwhelmed me as I realised just how much effort Abby had invested in supporting me on this assignment, making sure every detail was meticulously planned.

As my mind raced to process the information she had just shared, I found myself struggling to keep up with the rapid pace at which everything seemed to be falling into place. "How on earth did you manage all of this?" I blurted out incredulously, my mind still reeling. "I haven't even secured a job yet."

"I took care of it," she stated nonchalantly, as if it were the simplest thing in the world. "You got the job at the coffee shop. It's not glamorous by any means, but it will provide the necessary cover for your activities. You'll be working from 6 am till 5 pm, six days a week. And don't worry, the person who will be doing the job won't blow your cover. They've been given a high-end glamour so she will look identical to you as well as a full backstory that matches yours. I'll also be giving her daily debriefs to ensure there are no inconsistencies between what happens during the day and what goes on at the gyms and the fights."

I couldn't decide whether I should feel shocked, impressed, or downright terrified by her astonishing efficiency in sorting everything out while I was blissfully unaware, sleeping soundly. Her composure and capability were almost unnerving, leaving me in awe of her resourcefulness.

"Is this something you've done before?" I inquired, my voice betraying the intense curiosity that bubbled within me, barely contained. The intricacy and meticulousness of her plan were astonishing, leaving me to ponder the depths of her experience in these clandestine operations. I was eager, perhaps even a bit too eager, to learn more about the extraordinary lengths she had gone to ensure our success in this perilous venture.

She exhaled deeply, turning her gaze away, a flicker of shame clouding her eyes. "Unfortunately, yes," she confessed with a weary resignation. "Working for the vampire council demanded that I become proficient in these kinds of assignments. When chaos erupted in the paranormal world, it often meant there were bodies to contend with—bodies that simply couldn't be left to attract attention. When the vampire council needed someone to vanish without leaving a trace, the solution wasn't as simple as making them disappear overnight. It was far more discreet, more insidious. We would gradually extricate them from their lives, stepping into their existence and slowly, methodically, over weeks and months, erasing their presence from society. This method ensured their disappearance wouldn't raise alarm bells or prompt police investigations."

As I listened intently to her words, my heart felt as though it had plummeted into an abyss, sinking like a heavy anchor to the very depths of my chest. I absorbed the full weight and gravity of her revelation, coming to grips with the deep, shadowy world she had been so intricately entangled in and the immense burden it had inevitably placed upon her shoulders. The complexity of her reality was staggering, an intricate tapestry woven with threads of secrets and sacrifice, and I was left to grapple with how I would respond to this startling and unexpected disclosure. I was acutely aware that my response, whatever form it might take, would carry a significance for her that transcended mere words, touching upon the very core of who she was and what she had endured. It was a sobering moment, one that demanded careful consideration of the implications and the shared path that lay ahead for us both.

"Abby, you did what was necessary, and your actions may have brought closure to families who would have otherwise never found it," I began, my voice laced with a mixture of admiration and solemnity. My voice cracked slightly as I spoke, overwhelmed by the emotion welling up inside me. "I could never look at you with anything but admiration for that. You've shown a bravery and strength that is truly remarkable." I paused, allowing the gravity of my words to settle in the air between us. "But we can't waste any time now. You go be stealthy. I have some gyms to infiltrate. Let's meet for lunch in a few hours and share our progress."

"Okay," Abby replied softly, her voice carrying a quiet determination that mirrored my own resolve. We parted ways, each of us determined to make a difference, to carve out a small victory in a world fraught with challenges, all while avoiding the ever-present risk of getting caught in the process. The tension in the air was palpable, thick with unspoken fears and hopes, but we both knew what was at stake and were willing to take the necessary risks.

*

After a long and tiresome drive spanning several hours, I finally reached all the gyms listed on Paul's meticulously crafted guide. The very last gym was discreetly nestled in a shadowy back alley, heralding itself as the prestigious training ground for the region's most formidable fighters. Paul had assured me that if I could manage to gain entry, this particular gym would be perfectly suited for my training needs. It seemed like a promising option, especially considering it was conveniently just a 20-minute drive from the secure confines of the safe house.

As I manoeuvred my car into a parking spot near the gym, I couldn't help but notice its dilapidated state and overwhelming aura of neglect. The sign, once vibrant, was now cloaked in a thick layer of rust, and the windows bore an intricate web of cracks that extended like veins, creating an unwelcoming first impression that was hard to ignore. The entire structure seemed to groan under the weight of years without care, casting an aura of mystery and challenge.

Steeling myself with a deep, calming breath, I stepped into the gym, prepared for the possibility of being let down. The receptionist stationed at the front desk did little to alleviate this apprehension. He appeared dishevelled, with clothes soaked in sweat, and looked like someone who had never set foot inside a training ring. His eyes remained glued to his computer screen as I approached, exuding an air of indifference that was palpable.

But then, unexpectedly, his voice broke the silence, carrying a gentle and almost feminine tone that contrasted starkly with his rugged appearance. "What can I do for ya?" he inquired, his gaze never lifting from the digital display before him.

"Hey," I replied, attempting to draw his attention away from the screen. Despite my efforts, his focus remained unwavering. "I'd like a tour and membership, please. Paul sent me, mentioned that you guys are excellent for fight training."

At last, my words seemed to penetrate his bubble of disinterest, prompting him to finally look up and meet my gaze for the first time. His eyes were sharp, assessing, and his demeanour shifted as he posed a question laden with expectation. "Have you seen much action before?" The question lingered in the air, heavy with anticipation, as his piercing stare seemed to scrutinise my every expression for any sign of weakness.

Drawing myself up with resolve, I met his challenge with unwavering determination. "I have some experience, but I'm always searching for more opportunities to prove myself," I declared confidently, feeling a surge of determination course through me, fuelling my desire to demonstrate my capabilities.

He nodded slowly, maintaining a cautious expression on his face as if weighing every word carefully. "If you want to train here," he began, his voice steady yet firm, "you'll need to get approval from the boss first. Come back tomorrow at this exact time, and we'll see if you've got what it takes to join us." With those words, he smoothly slid a crisp card across the desk towards me. The card was clearly marked with an appointment date and time, leaving no room for error. "Don't be late," he added, his tone carrying a subtle hint of warning that suggested punctuality was not just expected but demanded.

Feeling a mix of frustration and determination, I let out a huff of annoyance, snatching up the card with a swift motion. I spun on my heel, my footsteps echoing slightly as I made my way out of the gym's dimly lit interior. Once outside, I paused for a moment, scanning the surrounding area with a keen eye for any potential surveillance spots where I might be able to inconspicuously spy on the regulars. However, the building was strategically tucked away, its layout making it nearly impossible for me to keep an eye on it without being seen myself. It was as if it was designed to discourage prying eyes, leaving me feeling somewhat defeated.

With a resigned sigh, I pulled out my phone and quickly typed a message to Abigail, letting her know that I was done with my initial reconnaissance and asked where she wanted to meet next. Her reply was brief and to the point, simply instructing me to head over to Ottimmo Bao Bao. As I made my way there, my mind raced with possible strategies and ideas for gathering information about the gym without drawing too much attention to myself. It was evident that gaining access to the inner workings of the gym was not going to be easy, but I was determined to find a way to do so, no matter how challenging it might prove to be.

After a quick search on my phone's map app to ensure I was heading in the right direction, I found myself approaching a charming little restaurant nestled snugly between two bustling shops. Its exterior was painted a cheerful, inviting yellow, and was adorned with large, open windows that offered a clear view of the lively street outside. As I peered through the glass, I immediately spotted Abby inside, waving at me from our table. She had chosen a spot that was strategically situated to provide a clear view of all entrances and exits, just in case any unexpected trouble arose.

As I stepped inside the restaurant, the comforting aroma of freshly-baked bread and simmering spices wrapped around me like a warm embrace, instantly making my stomach rumble with anticipation for the meal that awaited us. I navigated my way through the softly lit space, noting the inviting atmosphere that seemed to promise both solace and satisfaction. As I approached our designated table, Abby's radiant smile and the lively glimmer in her eyes greeted me with a warmth that washed away the stress of the day's many challenges. Her presence was like a beacon of hope and camaraderie in the midst of my otherwise hectic life.

I eased into the seat across from her, feeling a wave of relief as I settled into the cozy booth. The restaurant's ambiance, with its colourful paintings and photographs adorning the walls, and the gentle strains of music playing softly in the background, created the ideal setting for our discussion. It was the perfect spot to catch up and strategise about our ongoing project, a haven that allowed us to focus on the important matters at hand without distraction.

"So, how has your day been? Informative, I hope?" I inquired, my tone light and conversational as I leaned back, trying to absorb the comforting atmosphere around us. Abby's expression shifted subtly, her eyes twinkling with a blend of mischief and cunning, singling that she had much to share.

"Well, it has definitely been interesting," she replied, her voice carrying a hint of excitement and intrigue. She leaned forward, lowering her voice to draw me in. "Last night, while you were deep in slumber, I took the liberty of reaching out through my network, sending some feelers out there." Her words were laden with the weight of anticipation, and I could feel the energy of her dedication radiating from her.

"I informed them to expect a list from one of my trusted associates, making it clear that I am masquerading as one of my own employees." She shifted closer, her voice dropping to a conspiratorial whisper. "Even with glamour, I can't entirely erase my scent, so the faint traces they detect will be attributed to having spent so much time near me." Her meticulous attention to detail was evident, and I couldn't help but admire the thoroughness of her cover story. Given her history with the council, it was no surprise that she had planned everything so meticulously, leaving no stone unturned in her pursuit of the truth.

I leaned back in my chair, allowing Abby's words to wash over me, taking in the remarkable effort and meticulous planning she had invested in her intricate scheme. Despite the apparent exhaustion etched on her face, her unwavering dedication to unearthing the truth was undeniable. Each word she uttered was imbued with a fervour and commitment that was not only inspiring but also profoundly humbling. As we sat together, enveloped in the warm and inviting ambiance of the restaurant, I felt a surge of renewed purpose and determination, ready to confront the challenges that lay ahead, fortified by the knowledge that Abby would be by my side through it all.

She began to speak, her voice heavy with concern, the gravity of the situation weighing down her words. "It's much more grave than we initially thought," she said, her eyes meeting mine with a somber intensity. "This Paul character either doesn't know the full extent of what's happening, or he's deliberately withholding information. Given that he went straight to Alex about this, I would venture to say it's probably the former."

I leaned in closer, my curiosity piqued and my eagerness mounting, desperate for any details she had managed to uncover. "What do you mean? If it's worse than what we've been told, wouldn't there have been more reports by now?" I asked, my brow furrowing in confusion.

Abby shook her head, her frustration palpable, etched clearly across her features. "You would think so, but the only reason we even know about this is because of the recreational offshoot that's starting to surface. The cage fighting is just one aspect of a larger operation that we've only recently become aware of, thanks to Paul's intel."

My mind was a whirlwind of thoughts as I tried to digest this shocking new revelation. Without Paul's insider knowledge, we were truly lost, navigating blindly in the dark, groping desperately for answers in this perplexing and tangled case. But with the invaluable insights he provided, we finally had a glimmer of hope—a fighting chance to intervene and put a stop to whatever sinister activities were taking place before they spiralled irreversibly out of control and beyond our grasp.

Abby's voice was filled with tension, her words coming out in a low, urgent tone as she spoke, her eyes darting around the room nervously as if expecting someone to overhear. "The fight organisers are going to great lengths to keep the existence of this drug a tightly guarded secret, but rumours are beginning to spread like wildfire. There are whispers of the fighters showing unexpected strength, of their performance and development improving drastically between matches," she explained, her voice tinged with concern. She leaned in closer, her tone dropping to an even quieter whisper, almost as if she feared the very walls might hear. "But it wasn't just physical changes...there were disturbing reports of individuals experiencing drastic shifts in their personalities, becoming more aggressive and volatile, unpredictable even."

Abby paused for a moment, her eyes reflecting the turmoil within, as she took a shaky breath to steady herself before continuing the conversation. "Apparently, in order to keep them under control, they are being heavily sedated until the effects of the drug run their course," she explained, her voice tinged with a mix of frustration and concern. The weight of her words was palpable, hanging heavily in the air like a storm cloud, casting a shadow over our small table and painting a grim picture of the dangerous and shadowy world we were attempting to infiltrate. It was a world teetering precariously on the edge of chaos and darkness, where the lines between right and wrong were blurred beyond recognition.

"Are the humans the only ones affected by this insidious plan?" I asked Abby, my curiosity piqued by the gravity of the situation. I leaned in closer, eager to understand the full scope of what we were up against. She hesitated for a moment before answering, her eyes darting around the room as if searching for invisible threats lurking in the corners. Just when she was about to speak, our waitress suddenly appeared at our table, her timing almost comically perfect.

With a perky smile and a chipper tone that seemed out of place given the seriousness of our discussion, she shattered the tension in an instant. "Good afternoon, ladies! Can I interest you in anything while you peruse our menu today?" she chirped cheerfully, her presence a stark contrast to the somber mood that had enveloped us.

Before I could even begin to formulate a response, Abby confidently cut in, her voice steady and composed, as though she had rehearsed this moment countless times. "My friend here will have ginger and lemon tea, and I'll have a pot of blood lotus tea from your special menu," she declared with an air of unwavering certainty that left no room for doubt or hesitation. As the words flowed seamlessly from her lips, a subtle and almost imperceptible glance passed between Abby and the waitress, as if they were engaged in a silent exchange, a secret communication that spoke volumes without uttering a single word. The waitress, with a knowing nod, seemed to acknowledge this hidden message, as if they shared an understanding that transcended the obvious. She then quickly bustled off to fulfil our peculiar orders, her steps purposeful and efficient.

"Do I even want to know what you actually just ordered?" I inquired, a mix of curiosity and apprehension threading through my voice.

"It's just tea with a little blood in it," Abby replied nonchalantly, as if this were the most ordinary thing in the world. "I've been assured on previous visits that the blood is donated willingly, and the donors are rewarded handsomely for it," she added, her tone casual yet reassuring.

"Okay, as long as you're happy, and it's all legit," I responded, sensing her comfort with the situation. "But you were saying something about the other fighters," I prompted, eager to return to the pressing topic at hand.

Abby let out a heavy sigh, her shoulders visibly slumping as if burdened by an invisible weight. "As far as I can tell, every species that has been exposed to the compound more than a handful of times needs to be restrained," she explained, her voice tinged with a mix of sadness and frustration. "It gives them a huge power boost, a surge of strength that seems almost supernatural, but at what cost? The increase in strength also brings out their most primal instincts. They become more cruel and barbaric, stripped of any empathy or compassion, as though their very humanity has been eroded by this substance. It's like they're in a constant state of fight or flight, with flight no longer being an option," she continued, her voice heavy with the weight of her observations.

She paused for a moment, her eyes distant as she gathered her thoughts, like someone carefully piecing together a delicate but intricate puzzle. It was as if she were contemplating the profound gravity of what she had just shared with me. "It's utterly heartbreaking to witness the effects this compound has on them," she concluded, her voice tinged with a deep, resonant sadness and frustration that seemed to hang heavily in the air, echoing in the silence that enveloped us after she spoke.

The mere notion of being trapped in such a debilitating state of mind for an extended period was nothing short of terrifying.

Just imagining it could be enough to provoke drastic changes in a person's behaviour, altering their very essence. As these unsettling thoughts swirled in my mind, our waitress approached our table, balancing a tray of drinks with practiced ease. Despite her timely arrival, I found myself so consumed by these thoughts that I was unable to focus enough to place an order. Sensing my disarray, Abby took the initiative and kindly ordered on my behalf.

We sat in a contemplative silence for several minutes, the ambient sounds of the bustling café seeming to fade into the background. Abby watched me intently, her gaze steady and unwavering, much like a hawk observing its surroundings with acute awareness. Eventually, I reached for my cup of tea, the warmth of the porcelain grounding me as I took a slow, deliberate sip. The calming properties of the tea, infused with the refreshing scent of lemon and ginger, began to soothe my frayed nerves, offering a small measure of comfort in the midst of my inner turmoil.

"Well," I began, breaking the silence with a tone of genuine admiration that seemed to echo in the cozy ambience of the café, "you certainly gathered more information than I had anticipated." I savoured the aromatic blend before me, the citrus and spice melding together into a comforting embrace that lingered on my palate. "I've managed to arrange a tour of the main gym they operate out of for tomorrow," I continued, my enthusiasm growing with each word. "I'll be speaking with the owner about the possibility of registering there to train." I paused, my excitement palpable as I contemplated the next steps in our venture. "Now, I just need to find a suitable place where we can train together. Or have you already arranged something?" I asked Abby, eager to resume our conversation and make concrete plans for our training sessions together, envisioning the progress we would achieve side by side.

Abby's confident tone and determined expression caught my attention as she brought the cup of tea to her lips, her eyes glinting with a hint of mischief. I raised an eyebrow, unsure of what she had in store for me, curious and a bit intrigued by her assured demeanour.

"Don't worry about finding a place to train with me. I've taken care of everything," she declared casually, taking another sip of her tea as if it were the easiest thing in the world. I couldn't help but give her a skeptical look, a mix of surprise and curiosity playing across my features, as she nonchalantly sipped her tea, her calmness almost infectious.

"After we finish eating, I'll take you to a safe location for training," she explained, her voice steady and reassuring. "And I'll discuss the type of training you should do at the gym as cover," she added, her words sparking a sense of anticipation within me.

Just then, our waitress arrived with our food, her timing impeccable as the tantalising aroma of our meal wafted through the air, enveloping us in a delicious embrace. She asked if we needed any refills on our drinks, to which Abby politely declined with a soft smile. Once the waitress left, Abby gestured for me to dig in, her eyes twinkling with amusement.

My stomach grumbled audibly at the enticing sight of an impressive array of sides and a steaming bowl filled to the brim with katsu chicken elegantly nestled over a bed of fluffy rice. She had thoughtfully ordered it for me, knowing my penchant for such dishes. The aroma was intoxicating, a fragrant blend that made my mouth water uncontrollably. It was evident that waiting was not an option—I simply had to dig in right away. Meanwhile, Abby, ever the adventurer in culinary choices, had opted for something intriguing. Her plate was adorned with small bao buns, each exhibiting a captivating pale reddish-pink hue, which were both intriguing and slightly mysterious in appearance. With a sly, knowing smile, she leaned in and disclosed that these delectable treats, in an unexpected twist, also contained traces of blood. This revelation was unexpected, sparking a sense of intrigue and curiosity that lingered at the back of my mind. I made a mental note to delve deeper into this culinary curiosity with her later.

As I took my first bite, an explosion of complex flavours danced across my palate, a harmonious symphony of taste that was nothing short of pure bliss. Oriental cuisine had long held a special place in my heart, but this particular meal soared above and beyond my expectations, creating a new benchmark for delight. As we finished our plates, savouring the last morsels of our extraordinary meal,

Abby engaged in a brief conversation with our attentive waitress. To my surprise, she left a generous tip, one that far exceeded what I had anticipated for our delightful dining experience.

After leaving the cozy ambiance of the restaurant, Abby led us around the corner to a vehicle that appeared a world apart from the culinary sophistication we had just experienced. There, parked casually, was a very battered-looking jeep. Its rugged exterior bore the marks of time and adventure. "What the hell is this thing?" I couldn't help but exclaim, my voice tinged with disbelief.

Abby chuckled, her eyes sparkling with amusement as she unlocked the doors. "It's one of my cars," she explained, a hint of pride in her voice. "Completely off the radar and registered under a false name for security purposes. Pretty cool, huh?"

I stood there for a moment, feeling a wave of surprise wash over me as I struggled to reconcile the rugged, battered appearance of the vehicle with the tales it seemed to whisper. "Can it actually run?" I inquired, my voice dripping with doubt. "Honestly, it looks like it belongs in a junkyard."

Abby, with a touch of pride and affection in her voice, gently tapped the dusty hood of her beloved, aging jeep. "You might not believe it just by looking at her, but this old beast has gotten me out of more tight spots than I can even remember. Trust me, she can outdo some of the latest models on the market."

Skepticism still lingering, I arched an eyebrow as I settled into the well-worn seat, fastening the seatbelt securely across my lap. "If you insist. So, where exactly are we headed?"

With a mischievous twinkle in her eye, Abby flashed a grin and revved the engine, which responded with a deep, resonant growl that filled the air. "I mentioned that we're kicking off your training today, right? It's a good thing you brought your gym clothes because we've got a mountain of work ahead if we're going to transform you into a believable cage fighter by tomorrow." Just the thought of it sent a swirl of excitement and nerves twisting through my stomach. It promised to be an intense training session, to say the least.

In no time, we found ourselves pulling up in front of what looked like an abandoned warehouse. The place had a sinister aura, with its cracked concrete walls adorned with layers of graffiti and windows that were shattered and jagged. "Abby, where on earth have you taken us?"

"We're not too far from the safe house," she responded, her tone shifting to one of unexpected seriousness and authority. "This is just a secure spot I've arranged so we can prepare and train without any interruptions or prying eyes." Her voice was firm, almost business-like. "Now hurry up. We're wasting daylight, and you need to get your butt out of the jeep."

As I stepped out into the dim light of the late afternoon, my senses were immediately heightened, alert to every whisper of wind and shadow that flickered in the eerie surroundings. An unsettling feeling of unease crept over me, growing stronger with each step I took. This side of Abigail was one I hadn't encountered before—she was relentless, ever so strategic, and appeared ready for any challenge or threat that might unexpectedly emerge from the shadows.

We moved toward the weather-beaten exterior door of the building ahead of us. At first glance, it seemed like nothing more than a forgotten relic of the past, but as we approached, it became clear that appearances were deceiving. The door, though cleverly designed to look neglected, was in fact fortified with solid metal bars and equipped with a cutting-edge biometric keypad entry system. Surrounding us was a myriad of surveillance cameras and sensors, making me feel as if we were about to enter a high-security prison rather than an old, supposedly abandoned warehouse.

My curiosity, which had been simmering just below the surface, could no longer be contained. "Abby, what exactly are you keeping hidden in there?" I inquired, nodding towards the seemingly innocuous building that now seemed anything but ordinary.

A sly smirk danced across Abby's lips, and her eyes twinkled with a mixture of mischief and amusement as she replied, "Oh, just one of my many safe houses scattered around the world. I always ensure to have a few in close proximity whenever I plan on staying somewhere for more than a few weeks. You never know when danger might strike, especially in the unpredictable and perilous world of the paranormal."

A chill traveled down my spine at her words, prompting me to ask, "Are you certain this place is truly secure?"

With a flash of unwavering confidence lighting up her eyes, Abigail responded with conviction, "Until today, only one person knew about this location—me. So yes, I can assure you it's completely secure." Her assurance lingered in the air, a testament to her unshakeable confidence, as she deftly entered the code on the sleek biometric keypad. The door clicked open with a soft, mechanical whir, and with a sense of mystery still lingering, she led me inside. The threshold marked the entrance to a hidden world, a world that had been known only to her until that very moment.

Abigail guided me through the initial entrance of the building, where grand doors swung open to reveal a sleek and sophisticated conference area. The polished floors gleamed under the ambient lighting, and modern furnishings exuded an air of professionalism and formidable power. The space was meticulously designed, every detail contributing to the aura of efficiency and authority. Yet, as we proceeded deeper into the building, the atmosphere underwent a dramatic transformation. The back area presented a stark contrast to the front—a cluttered and well-stocked armoury filled the room. Guns, knives, and various other weapons were mounted on the walls like lethal works of art, their presence both intimidating and awe-inspiring. The remainder of the space was occupied by practice combat dummies, chart tables, high-tech computers, and several large display screens that flickered with strategic data. This was no ordinary conference centre; it was a clandestine base for covert operations, a hub of strategic planning and execution.

A thrill of excitement mingled with a ripple of apprehension as I absorbed my surroundings. If anyone needed to orchestrate their own private war, this was undoubtedly the place to do it. Abigail moved with purpose and precision around the room, her motions fluid as she switched on computers and meticulously checked the building's comprehensive security grid. Her confidence was palpable, each gesture underscoring her command over this secretive domain.

After a few moments of careful observation, she nodded in satisfaction, her expression radiating a quiet triumph that spoke volumes about her confidence in the plan we were about to execute. She turned to me with a small, knowing grin that seemed to hold secrets of its own, and said, "Okay, the perimeter's secure, and it doesn't look like anyone followed us here. There's a bathroom just past the weapons rack, so go ahead and get changed into something more suitable. Then, I want you to start on a quick warm-up while I finish up with some preparations here. Once I'm done, we'll get down to business." Her words, though calm and controlled, were suffused with assurance and authority, each syllable reinforcing the fact that she was the one in charge, the one who knew exactly what needed to be done. Yet, her confidence only served to heighten my awareness of how out of my depth I truly was in this situation. Despite this looming realisation, I steeled myself, pushing aside any lingering doubts or trepidation that threatened to undermine my resolve.

I made my way to the small, sparsely decorated bathroom she had indicated. The space was utilitarian, with white tiles adorning the walls, although some were slightly chipped, hinting at years of use. A faint smell of bleach lingered in the air, a testament to its recent cleaning. The bathroom was equipped with the bare essentials: a cramped shower stall that seemed to have seen better days, a basic toilet, and a sink with rusted faucets that had clearly withstood the test of time. Despite its simplicity and wear, the bathroom served its purpose perfectly for what I needed at that moment.

Changing quickly into my workout clothes, I emerged back into the main room, feeling the coolness of the air against my skin. I began to stretch, methodically working through each muscle group, trying to prepare my body for the physical demands that lay ahead. As I moved through my routine, I couldn't help but feel a sense of dread wash over me, a foreboding that clung to my thoughts like a shadow. Abby's sly smile, which she wore with a certain air of mischief, told me that this would not only be an educational experience but one that she would take great joy in orchestrating. Steeling myself for the pain and challenge to come,

I continued with my stretches, focusing intently on limbering up my muscles to the best of my ability. Each movement was deliberate and precise, as I sought to prepare my body for the rigorous demands that lay ahead. After about ten minutes of concentrated effort, during which I tried to clear my mind and centre my thoughts, Abby finally approached me. Her confident demeanour was unmistakable, and there was a glint in her eye that left no doubt about her intentions. She was ready, resolute in her determination to push me beyond the limits I had come to know. With a resigned sigh, I braced myself for the inevitable soreness and discomfort that awaited me at the end of this gruelling session.

Abby's piercing gaze locked onto mine, a silent command demanding my full attention. Her eyes bore into me, as if willing me to grasp the seriousness of what was about to unfold. "Jess," she said firmly, her voice carrying a sense of urgency that resonated deep within me. "I know you're a capable fighter, there's no question about that, but this is a whole different type of combat altogether. It's not something you've been trained in or experienced before, and it requires a different mindset."

She paused for a moment, allowing her words to sink in while she gave me a searching look, as if probing the depths of my resolve. "I spoke to Hargreaves about your previous training," she continued, her tone becoming more insistent. "He confirmed that you have the skills, but there's something holding you back. You hesitate to attack, and that just won't work in the arena." Her voice was stern and commanding, a force willing me to understand the gravity of the situation that lay before me.

A wave of unease washed over me at the thought of causing pain intentionally. The footage we had watched together earlier replayed in my mind, a stark reminder of just how brutal and unforgiving this type of fighting could be. Each strike, each blow, was delivered with a merciless precision that left no room for hesitation or doubt. But Abby wasn't finished yet, her determination unwavering.

"You need to let go of that passive mindset," she continued with unwavering resolve, her gaze fixed intently on mine as if trying to drill her words deep into my soul. "Fight with everything you've got, every ounce of strength and determination within you. You're not just fighting for a win; it's about survival, about proving to yourself that you can overcome anything thrown your way." Her words reverberated in the silent room, each syllable a challenge that demanded to be confronted and tackled with all the energy I could muster.

"This isn't a game, Jess. It's survival." Her words struck me with a force that was almost physical, hitting like a punch to the gut, making the remnants of the lunch I had overindulged in churn uncomfortably in my stomach. Despite my initial resistance and the instinct to dismiss her words, I couldn't deny their truth. To survive the daunting task ahead, I would have to dig deep, tapping into a primal side of myself that I had always approached with fear and trepidation. My stomach twisted and turned, a turbulent sea of nerves and apprehension swirling within me, but somewhere deep inside, a flicker of fierce determination began to ignite and grow. This might not be my usual style of combat, but I was steeling myself, ready to do whatever it takes to emerge victorious in the end.

Abigail's voice was firm and unwavering as she set the plan into motion, "Jess, these fighters are trained to attack relentlessly and take blows without flinching. That's what we're going to focus on today." With a determined and resolute look in her eyes, she continued, "You and I will engage in repeated 5-minute matches, recording each one so we can analyse them comprehensively later. This will allow me to pinpoint exactly which areas you need to improve and develop. Now, let's begin."

The moment Abigail finished articulating her plan, she launched into action with a swift right hook aimed precisely at the side of my head. Instinct took over as I raised my arms in a protective stance to block her attack. Her movements were fluid, graceful, and calculated, as if she were executing a perfectly choreographed dance. She quickly pivoted, using the momentum to bring her left elbow crashing down forcefully onto the back of my neck, driving me down to my knees with a precision that left me vulnerable.

Before I could even catch my breath or regain my footing, she launched into another assault, delivering a powerful kick aimed directly at my midsection. The sheer force of the impact felt like a battering ram crashing into me, sending me sprawling across the floor. I landed in a crumpled heap, gasping desperately for air, every breath a struggle. My mind raced as I tried to regain my composure, to steady myself and brace for whatever she might throw at me next.

Abby let out a deep sigh and lowered her clenched fists, breaking the tense atmosphere that had settled between us. "Okay," she said, her voice calm yet authoritative, "that wasn't quite five minutes, but let's take a moment to review." Still struggling to catch my breath, I could only manage to growl out my frustration. "What the hell do you mean by 'let's review'? You didn't even give me a chance to find my bearings." I fought to stand on my shaky legs, attempting to mask the pain that radiated through my body. Abby, in stark contrast, stood with a confident and relaxed stance, while mine was hunched over, trembling with exertion.

"That's the point of fighting," she explained calmly, her words slicing through the air with precision. "Your opponent won't give you a moment to rest. They'll keep attacking relentlessly until you can't keep up. And just so you're aware, I've been holding back this whole time." The realisation hit me like a punch to the gut, leaving me unsteady as I winced at the memory of my lacklustre attempts at defence. "What do you mean you pulled your punches?" I asked, bewildered and a little frightened by the thought of her full strength.

She gazed at me with a mixture of disappointment and concern in her eyes, a look that seemed to pierce through my defences. I couldn't even begin to imagine the kind of impact a full-strength hit from her would have. "Come on, go sit down," she instructed, gesturing towards one of the terminals where two chairs were set up in front of it. "We'll review and then start again."

Reluctantly, I obeyed, knowing full well that there was no escaping this gruelling training session. As I settled into the seat, Abby began to pull up footage on the monitor, revealing the setup of several internal cameras that had been tracking my movements. Abigail explained that this would allow us to meticulously break down my fighting style, analyse my weaknesses, and make the necessary adjustments to improve my techniques. The thought of going through it all again was daunting, but I knew it was the only way to become stronger.

For the remainder of the day, we settled into a steady rhythm that became almost second nature: combat, review, and repeat. Each session with Abigail was a meticulous dance of movement and critique. She would pause frequently, pointing out specific moments where my footwork faltered or instances where I missed an opportune moment to strike. Her keen eye caught every flaw, and her guidance was both relentless and invaluable. By the time the day drew to a close, my muscles felt like they had been put through the wringer—hot, drenched in sweat, and achingly fatigued. Yet, as I glanced over at Abigail, she seemed unfazed by the physical demands of the day, not even slightly winded.

"Go get a shower," she instructed with her usual calm authority. "I'll wait here, then we can return to the house." The mere thought of a warm, soothing shower was like a beacon of hope at the end of such a gruelling day of training. Despite the exhaustion, a part of me was acutely aware that tomorrow would usher in another day of rigorous training under Abigail's watchful and demanding guidance, pushing me to my limits and beyond.

Letting out a deep, frustrated grunt, I trudged away from the training area. My muscles screamed in protest with every step, and my mind was a whirlwind of exhaustion from the constant drills and sparring matches. Once I reached the sanctuary of the bathroom, I locked the door, turned on the shower, and allowed the steamy water to cascade over me, soothing my aching body for a blissful twenty minutes. The stress of the day slowly washed away as the water enveloped me, leaving me feeling somewhat rejuvenated. After rinsing away the grime and tension, I dressed and returned to meet Abby at the jeep, where she was waiting patiently.

As we drove back to our house, the silence was thick with unspoken thoughts and the hum of the engine. I couldn't shake off the growing anxiety about my chances in the upcoming arena competition. "Do you really think I have a shot, Abby?" I finally asked, the doubt in my voice betraying my inner turmoil.

"If I didn't believe in you, I would have pulled the plug already," she reassured me with a confident smile that lit up her face. "It won't be easy, but I know you can do it. Just make sure to get some rest tonight. You'll need all your energy for tomorrow's training." Her words were a balm to my frayed nerves, instilling a renewed sense of determination.

We arrived at the house later than we had anticipated, finding it cloaked in silence as everyone else had already retired for the night. The weight of exhaustion settled over us like a heavy blanket as Abby and I headed straight to our room, eager for the comfort of our beds.

"I will try not to drool on you while I sleep," I joked, attempting to lighten the mood as we crawled into bed together. She laughed, a sound that was both familiar and comforting, before turning her attention to her phone. The soft glow of the screen illuminated her face in the darkness of our shared room, as she scrolled through messages and updates from our team.

Closing my eyes, I made a conscious effort to push away any lingering fears or doubts, focusing instead on the importance of a good night's rest before another intense day of training. As I drifted off to sleep, the rhythmic sound of her breathing beside me was a soothing reminder that I wasn't alone in this journey.

CHAPTER 7

Gym Anxiety and Unexpected Training

My muscles were still sore from the gruelling workout Abby had put me through the previous day, and that soreness only heightened my apprehension about my upcoming appointment at the gym. The very idea of having to simulate training, followed by the reality of actually working out with Abby, twisted my stomach into knots of anxiety. Determined to gather my composure, I arrived at the gym a full 10 minutes early, hoping that a few moments of solitude might help steady my nerves before the appointment began.

As I stepped through the entrance, the familiar musty odour hit me immediately, mingling with the dim lighting to create an atmosphere that felt almost oppressive. The stifling heat seemed to wrap around me like a heavy blanket, adding to my growing sense of unease.

The same indifferent guy from the day before was stationed at the front desk, his demeanour as apathetic as ever, with his eyes glued to the computer screen in front of him. I stood there for a moment, unsure how to proceed, before finally deciding to tap my knuckles lightly on the counter to draw his attention.

"Excuse me," I ventured, my voice striving for steadiness even as my insides fluttered with nervous energy. "I'm not sure if you remember me, but you set up an appointment for me."

The fluorescent lights overhead flickered intermittently, casting a sporadic glow over the room as I fidgeted uneasily, waiting for any sign of recognition or acknowledgment from him. In the background, the faint sounds of weights clanking and distant voices reverberated through the closed doors, serving as a reminder of the bustling activity beyond.

Eventually, after what felt like an interminable wait, the guy finally, and with excruciating slowness, peeled his gaze away from the computer screen. His eyes, which looked like they had been glued to the glowing rectangle for ages, met mine with an expression that was the epitome of boredom and indifference. It was as if I were nothing more than a mundane interruption in his otherwise uneventful day. His piercing gaze scanned me meticulously from head to toe, sizing me up with a critical and scrutinising eye. I felt like an ant under a magnifying glass, exposed and vulnerable, as he remarked in a monotone voice, "Yeah, I remember you. You're one of Paul's fighters, right? Head to the back office. The boss is waiting for you." His mesmerising tone was a clear indication that he didn't regard me as someone deserving of any significant attention.

With a lazy and indifferent wave of his hand, gesturing vaguely in the direction I needed to go, he shifted his attention back to the mesmerising glow of the screen in front of him, a screen that seemed to command his full and unwavering devotion. As I proceeded past the front desk, my eyes widened in sheer astonishment at the scene that unfolded before me. The gym was unlike any other facility I had ever encountered in my life. It was a sprawling arena of physical prowess, where various combat cages were meticulously arranged. Each cage housed intense and rigorous training sessions, where trainers and fighters engaged in a dynamic dance of strategy and strength, creating a symphony of grunts, shouts, and the occasional dramatic clatter of bodies hitting the mats with resounding force. The standard weight-lifting equipment lined the walls like sentinels, but it was the vibrant energy and unique aura emanating from this place that truly set it apart from the rest. A palpable intensity filled the air, an electric charge that seemed to pulse and thrum through every corner of the gym, sending an involuntary chill racing down my spine. It was a place where dedication and determination were not merely abstract concepts; they were tangible, almost as if you could reach out and physically grasp them from the air.

I cautiously navigated my way through the gym, careful not to make direct eye contact with the skilled and formidable fighters who surrounded me. Their muscles glistened with sweat, evidence of their fierce and relentless dedication as they trained with unwavering determination. I couldn't help but feel a surge of nervousness coursing through my body as I made my way towards the back office, fervently hoping to make a favourable impression on whoever awaited my arrival there.

Finally, as I reached the far end of the gym, my eyes were irresistibly drawn to the office that the receptionist had pointed me towards. It stood apart from the rest of the gym, a distinct entity with a sizeable one-way window that provided a commanding view of the bustling practice area. I assumed it was designed this way so the occupant could have a clear, unobstructed view of any potential fighters in action.

Taking a long, steadying breath to quell the storm of anxiety inside me, I stepped cautiously toward the imposing door, each movement deliberate as if weighed down by the gravity of the unknown. With a firm, resounding knock—a sound that echoed through the expanse of the gym—I paused briefly, listening as it was followed by a cacophony of shifting chairs and the rhythmic thud of footsteps drawing nearer from the depths of the adjoining office. In an instant that felt like the prelude to an ambush, the door burst open with a force I hadn't anticipated, revealing a man whose very presence shattered every expectation I had carried.

He was not merely a figure in the doorway; his lean, muscular build spoke of countless hours sculpted by discipline and physical rigour. Every inch of him exuded a primal strength, his body fat barely perceptible beneath his taut skin, as though he were carved from stone and honed for combat. His stance was alert and defensive, each movement betraying the readiness of a seasoned warrior perpetually on the lookout for an unforeseen threat. His sharp, grey eyes scanned his surroundings with a predator's focus, absorbing every minute detail with an almost inhuman precision. Even the deliberate cut of his close-cropped hair, seemingly fashioned to thwart any chance of an adversary seizing it during a skirmish, contributed to his aura of danger. In another context, clad in a pair of jeans and a casual hoody, he might easily have blended in with the crowd, but on the hardwood of the gym floor, he radiated overwhelming power and volatile energy.

Fear gripped me as my body shuddered in the presence of this formidable sentinel. His broad, solid shoulders and the taut, rippling muscles that dominated his frame were tangible evidence of a force that could dismantle me with a mere thought. I felt a morbid respect, and a terror, knowing that one misstep could unleash a power capable of reducing me to little more than a forgotten whisper in the wind. Yet, as I dared to meet those steely grey eyes, I discerned a flicker of something deeper—an almost imperceptible rage simmering just beneath the surface, restrained but ready to erupt.

"Come in," he commanded with a gruff, no-nonsense tone, his hand motioning for me to step further into the sanctum of his office. "You must be the new talent. Paul has been talking about you. My name's Kane, and I'm the owner of this gym." His words, edged with both authority and a hint of admiration, filled the space like a challenge and an invitation all at once.

I hesitated only briefly before entering the room, each step underscored by the stark contrast between my diminutive form and the overwhelming presence before me. Kane directed me to settle into a chair placed across from his imposing desk—a simple piece of furniture that now seemed to dwarf me in its stoic pragmatism. I sat, trying desperately to mask the cascade of anxiety that threatened to spill over, while my heart pounded a frantic rhythm within my chest.

After what felt like an interminable pause, I gathered every ounce of courage and let it manifest in a tone that belied the nervous flutter within me. With a smile that faltered under the weight of the situation, I said, "Hi, I'm Jess." My voice, bubbly though measured, fought against the palpable tension in the room as I continued, "I'm really happy to meet you. Paul gave me a list of gyms to check out, but something about this one—this vibe—completely drew me in."

In that brief, yet seemingly eternal moment, as the cascade of words spilled unbidden from my lips, I instantly regretted each and every syllable that had escaped me. The gym, far from the warm and welcoming refuge I had imagined, loomed as a formidable and oppressive fortress, laden with an undercurrent of raw, volatile energy. It was as if the air itself was charged with an electric tension, a ticking time bomb poised to detonate at any given moment. Despite the turbulent storm of emotions swirling within me, I meticulously masked them all, resolute in my determination that Kane must never catch even the slightest glimpse of the apprehension gnawing at the edges of my composure.

A sly, knowing grin slowly unfurls across his face, as though I had just uttered the punchline of a particularly amusing joke. "Haha, yeah," he chuckles, the sound resonating with a confident ease. "He mentioned he sent you to a few other places, but I had a feeling you'd wind up here eventually. You see, I boast one of the most prestigious ratings in the world for producing top-notch fighters and orchestrating unparalleled shows." Each word drips with unmistakable pride, a testament to his self-assured prowess and the empire he had meticulously built.

"So, I hear you have some experience in cage fighting. Is that accurate?" His eyes, alight with an eager anticipation, lock onto mine as he leans in closer, clearly impatient to hear my response.

I nodded deliberately, making an effort to uphold the meticulously crafted facade of my invented backstory. "Yeah," I responded, infusing a subtle yet deliberate hint of cautious confidence into my words, "I've had a few bouts in smaller arenas, but nothing that would really stand out. I'm in search of a greater challenge, something that can really push my limits."

His next question caught me off guard slightly, as I hadn't anticipated him showing such interest. "Okay, so what disciplines have you worked with before?" he inquired. Fortunately, I had spent time studying various martial arts under the guidance of Hargreaves, absorbing bits and pieces from different styles, which I had strategically included in my backstory.

"I've had some experience with jujitsu, kickboxing, and Muay Thai," I replied, attempting to project confidence despite my limited formal training. "However, in my previous bouts, I never really focused on mastering one particular style. It was more of an eclectic mix of punches and kicks that saw me through the fights." As I spoke, vivid memories surged through my mind—recollections of the chaotic adrenaline rush during the warehouse raid and the intense battle with the wendigo. Even now, the effects of that fight linger within me, like echoes of a storm that refuse to fade, but I couldn't allow Kane to detect any sign of vulnerability.

"Alright," he said with a tone of authority, "quickly change into your training gear and meet me by the cages. I need to assess what I'm working with. If you manage to impress me, we can have a detailed discussion about setting up a comprehensive training schedule. Did Paul happen to mention that it might take a few weeks before I can secure a match for you?" His words were direct and left little room for negotiation.

I was momentarily taken aback by his boldness and straightforward nature but nodded in understanding. "Yes, he did mention that. He said it could be anywhere from 4 to 6 weeks, correct?"

He gave a curt nod, his expression unwavering, and replied, "That timeframe depends entirely on how well you train. These cage fights aren't your average bouts, so we need to ensure that whoever we put in there can truly entertain the crowd and hold their own. Now hurry up and change. Our time is limited, and we need to make every second count."

The changing rooms were sleek and modern, equipped with all the necessary equipment for a professional fighter. It was clear that the world of cage fighting paid much better than I had originally thought, given the luxurious amenities available.

Emerging from the changing rooms a few minutes later, I made my way over to Kane with a mix of eagerness and apprehension. "So, what's your plan for training me?" I asked tentatively, noticing the permanent scowl etched onto his face. I couldn't quite tell if it was directed towards me or if it was simply his default expression, one that he wore like a second skin.

"First," he growled, his voice low and gruff like gravel underfoot, "I want you to spar with a few other fighters from different disciplines so I can observe your technique. Remember, your opponents are human, so make sure to pull your punches. Our goal here is training, not injury. I'm just interested in seeing how you fight. Winning isn't the focus right now."

With a nod of understanding and acceptance, I cautiously stepped into the cage, my muscles coiled with tension and ready to respond to whatever challenge lay ahead. Abigail's motivational words reverberated in my mind, urging me to abandon thoughts of defence and restraint, and instead to channel my energy into pure offence. This was the mantra I clung to, a mental anchor as I braced myself for the imminent onslaught.

Kane, the authoritative figure overseeing the match, barked out orders to one of the fighters standing nearby. This fighter was a towering giant of a man whose sheer presence seemed to fill the entire room with an overwhelming intensity. He was easily twice my size, exuding an air of unshakeable confidence as he confidently entered the cage. His eyes locked onto mine, and he cracked his knuckles with a bravado that was both intimidating and strangely invigorating, setting the stage for our impending confrontation.

My opponent moved with a saunter around the cage, his every step radiating confidence and raw power. He gave me a slight dip of his head, a silent acknowledgment that he would be the one challenging me in this fierce battle. Without any further warning, the sharp clang of the starting bell pierced the air, signalling the official commencement of our match. I had trained rigorously for this moment with Abby just the day before, preparing meticulously for any tactics my opponent might employ against me.

As I had anticipated, my opponent attempted a rapid rush, hoping to catch me off guard with his aggressive advance. However, I had foreseen his move and noticed the moment he lowered his defence as he lunged toward me. Seizing the opportunity, I deftly sidestepped to my left just before he could strike, and with precision, I launched a powerful kick aimed at his abdomen. My intention was to incapacitate him without causing any serious harm, using his own momentum to my advantage.

As my kick connected with a decisive impact, I followed through with the movement, sending my opponent stumbling backward with a loud, involuntary grunt that echoed throughout the cavernous arena. His body seemed to crumple as he clutched at his stomach, desperately gasping for breath, each inhale laboured and pained as the force of the blow took its toll on him. The sound of the bell ringing once again reverberated through the space, signalling the conclusion of the intense match. My opponent, overcome by the force of the encounter and perhaps the bitter taste of defeat, collapsed to the ground, groaning in discomfort as he tried to reconcile with the loss.

It was a profoundly satisfying victory, one that filled me with a sense of achievement and gratitude. I knew deep down that I owed this triumph to Abby's invaluable guidance and unwavering support. Without her help, her rigorous training sessions, and her strategic insights, I would not have been able to execute such a calculated move with the precision and effectiveness that had won me the match.

Feeling confident and riding the high of victory, I approached Kane once again, my steps imbued with a newfound swagger. "Who's next?" I asked, my voice carrying a hint of bravado that matched my mood.

"Not bad, kid," Kane remarked with a sly grin stretching across his face. He seemed both impressed and entertained by my performance. "But let's try something a little more challenging," he suggested, his tone tinged with a playful challenge.

He called out to everyone in the gym, his voice booming and commanding attention. The buzz of activity around us ceased almost instantly, as all eyes turned to him, curious about what was to come. "Listen up, folks. I have a special training exercise for you today," he announced, piquing everyone's interest. "It's a one-on-one challenge with this newbie here," he continued, gesturing towards me with a nod that seemed to place me squarely in the spotlight. "The first person to take her down will win £1,000 cash."

The announcement created a frenzy of excitement, a palpable energy that swept through the gym like a wave. Soon enough, there was a line of eager participants, each one buzzing with anticipation, waiting to have their shot at taking me down and claiming the prize money.

"Now, kid," Kane turned to me with a mischievous glint in his eye, one that hinted at both the challenge and opportunity ahead of me. "You have two options. You can run away and admit defeat, or you can face your challengers head-on. If you can hold your own against them all for as long as they're willing to keep trying, you'll earn yourself a spot in this gym and a place on our fight list."

My mouth hung open in shock, disbelief washing over me. He couldn't be serious, could he? To take on every single person in this gym one-on-one would be an enormous task, potentially taking all day and testing me to my very limits. But then I caught sight of him smirking at me, a silent dare in his expression, challenging me to back down.

I squared my shoulders, summoning my resolve and determination. Meeting his challenge head-on, I declared with confidence, "I'm in." This was my chance to prove myself, to show not just Kane but everyone in the gym what I was capable of, and to earn my rightful place among these skilled fighters.

***

My time at the gym transformed into an epic, seemingly endless battle of endurance, as I faced off against fighters hailing from various martial arts disciplines. Each warrior took their turn to unleash a relentless wave of attacks upon me, their intensity unwavering and their determination palpable. Kane stood on the sidelines, his voice booming with words of encouragement to his warriors as I defended myself with all the strength and skill I could muster. These combatants appeared to possess an insatiable thirst for the thrill of the fight, never abandoning their objective to bring me down and claim the ultimate prize for themselves. Over time, I had come to recognise several of these fighters, their faces familiar as they returned time and again, driven by an unyielding desire to achieve victory. However, it seemed the whispers of this clandestine tournament had spread beyond the usual crowd, as I began to notice unfamiliar faces appearing, as if reinforcements had been summoned to join the fray.

For an excruciating four hours, I endured this punishing ordeal, my body gradually succumbing to fatigue and growing increasingly bruised under the unending barrage of powerful blows. Yet, I refused to succumb to defeat, relying on my agility and sharp reflexes to dodge incoming attacks while expertly identifying and exploiting weaknesses in my opponents' defences to deliver counterstrikes. The young kickboxer I was currently engaged with was particularly fierce and unrelenting in his assaults, but I skilfully turned his aggression to my advantage, countering with precision strikes that disrupted his rhythm and flow.

After what felt like an eternity, Kane mercifully called an end to the gruelling training session. My body was drenched in sweat, and my muscles throbbed with the deep ache of exhaustion. "Okay kid," Kane addressed me, his voice carrying a note of genuine surprise. "You said your name is Jess, right?"

"Yeah, that's me," I managed to reply, my breath coming in ragged gasps as I struggled to regain my composure.

"Well, you just saved me a £1,000 payout and taught these chumps a valuable lesson on the dangers of underestimating their opponents. Honestly, I wasn't expecting much when you first walked in here. You don't exactly give off the impression of someone who can take a hit and rise back up. But look at you now—four hours later and you still look like you're ready for another round," he chuckled, a hint of admiration in his eyes. "So be here tomorrow evening, and we'll officially begin your training."

"Wait, that's it? Just like that?" I questioned, my voice laced with incredulity. I couldn't quite believe the abruptness of the situation. "Aren't you going to discuss a training plan or anything at all?"

Kane grinned, a mischievous glint lighting up his eyes, betraying his excitement. "Oh, don't worry about that. We'll have plenty of time to go over all the details tomorrow," he assured me, though his tone was dismissive. "For now, you can just bugger off. I've got work to attend to." With that, he turned on his heel and stormed off towards his office, the door slamming shut behind him with a definitive thud.

As the sound of the door echoed in the room, the weight of his words began to settle over me like a heavy blanket. The magnitude of what I had achieved today slowly dawned on me. I had completed stage one of the infiltration mission, and now the challenge lay in surviving the aftermath.

I stood there, momentarily stunned by Kane's abrupt departure. The air around me felt thick with a mix of disappointment and confusion, and I couldn't shake off the feeling of someone's presence looming behind me. A soft clearing of the throat broke the silence, urging me to turn around. There stood a man, an easygoing demeanour about him.

"Don't worry about him," the man said with a chuckle, extending his hand towards me. "He's always in a foul mood unless he's just won big on the fights." His relaxed manner put me at ease. "Name's Mal. You're probably not familiar with me since I'm one of the guys you've been beating on for the last few hours."

I shook his hand, trying to piece together where I might have seen him. "Oh, right, Mal. Sorry, it's been quite a long night," I replied, attempting a smile.

"Yeah, you've pretty much taken down all the regulars now," he remarked with a casual shrug, as if it were no big deal.

His words flattered me more than I expected. "Wow, really? I guess I was too caught up in the fights to notice," I admitted, feeling a sense of pride.

Mal's lips curled into a mischievous grin, his eyes twinkling with a mixture of amusement and genuine admiration. "Honestly," he began, voice low and full of frank honesty, "most of us were just trying to figure out how to beat you." He paused momentarily before adding, "I even heard that a gym-wide text went out, announcing that Kane would offer a hefty payout to anyone who managed to take you down."

A laugh bubbled up from deep within me as the scattered pieces of the puzzle clattered into place. "That explains so much," I admitted, nodding in understanding. "I was beginning to wonder why Kane himself seemed dismissive of me earlier."

Mal's kind reassurance cut through the tension that had been steadily building inside me, a pressure spawned by a gnawing anxiety over my performance in the fight. I returned his smile with gratitude, then took a moment to really study my opponent in the flesh. From his muscular frame to the self-assured way he held himself, it was evident that he had spent countless hours mastering the art of combat. And there I stood, someone who had barely managed to survive each gruelling round, yet had somehow emerged victorious in the end.

"I wouldn't say I was absolutely dominating out there," I said with a modest chuckle, trying to downplay my own efforts.

Raising a playful eyebrow, Mal remarked, "Maybe not, but you definitely have some serious skills."

As he spoke, his battered appearance told its own story of endless battles fought. His nose, clearly having suffered more than one break and never fully mended, and the network of bruises and minor cuts marring his skin painted the picture of someone who lived for the fight.

Feeling a wave of concern mixed with camaraderie, I gestured toward a rather conspicuous bruise on his jaw. "I hope I didn't make any of your injuries any worse," I said, my voice tinged with genuine worry.

With a casual nonchalance, Mal lifted his shirt, revealing a web of scars that crisscrossed his chest and abdomen, each mark a silent testament to past encounters. "Oh, these?" he laughed softly. "They're nothing. They're nearly healed. Kane will let me get back in the ring once they're sorted out." His tone gradually shifted, growing more serious as he continued, "He's incredibly strict about that. If you're not absolutely at 100%, you can't get into the cage. And when it comes to the special fights, he's even more meticulous. Full X-rays and blood tests are standard procedure to ensure you're fit enough to put on a show."

My curiosity got the better of me, and I leaned in slightly. "Have you ever been in one of those special matches before?" I asked, genuinely intrigued by the undercurrent of tension that his words carried.

"Yeah," Mal replied after a brief pause, his voice now holding a hint of hesitation. "But honestly, we're not really supposed to talk about it. My last match was a special one, and I ended up being sidelined for about 10 weeks. The doctors are insisting I take a longer break, but you know how it is—if I'm not fighting, I'm not earning." He let his words linger for a moment before adding with a more upbeat tone, "I've got another match coming up in a few weeks though. So if you ever need someone to spar with, just give me a shout. I could really use the practice." With that, Mal slung his bag casually over his shoulder and began making his way off to change, his confident stride leaving no doubt about his experience in the ring. Well, that was definitely informative. I should head out before people start asking a question. I headed for a warm shower and change before heading out

**

The safe house came into view, a beacon of relief after a day that had tested every ounce of my endurance. Each step toward the entrance felt like a monumental effort as my muscles screamed in protest, weighed down by fatigue. All I wanted was to collapse into the soothing embrace of my bed. With a deep, weary sigh, I pushed open the door, feeling the cool air of the hallway wash over me as I dragged my feet down its length.

Turning the corner, I was met with an unexpected sight that stopped me in my tracks. Abby, with her elegant figure stretched comfortably across my bed, was engrossed in her phone. Her expression was one of serene tranquility, exuding a peacefulness as if she were untouched by any troubles. In that moment, sleep no longer occupied my thoughts as I became entranced by her effortless beauty, her presence a calming antidote to my chaotic day. As the door creaked behind me, announcing my arrival, her eyes lifted to meet mine. Instantly, a radiant smile illuminated her face, as if my appearance was the highlight of her day.

However, her gaze soon shifted, taking in the sorry state of my appearance. Concern replaced her earlier carefree demeanour as her warm brown eyes scanned the bruises and cuts marking my face. My features were a mess—swollen and bruised, a split lip oozing blood, and my hair, once neatly in place, now a disheveled tangle. Deep scratches marred the skin of my arms. "What happened?" Abby gasped, her voice a mixture of shock and worry as her hand reached out, fingers brushing gently against the bruises on my cheek.

"I'm okay," I attempted to reassure her, though my voice lacked conviction, the pain simmering beneath my skin making it hard to sound nonchalant. "I've secured a spot at the gym. I have my first session tomorrow evening," I added, trying to steer the conversation away from my injuries.

Abby wasn't about to be easily dissuaded. As if her inner resolve had ignited a fiery determination within her, her tone sharpened and grew more insistent with every passing moment. "What happened?!" she demanded once again, her eyes locking onto mine with an intensity that brooked no interruption. She was unwavering, adamant that no detail would go unspoken until the entire truth was laid bare.

I exhaled a heavy, resigned sigh, feeling the weight of the moment press down on me as if it were a physical burden. Slowly, and with a palpable reluctance, I uttered the name that set every nerve on edge: "Kane." That single word held enough power to spark a blaze of anger within me, and I could feel my fists clench against my sides as memories of past encounters flared up like embers in the dark.

"In short," I began, my voice mingling defiant pride with a trace of melancholy, "the guy who runs the place decided I needed to be tested. So, I've been thrown into a series of brutal fights. They even put up a £1,000 prize for the first person brave—or foolish—enough to take me down." Despite the persistent ache that throbbed in every muscle, a subtle glimmer of pride shone through as I recounted the day's challenges.

Abby's gaze was fixed on me with an unspoken mix of awe and admiration, her features softening as she absorbed every word. "Abby, don't worry about it," I reassured her, my tone laced with the confidence of someone who had faced down intimidating odds before. "I've taken on every challenger, over and over again. And besides, they were all merely human—nothing monstrous lurking in their shadows." But even as I offered my assurances, her face betrayed a lingering apprehension, her brow knitted together in quiet dismay.

"I understand your fears," I continued, earnest in my attempt to ease her troubled mind. "But trust me, I know how to handle myself." For a moment, a look of almost childish disappointment flickered across her face—a pouting expression that recalled a little girl sulking when she didn't get her way. That glimpse of vulnerability drew a genuine laugh from me, a sound that burst forth and filled the room with an unexpectedly joyful energy despite the tension that hung in the air. In that laughter, I found solace and gratitude for Abby's presence—she was my constant reminder not to take life's perils too gravely, to always find humour even when the stakes were at their highest.

Meeting her worried eyes, I felt an inner duty to reassure her and allay her anxieties. "I know it isn't easy to swallow," I said firmly, "but I've defeated them all and come out on top. You don't need to worry about me." I explained that my training session with them would begin tomorrow evening—a critical juncture in a plan carefully laid out to preserve my cover. Yet, deep down, I understood that tomorrow would mark a crucial day; a day that would test every ounce of my preparedness for the unforeseen challenges that might be hurled my way.

"You'll have the whole of tomorrow dedicated to what I call my real training," I elaborated, emphasising that every moment would be spent building the skills necessary to overcome any obstacle. "Consider it a preparation for anything and everything they might try to throw at me." Though Abby nodded in reluctant understanding, determination still shadowed her expression as she issued a final warning: "Fine, but know this—the training I'm putting you through will be intense. Get some rest tonight because tomorrow is going to be a gruelling day."

With that, she slipped away silently, leaving me alone with my thoughts and the weight of the day's events. As I stood there, the gravity of my mission pressed heavily upon my shoulders. Amid the quiet solitude, I resolved to clear my cluttered mind and steal what rest I could, all while the looming test of my skills and strength awaited like an approaching storm on the horizon.

CHAPTER 8

Nightmare Training

Before the sun had even begun to cast its first gentle rays upon the horizon, my inaugural day of training was already set in motion. The tranquility of the early hours was shattered as I was jolted awake, my heart pounding fiercely within my chest, each beat resonating like a drum in the silence of the room. My entire body was drenched in a cold, clammy sweat, as if I had been submerged in an icy pool during the dead of night. The echo of my own screams hung in the dimly lit room, lingering like a ghostly presence, remnants of a nightmare so vivid and terrifying that it seemed to claw at the fragile edges of reality itself.

Once again, I found myself tormented by the spectre of Jeremiah's twisted experiments, haunting me relentlessly even in the sanctuary of sleep, where dreams are supposed to provide solace and escape. My hands trembled uncontrollably, betraying the turmoil that raged within me, and I reached out desperately for Abigail, seeking solace in her presence, a lifeline in the storm. Despite the chaos that swirled around us, she remained a beacon of calm and steadiness, her touch as soothing as a gentle lullaby that could quell even the most oppressive stillness.

Trying to regain a semblance of composure, I forced myself to feign a casual stretch, my muscles protesting as I moved. I suppressed a yawn that threatened to escape my lips, an attempt to mask the anxiety that churned in my gut. In a tone that I hoped sounded more relaxed than I felt, I inquired about the time, my voice barely above a whisper. The room remained shrouded in darkness, its shadows deep and impenetrable, yet the tension in the air was unmistakable, a silent acknowledgment of the challenges that awaited us, lurking just beyond the horizon.

"It's time for you to get ready," Abigail's voice broke through the silence, carrying an undertone of urgency that was impossible to ignore. Her words were low but firm, each syllable imbued with the weight of impending responsibility. With a determined grace, she rose from the bed, her movements purposeful and deliberate as she made her way toward the door. "We have a lot of training ahead of us and not much time to do it," she continued, her words hanging heavily in the air, a solemn reminder of the arduous path that lay before us. The gravity of her statement resonated deeply within me, underscoring the seriousness of our mission and the limited time we had to prepare for it.

Glancing at the clock on the nightstand, its pale digits glowing 3:00 A.M., I felt the world around me suspended in hushed anticipation. The room lay swathed in deep shadows, broken only by the moon's silvery glow seeping through heavy drapes. Pools of light danced on the faded wallpaper, weaving shifting patterns that seemed to pulse in time with my racing heart. A jolt of adrenaline coursed through my veins as I realised there was no point in drifting back into slumber; some urgent part of me demanded I rise and act. Pushing aside the lingering tendrils of my nightmare—flashes of darkness and unspoken fear—

I swung my legs over the side of the bed, muscles taut beneath damp sheets, and stood up. My limbs trembled slightly, half-woken by the residue of a nightmare that still clung to my thoughts like cobwebs. Determined to shake off the last vestiges of that fitful slumber, I crossed the room in long strides and plunged into a cold, bracing shower. The icy water cascaded over me, each drop a stinging reminder of reality, flushing away the haze of dreams. My lungs filled with chilly clarity, and I felt as though I might emerge from that spray fully reborn—fierce, alert, unbreakable.

Towel-dried, dressed and now anchored firmly in wakefulness, I padded down the silent corridor toward the kitchen. The floorboards creaked softly underfoot, and the low hum of the refrigerator was the only sign of life. There, perched casually on the corner of the oak table, was Abby—her silhouette outlined by the café's single overhead bulb. She held a porcelain mug between her palms, steam spiralling upward like a ghostly signal. "You're going to need this," she said, her voice calm yet edged with expectation, as she offered me the steaming brew.

I accepted the mug, the warmth searing through my cold fingers. Bringing it to my lips, I inhaled deeply: the coffee's aroma was rich and chocolatey, with just a whisper of smoke that teased awake every slumbering nerve. The first sip was sharply bitter, a jolt to my system, but it settled into something smooth and grounding as it slid down my throat. I closed my eyes and savoured it, feeling the warmth expand from my chest outward, bolstering my resolve.

Abby rose, setting her own mug aside, and motioned for me to follow. We stepped out into the pre-dawn chill, the air crisp enough to make each breath visible. Around us, the world was eerily still—no birdsong, no distant cars—just the soft, rhythmic crunch of fallen leaves under our sneakers. The faint glow of street lamps cast long, skeletal shadows across the pavement as we made our way toward the training grounds.

With each step, my excitement mounted. My heart pounded in time with the echo of Abby's strides. She moved with purpose, her shoulders squared, every muscle taut with anticipation. Then she halted and turned, her piercing gaze locking onto mine. In that instant, the faint rustle of the night fell away, and all I could feel was the intensity radiating from her eyes. "You need to understand exactly what you've signed up for," she said, her tone low and unflinching.

"This training won't just challenge your body—it will test your mind, push your limits, and forge you into something stronger than you ever believed possible," Abby declared with an intensity that made each word resonate deep within me. The gravity of her statement settled around me like an impenetrable armour, weighing heavily on my shoulders and fortifying my resolve. I nodded, acknowledging the monumental task ahead. My remarkable healing abilities might allow me to recover faster than most, but Abby was determined to push me beyond every comfort zone and surpass every boundary I had ever known. She drew in a long, deliberate breath, her posture as unwavering as her resolve. "And just so we're clear," she continued, her voice firm and unyielding, "we leave at whatever time you wake up. No excuses." The finality in her words was absolute, leaving no room for debate or hesitation. As I met her unwavering gaze, I felt a steely determination rise within me: whatever challenges lay ahead, I would not back down.

As we prepared to move forward, Abby's tone softened slightly, a hint of concern creeping into her voice. "Hopefully, by the end of our sessions, and what ever you do at Kain's gym in the evening you will be so physically exhausted that it will keep any nightmares at bay," she added, her words tinged with genuine care. The thoughtfulness in her statement struck a chord within me, and as we walked towards her jeep, I couldn't help but feel a deep sense of gratitude for her consideration. She had recognised the torment of my nightmares and was trying to help me in her own unique way.

Initially, I felt a surge of outrage at the prospect of being pushed to the brink of exhaustion every single day. The idea seemed almost insurmountable, a daunting challenge that loomed over me like a towering wave. But as I let her words sink in, I realised that this rigorous training was ultimately for my own good, a necessary path to becoming the best version of myself. Just as I was about to voice my thoughts, Abby continued, her voice infused with a playful yet determined edge. "Now get your ass in. I have a fun day planned," she said with a smirk, gesturing for me to climb into the passenger seat of her jeep. Despite my initial apprehensions, I couldn't help but feel a rush of excitement and anticipation for the adventure Abby had in store for us today.

***

Abby's assurance had been no idle boast. From the moment I stepped into the dimly lit training hall, she drove me unrelentingly through one punishing exercise after another. We shadow-boxed under the flickering fluorescent lights, drilled combinations until my arms trembled, and studied every nuance of our previous sparring sessions on the gritty projection screen. Abby's singular aim was to remould my cautious, defensive instincts into an all-out, attack-first mentality. As the hours dragged on, each jab and cross sent fire through my muscles, and my lungs rasped with every breath. Sweat pooled at the base of my skull and trickled down my spine, but Abby—eyes aflame with fierce resolve—pressed on like a merciless storm.

Then, without warning, she froze mid-stance, head thrown back, and unleashed a guttural roar that reverberated off the concrete walls. "Jess, cut it out with this half-hearted nonsense!" she bellowed, voice raw with impatience. "You think you can tiptoe into the ring like you're cradling a porcelain doll? These opponents are bloodthirsty. You want to survive? You need to maul them like your life's hanging by a thread." Launching into a low, predatory crouch, Abby snarled so fiercely that my spine snapped upright in alarm. Gone was the playful, sardonic vampire I'd come to adore, smouldered replaced by an apex hunter, primed to rip any challenger limb from limb.

A tightening coil of fear and determination wound itself around my chest. I inhaled sharply, tasting the metallic tang of my own adrenaline, and squared my shoulders for another bout. Under Abby's uncompromising gaze, I channeled every scrap of instruction she'd ever given me—footwork, feints, explosive power. I drove each strike forward with every ounce of strength I could muster, feeling my muscles bulge and pulsate as though they had lives of their own. But Abby didn't just test my body—she assaulted my mind, demanding unwavering focus the way a general demands loyalty.

Watching her move was like witnessing a force of nature. I understood then why the vampire council had hand-picked her as an enforcer. Her legs coiled like springs before she launched a devastating roundhouse kick aimed straight for my temple. My reflexes screamed to raise my guard, but Abby had drilled into me the art of relentless offence so instead of retreating, I pivoted on my heel and delivered a fierce kick to her standing leg. Abby staggered, crashed to the mats, and for a heartbeat I thought I'd broken her leg. But barely a heartbeat passed before she sprang up again, her expression alight with exhilaration, and resumed her assault as though she'd never fallen.

Blow for blow, we clashed like titans. My gloves thudded against her ribs, hers smashed into my ribs, my guard, my shoulders. The minutes stretched into an eternity of pain and adrenaline, and just when I felt my will fracturing, Abby finally eased off. She straightened, chest heaving, and motioned me to step back.

"That's a hell of an improvement," she remarked, her voice carrying a note of admiration as she wiped the sweat from her brow with the back of her glove. Her eyes had a glint of satisfaction, a silent acknowledgment of the hard work that was finally paying off. "Take a five-minute break. We will go again in a minute."

A ragged laugh of relief escaped my lips, and I half-pleaded, half-shouted, "Go again? Are you joking? I'm utterly spent!" My voice cracked under the weight of exhaustion, yet beneath the weariness smouldered a spark of pride. Despite Abby's relentless training regime that left me feeling battered and bruised, it also ignited a newfound fire within me—a resilient determination that refused to be extinguished.

"Yes," Abby replied with unwavering resolve, her tone firm and unyielding. "We will go again and again and again until I say we are done. You are the one who insisted on not stopping this operation, so I'm going to train you so hard that we will see it through to the end. Even if that means beating your cute ass black and blue. Now take a break, then we will review."

With a sigh, I made my way to the designated rest area, my muscles protesting with every step. Grumbling under my breath, I couldn't help but reflect on the rigorous journey ahead, a journey that demanded every ounce of my strength and determination. Yet, amidst the complaints, there lingered an undeniable sense of purpose, a drive to push past my limits and achieve what seemed impossible just days ago.

***

My body felt like a raging inferno, consumed by the relentless intensity of the physical training regimen that Abby had subjected me to over the course of 12 punishing hours. She had pushed me right to the brink of my physical and mental limits, extracting every last ounce of strength and endurance from my utterly exhausted muscles. As I hobbled towards Kane's gym for what was to be my first session there, each step I took felt like a monumental feat of endurance and determination.

The imposing glass doors of the gym loomed before me, towering and almost impenetrable in their presence. With a deep, steadying breath, I gathered my courage and pushed them open, stepping inside the bustling establishment. The air was thick, almost suffocating, with the pungent stench of sweat, mingling with the sounds of weights clanking and people grunting as they pushed themselves to their limits. I navigated my way through the crowded lobby, every fibre of my being tensed with anticipation, fully aware that I was about to face yet another brutal session under Kane's notoriously unforgiving guidance.

As I approached the reception desk, I was met with the cold indifference of the front desk attendant. His eyes barely flicked up from his computer screen, and his bored expression made it clear that he had no interest in my presence there. With a curt nod, he directed me towards the back of the gym, mumbling in a monotone voice, "Walker's waiting for you." His words seemed devoid of any warmth or encouragement, reinforcing the idea that this was a place where pain and punishment reigned supreme, and any sense of welcome was conspicuously absent. I steeled myself for what lay ahead, knowing that I was about to embark on a journey that would test every aspect of my being.

I nonchalantly shrugged off his indifference, my emotions unaffected by his dismissive attitude. As I confidently walked towards the back of the gym, my eyes were immediately drawn to a towering figure who exuded a strong presence. His muscular frame and confident stance immediately marked him as a fighter, someone not to be messed with.

He scanned the room with sharp, assessing eyes, taking in every person around him with ease. No one dared to approach or even make direct eye contact with him. He was in control here, a powerful force that demanded respect.

I halted precisely outside his kill zone, muscles coiled. "You must be Walker."

He pivoted, a predator's smile slashing across his face. Fantastic—another alpha who found me entertaining. "And you must be Jessica," he growled, voice like gravel over steel. "Don't worry, kid, I'm not gonna bite." Yet. The unspoken threat hung between us as he jerked his head toward a door. I tracked his every movement—the brutal architecture of muscle beneath fabric stretched to breaking, eyes that calculated weaknesses with machine precision. He yanked open a door marked "Staff Only," the hinges screaming in protest. My skin crawled as I slipped through, every instinct shrieking as my back remained exposed for that split second.

The stairwell plunged like a throat into hell, each step down a vertebra in the spine of some buried leviathan. I froze at the precipice, jaw slack. Walker rammed his shoulder past me. "Move. Sub-level 20. Now." The concrete swallowed us whole. Fluorescent lights spasmed overhead, transforming our shadows into writhing demons that clawed at walls weeping with toxic condensation. Twenty floors down. Twenty heartbeats closer to damnation. Each landing revealed corridors that twisted away like severed arteries, lined with vault doors that vibrated with contained violence. The air scorched my lungs—ammonia, copper, fear—as we plummeted deeper. My eardrums threatened to rupture from the pressure until we came to a halt before a door branded "Sub-Level 20" in bleeding crimson. My heart slammed against my ribcage like something feral caged inside me.

Walker surged forward like a tidal wave, his massive frame swallowing the distance between us. His boots crashed against the metal flooring, reverberating like cannon fire as he led me to a door pulsing with ominous red warnings: "AUTHORISED PERSONNEL ONLY." The letters hammered with an unsettling rhythm, as if alive with their own heartbeat.

My mind was a storm of thoughts as we closed in. Was this where the insidious drug was being manufactured? Were we finally on the brink of shattering this labyrinthine case? I was so consumed by the chaos in my head that I failed to notice when we reached our destination. Walker's gruff voice cut through my mental fog like a whip.

"Well, come on," he growled, his impatience sharpening each syllable. "You're not here to daydream, let's get moving." Jolted, I stumbled after him into the room, wrestling with my frayed nerves to concentrate on the mission.

As I stepped through the threshold, I was blindsided by the sight before me. In my wildest nightmares, I could never have conjured something so bizarre. Frozen in the doorway, words deserted me in the face of such staggering revelation.

"What, you've never encountered a realm corridor?" Walker's voice sliced through my stupor, smashing my train of thought.

"I am familiar with pocket realms, if that's what you're asking," I shot back, my voice defensive, betraying a flicker of awe despite my efforts to mask it.

Walker's face contorted with rage. "Listen, you idiot," he snarled, jabbing a finger so close to my face I could feel the heat radiating off it. "This isn't some goddamn tourist attraction. One wrong door and they'll be scraping what's left of you off the walls. Each portal leads somewhere Kane doesn't want you. Ever." His eyes burned into mine, pupils constricting to pinpoints. "Cross that line and you're dead. Not hurt. DEAD. Understand?"

I plunged after him, throat closing as the pocket realm devoured us. The air hit my lungs like liquid nitrogen—first freezing my chest solid, then shattering it into burning fragments. Each breath felt like swallowing glass. My eardrums ruptured and healed in microseconds as reality compressed us through its fist.

The doorway vomited us into hell. A twelve-foot giant—its granite skin cracked with glowing veins—roared as it pulverised a weight rack into dust. Razor-winged sprites shrieked past my face, their wings slicing my cheek before I could flinch. Blood-red mist writhed overhead, something massive thrashing within it, howling with such primal rage my knees buckled. Weights that could crush buildings lay embedded in the floor beneath machines that pulsed with energy that made my teeth vibrate and my vision blur. The stench hit me like a physical blow—ozone and alien musk so potent It could make your nose bleed. A creature skittered across the wall, its limbs multiplying as I watched, each ending in dripping hooks.

Walker's fingers clamped onto my shoulder like a vice. I spun around, a snarl ripping from my throat, my teeth bared like a cornered animal. "WHAT?" I roared, saliva spraying with every word.

"Focus or die," he seethed, his eyes blazing with an intensity that could melt steel. "This is your life now. Every single day. You either cancel everything else or I cancel you. I've seen your fights—nothing but raw potential squandered." He let go of me with a shove, striding past the writhing, nightmarish silhouettes I refused to acknowledge as fighters.

We walked on in a suffocating silence, the crunch of gravel beneath our feet echoing like a countdown to some inevitable doom. My palms were slick with sweat, my heart pounding a relentless drumbeat in my chest. The oppressive quiet was unbearable, a weight I couldn't shoulder any longer.

"Are we going to keep dragging our asses through this hellish silence, or are we actually going to train?" I snarled, my knuckles whitening as I clenched my fists.

Walker's head snapped toward me, eyes flashing like a predator's. "We're here." He jerked his chin toward a massive circular pit carved into the earth, its sand stained rust-brown with what could only be blood. Ancient-looking symbols were carved into the stone rim, pulsing with faint blue light.

He vaulted over the edge, landing in a crouch that sent sand exploding outward. The ground beneath me trembled as he straightened to his full height. "Sit," he commanded, dropping cross-legged into the sand, his massive frame folding with unexpected precision. Despite his stillness, every muscle in his body remained coiled, ready to unleash violence in an instant.

I slid down into the pit, keeping my distance. The sand burned hot against my palms as I settled across from him, my spine rigid. His eyes dissected me, calculating weaknesses.

"I watched the footage of your audition fight," he growled, his voice grating like steel on granite. "Decent foundation. You survived against humans who've bested some lower-level paranormals." His lips twisted into a snarl that was far too savage to be called a smile. "But the arena will devour you whole."

"Your fighting style resembles an impenetrable fortress, always entrenched in defence. Every move is a calculated manoeuvre, cautiously avoiding unnecessary risks. While this shields you from harm, it binds you, preventing you from seizing the moment to strike with lethal force. Your agility is unmatched, allowing you to zip with lightning speed and elude most attacks. Yet, in these merciless arenas, mere survival is akin to defeat. To truly obliterate your foes and claim victory, you must demolish your defensive barriers and embrace a relentless, savage assault. Discard your caution and unleash the untamed beast that snarls within!

"Every. Fucking. Day." Walker slammed his fist into his palm with each word. "We're going to break you down and rebuild you until your bones feel like razor wire and your blood runs like battery acid. You think you're fast? You'll be a goddamn ghost. You think you're flexible? You'll fold yourself into shapes that would make a contortionist vomit."

His eyes burned into mine. "I've lined up fighters who've ripped spines out through throats, who've pulverised concrete with bare knuckles. After seeing your little performance yesterday, they're placing bets on which one gets to be the first to make you scream. Some want to keep pieces as souvenirs."

My face must have drained white. Walker's lips twisted into something feral. "Relax, kid. I won't let them permanently maim you. But pain?" He leaned in close enough I could smell copper on his breath. "Pain is your new best friend."

"What about Kane?" I managed, throat dry as sandpaper.

"Kane wants you in the ring yesterday. Something's lit a fire under him." Walker's eyes narrowed. "Whatever you did, he's obsessed with seeing you bleed for it."

"Will we always train here?" I asked, desperate to change the subject.

Walker's laugh was like gravel in a garbage disposal. "Fuck no. Tomorrow might be quicksand that'll swallow you to your neck if you stand still. Next day, ice slick as glass over a hundred-foot drop. After that? Maybe we'll fight in actual lava." His grin widened. "Kane doesn't just want you to fight. He wants you to suffer spectacularly."

I couldn't help but be impressed. "How in the world does he pull that off?" I asked, genuinely curious.

"It's not my job to know," he replied nonchalantly, showing no interest in my question. "My only concern is making sure you put on a good show."

With a firm tone, he continued, "Now let's get started. We'll go through the fundamentals of strikes and grappling-based moves. And as of today, let's remember: no blatant defence. I want to see you constantly on the attack." His words were like a battle cry, igniting a fire within me. The training area was filled with the sounds of grunts and thuds as we practiced our moves, each one executed with precision and determination. With every strike and counter, I could feel myself getting stronger and more confident in my abilities.

***

My body ached and protested as I dragged myself out of the gym after my gruelling training session with the walker. Every muscle screamed in protest, and I could feel bruises forming on every inch of my skin. Despite my accelerated healing abilities, the intensity of my training sessions with both the walker and Abby was taking its toll. The techniques they were teaching me were daunting, to say the least.

As I entered my new home, I bypassed my housemates and made a beeline for my room, hoping that Abby would have some food waiting for me. My steps were heavy and laboured as I trudged to the door and pushed it open with a sigh of exhaustion.

To my delight, Abby was sprawled out on the floor amidst an array of takeout containers. A growl rumbled in my stomach at the sight of all that delicious food. "I figured you'd be hungry," Abby said with a grin. "Dig in and tell me how brutal your training was."

I didn't need to be told twice. Without hesitation, I pounced on the food like a famished animal. Each bite brought a burst of flavour to my taste buds, and I couldn't help but let out a moan of pleasure. Abby waited patiently until I had devoured everything in front of me before speaking again.

"Well, I knew you would be ravenous, but that was quite impressive," she stated with a matter-of-fact tone. I felt my cheeks flush as I quickly wiped my mouth, hoping I didn't have any food stuck on my face. "I knew training like this would be tough, but I am famished. The guy they paired me with is almost as difficult as you."

Her eyebrow raised inquisitively, her eyes sparkling with curiosity and a hint of playful teasing. I shifted uncomfortably under her gaze, suddenly feeling self-conscious about the intensity of the training I had just endured. Yet, at the same time, a sense of pride swelled within me for keeping up with such a demanding routine.

"His methods were focused on grappling and strikes. He believes that honing my reflexes and speed will be more advantageous than building strength. And as you suggested, he wants to abandon defence altogether. According to him, the patrons pay to see something thrilling and bloodthirsty - not cautious and defensive."

"Well, he certainly sounds like a charming individual," she remarked dryly. "Why don't you take a warm shower to ease those tense muscles? Once you're finished, I'll give you a deep tissue massage to help relieve any lingering soreness. Then, you can finally get some well-deserved rest."

A sigh of relief escaped my lips at the thought of a hot shower and a rejuvenating massage. "That sounds absolutely heavenly." I moaned

CHAPTER 9

Midnight Adventures with Abby

The darkness of the night still enveloped the world as my day began, long before the rest of the city stirred from their slumber. With Abby, by my side, we would trek through the deserted streets until reaching the abandoned warehouse on the outskirts of town. The walls were lined with a dizzying array of equipment that seemed to glimmer in the faint light filtering through the windows. It was our secret haven, away from the watchful eyes of society where we could focus solely on our training.

Abby was my mentor and guide, pushing me beyond my physical and mental limits every day. She showed me techniques and stances that I never thought possible, her expertise and dedication guiding me towards becoming a formidable fighter. But it wasn't just brute strength and aggression that she taught me; Abby incorporated elements of dance and yoga into our workouts, much to my initial disbelief. Yet as each day passed and I felt myself becoming stronger and more agile, I couldn't deny the effectiveness of her unique methods.

Despite my initial frustration with Abby's strict training regimen, I couldn't deny the evident results. Under her guidance, I was improving at a rapid pace, becoming stronger and more skilled day by day. There were times when I felt like I had no say in my own training, but I knew deep down that Abby had my best interests at heart. So I followed her instructions diligently, trusting in her vast knowledge and experience to mould me into the best version of myself.

As yet another gruelling day of training with Abby ended, I made my way to Kanes Gym for official training. While my workouts at the gym were progressing well, they were nothing compared to the intense and secret training sessions I underwent with Abby. Ever since our first introduction at his office, I rarely saw Kane at the gym. Instead, every day that I arrived, I was whisked away to a back storage area that led down to a hidden pocket realm designed specifically for supernaturals to train. The equipment there was unlike anything I had ever seen - weights that could crush a human with ease - and it was constantly bustling with all sorts of supernatural beings. Some I couldn't even identify, their forms so bizarre and otherworldly.

My time at this underground facility was split between building up my strength and endurance with heavy weights, allowing me to take hits from opponents without faltering, and perfecting my fighting forms under the watchful eye of Walker - the guy assigned as my trainer. He would patiently teach me new moves before pitting me against larger, faster, and stronger opponents in sparing matches. And after one particularly brutal session where I found myself gasping for air on the ground, completely exhausted and battered, something inside me snapped.

I turned towards Walker, anger blazing in my eyes as I hissed out accusations.

"Walker," I seethed through gritted teeth, "are you trying to fucking kill me or something? I know I may not be your first choice of fighters, but that was beyond ridiculous. If you hadn't finally called a halt to the match, I'm pretty sure my back would have been broken by that troll." I pointed towards the hulking creature that was now strutting away, looking like a victorious champion.

But despite my outburst, I knew deep down that this intense training was necessary if I wanted to survive in the pit. And as much as it pained me in the moment, I couldn't deny the thrilling rush that came with every hard-won victory as I spared.

"Lower your damn voice, kid," growled Walker, his dark eyes burning with frustration. "And show some goddamn respect. Look, I'm being hard on you because I don't want to see you end up dead. i've been warned that Kane wants to see you in his office before you leave today, and I've been given the next 48 hours off."

I clenched my jaw, already bristling at his condescending tone. "Okay, what the hell does that even mean?" I snapped back, trying to match his intensity.

Walker let out a heavy sigh, rubbing a hand over his cropped hair. "Think about it, kid. You've been training here for weeks now. And not once has Kane asked to speak with you. But now he's calling you into his office. That means one thing – you've made it onto the roster. You have a fight."

A surge of excitement rushed through me at this revelation, making me grin like the Cheshire Cat. Finally, after all this gruelling training, I would get a chance to prove myself in the arena. But Walker quickly extinguished my joy with his next words.

"Don't look so damn happy about it," he snarled, his expression stern and unrelenting. "You're not ready for the arena yet. That sparring match with the troll should have shown you that. And I told Kane as much, but he's ignoring my recommendation."

My heart sank at his words, my grin fading as fast as it had appeared. "What do you mean I'm not ready?" I demanded, my pride stinging from his criticism. "And you were the one who told me not to go full strength against him!"

But Walker just shook his head, his gaze unwavering as he stared me down with a mix of pity and disappointment.

But Walker just shook his head, his piercing gaze never wavering as he stared me down with a mixture of pity and disappointment. His words cut through the air like a sharp blade, each one landing heavily on my shoulders as I struggled to meet his unwavering stare.

"You still have a lot to learn, kid," he said gravely, his voice laced with a hint of exasperation. "I specifically told you not to go full strength in here. This place is filled with trainers and fighters who are constantly analysing your every move, looking for any weakness they can exploit if one of their own fighter were to come up against you . And that troll you faced? He's not even ranked to fight. He just comes here to train so he can brag to his buddies at the pub that he trains with cage fighters. But that doesn't excuse the fact that you had so much difficulty taking him down. You can pretend all you want to be a weak damsel, but don't try it with me."

"I don't know what..." I stammered, trying to come up with some sort of excuse.

"Save the bullshit, kid," Walker interrupted, his tone stern and unyielding. "I may be old, but I'm not blind. I know that you're not what you claim to be. You've been doing outside training to get stronger quickly, and that's a good thing. But don't think you're fooling me. Now listen up - take the next few days and rest. No more training, no more pushing yourself until the match. You need to be at your absolute peak because this match is going to be challenging. And as an added precaution, I'll be working your corner during the fight so there won't be any funny business with people trying to sabotage you by spiking your water."

Well, shit. I had to give it to the guy, he was definitely perceptive and had my best interests at heart.

"Thanks, I guess," I muttered, feeling a mix of frustration and gratitude towards Walker's tough love approach.

"Don't mention it," he growled through gritted teeth. "Now get out of here so I can finally enjoy my time off." His shoulders tensed as he stalked away, not bothering to look back.

After a quick, invigorating shower to wash off the sweat and blood from my intense sparring match with the troll, I made my way to Kane's office. His door was slightly ajar, and I could hear him bellowing into his phone. With a deep breath, I knocked on the heavy wood, causing it to creak in response. "It's open," came the gruff reply. Pushing the door open with more force than expected, I stepped into the room, ready for whatever news or orders he had for me.

But before I could even close the door behind me, he snapped at me without looking up from his desk, "Just stay there. I have a match set for you this Saturday." My heart skipped a beat as adrenaline surged through my veins. This was what I had been training for - my chance to prove myself in the fighting ring. Kane continued gruffly, "Be here at nine pm sharp. Paul will bring you a fighter's uniform. And make sure you are not late." His tone left no room for argument.

With a dismissive wave of his hand, he added, "And don't show your face here until then. Get some rest so you'll be at 100% on fight night." Feeling both excited and nervous, I nodded quickly and let myself out of his office.

As I left the gym, my muscles quivering from an intense workout, I immediately pulled out my phone and dialled Abby's number.

"Jess. What's going on? I just saw you on the surveillance footage leaving the gym."

Her voice was filled with concern. "Jess, tell me what happened. Are you okay?"

I took a deep breath before replying. "I was summoned to Kane's office. Looks like I have a fight scheduled for this Saturday."

There was a long pause before Abby spoke again. "Jess, get to the warehouse now. I'll meet you there."

Before I could ask any questions, the line went dead. The urgency in her voice made me realise that I needed to hurry.

I quickly stuffed my phone in my bag and headed towards the warehouse district, adrenaline pumping through my veins as I prepared for whatever lay ahead.

***

As I arrived at the dimly lit warehouse, my heart rate accelerated at the sight of Abby waiting outside. Her usually calm demeanour was replaced with a rigid stance and furrowed brow, hinting at an underlying anger. Confused and concerned, I approached her.

"Hey, what's going on? I thought this is what we wanted," I said, trying to diffuse any tension.

"Wait till we get inside, then we can talk," she replied curtly.

My gut churned as her strange behaviour set me on edge. As we entered the building, I scanned my surroundings cautiously, wary of any potential danger. Though nothing seemed out of place and no one was lurking in the shadows, I couldn't shake off the uneasy feeling creeping up my spine. As Abby locked the door behind us, I could visibly see the tension leaving her body.

"Okay, you need to tell me what's got you so freaked out," I urged, my voice betraying a slight tremor of fear.

The tension in the air was thick as she spoke. "They've got you fighting already," her voice trembled with fear. "That's what's freaking me out." I could see the worry in her eyes and it only made my own nerves escalate. "Not hearing it from Paul is sending up red flags," she continued, almost pleading with me.

"You aren't ready," her words were like a stab to my heart. "I think we should pull you out of the fight." Her body radiated nervous energy, her hands shaking by her sides.

My fury burned within me at her suggestion. "What do you mean you want to pull me out of the fight?" I practically screamed, my emotions taking over. "That's not your call. You are here as backup." My voice was laced with anger and frustration. "I'm sure Paul is updating Alex on everything. I will only stop this assignment when he says so." I had been working my ass off preparing for this, and I wouldn't let all that hard work go to waste because of someone else's doubts.

Abby stepped back, her hands raised in a gesture of surrender. Her eyes flickered with concern and fear as she spoke. "Jess, I know you're making progress, but something doesn't feel right. You haven't heard from the contact. Are you sure you're ready to take a beating?" Her voice trembled slightly and I could see the worry etched on her face.

I took a deep breath, trying to push down the memories that threatened to resurface. "It's fine, Abby. I've taken beatings before, trapped in that cave with Jeremiah conducting his twisted experiments on me. I survived that, I can handle a few more." But even as the words left my mouth, my body tensed at the thought of enduring physical pain again. The scars may have healed, but the wounds were still fresh in my mind.

Abby's gentle touch on my cheek sent shivers down my spine. I closed my eyes and took a deep breath, trying to calm the racing thoughts in my mind. But her words cut through me like a knife, reopening wounds that had never fully healed.

"You still have nightmares about what happened in those caves," she said, her voice laced with sadness and concern. "I'll admit, I had my suspicions before this assignment, but seeing you sleep and how much pain you radiate as you relive those events...the screams that escape your lips, it's enough to wake the dead." She paused, her hand still resting on my face.

My cheeks burned with embarrassment and shame. I couldn't even look at her, knowing she saw me as weak and broken. I could practically hear her thoughts: 'How can she be a successful agent if she can't even handle her own past?' It was a thought that had plagued me since the day I started working for the agency.

But Abby didn't understand. She didn't know what it was like to live through the horrors from that time in my life, to have them haunt your every waking moment and invade your dreams. If it wasn't for the soundproofing in the rooms at the halfway house, the police would likely be called every night due to my screams.

As much as I tried to bury those memories and move on, they continued to suffocate me, reminding me of my own weakness and vulnerability. And now, as Abby looked upon me with pity and disappointment, I felt more exposed than ever before.

Tears streamed down my face as I buried my head into her chest, seeking comfort in her warm embrace. Her gentle touch and soothing words were the only things keeping me from breaking apart.

"Jess, I just want to protect you from more trauma," she whispered, tightening her hold on me. My heart ached at the thought of causing her any pain or worry, but I couldn't back down now. Not when so much was at stake.

"You don't need to protect me," I said, my voice muffled against her skin. "I signed up for this and knew what I was getting myself into. I knew it would be hard, but someone has to stop them." Anger bubbled up inside of me at the assumption that I couldn't handle this mission. But at the same time, I was touched by her concern for my well-being.

Taking a deep breath, I closed my eyes and allowed myself to fully immerse myself in her scent - a comforting mix of lavender and vanilla. A sudden wave of peace washed over me, and for a moment, all the worries and fears faded away.

"Please don't try to stop me from doing this," I pleaded with her, my voice shaky but determined. "I will do this with or without your support, but I would much rather have you on my side. This will be hard enough, and I don't want to endure it alone."

She pulled away slightly, cupping my face in her hands as she gazed into my teary eyes. "Fine," she conceded with a sigh. "But I agree to this under protest. And after the match, I will be even stricter with your training."

I smiled through my tears, feeling grateful for her understanding and support. With her by my side, I could face anything that came our way. Together, we would fight and protect each other until the very end.

CHAPTER 10

Nervous Anticipation

Despite Paul's assurance that he had notified Alex about the upcoming match, I couldn't shake off the nervous energy that consumed me. The phone call with Paul from earlier played on repeat in my mind, his agitated voice causing Abby and I to exchange worried glances.

"Of course I've given him an update on the case," Paul snapped impatiently over the line, his frustration palpable even through the phone. "Do you think I would neglect such an important detail?"

I muttered an apology before quickly changing the subject. "Okay, well, can you tell us anything about my first opponent?" The match-ups were ment to be kept secret until the actual fight, but I figured Paul must have some inside information on who I would be facing.

"My sources have informed me that we are up against a formidable foe," Paul muttered with disgust. "They call him a mongrel, a mix of lesser elf, shifter, and human blood. His ancestry is murky at best, but one thing is clear - he possesses enhanced physical abilities, namely strength and speed. And as an added bonus, he's long-lived, and as a result will have more experience than you" Paul scoffed with a bitter laugh.

My heart dropped at the thought of facing such a powerful opponent, especially with the added challenge of limiting my own abilities. But there was no backing out now. This was my chance to prove myself in this brutal fighting ring.

"From what I've gathered, he has been fighting for at least a century. He knows what he's doing and will stop at nothing to defeat his opponents. Are you sure you're ready for this?" Paul asked, clearly doubting our chances.

I took a deep breath and steeled myself for the inevitable battle ahead. I may not have much experience or magical ability, but I had determination and a strong will to survive on my side.

"Thank you for your information, Paul. I'll be ready," I replied confidently.

Paul abruptly ended the call, leaving both Abigail and me in silence. We knew the stakes were high and failure was not an option. It was time to prepare ourselves mentally and physically for the fight.

***

I approached the entrance to the gym, my heart racing with anticipation and nerves. Paul stood outside, his usually confident demeanour replaced with a sickly pallor. His face was unshaven, dark rings encircling his bloodshot eyes, a clear indication that he had not been getting much sleep lately. "Hey Paul," I greeted him cautiously, my concern evident in my tone. "Are you feeling alright?"

He shot me a cold glare and let out a low growl. "Do I look okay to you?" he snapped back, his words laced with bitterness. I could smell the sharp tang of alcohol on his breath, a telltale sign that something was definitely wrong. But before I could press further, he grabbed my arm roughly and began to drag me away from the gym entrance.

"Just keep your fucking voice down and follow me," he hissed through clenched teeth. I swallowed hard and nodded, too scared to argue or question him any further. As we made our way towards his car, my mind raced with worry and confusion. What could have possibly happened to make Paul act this way?

Silence hung heavy in the car as we drove away from the gym, the only sound coming from the tight grip Paul had on the steering wheel, his knuckles turning white from the pressure. I couldn't help but sneak glances at him, trying to decipher the turmoil that was clearly visible on his face. His jaw was clenched with anger and pain, and it was clear that whatever was happening was tearing him apart inside.

After what felt like an eternity, he seemed to relax slightly and I saw a flicker of vulnerability in his eyes. "Is it okay for me to talk now, or are you going to continue giving me the silent treatment until you serve me up to get my ass kicked?" I asked, unable to resist making the snide remark.

He winced visibly at my words before responding with a hint of bitterness in his voice. "Look, we couldn't talk out there without risking being overheard. And if you must know, I'm not okay. Nothing is going right. Some of my fighters have gone missing. That's why you got bumped up on the roster. Alex isn't happy about it and I've been stonewalled by my usual contacts." He took a deep breath before continuing, "The only silver lining is that your opponent has been changed. You'll be fighting a relative unknown. He's had a few fights under his belt and he's good, but he's still human. He shouldn't be able to inflict any serious damage on you. But it also means that your plan of losing has gone out the window. It would be better if you win this fight, but make it look like a struggle."

His words landed with the impact of a blow to my stomach. I understood the importance of losing this fight - it was crucial for me to attract those who would offer enhancement products. But now, not only did I have to win, but I also had to make it look like a struggle. All because someone had gone missing and Paul's entire world was falling apart.

My thoughts tumbled out in a chaotic frenzy, my mind struggling to keep up with the onslaught of questions pouring from my mouth. The man in front of me remained unmoved, his expression giving away nothing as he listened to my frantic inquiries.

"What do you mean they changed who I'm fighting? And why am I only hearing now that you've had fighters go missing? Do you think they know we are investigating them?" My voice was laced with frustration and disbelief, my heart pounding in my chest.

He took a deep breath before responding, his tone tinged with annoyance. "No, if they thought I was a snitch, I would be dead. It's a pain in my ass, but it's not unheard of for fighters to just up and leave all the time. These were some of my best fighters, so I've taken a big hit on my business."

Despite the tense situation, I couldn't help but feel sorry for him. "Is there anything I can do to help? Maybe I can ask around about your fighters to see if anyone knows why they left." My offer was genuine, though I knew deep down that it wouldn't yield any results. The few fighters I had met so far had all been cagey and closed off, unwilling to reveal any information. It made sense - you don't want to get too friendly with the people you're about to fight.

He shook his head, a small smile tugging at the corners of his lips. "No, it's okay. It's not your problem. You'll only bring more attention to yourself than necessary. I'll just have to start scouting for new talent, so you might see me hanging around the gym more often."

He stopped speaking for a moment before adding as an afterthought, "On the phone, I meant to ask you who they have you training with." His question made me tense up, but I managed to force a smile and appear nonchalant.

"Just some guy named Walker," I replied. "He's intense and almost as strict as a drill sergeant when it comes to training. He's not much to look at, but he definitely knows his stuff." I looked at Paul for a reaction, but he gave none.

The rest of the drive was spent in silence, and soon we arrived at an abandoned industrial area. Cars were already lining up, and elegantly dressed individuals were greeting each other with hugs or kisses on the cheek and handshakes. The contrast between their beauty and the rundown location was striking. Paul drove towards what appeared to be a back entrance for employees at one of the larger buildings.

The sound of Paul's voice shattered the eerie silence that enveloped me, dragging me back to reality. I blinked, trying to shake off the fog of my thoughts and focus on the task at hand.

Paul slammed his car door and strode across the gravel carpark, each step crunching urgently beneath his feet. "Let's move, Jess. Your fight's about to start and you're not even ready yet."

I could feel the urgency in his voice, and it only added to the butterflies fluttering in my stomach. With determination in my heart, I followed closely behind him as we made our way towards the abandoned warehouse where tonight's underground fighting match would take place.

The uneasy feeling in my gut only grew stronger as we ventured deeper into the dark interior of the building, rusted metal doors creaking open with each step we took. Finally, we arrived at a small changing area tucked away deep in the bowels of the warehouse.

"Here," Paul said, handing me a heavy gym bag. "You can change in here."

I was grateful for his consideration as I entered the cramped room and closed the door behind me. My heart was racing with nervous anticipation as I rifled through the bag, revealing a black sports bra and leggings emblazoned with a fierce Phoenix insignia. I couldn't help but wonder if it was Paul's team logo or something else entirely. But one thing was for sure - it made me feel powerful.

With shaky hands, I quickly shed my street clothes and slipped into the tight-fitting gear. As I adjusted the straps on my bra and tugged at the fabric of my leggings, my mind raced with doubts and fears. This wasn't just any fight - it was my first underground match. But despite my nerves, there was a fire burning within me, fuelling my determination to prove myself in the ring. I took a deep breath and steeled myself for what was to come.

Just as I finished dressing, there was a tentative knock on the door.

"Yeah, who is it?" I called out, my voice betraying just a hint of nervousness.

"It's just me," Paul's muffled voice came from the other side. "Are you decent?"

I couldn't help but be surprised by his consideration for my modesty, and a small smile tugged at my lips before I answered, "Yeah, come in."

He strode into the room with a purposeful gait, carrying a bundle of essential hand wraps and a set of foot grips. With a swift toss, he threw the foot grips to me and commanded, "Put these on, and I will wrap your hands when you're finished." As I complied with his request, I couldn't help but notice an air of heightened anxiety emanating from him. It was almost palpable, like a tangible cloud hovering around his body.

"Are you going to tell me what's causing your anxiety to spike so high, or is it meant to be a surprise?" I half-joked, attempting to lighten the mood. Flashing him a smile, I reassured him that I was only playing around. He began wrapping my hands with surprising care and tenderness - qualities I wouldn't have expected from someone in his line of work.

"The match has undergone some last-minute updates," he finally breathed out in a hushed tone.

"Okay," I replied, my mouth suddenly parched and unable to swallow the lump forming in my throat. "What are the changes, and how will they affect the fight?" The fear in my voice was unmistakable.

"No weapons. Enhancers are still allowed, but no additional weapons." That wasn't an issue for me; I had no intention of using any weapons in the first place. "You can't surrender. It's knockout or death." This declaration caught me completely off guard. In the briefing for this mission, I had been made aware of fatalities among fighters, but it had been portrayed as a rare occurrence in the files. Now knowing that it was a very real possibility, my heart rate quickened and my palms began to sweat.

Paul's solemn expression told me that he had more bad news to deliver. I braced myself for the worst and urged him to share it with me.

"Your opponent has been drugged," he finally said, confirming my suspicions. My heart sank at his words. No wonder the guy looked like he had just eaten a bowl of cat shit instead of his morning cereal. My stomach clenched into a knot. First an underground death match, and now this—my opponent pumped full of whatever chemical cocktail was making the rounds. I closed my eyes and inhaled slowly through my nose, counting to four before releasing the breath. When I opened my eyes again, Paul's face remained grim, confirming what I already knew. "So he's juicing with that new stuff," I said, my voice sounding hollow even to my own ears. "Guess my chances just went from slim to practically non-existent."

As I sat in the changing room, Paul looked at me with concern etched on his face. "Let's revert back to the original plan," I continued, trying to keep my voice steady. "We'll put on a show and I'll lose in a way that will send a message to the drug dealers that if I had their Drug, I could have won."

Despite my attempt at confidence, I knew Paul could see through it. But now, even he couldn't hide his disappointment and worry. "Is there anything else I need to know?" I asked, hoping there was some loophole or solution we hadn't thought of yet.

Paul wordlessly shook his head as he focused on wrapping my hands. He knew what this meant. "You know I can call off the fight," he pleaded, desperation evident in his voice. "Just forfeit and we can deal with the consequences later."

I appreciated his concern, but I couldn't back down now. This wasn't just about winning or losing a single match - it was about setting myself up to take this operation down "If we don't take a stand against this drug, who else will?" I replied firmly. "I've made up my mind. I'm seeing this through."

I tried to give Paul a reassuring smile, but deep down, I knew he didn't fully believe me. As my hands were tightly wrapped, I could hear murmurs from the commentator and the spectators outside. Paul left me alone in the changing room with clear instructions to walk down the concourse once they announced my name and into the arena.

My heart raced as I waited to hear my name being called, fully aware that the situation had changed again and i needed to lose this fight. I could already feel the pain and injuries I would suffer for very little reward. But backing out now was not an option - I had a chance to gain some first hand intel with a fighter exposed to the drug I might be able to glean some information about its effects. With a deep breath, I confidently waited by the door leading to the concourse, prepared to face whatever challenges awaited me in the arena. My determination and strength surged as I prepared to step into the arena, ready to not only fight for myself but for all those who have been affected by this drug.

***

My heart raced and my stomach churned as I paced the small waiting area. Each step felt like I was treading the perimeter of a cage. The memories of Jeremiah flashed through my mind, making my muscles tense with nervous energy. I clenched and unclenched my fists, trying to steady my breathing. Suddenly, a booming voice cut through the silence.

"LADIES AND GENTLEMEN, WELCOME TO TONIGHT'S HIGHLY ANTICIPATED EXTRAVAGANZA. WE HAVE A NEWCOMER WHO HAS BEEN CREATING QUITE THE BUZZ IN HIS RECENT MATCHES. LET US GIVE IT UP FOR MAL!"

The crowd erupted into a deafening roar, chanting his name over and over. My stomach dropped. Could it really be Mal from the gym? The same Mal I'd met the first day?

"AND NEXT, WE HAVE JESS," the announcer continued. "SHE IS A FIRST-TIME COMPETITOR, BUT I'VE BEEN ASSURED THAT SHE'S A LITTLE FIRECRACKER AND MIGHT JUST CAUSE AN UPSET TONIGHT."

A few half-hearted claps greeted my entrance, scattered like reluctant raindrops against the thunderous ovation Mal had received. I made my way down the sloping concrete ramp toward the arena floor, each step bringing me closer to what looked more like an opera house than a fighting pit. Ornate gold-leafed box seats lined the perimeter, where men in tailored suits and women dripping with diamonds leaned forward on velvet-cushioned railings. Between the seating tiers, spectators in evening wear clustered around illuminated cocktail booths, martini glasses catching the light as they laughed and placed bets on my demise. The contrast was jarring—their civilised veneer barely concealing the barbarism beneath.

As I stepped through the final archway onto the sand, the atmosphere changed. The air grew thick with the metallic tang of dried blood and acrid sweat that no amount of expensive air freshener could mask. My lungs seized, refusing to take a full breath. The bright spotlights momentarily blinded me, but as my vision adjusted, I could see the crowd's faces transform—pupils dilating, lips pulled back in anticipation, perfectly manicured hands gripping seat edges. Their collective hunger hit me like a physical force—thousands of eyes fixed on my flesh, their chants building into a rhythmic, primal roar that vibrated through the soles of my feet and into my bones. "Mal! Mal! Mal!" they bellowed, voices merging into a single monstrous entity.

My legs carried me forward mechanically while every rational thought screamed retreat. Each step across the arena floor felt like moving through quicksand. I had signed up for this mission knowing the risks, but nothing in the briefing files had prepared me for this reality—the smell of copper and sweat, the deafening roar, the certainty of violence.

The open expanse of sand stretched before me, thirty yards of pristine beige that would soon be stained crimson. At the opposite end stood Mal, hunched and trembling, his powerful arms secured by gleaming metal restraints anchored to the floor. His face—the same face that had smiled warmly at me in the gym just days ago—was now contorted into something inhuman. Veins bulged across his forehead and neck, his pupils so dilated they nearly swallowed the irises. When our eyes locked, I saw no recognition there, only a feral hunger and desperate fear that made my stomach clench. Whatever drug they'd given him had hollowed out the man I knew and filled the shell with something primal and terrified.

I tried to remind myself that this wasn't the same man I had met just a few my first day at Kanes gym, who had shown me kindness and camaraderie. This was a savage beast, ruled by the drug for one purpose only - to kill and win in this brutal arena.

My opponent strained against his restraints, his screams causing tears to well up in my eyes. I couldn't bear to see someone I knew, once a gentle soul, turned into a bloodthirsty creature for the entertainment of others. But this was the reality of our world now - a cruel and barbaric society where gladiator fights were normal source of entertainment.

I had been preparing for this moment. But Watching footage of these fights was one thing, seeing it in person was an entirely different experience. Yet, I couldn't dwell on that now. The sound of the bell signalled the start of our fight, and I had to push all thoughts and emotions aside, focusing solely on survival.

An audible click signalled that Mal's restraints had been released, and the chains withdrew into the ground. He wasted no time savouring his newfound freedom and let out a spine-chilling scream as he charged towards me. It took him just a few seconds to build up speed, but as he drew closer, he seemed unstoppable. A freight train of muscle and bone barreling toward me at inhuman speed. Veins pulsed beneath his skin like live wires, and his eyes—God, his eyes—had gone completely black, pupils blown so wide I couldn't find the man I'd met at Kane's anywhere in them.

I pivoted left, my heel digging into the sand, but Mal tracked the movement with predator precision. His fist connected with my shoulder—just a glancing blow—but the impact reverberated through my body like I'd been hit with a sledgehammer. My collarbone creaked in protest. I stumbled backward, sand shifting treacherously under my feet, and in that split-second of vulnerability, his leg whipped around in a perfect arc.

The kick connected just below my ribcage with such force that my body left the ground entirely. I sailed through the air, a weightless moment of terror, before slamming into the arena wall. The concrete cracked behind me—or maybe that was my spine. Blood filled my mouth as the crowd's roar crescendoed into something primal and hungry. Through blurred vision, I saw them standing, drinks forgotten, faces contorted in ecstasy at the violence. They weren't people anymore but a single, pulsing organism feeding on my pain, thousands of mouths opening and closing in unison with every blow I took. And Mal the man who'd once offered me gentle encouragement was stalking toward me now with predatory grace, wasn't a person either. His eyes had gone completely black, like windows into an abandoned house. Whatever drug they'd pumped into his system had hollowed him out completely, leaving only a perfect killing machine in human skin.

Blood pooled beneath my tongue as I struggled to my feet, one knee buckling. The concrete wall behind me had cracked from the impact of my body. My ribs screamed with each shallow breath. Mal circled closer, muscles twitching beneath skin that had taken on an unnatural sheen.

"Mal," I gasped, spitting crimson onto the sand. "It's me. From Kane's. Remember? we met my first day"

He lunged with inhuman speed. I barely rolled away, feeling the wind of his fist as it punched into the wall where my head had been, leaving a crater in solid concrete. The crowd's roar intensified, the sound pressing against my eardrums like a physical weight.

"Please," I whispered, though I knew it was useless. The Mal I knew was gone, replaced by this feral creature pumped full of combat drugs. My only chance was to fight with everything I had left. I centerer my weight despite the white-hot agony lancing through my shattered ribs and raised my trembling fists.

I spat a mouthful of blood onto the sand and locked eyes with a woman in the front row—her champagne glass frozen halfway to crimson-painted lips, diamonds glittering at her throat like ice chips on a corpse. Let her see what she paid for. Let her wear the memory of my death like those cold jewels.

Twenty feet away, Mal's massive chest heaved, muscles twitching beneath skin stretched too tight, veins writhing like blue worms beneath the surface. The drug had turned his sweat caustic—I could smell it from here, chemical and wrong, like burning plastic and ammonia. His earlier punch had left a six-inch crater in solid concrete that would have been my skull. With each laboured breath I took, bone fragments grated where my ribs had splintered beneath his last kick, sending lightning bolts of pain through my nervous system. The crowd's roaring faded to white noise as my vision narrowed to just Mal—just the threat—just survival. I forced my left knee to lock despite the grinding sensation of torn cartilage, raised my fists higher, and charged.

My right arm hung useless, shoulder wrenched from its socket when Mal had caught me mid-dodge. The joint throbbed with each heartbeat, a metronome of agony keeping time with the fight. My dominant hand dangled like dead weight. Every movement sent fresh waves of nausea through me as torn ligaments screamed in protest.

Blood and sweat stung my eyes as I circled him, searching for an opening. The plan was clear: lose convincingly without revealing my true purpose. One clean hit to his liver would trigger his drug-fuelled rage—enough to knock me out without killing me. The dealers watching from their VIP boxes needed to believe every second of this performance. My lungs burned as I ducked another wild swing, the displaced air from his fist hot against my face. My body was shutting down system by system, but my mind remained razor-sharp. Three more minutes. That's all I needed to survive. Three minutes to make this loss look real enough to get dealers interested in me. Three minutes before darkness would be a mercy.

The roar of the crowd surrounded me as I fought my way through the ring, dodging and weaving through Mal's wild and reckless punches. In his fury, he was leaving himself open and over-extending with each strike. A glimmer of hope sparked in my mind as I noticed the pattern - if I could just evade his next attack, I could score a solid hit to his vulnerable ribs. It was a risky move, If I was lucky, it could cause him enough pain that he would lash out and knock me out. With determination coursing through my veins, I braced myself for his next assault. As soon as he swung, I moved in swift and calculated movements, making it appear as though my body was slow and uncoordinated. But with precision and force, I landed a blow to his side that elicited a satisfying cracking sound. I couldn't help but grin with satisfaction. However, my moment of triumph was short-lived as I looked up to see Mal's face twisted in a terrifying mixture of pain and rage. Before I could react, he let out a blood-curdling scream and went completely berserk. The world spun around me as he unleashed a flurry of frantic attacks, and before I knew what was happening, everything went black

CHAPTER 11

Anxious Waiting

****Abigail***

My thoughts raced like a runaway train as I paced back and forth in our bedroom room, anxiously awaiting any news about the fight. Every tick of the clock felt like an eternity, each second dragging on with agonising slowness. I knew it was foolish to worry so much, but I couldn't help it. She had insisted on going alone, despite my protests. What if something went wrong? What if she got hurt? The mere thought of her being in danger without me there to protect her filled me with a burning mixture of anger and guilt.

I should have put my foot down and refused to let her go through with this reckless plan. I knew it was dangerous from the moment she mentioned it, but I convinced myself she could handle it. Or at the very least, I should have talked to Alex about my concerns beforehand. But no, I let her stubbornness and determination cloud my judgment, silencing my own instincts. And now, here I was, pacing like a madwoman across our bedroom floor, unable to do anything but wait and hope for the best while imagining the worst possible scenarios playing out in vivid detail.

If anyone dares hurt her, they will regret it for the rest of their miserable existence. My fists clenched involuntarily at the mere thought of someone laying a finger on her, my nails digging crescents into my palms deep enough to draw blood. I promised myself that if she came out of this unscathed, I would personally make sure whoever dared to cross her paid dearly for their actions. After all these centuries, I've learned patience when it comes to vengeance—and I have all the time in the world to make them suffer. The thought of their screams brought a cold smile to my lips as I imagined their blood coating my hands, their pleas falling on deaf ears. I've perfected the art of making pain last, drawing it out until death becomes a mercy they beg for but never receive.

But then again, what if my own actions put her in harm's way? The inner conflict tore at me as I cursed myself for not being more proactive in keeping her safe. If only I had been more insistent on going with her, or had taken the time to address my concerns before it was too late. My fingernails scraped against my palms as I clenched my fists tighter, drawing tiny crescents of blood that healed almost instantly—a cruel reminder of my immortality while she remained vulnerable.

As I continued to pace back and forth, my footsteps wearing an invisible path in the carpet, my mind racing with possibilities and regrets, all I could do was hope and pray that she would come out of this unharmed. The clock on the wall seemed to mock me with each tick, reminding me of how fragile life could be. For if anything happened to her...I don't know how I could live with myself. The weight of three hundred years of existence would become unbearable without her light to guide me through the darkness.

My mind was consumed with these dark thoughts, and I shuddered as the thirst for blood grew stronger within me. It had been centuries since I last felt this urge, and it was difficult to control. My fangs threatened to descend, pressing painfully against my gums as my vision sharpened and my senses heightened—the predator within me awakening after a long slumber. The beast inside me whispered seductively of the relief that would come with giving in, with hunting down whoever had put her in danger and tearing them apart limb from limb.

Just as I was starting to calm myself, a quiet knock on the door interrupted my thoughts. "Abigail, it's me," came Nixie's tiny voice. "Door's open, Nixie, come in," I said, trying to sound upbeat despite my inner turmoil.

As Nixie swept into the room, her usually rosy complexion was drained of colour and her eyes were wide with fear. She clutched a phone to her ear and whispered, "I have Paul on the line. It's about Jess."

Without a moment's hesitation, I swiftly moved to Nixie's side and forcibly snatched the phone from her trembling hand before she could protest or pull away. The voice on the other end belonged to Paul, our informant. My grip on the phone tightened as I braced myself for whatever news he was about to deliver.

"Paul, what happened? Where is Jess?" I demanded in a commanding tone, my mind racing with worry and fear for my friend.

"It's bad," Paul's voice crackled through the phone. "I have her, and I'm coming to you. She needs a healer like now, so clear some space and make sure everything is safe when I arrive." With those ominous words, the line went dead.

Nixie stood beside me, visibly shaken and still clutching her own phone tightly. "Did you hear all of that?" I asked her, my voice now cold and detached as I struggled to keep my emotions in check.

"Umm, yes...yes, I'm on it," Nixie stammered, her hands still trembling with fear. "I'm a healer. When she arrives, bring her straight to the kitchen. I will gather lunette and prepare everything for her treatment. You will need to carry her from the car, and make sure Paul comes in with you. I will need him to tell me exactly what happened and if any magic was involved or if she was harmed by enchanted weapons." Nixie's words spilled out quickly, her fear evident in every shaky syllable.

My heart constricted painfully at the mere thought of Jess being in danger. The possibility of her being injured or under some kind of dark magical attack was enough to send my mind spiralling into a frenzy. But there was no time for my worries or fears; we needed to act fast if we wanted to save her.

With grim determination, I nodded at Nixie's instructions and focused all of my energy on preparing for Jess's arrival. She sprinted off to gather the necessary supplies and tools while I made my way to the door. Every second that passed felt like an eternity as I paced back and forth, mentally going over every scenario and outcome.

After what felt like an eternity, the distant growl of an engine broke the silence. Paul's black sedan screeched to a halt in front of the house, tires kicking up gravel in its wake. Without wasting a moment, I bolted down the porch steps and flung open the passenger door. The metallic stench of blood hit me before I could even see her. Jess lay crumpled across the seat, unconscious and barely breathing. My hands trembled as I carefully slid my arms beneath her broken body. When I lifted her from the car, my heart plummeted to the pit of my stomach. She was barely recognisable beneath the congealing layers of blood and mangled flesh. Her right arm hung at an impossible angle, bone fragments jutting through torn skin. Her once beautiful face was now a swollen mass of purple bruises and split flesh, her left eye completely sealed shut. A jagged laceration ran from her hairline to her jaw, still weeping crimson. Her chest rose and fell in shallow, uneven bursts that whistled through what must have been broken ribs. But there was no time to catalog the horrors inflicted upon her body. Every second that ticked by was another second closer to losing her forever. Every second counted now. I burst through the front door with Jess cradled against my chest, her blood seeping through my shirt and sticking the fabric to my skin. The metallic scent filled my nostrils as I shouted for Nixie. Her weight, normally so solid and strong, felt frighteningly light in my arms.

"Kitchen! Now!" Nixie's voice echoed from down the hallway.

My vision tunnelled as I carried Jess through the house, past the antique grandfather clock whose ticking seemed to mock the precious moments slipping away. Each laboured breath she took whistled through what must be broken ribs. The sound tore at my composure.

When I reached the kitchen, Nixie had already transformed the space. The oak dining table was cleared and covered with a white sheet. Mason jars filled with strange greyish-coloured liquids lined the counter, and bundles of herbs hung from hooks above.

I laid Jess down as gently as possible, wincing as she let out an unconscious moan. Her skin had taken on a greyish pallor beneath the blood and bruises. The jagged laceration across her face continued to weep crimson, and her right arm lay at that impossible angle, white bone fragments jutting through torn flesh.

"Please," I begged, my voice cracking as I looked from Nixie to Paul and back again. "Do whatever you can to save her." Tears I couldn't control spilled down my cheeks.

Nixie's hands hovered over Jess's broken body, her expression shifting from horror to clinical assessment. "Wait," she commanded, her tone leaving no room for argument. "Before I begin, I need to know exactly what we're dealing with. Was magic involved? What kind of spell or enchantment caused this?"

The question hit me like a physical blow. This wasn't magic. This was simple, brutal human violence—somehow worse in its mundane cruelty.

"No magic," I spat through clenched teeth, my fangs threatening to descend. "Just one hell of a beating." The rage building inside me was becoming uncontainable, a living thing clawing to get out. If I stayed, I might destroy something—or someone.

I backed away from the table, my hands trembling uncontrollably. "Help her," I managed to whisper before turning and stalking toward the door, my fingernails digging crescents into my palms.

I reached the front hallway when I sensed movement behind me. Paul had followed, his footsteps hesitant on the hardwood floor. His face was a mask of guilt and shame, eyes downcast, shoulders hunched as if expecting punishment. The rage that had been simmering inside me boiled over in an instant. Without conscious thought, my hands flew to his throat, fingers curling around his windpipe. I felt the familiar prickling sensation as my nails elongated into razor-sharp claws, the transformation I'd spent years learning to control now happening involuntarily. The tips pierced his flesh just enough to draw pinpricks of blood that welled against my fingertips.

"How could you let this happen?" I slammed him against the wall, hard enough that a framed photograph crashed to the floor, glass shattering. My voice emerged as something barely human, a guttural snarl that revealed too much of my true nature. "You were supposed to protect her. That was your only job."

His eyes bulged as he clawed weakly at my wrists. The desperate wheezing sounds as he struggled for air satisfied something primal in me. I squeezed harder, watching his face turn from red to purple, feeling the rapid flutter of his pulse beneath my thumbs. For a moment, I revelled in this display of power, this small vengeance for Jess's broken body.

Then, like a bucket of ice water, clarity washed over me. This wasn't helping Jess. Paul was our only witness, our only source of information. With tremendous effort, I uncurled my fingers from his throat and stepped back, my chest heaving with exertion and barely contained fury.

Paul collapsed in a heap on the floor, one hand massaging his bruised throat while the other braced against the floorboards. He coughed violently, each hack sending spittle onto the polished wood. When he finally looked up at me, his eyes were wide with terror and confusion, as if seeing me—truly seeing me—for the first time.

"I expect an answer," I demanded, my voice still rough with anger but now controlled, deliberate. I crouched down to his level, close enough that he couldn't escape my gaze. "What exactly did they do to her? Every detail, Paul. Now."

After several more ragged breaths, Paul began to recount the events of the fight. The organisers had changed the rules at the last minute, he explained, it was knock out or death. My stomach twisted as he described how Jess had refused to withdraw despite the dangerous new conditions. Her stubborn streak had always been a mile wide—it was what had drawn me to her initially, that unflinching determination that bordered on recklessness. Even now, with her lying broken in the next room, I couldn't help but feel a conflicted admiration for her courage, foolish as it might have been. The image of her standing in that underground ring, fists taped and raised against an opponent twice her size, made my chest ache with both pride and fury.

Paul's voice cracked as he described her final attack. "She feinted left, then came in with an uppercut that nobody saw coming," he said, mimicking the motion with his own fist. "You could hear the guy's ribs shatter from across the room—this sickening wet crack that made half the crowd wince." He swallowed hard, his Adam's apple bobbing. "Normally, that would've dropped anyone. Should've ended the fight right there."

"But this guy wasn't normal," I prompted when Paul fell silent.

He shook his head, eyes distant. "It was like... like the pain flipped some switch in him. His eyes went completely blank. Before anyone could react, he tackled her to the ground and just... just kept hitting her. Over and over. Blood everywhere." Paul's hands trembled as he pantomimed the brutal assault. "security couldn't pull him off. Took six security guards to restrain him. They pumped him so full of tranquillisers he should've been comatose, but he was still fighting against the restraints when they dragged him out."

Paul leaned forward, elbows on his knees, voice dropping to a whisper. "Everyone thought she was gone. The medic took one look and shook his head. But then—" his eyes widened at the memory "—her fingers twitched. Her eyelids fluttered open, and I swear to God, she tried to push herself up. Still wanted to finish the fight." He ran a hand through his sweat-matted hair. "I didn't think twice. I scooped her up and ran through the crowd, past security, past everyone. Her blood soaking through my shirt, and she's whispering 'Put me down' the whole time." His voice broke on the last words. "Who does that? Who takes that kind of beating and still wants to get back in the ring? I've never seen anything like it in my life."

I stood there In shock at what Paul had told me. I couldn't wrap my head around the fact that someone would willingly inflict such harm on another human being. And yet, Jess had faced it head on, refusing to back down even when she knew what she faced. As I recalled the feel of her battered body in my arms, I couldn't help but feel a mixture of anger and admiration for her unbreakable spirit. Her will to survive and fight another day was stronger than any opponent they could have put in front of her. I couldn't help but feel an overwhelming sense of protectiveness towards this strong, stubborn woman who always seemed to find a way to surprise me with her strength and resilience.

Paul paused and took a deep breath before continuing. "I monitored her breathing as best I could," he said, his voice strained and weary. "And I'm sure she hadn't stopped. And although it was faint, she still had a heartbeat." His eyes flickered down to the ground as he spoke, his thoughts clearly consumed by the traumatic events that had just occurred.

"I think she had started to heal, too," he added gravely, his hand reaching up to rub at his tired eyes. "By the time we got here."

I didn't know when it started, but suddenly Paul was holding out a tissue towards me. Confused, I looked at him questioningly. But before I could even ask why, he simply said, "To wipe the tears away." It then dawned on me that I had been crying without even realising it.

"Stay here," I instructed firmly. "We need to talk more once I know Jess is okay."

Leaving him slumped on the hardwood floor of the hallway, I trudged back towards the kitchen. Each step felt like wading through thick, heavy mud as my mind raced with worry for Jess's well-being. The once vibrant and welcoming atmosphere of our home now felt desolate and cold.

"How is she?" I couldn't help but blurt out as soon as I entered the kitchen.

Nixie was the first to respond, her soft voice tinged with concern, "She's stable, but it will take time for her to fully recover. What happened to her?"

I didn't want to answer that question, but I knew I had no choice; fate seemed to be pushing me in a certain direction. They had saved Jess. Perhaps it was time for me to trust them. The scent of freshly brewed coffee filled the room, mixed with the faint aroma of herbs and spices from Nixie's potion-making. The soft glow of candlelight illuminated the countertops, casting shadows on the neatly stacked dishes in the sink. Despite the chaos that had just unfolded, there was a sense of calmness in this familiar space. My heart ached at the thought of what Jess had gone through, but I knew we were in good hands now.

"I will do my best to explain everything later. Can you keep an eye on her for now and let me know about any changes?" I ask, hoping they will agree.

She gives Lunette a quick glance before nodding. "Okay, but we expect to be kept in the loop. You're lucky we have the skills to help her."

"Thank you, and I promise once Jess wakes up, we will tell you everything that's going on." I feel guilty for possibly involving two innocent people in our investigation, but I know I owe them the truth.

"But for now," I continue, "I have another guest to attend to." As I finish speaking, I hear an audible gulp from Nixie.

I turn back to Paul, who is still slumped on the floor. "Get up and come to the living room with me. We have a lot to discuss, and I would prefer to be comfortable while you tell me everything you know."

I don't wait for him to get up; instead, I lead him to a cozy armchair and gesture for him to sit on the sofa across from me. "I'm waiting," I say firmly, making sure my authority fills the room.

"I...I don't know what happened. Honestly, I thought it was just going to be a routine fight. I never expected this." He gestures at his blood-stained clothes with disgust written all over his face.

"Start from the beginning and leave nothing out," I command.

It was going to be a long night, but I was determined to make the most of it.

CHAPTER 12

Awakening to Pain and Purrs

Jessica*

A throbbing pain pounded relentlessly in my skull, each pulse like a hammer striking an anvil behind my eyes. The fluorescent lights above me seemed to flicker and swim, making it nearly impossible to think clearly. My entire body felt as if it had been run over by a bulldozer, then backed up on and crushed again for good measure. Every inch of me screamed in agony, but the pain itself was strangely reassuring—a definitive sign that I was still alive. Slowly, through the fog of discomfort, I became aware of a soft, rhythmic purring sound coming from my left side. It was Argus his orange-striped body curled into a perfect circle against my ribs, his chest vibrating with each contented breath.

With great effort, I attempted to sit up and reach for him, my fingers stretching toward his warm fur for comfort. But the simple movement sent sharp, electric shooting pains radiating from my core throughout my battered limbs. A brief, ragged scream escaped my lips before I could stop it, the sound tearing from my throat like barbed wire. Argus leapt away in alarm, his claws digging briefly into my side as he scrambled off the makeshift bed. Suddenly, the door burst open and three familiar figures rushed into the room—Abby, Lunette, and Nixie—their exhausted faces instantly transforming with huge, relieved smiles when they saw me conscious. Abby reached me first, her normally composed face now streaked with tears that left glistening trails down her ashen cheeks. She wrapped her trembling arms around me with surprising strength, fingers digging into my shoulder blades as though I might dissolve into mist if she loosened her grip even slightly. The familiar scent of her lavender shampoo mingled with the metallic tang of blood that seemed to permeate the air around us.

"Jesus Christ, Jess," she whispered, her voice cracking. "It was touch and go for hours. Your heart stopped twice. I thought" She pulled back just enough to meet my gaze, her bloodshot eyes searching mine. "I knew you would pull through, but don't you dare pull a stunt like this again. I can't—we can't lose you."

Behind her, Lunette and Nixie exchanged glances before letting out strained chuckles that sounded more like relief than actual amusement. Lunette's usually immaculate makeup was smudged beneath her eyes, while Nixie's fingers nervously twisted the silver rings adorning her hands.

As my vision cleared further, I took in my surroundings with growing confusion. I was sprawled across our kitchen table, the same one where we'd shared meals and late-night gossip sessions was now serving as a makeshift operating table. A once white blanket, now stained crimson in alarming patterns, covered my lower half. Medical supplies were scattered across the counter: gauze packages torn open, bloody cotton swabs, and several empty syringes that made my stomach turn.

"What..." My voice emerged as barely more than a rasp, my throat feeling like I'd swallowed broken glass. I swallowed hard and tried again. "What happened? How did I end up here? "The last thing I remember is the fight—that final punch and then..." I trailed off, fragments of violent memories flashing behind my eyes like a broken film reel. The taste of copper flooded my mouth as I recalled the sickening crunch of bone against knuckle. "Everything went dark." My fingers instinctively reached for my ribs, finding them tightly bound with bandages beneath the thin fabric of a shirt that wasn't mine. The pain radiated outward with each shallow breath.

Abby's grip on my shoulders tightened protectively. Her eyes, went from warm and welcoming to something darker more predatory, and a low growl rumbled from deep in her chest. I'd never seen this reaction from her before, the way her human features seemed to sharpen, how her muscles coiled with barely contained energy. I could almost see the monster in her fighting to get out.

"Abby, calm down. I'm okay," I whispered, placing my palm against her cheek. The contact seemed to anchor her, pulling her back from the edge of something primal. "But I need to know what happened. All of it."

She inhaled deeply, nostrils flaring as she fought for control. After a moment, Abby's posture softened. She pulled a chair close to the table where I lay and collapsed into it, suddenly looking exhausted. Her fingers combed through her wild hair, revealing the dark circles beneath her eyes.

"I got a call from Paul shortly after the fight ended," she began, voice hoarse. "You were in terrible condition—internal bleeding, possible skull fracture—from the little I could get out of the rat bastard before he fled." The last words came out as a snarl, her upper lip curling to reveal teeth that seemed too sharp in the harsh kitchen light. "Your opponent was given the compound in a massive dose, way beyond what anyone should survive. Apparently, you were doing okay at first. The fight was heading exactly in the direction we wanted." Her eyes met mine, filled with a mixture of pride and terror. "You went for a final attack to make everything look legitimate—a perfectly executed move that would have ended any normal fight. But then something changed in him. suddenly you weren't fighting a man anymore."

From what I have been told, everyone in the pit heard the impact. You must have broken at least one, if not a lot more of the guy's ribs. The next thing anyone knows, he was using you as a human punch bag, and they had to shoot him with tranquillisers to take him down."

As Abby recounted the details, my mind began to fill with fragments of memory. Images of the fight flashed before me, each one more intense than the last. "If this is what I'll be up against, I'll need to push myself even harder," I declared with determination, my voice echoing through the room.

As I lay on the blood-soaked table, trying to process the events of the past few hours, a loud knock at the door shook the entire house. The sudden sound startled me into action, but Abigail placed a calming hand on my shoulder, silently instructing me to stay put. With a nod of understanding, she led the other two towards the front door, leaving me alone with the plump and purring cat for company. Its soft fur and gentle purrs provided a comforting contrast to the tense atmosphere that had been in the room.

For a brief moment, I allowed myself to relax and let go of the fear and adrenaline that had been coursing through my body. But just as quickly as it had come, it was shattered by raised voices from down the hall, causing me to resign myself to the fact that I wouldn't be getting any rest anytime soon. With a groan, I stood up from the table, wincing at the pain in my bruised and battered body. The blanket slipped off of me, revealing my clothes still stained with dirt and blood from the fight. As I inspected my body, I winced at the sight of purple and green bruises blooming across my skin. My face in particular throbbed with pain, but I was grateful that I couldn't see my reflection in that moment.

Taking a deep, shaky breath, I mustered up what little courage I had left and forced myself to leave the safety of the kitchen. Each step felt like wading through quicksand, but as I moved further away from the chaos behind me, I found my footing becoming more sure. My heart raced as I made my way down the dimly lit hallway towards the front door, my mind swirling with fear and questions.

"What in the hell do you think you're doing? Get back to the kitchen and stay there," Abby barked with such authority that a part of me wanted to obey and retreat back to the safety and familiarity of the kitchen. But another part of me, fuelled by curiosity and a need for answers, pushed me to stand my ground.

I waved her off dismissively, trying to conceal the unease that was bubbling within me. "I'm fine, just feeling a little unsteady on my feet. But who are you yelling at out here?" That's when I noticed him, Walker standing tall with his chest puffed out as if he was preparing to charge into battle.

I stood before him, battered and bruised from the events that had just unfolded. The wounds on my body ached with every movement, but I refused to let them slow me down. My eyes met his, and I could see the mix of emotions swirling in their depths.

There was relief, no doubt, at seeing me still alive after everything that had happened. Confusion, perhaps, at the sight of me holding a fussy cat in my arms. But most of all, there was a hint of lingering rage that seemed to barely be contained within him.

My heart clenched at the thought of the pain I had caused him. I never wanted to hurt anyone. As I spoke, urging us all to move to the garden and resolve our conflicts like mature adults, I saw the tension slowly leave his body. A flicker of a smile crossed his lips before he nodded in agreement.

The others followed suit, though they insisted on me cleaning up first. And looking at myself in the mirror, I couldn't blame them. My face was a patchwork of bruises and cuts, looking like something out of a horror movie. The memory of what transpired earlier made me shudder.

With Abby's help, I stumbled my way to the bathroom where she turned on the shower for me. As I stood under the warm water, letting it wash away the grime and blood from my skin, I took stock of my injuries. To my surprise, most of them were already healing rapidly - a testament to my growing powers.

It would have taken weeks or even months for a normal person to recover from such trauma, but for me, it would only be a matter of hours. Absentmindedly rubbing some healing salve onto my skin, I couldn't help but marvel at how far my powers had come. Just a few months ago, I would have been completely helpless in a situation like this.

"How long has it been since I've been back here?" I asked Abby, breaking the silence that had settled between us.

"About 5 or 6 hours," she replied softly, her expression filled with genuine sadness.

I couldn't believe it had only been a few hours. It felt like a lifetime ago when everything seemed to spiral out of control. "My healing abilities are getting stronger," I mused, more to myself than to Abby. "This kind of punishment would've taken days to heal before."

As i looked at my battered reflection in the mirror, I couldn't help but feel grateful for my powers Despite all the challenges and dangers that came with them, They were a part of who I was now, and I had to learn to accept and embrace them

Abby's pleading words echoed in my mind as I lay there, battered and bruised from the latest mission. "Jess, please reconsider. I can't bear to see you like this." Her tear-streaked face was a stark contrast to her usual composed demeanour. But I couldn't back down now.

I reached out and gently brushed away the lone tear that rolled down Abby's cheek. "I'm sorry, Abby. I know I shouldn't have put you through this, but I can't just walk away from this assignment." It pained me to see her so distressed, but I couldn't let her convince me otherwise.

"You didn't see what that drug did to Mal," I continued, my voice filled with conviction. "He's human, he shouldn't have been able to move the way he did, or hurt me with his bare hands. These maniacs are turning people into mindless animals. It's worse than anything Jeremiah ever did."

At those words, I felt a shiver run down my spine. The memories of my time trapped with Lyn flooded back, bringing with it a wave of fear and helplessness. But even then, I had still clung onto my free will, finding refuge in my own mind. Now, seeing others stripped of that choice, it only fuelled my determination to bring these criminals to justice.

As Abby leaned in, our heads touching as we both shed silent tears, I knew she understood. She knew why I couldn't just walk away from this mission. And yet, it pained me to think of her having to witness more of the horrors that awaited us.

"I'm sorry," I whispered once again, my voice catching on the words. The bruises on my face throbbed as I spoke, a physical reminder of what we were up against. "But this is something I can't just turn my back on. These people—what they're doing—it's monstrous. If you want to leave and report everything to the agency, I won't hold it against you. But for me, I'm in this until the end, whatever that might be."

Abby's chest rose and fell with rapid, shallow breaths. Her hands trembled visibly as she gripped the edge of the counter, knuckles whitening. The fluorescent bathroom light cast harsh shadows across her face, highlighting the dark circles under her eyes from worry.

"You still don't understand, do you?" Her voice cracked, the sound raw and vulnerable in the small space between us. She pushed herself away from the counter and stepped toward me, her movements deliberate despite her shaking. Her eyes those deep amber eyes I'd come to know so well searched mine, looking for something I wasn't sure I could give her.

And then she did something that stopped my racing thoughts completely. Abby leaned forward, one hand coming up to cradle my battered cheek with unexpected gentleness, and pressed her lips against mine. The kiss was soft, tender, careful of my split lip, yet unmistakably filled with all the unspoken feelings she'd been holding back.

When she pulled away, her eyes remained closed for a moment longer, as if memorising the sensation. "I can't leave," she said, her voice barely above a whisper, her breath warm against my still-tingling lips. "Being away from you is unbearable. and I won't do it. Despite your infuriating stubbornness and that reckless streak that gives me anxiety, I can't imagine not being by your side through this." Her eyes opened, a hint of her usual spark returning. "Besides, who else would watch over you and save you from your own damn recklessness?"

She let out a small laugh then, the sound brightening the sterile bathroom like unexpected sunlight through frosted glass. Her hand moved from my face to deliver a playful smack to my backside, the sudden shift from tenderness to teasing so quintessentially Abby that it made my heart ache with a bittersweet longing I couldn't quite name.

"Now go shower," she ordered, pushing me toward the bathroom door with gentle insistence. "You smell like a crime scene. Blood and sweat and whatever that warehouse was coated in." Her nose wrinkled, but her eyes never left mine.

I closed the door behind her but could still sense her presence on the other side, keeping watch. As I undressed, wincing at each movement that pulled at my injuries, I caught sight of myself in the mirror—a canvas of purple bruises blooming across my ribs, dried blood crusted at my hairline, dirt embedded in my knuckles. I barely recognised myself.

When I stepped under the cascading hot water, letting it sluice away layers of grime and evidence, my mind wasn't consumed with our mission or even my injuries. Instead, I replayed the moment Abby's lips had pressed against mine—soft yet certain, tasting faintly of salt from tears neither of us had acknowledged, carrying the weight of something unspoken but unmistakable between us.

The steam rose in thick clouds around me, creating a cocoon of isolation and intimacy. The bathroom transformed into a sanctuary where time seemed suspended. Water drummed against my shoulders, working its way into my tense muscles, washing pink rivulets down the drain. In that moment, nothing existed beyond these tiled walls except the knowledge that Abby waited just beyond them, and she wasn't going anywhere.

Our bond felt unbreakable, forged in fire and sealed with that kiss. with in these walls i existed in my own little world, separate from everything else—from the drug dealers, from the agency, from whatever awaited me outside. But reality hovered at the edges of my consciousness, hanging heavy like storm clouds ready to burst. I couldn't hide in this steamy sanctuary forever. Soon, I would have to face those waiting outside and explain what I was really doing here and why Abby and I had lied to them, why we'd put ourselves in danger. The thought made my heart race and my stomach churn with anxiety.

But for now, with warm water washing away the last traces of dried blood from my body and Abby's kiss still tingling on my lips, I couldn't bring myself to care about any of that. All that mattered was Abby and this fragile, beautiful thing growing between us. Despite whatever challenges loomed on the horizon, I knew with absolute certainty that as long as I had Abby by my side, I could face anything, fight clubs, enhancement drugs , agency politics, or my own demons.

So I took my time in the shower, savouring each moment of this stolen peace, letting the water heal what it could while my thoughts drifted between memory and possibility. When I finally turned off the water, my skin was flushed pink and my mind was clear. Whatever waited for me beyond that door, I would face it.

***

The hot shower soothed my battered body like a healing spell, steam rising around me as water cascaded over purple bruises and raw skin. Each droplet seemed to carry away fragments of pain, dissolving the exhaustion that had settled deep in my bones. I lingered longer than necessary, savouring the temporary reprieve before reluctantly shutting off the water. Towelling dry with careful movements, I slipped into the softest clothes I owned—well-worn yoga pants with a frayed waistband and an oversized navy hoodie that hung past my hips, enveloping me in its comforting embrace.

The night air greeted me with unexpected warmth as I stepped into the garden, moonlight casting silver patterns across the flagstone path. Abby followed several paces behind, her footsteps deliberately silent, her presence both protective and predatory—a vampire's natural state. The garden's fragrance of night-blooming jasmine couldn't mask the tension that hung in the air.

Walker, Lunette, and Nixie sat arranged in a half-circle of patio chairs, their faces illuminated by strings of fairy lights draped through nearby trees. Each clutched a beer bottle, condensation dripping down the amber glass. No one spoke. No one moved. Three pairs of eyes tracked my approach with varying degrees of suspicion and concern.

I lowered myself gingerly into the remaining chair, wincing as my ribs protested. The wicker creaked beneath my weight, the sound unnaturally loud in the silence. Reaching into the nearby cooler, ice water sloshing against my fingers, I extracted a beer and popped the cap with practiced ease. The bitter scent of hops wafted up as foam bubbled at the bottle's neck.

"So," I finally said, taking a long pull from the bottle to steady my nerves, "I guess I owe you guys an explanation." The words hung in the humid air between us, inadequate but necessary.

Walker's face tightened, jaw muscles flexing beneath stubbled skin. "That's an understatement if I've ever heard one," he grumbled, tilting his bottle back for a deep swallow. His Adam's apple bobbed as he drank, eyes never leaving mine over the rim.

Abby settled beside me, her body coiled with tension. She fixed Walker with a glare so intense it seemed to lower the temperature around us. Her lips pulled back slightly, not quite revealing fangs, but the threat was unmistakable.

Walker set his bottle down with deliberate care. "Cool your tits, vampire," he retorted, leaning forward with elbows on knees. "I'm not here to cause trouble." He gestured toward me with his bottle, amber liquid sloshing inside. "But I want answers. This kid shouldn't even be conscious after the beating she took, let alone walking around like it was nothing more than a rough sparring session. She should be in intensive care, if not the morgue." His eyes narrowed, flicking between Abby and me. "And I'm especially curious why she's hanging around with a member of the vampire council—and a high council enforcer at that."

"Well, fuck me sideways," I blurted, shock momentarily overriding my pain. My gaze ping-ponged between them, trying to process this new information. "You two know each other?" The revelation shifted the ground beneath me, connections I hadn't anticipated suddenly materialising in this already complicated web.

Silence descended again, heavier than before. Nixie fidgeted with her bottle label, peeling it in thin strips. Lunette stared into the darkness beyond our circle of light. Walker and Abby locked eyes in what appeared to be a silent battle of wills.

Finally, Abby broke the standoff. "It's complicated," she muttered, her voice low and edged with warning. The moonlight caught the sharp angles of her face, casting half of it in shadow. "And it's not important right now." Her cool hand found mine under the rough wooden table, squeezing once—both reassurance and caution. Her touch sent an electric current up my arm, a reminder of our connection amid this tense confrontation.

"Complicated or not, I deserve to know," I pressed, leaning forward despite the protest from my ribs. My curiosity burned hotter than the pain radiating through my body. The fairy lights strung above us reflected in everyone's eyes, turning them into constellations of secrets.

Walker took a long pull from his beer, then set it down with deliberate precision. The bottle made a hollow sound against the stone patio. He ran a hand through his disheveled hair before finally speaking up, his voice gravel-rough with reluctance.

"Abby here is—or at least was—a part of the vampire high council enforcers," he said, gesturing toward her with his bottle. "Not just any enforcer. One of their elite. The kind they send when they want problems permanently solved." His eyes never left Abby's face as he spoke, watching for her reaction like a hunter tracking prey. This wasn't news to me, but Nixie and Lunette exchanged wide-eyed glances across the circle, their expressions shifting from confusion to betrayal. The fairy lights cast dancing shadows across their faces, highlighting their shock. We hadn't exactly told them the truth about who we were and why we were really there. The weight of our deception hung in the humid night air, as tangible as the scent of jasmine that drifted around us from the flowering vines that climbed the garden trellis.

Abby let out a heavy sigh, her shoulders dropping slightly. She traced the rim of her untouched beer bottle with one pale finger before speaking. "Walker and I have had the occasional run-in with each other over the years," she admitted, her voice cool and measured. "But it's irrelevant to this conversation. Let's just say I know he's a good person and someone I believe we can trust." The admission seemed to cost her something, a small concession in what I suspected was a long history.

With that reluctant reassurance hanging in the air, I took a deep breath and opened up about everything—the real reason we were there, about the enhancement drug circulating through the fight clubs, about the shadowy figures we suspected were behind its distribution, and finally, about what I was. The words tumbled out in a rush, my voice growing steadier with each revelation, as if unburdening myself of these secrets was physically lightening my load.

Walker listened intently, his expression shifting from suspicion to understanding. When I finished, he nodded slowly, pieces falling into place behind his eyes. "Well, that explains why you can take that beating and already be this healed and upbeat," he said, gesturing to my bruised but remarkably functional body. "We will need to keep you out of the gym for at least a few days, so it doesn't raise too many questions about your miraculous recovery."

His use of "we" didn't escape my notice. Walker leaned forward, elbows on his knees, his tone brimming with confidence and determination as he continued. "No one will question a few days off after the beating you took. It gives us time to regroup and plan our next move." His presence immediately commanded attention, filling the small garden with an energy that transformed our little group.Without asking permission or waiting for invitation, he had somehow become an active part of our assignment, stepping into our dangerous world as if he'd always belonged there. His presumption shocked me to my core. "What do you mean 'we'?" I stammered, my voice cracking slightly.

Walker leaned forward, the fairy lights casting deep shadows across the hollows of his face. "Kid, I can't just sit by and watch someone like you take on this dangerous mission with only a vampire for backup. I'm in," he stated firmly, his calloused hands gripping his beer bottle so tightly I thought it might shatter. "I'll do everything I can to help. And I assume you have a training area outside the gym where Abby has been working with you?"

Abby's posture shifted subtly—a predator recognising another apex hunter entering her territory. "I have a spot where we train together, yes," she replied with a measured grin, her eyes glinting with something that wasn't quite excitement but closer to calculation. The night breeze lifted a strand of her dark hair, and she tucked it behind her ear with deliberate casualness.

"Excellent," Walker said with a decisive nod, setting his empty bottle on the patio with a hollow clink. "Because I'm joining your training sessions from now on. We'll make more progress if we're all following the same training plans." The determination in his voice matched the intensity burning in his eyes—eyes that had seen combat, that understood violence in ways I was only beginning to comprehend. He was ready to fight alongside us, and despite my initial resistance, warmth bloomed in my chest at his willingness to risk everything for a cause that wasn't his.

As Abby and Walker continued to bicker about training schedules and fighting techniques—her voice cool and precise, his gruff and insistent—I sank deeper into my chair, the wicker creaking beneath my shifting weight. The realisation settled over me like a heavy blanket: this journey would be longer and more arduous than I'd imagined. Each word they exchanged about proper stance and kill techniques hammered home how unprepared I truly was. My ribs throbbed in painful agreement.

Desperate for some reassurance away from their tactical planning, I pushed myself up with a wince and limped toward Lunette and Nixie at the far end of the patio. They sat beneath a trellis of climbing jasmine, its white flowers luminous in the moonlight, petals occasionally drifting down around them like tiny stars. The sweet fragrance intensified as I approached. Their faces, half-shadowed by the vines, turned toward me with expressions I couldn't quite read.

"You both have been unusually quiet during all of this," I said, lowering myself carefully onto a weathered wooden bench across from them, trying not to grimace as my bruised ribs protested. My fingers nervously traced the peeling paint along the bench's edge. "I know I kept things from you. Big things. I just I need to know if we're okay."

The question hung between us. A moth fluttered around the string of fairy lights above, casting erratic shadows. Lunette's silver rings caught the light as she folded her hands in her lap, her dark eyes lifting to the vast expanse of stars overhead. The constellations reflected in her gaze seemed to hold the weight of her thoughts.

"I've been thinking about trust," she finally said, her melodic voice barely above a whisper. "About what it means to keep secrets from those you care about." She leaned forward, moonlight illuminating half her face while leaving the other in darkness. "I don't need to forgive you, Jess. Your deception wasn't born from selfishness—you were trying to shield us from danger. I understand that kind of protection." Her fingers reached across the space between us, not quite touching mine but bridging the gap. The jasmine-scented breeze stirred her dark hair as moonlight caught the silver rings adorning her slender fingers. "But now, let us help you," she whispered, her voice steady with conviction. "We may not be fighters like Abby and Walker, but we have our own strengths. Nixie's intuition can sense danger before it arrives. My connections stretch through three counties—people who owe me favours, who know things. Don't carry this burden alone anymore."

Nixie nodded, the fairy lights reflecting in her amber eyes. She leaned forward, her colourful bracelets jingling softly. "We're already involved," she added, her usually playful tone replaced with something harder, more determined. "Keeping us in the dark only puts us in more danger, not less."

A wave of emotion crashed over me—gratitude, relief, and something deeper I couldn't name. My vision blurred as tears gathered. The weight I'd been carrying since this assignment began seemed to lighten, distributed now across shoulders willing to bear it with me. My bruised ribs ached with each shuddering breath.

"I don't deserve friends like you," I managed, my voice cracking.

Lunette's expression softened. "That's not how friendship works."

With everything finally in the open and emotions running high, exhaustion hit me like a freight train. My body, already taxed from the fight and healing, began to sway. The garden around me tilted and spun, fairy lights stretching into golden streaks across my vision.

"She's about to collapse," Nixie said sharply, already on her feet. She slipped a supportive arm around my waist, careful to avoid my injured ribs.

Abby appeared at my other side, her cool fingers checking my pulse. "Too much, too soon," she muttered. "Let's get her to bed before she falls over."

They guided me through the house, my feet dragging across the worn floorboards. Each step sent pain radiating through my battered body. By the time we reached my room, I could barely keep my eyes open.

Abby pulled back the covers while Nixie helped me sit on the edge of the bed. With gentle efficiency, Abby removed my shoes and eased me down onto the cool sheets. She tucked the blanket around me with surprising tenderness, her movements precise yet caring.

"Rest now," she said, her voice uncharacteristically soft. "We'll figure everything out tomorrow."

As they slipped from the room, the last thing I saw was moonlight streaming through the window, casting silver patterns across the ceiling. Then the blackness of sleep enveloped me completely, washing away all worries and fears. For the first night in weeks, I surrendered to slumber without resistance, knowing I wasn't alone anymore.

CHAPTER 13

Resilience in the Ring

Two weeks had passed since I last stepped foot into the Kanes gym. My body had miraculously healed from all of the injuries I sustained during my disastrous fight with Mal. the broken ribs that had made each breath a stabbing agony, the dislocated shoulder that had hung uselessly at my side, the deep gash above my left eye that had painted half my vision crimson. Even now, when I closed my eyes at night, I could still see his twisted smile as he pummelled me, could still taste the metallic tang of blood filling my mouth. But despite my swift recovery. a recovery that should have taken months, not hours. I still needed to maintain the facade that I was still recovering, wincing at phantom pains whenever Kane's men were watching, dragging my right leg slightly as if the knee hadn't fully healed.

Meanwhile, Abby and I continued our secret training in the abandoned warehouse on the edge of town, its concrete floor stained with years of oil and my fresh sweat. These training sessions were more intense than ever before, with Walker now insistent on joining in, his massive frame casting long shadows across the floor as he demonstrated how to break a chokehold or slip past a guard. The daily punishment my body was taking was pushing my healing abilities to their absolute limit. Each night I collapsed onto my thin mattress, muscles screaming, skin mottled with fresh bruises that would fade by morning only to be replaced by new ones. My knuckles remained perpetually split and scabbed, and a persistent ringing had taken up residence in my left ear. By the end of each day, I was so exhausted and drained that I barely had the energy to shower before falling into a dreamless sleep. Yet somehow, when

Abby woke me at 5 AM, I found the strength to drag myself up and repeat the same gruelling routine. It was like a never-ending cycle of pushing myself beyond my limits, breaking myself down only to build back stronger—a necessary crucible if I was going to survive whatever Kane had planned for me next. My body was becoming a weapon, honed through pain and repetition until even the simplest movements felt deadly.

Despite whatever tumultuous history may have existed between Walker and Abby, they didn't let it interfere with my instruction. In fact, it seemed to fuel their competitive spirits, each pushing themselves harder in an effort to outdo the other. Abby would demonstrate a technique with perfect form, only for Walker to immediately show a counter that rendered it useless. Then Abby would modify her approach, adding a feint or changing the angle of attack. Their silent battle played out through my training, and I absorbed every lesson born from their rivalry.

But today was different. Walker was absent. While I didn't miss the constant bickering between him and Abby, his towering figure had become a reassuring presence during our training sessions. Without him there, a feeling of unease crept over me, like missing the weight of armour before stepping onto a battlefield.

As the day wore on, Abby and I engaged in a fierce sparring match. The warehouse echoed with the sound of our laboured breathing and the squeak of our shoes against the concrete floor. My focus was laser-sharp, tracking her every move and anticipating her attacks by analysing her breathing and body language. I noticed how her right shoulder tensed slightly before she threw a punch, how her weight shifted almost imperceptibly before a kick. Beads of sweat dripped down her neck and plastered strands of her dark hair to her forehead. Her eyes scanned me like an eagle, searching for any hint of an opening, any momentary lapse in my defence she could exploit.

But I stood firm, using my training to block and evade until she made a mistake. The muscles in my arms burned from deflecting her strikes, and my lungs ached for more oxygen than I could give them. And then, in an instant, our movements shifted. She lunged forward with a right hook that left her centre exposed for just a fraction of a second. I dropped to the ground and swept her legs out from under her, feeling the impact travel up my shin as my leg connected with hers. With expert precision, I pinned her to the mat with practiced precision, my forearm pressed against her throat just hard enough to restrict her breathing without cutting it off completely. My knee dug into the soft flesh of her stomach, and I could feel her abdominal muscles tense beneath me as she struggled. The warehouse's fluorescent lights cast harsh shadows across her face as I raised my free hand, fingers curled into a tight fist, knuckles still raw from our earlier drills. The finishing blow hovered in the air between us, suspended in that moment of decision.

Abby's eyes—those unnaturally bright amber eyes that marked her as something other than human—locked with mine. For a heartbeat, I saw something flicker there—not fear, never fear with her—but perhaps a glimmer of pride. She raised her hands in surrender, palms facing outward, her chest heaving beneath my weight as sweat beaded along her hairline and trickled down her temple.

"Okay, I'll admit it," she conceded begrudgingly, her voice slightly raspy from the pressure on her throat. "You're getting a lot better." She pushed against my shoulder, and I eased back, releasing her from the pin. As she sat up, she rubbed her neck where my forearm had been. "But remember, in the arena your opponent won't give you time to analyse their movements. They'll be coming at you without hesitation, so you need to analyse and adapt on the fly. Don't commit to an attack until the very last moment—that hesitation I saw before you swept my legs? That'll get you killed."

I nodded, absorbing her critique as I wiped sweat from my brow with the back of my hand. My muscles ached pleasantly, the kind of pain that signified progress rather than injury. Just as we caught our breaths and prepared for another round, Walker's deep voice echoed throughout the cavernous space.

"Ladies," he said with that infuriating smirk of his as he strolled into view, his massive frame casting a long shadow across the training mats. His dark hair was slicked back, and his leather jacket creaked as he moved. "I have some news."

I looked around in surprise at his sudden appearance, wondering how someone so large could move so quietly when he wanted to. The air in the room seemed to shift, growing tense with the electricity that always sparked between Walker and Abby.

As we got up from the mats, my legs still trembling slightly from exertion, I couldn't help but ask, "How long have you been watching?" I grabbed a towel from the nearby bench and dabbed at my face, trying to appear nonchalant despite my curiosity.

His eyes, the colour of storm clouds, were filled with amusement as he replied, "Long enough to see you kick that vamp's ass." He jerked his chin toward Abby, using the slang term for vampires that I knew she despised.

I turned to see Abby walking away, her shoulders rigid with annoyance. Without breaking stride or looking back, she raised her arm and gave him the middle finger, the gesture somehow both casual and venomous. Despite her tough act and the obvious tension between them, I knew she was just as proud of my takedown as he was—maybe even more so, since she'd been the one to teach me that particular move.

"Well, she may not show it," Walker continued, lowering his voice conspiratorially as he stepped closer to me, close enough that I could smell the faint scent of pine and gunpowder that always seemed to cling to him, "but that was a damn good takedown. Fighting a vampire is no easy feat, even in training. Their reflexes are twice as fast as ours, and their strength..." He whistled low, the sound echoing in the cavernous space. "You should be proud," he added with a beaming smile that crinkled the corners of his eyes and momentarily softened his usually hard expression, revealing laugh lines that hinted at a life before all this—before vampires and training and whatever history he shared with Abby.

The tension between Abby and the towering figure before me was almost tangible, an invisible force field that crackled with unresolved emotions. Every molecule of air between them seemed charged, like the atmosphere before a thunderstorm. Any time they were in the same room, I couldn't help but wonder about their past and if there was some unfinished business between them—

something more than professional rivalry. The way they circled each other reminded me of predators sharing territory reluctantly, both too dangerous to challenge directly. The air seemed thick with unspoken words and lingering glares, years of history compressed into pointed silences and barbed comments.

"Are you ever going to tell me the story between the two of you?" I asked, my voice laced with curiosity as I wiped sweat from my forehead with the back of my hand. My muscles ached pleasantly from the exertion of the takedown. "Or will I have to keep dealing with your childish antics until the end of time? Because honestly, it's getting old."

I raised my voice so Abby could hear me over her retreating figure, her steps echoing against the concrete walls, each footfall deliberate and graceful despite her obvious irritation. Her shoulders tensed at my words, and she paused mid-stride, turning just enough to reveal the sharp profile of her face. Her reply came in a sarcastic tone, dripping with bitterness that seemed to have fermented over years. "Not my story to tell, love. Maybe if you ask the jackass nicely, he will grace you with it. Though I wouldn't hold my breath waiting for honesty from him."

I gave Walker a pointed look, silently urging him to speak up, to finally clear the air that had been thick with tension since day one. His jaw clenched, a muscle twitching beneath the stubble that darkened his cheeks. He simply shrugged in response, rolling his massive shoulders as if physically shaking off the weight of my question. "Maybe another time, kid," he said dismissively, though something flickered in his storm-grey eyes—regret, perhaps, or a deeper pain. "At the moment, we have more important things to discuss." His tone shifted, becoming all business, the brief moment of warmth evaporating like morning dew.

Abby's voice, urgent and filled with concern, broke through the silence beside me. She moved like a lightning bolt, crossing the distance between us in a blur of motion that still, even after weeks of training, made my eyes struggle to track. One moment she was walking away, the next she stood at my side, her amber eyes fixed on Walker with an intensity that could have melted steel. She surprised me once again with her speed, and I couldn't help but wonder if I would ever truly get used to the supernatural abilities of the beings I now found myself surrounded by.

"What's happened?" she asked, her amber eyes searching his for answers, her body tensing like a predator sensing danger.

Walker ran his calloused hand through his dark hair and took a deep breath before answering, his shoulders visibly tightening beneath his leather jacket. "Kane has been asking about your recovery," he said, voice dropping to a near whisper that somehow felt louder than a shout in the cavernous training room. "But trust me, it's not out of genuine concern. You're a hot commodity right now his new star. The clients who bet thousands on these fights are begging to see you in action again. He's already arranged your next match." He paused, jaw clenching. "In just three days."

The weight of his words hung heavily in the air between us, settling like lead in my stomach. This wasn't how things usually worked in the underground fighting circuit. All the intelligence we'd gathered indicated there were supposed to be thorough medical evaluations and at least two weeks of recovery and training before any fighter could step back into the ring after injuries like mine. But Kane seemed to be rushing things, skipping over the necessary precautions that kept fighters his investments alive and functional.

"Why the sudden rush?" I asked, trying to keep my voice steady despite the cold fear that was rising in my chest like floodwater.

"It's not normal," Walker confirmed, his storm-grey eyes darkening as they followed my movement. "Normally fighters have at least fifteen days to prepare before their next match. And they're required to pass all sorts of medical checks beforehand blood work, physical evaluations, cognitive tests." He crossed his massive arms over his chest. "Something's off about this whole situation."

I scowled, my brow furrowed with concern as I spoke, tasting the metallic tang of anxiety on my tongue. My split lip throbbed in time with my heartbeat. "Well, apart from this being quite an unusual situation, can you provide any information about my opponent? Fighting style? Weaknesses? Anything?" Despite trying to sound confident, my voice betrayed me with a slight tremor. I couldn't shake the feeling of dread coiling in my gut at the thought of facing someone new so soon after my loss. The memory of my last fight flashed before my eyes the sickening crunch of bone, the copper taste of blood flooding my mouth, the roar of the crowd becoming distant as darkness threatened to claim me.

"From the constant chatter at the gym, it seems that Kane's brought in a fighter from another branch of his business," Walker said, running his hand through his hair, a nervous habit I'd noticed whenever he was withholding information. "And it's not someone local. No one seems to know them, not even the veterans who've been around the circuit for years. To make matters worse, I haven't been given the chance to meet them, which is unusual. Normally, I'd at least get a glimpse during training sessions." His eyes darted to Abby, a silent communication passing between them that I couldn't decipher.

Abby's voice broke through the tense silence, her words chosen with care as she spoke. Her fingers drummed against her thigh—the only outward sign of her agitation. "Do you truly believe that they are oblivious to Jess's investigation? Could this be a trap?" Her question hung in the air, heavy with suspicion and unease. The fluorescent lights overhead cast harsh shadows across her face, making her amber eyes appear almost predatory.

Walker took a moment to carefully consider his response before answering, his massive frame shifting as he leaned against the wall. The leather of his jacket creaked with the movement. "I believe he is testing her," he replied thoughtfully, his voice dropping to a near-whisper that forced us to lean in closer. "Despite her defeat in their last match, she held her own against Mal and managed to survive his brutal attacks, even though he was pumped full of the drug. That's impressive by anyone's standards, and Kane knows it." He paused, his storm-grey eyes meeting mine with an intensity that made me shiver. "But above all else, he is a shrewd businessman and knows how to manipulate the situation for his own gain. By pitting two unknown fighters against each other while keeping any information about them limited, he creates a buzz and generates more interest from the public. The mystery drives up betting, and the higher the stakes, the more money flows into his pockets." His calloused fingers tapped against his thigh as he added, "At least, that is what I am hoping for." His voice was tinged with doubt, but I clung onto the small glimmer of hope that this could be our chance to finally uncover more information about the mysterious organisation behind the Arena and the drug. The weight of our mission pressed down on my shoulders like a physical burden, and I rolled them back, trying to ease the tension that had settled there like a second skin.

Abigail's voice sliced through the tense silence, her words sharp enough to make both Walker and me flinch. "I want to be there!" She stepped forward, amber eyes flashing dangerously in the fluorescent light of the training room. Her fists clenched at her sides, knuckles white with tension.

"She shouldn't step foot into that arena again without me by her side," she continued, each syllable precisely enunciated as if carving the declaration into stone. "And if you even think about vetoing this, Walker, I will shut down this whole fucking operation myself. Is that clear?" The force behind her statement made the air in the room feel suddenly charged, like the atmosphere before a lightning strike. I'd seen Abby angry before, but this was different—this was calculated fury wrapped in absolute certainty.

Walker's massive frame seemed to shrink slightly under her gaze. He ran a hand across the stubble on his jaw, the scratching sound audible in the silence that followed her ultimatum. "I think I can get you a ticket to the match," he reluctantly agreed after a moment, his storm-grey eyes darting between us. "It won't be great access—probably somewhere in the upper tiers—but if you insist on going, it will at least be a good place to look out for anyone peddling the drug and maybe pick up some gossip." He shifted his weight, leather jacket creaking as he crossed his arms defensively. "But you need to understand that you can't interfere until the match is called. If you blow your cover, we lose our only chance at infiltrating Kane's operation."

"I get it," Abby replied, her demeanour transforming with unsettling speed. The rage that had been radiating from her just seconds before was now contained, crystallised into something colder and more dangerous. She smiled thinly, tucking a strand of hair behind her ear with deliberate slowness. "I'll be good and sit on my hands," she assured him, her voice honey-sweet in a way that made my skin crawl. "However, I'll be keeping an eye on everyone there. And if anything happens to her..." She trailed off, letting the threat hang heavily in the air between them. The fluorescent lights caught the amber of her eyes, making them glow with an almost supernatural intensity as she leaned closer to Walker. "I'll make sure every single person connected to this drug and these fights suffers a disturbing death. I'd happily face Tartarus for the blood bath I leave behind.

Without a word of warning, Abby pivoted on her heel and strode purposefully away. leaving a charged silence in her wake. The air seemed to thicken as she disappeared from sight, and a low hum of tension settled over the room an unspoken reminder that Abby brooked no challenge. I found myself quietly thankful for her fierce loyalty; in this place, having her on my side felt like a precious shield against whatever lay ahead.

My attention shifted to Walker, who stood just a few feet away, his shoulders drawn tight with anxiety. Abigail's parting remark had clearly rattled him: the usual ruddy flush of his cheeks had drained to a paper thin pallor, and I could see a slight tremor run through his right hand. He gripped it into a fist, knuckles whitening as he forced himself to breathe evenly. The moment our eyes locked, he snapped his hand open and cleared his throat, as if to mask the turmoil behind his forced composure.

"All right, kid," he said, voice unnaturally bright. There was an edge of steel beneath the forced cheerfulness. "My turn to spar with you. And trust me, I won't pull any punches this time." He paused, letting the weight of his words settle. "Paul's going to want a face-to-face. And believe me, we'll hear from him sooner rather than later. so you looking a little worse off will help convince them that your still recovering"

A surge of adrenaline shot through me, my heart pounding at the prospect of going all out against Walker's full strength. There was no backing down, though not if I wanted to survive in this cutthroat environment. I inhaled deeply, planting my feet firmly on the cracked gym floor, and raised my guard.

Before I could steady my thoughts, Walker was upon me like a whirlwind. His first strike came faster than I anticipated, a blur of motion that forced me back several steps. The sting of impact radiated up my arm, jolting my senses into sharp focus. I adjusted my stance, slipping and bobbing beneath his next barrage of blows. Each narrowly avoided punch bolstered my resolve; I could feel my confidence growing with every block and evasion.

Seizing a momentary opening, I countered with a swift jab to his side, the meat of my fist connecting cleanly against his ribs. He grunted, shifting his weight, and I pressed the advantage, weaving beneath his next swing to land another solid hit to his thigh. For what felt like an eternity, we traded blows in a relentless dance of offence and defence. sweat beading on my brow, breath coming in controlled bursts.

Then, like a guardian from the shadows, Abigail reappeared in the doorway, her expression grave. She stepped forward, folding her arms. "Paul just called," she announced, voice low and urgent. "He and Kane want to see you right now.

At the mention of their names, my chest tightened with equal parts dread and anticipation. This was the moment to prove myself to show Kane that I belonged. Without hesitating, I rubbed a hand over my bruised knuckles, exchanged a quick nod with Abigail, and made my way toward the locker room. The metallic scent of sweat and liniment clung to the air as I headed for the showers, each step echoing with the promise and peril of whatever awaited me on the other side.

***

With aching muscles and bruises decorating my body like a violent watercolour, I stumbled into the bustling gym. My ribs throbbed where Walker had landed a particularly vicious right hook, and the cut above my left eye had finally stopped bleeding but still pulsed with each heartbeat. The last few hours of training with Walker and Abby had been brutal beyond measure. Walker hadn't held back—each calculated strike designed to leave marks that would convince Kane of my supposed recovery period.

"You need to look the part," Walker had said earlier, circling me like a predator. "Kane needs to believe you're still healing." Then he'd unleashed a flurry of precisely placed blows that hurt like hell but wouldn't impair my actual fighting ability.

Compared to Abby's clinical precision, Walker was a true savage—inflicting just enough pain to make me suffer without causing lasting damage. It was a masterclass in controlled violence.

As I made my way through the chaos of the gym, past fighters skipping rope and pounding heavy bags, I reminded myself that these injuries were merely cosmetic. They would heal quickly with rest and proper nourishment. By morning, thanks to my enhanced physiology, I would be 100% recovered and ready for more. I needed to be in peak condition for whatever awaited me in the arena.

The gym pulsed with activity—the rhythmic thud of gloves against leather, grunts of exertion, and the occasional shout of encouragement from trainers. The front desk employee with the perpetual five o'clock shadow, greeted me with a brief nod before returning to his clipboard. I continued toward Kane's office at the far end of the facility, my footsteps slowing as I approached the imposing black door.

As I drew closer to Kane's office, the muffled sound of raised voices penetrated what were supposed to be soundproof walls. I slowed my approach, glancing over my shoulder to confirm I was alone in the corridor. Heart quickening, I pressed my ear against the cool metal surface of the door, the vibrations of angry voices traveling through my skull.

"This is fucking ridiculous, Kane," came Paul's voice, tight with barely controlled rage. "She hasn't even been cleared by medical, and you're throwing her back in? That animal nearly killed her last time! Her ribs were practically shattered!"

"Are you going soft on me, Paul?" Kane's voice oozed contempt, the words drawn out like he was savouring them. "Since when do you give a fuck about the fighters? They've always been commodities to you walking, bleeding ATMs."

"It's not about the goddamn money," Paul shot back, his voice rising. Something crashed—maybe a fist on the desk. "It's about you cutting corners with these lineups. They're reckless. That fight last night wasn't a match; it was an execution. Ramirez had zero chance from the start, and that sadistic bastard you put him against spent fifteen minutes carving him up for fun. The ref should have stopped it after the second round."

I pulled back slightly, a cold knot forming in my stomach. Kane was putting me in another fight soon against someone who might be even worse than my last opponent. My bruised ribs throbbed at the thought.

Taking three deep breaths to steady myself, I smoothed my expression into one of neutral confidence and knocked firmly on the door.

"Come in," Kane's voice called out, suddenly businesslike.

I pushed open the heavy door and stepped inside. Kane lounged behind his massive mahogany desk, one ankle crossed over his knee, looking completely unconcerned about being overheard. Paul sat opposite him, shoulders hunched forward, head slightly bowed. From my angle, I could see the muscle in his jaw working overtime, his knuckles white where they gripped the armrests of his chair. The tension in the room was thick enough to choke on.

"Jess," Kane said with a smirk, baring his teeth like a deranged Cheshire cat. The sight sent shivers down my spine, but I refused to let him see that he could intimidate me. "It's so lovely to see you thriving. Looks like you've recovered nicely from your last match." His eyes scanned my body, taking in the fresh bruises Walker had strategically placed, the cut above my eye, the way I favoured my left side when I moved.

I let his words hang in the air for just a moment, maintaining an air of indifference. The office smelled of expensive cologne and leather, with an undercurrent of sweat that never quite left a fighting gym, no matter how upscale. I squared my shoulders despite the pain.

"Yes, I'm basically back to normal. I was actually planning on resuming training in the next day or two, if that's acceptable?"

I could hear Paul huffing disapprovingly in the corner. He shifted in his seat, the leather creaking beneath him like a child having a tantrum. Kane's smile widened at my response, revealing a gold molar at the back of his mouth that caught the light from the overhead fixtures.

"I am thrilled to hear that, Jess." Kane's voice dripped with false sincerity. "But unfortunately, I must ask you to hold off on training for a few more days."

My confusion must have been evident on my face because he continued without skipping a beat, leaning forward hands pressed against the polished mahogany surface of his desk. The gold signet ring on his right pinky caught the light as he moved.

"Your last match was such a smashing success that our loyal patrons have been clamouring for more. The betting pool was unprecedented." He paused, savouring the moment like a predator toying with wounded prey. "So, I have arranged for your next fight this Thursday evening."

Kane's eyes cold and calculating beneath heavy lids glinted with satisfaction. He ran his tongue across his bottom lip, no doubt already counting the hefty sum he'd be earning from my next bout. The bruises Walker had strategically placed across my body throbbed in protest, but knowing the information in advance made it easier to show no weakness or reluctance.

I plastered on a fake smile and nodded, suppressing the anger and disgust rising within me like bile. "Of course, whatever you think is best," I replied, my voice steady despite the storm raging inside.

Kane's grin widened even further. "Excellent. In the meantime, I want you to relax and recover as much as possible before the fight. We can discuss your training regime after Thursday's match." His tone made it clear this wasn't a suggestion but a command.

As if on cue, Paul stood up from his leather chair and strode purposefully towards the heavy oak door, the floorboards creaking beneath his weight. "Jess, if I could have a word outside," he said in a low voice, his sharp features contorted into a stern expression. The muscle in his jaw was still working overtime.

Kane, who had shifted to lounging lazily on his chair, merely waved his hand in a dismissive gesture, not even bothering to spare me a glance as he reached for his phone. My insides boiled with resentment as I forced myself to maintain composure while leaving Kane's luxurious office, the scent of his expensive cologne lingering in my nostrils.

This assignment was turning out to be nothing like I had imagined. Instead of a straightforward undercover operation, I found myself caught in an intricate web of calculated moves and manipulation, where fighters like me were merely pawns in Kane's bloody chess game. The walls of the corridor seemed to close in around me as Paul waited, his expression unreadable beneath the harsh fluorescent lighting that cast shadows across his weathered face.

I followed Paul through the gym's exit, the cool evening air a welcome relief after the stifling tension of Kane's office. He gestured wordlessly toward his sleek black Audi parked in the reserved spot near the door. Once inside, I watched as he gently closed his door and exhaled deeply, his broad shoulders visibly relaxing as he leaned back against the leather seat. The scent of his sandalwood cologne mingled with the car's new leather smell. I gave him a moment to compose himself, studying his profile as he stared straight ahead through the windshield, his fingers drumming lightly against the steering wheel.

My heart pounded against my bruised ribs as I finally broke the silence. "So do I at least get to know who I'll be fighting?" The question had been burning in my mind since leaving Kane's office. I held my breath, watching Paul's reaction carefully.

As expected, he gave a firm and resounding no, his jaw tightening as he turned to face me. The streetlight illuminated the lines of exhaustion etched around his eyes. "Unfortunately, Jess, I don't have any more intel on your opponent other than they are from another branch of his operation. The first time you will meet is in the arena." His tone was resigned, the words hanging heavy between us, as if he had already given up hope for me.

I let out a disappointed sigh. Going into the fight completely blind was not ideal, especially with only days to prepare. Paul seemed to be losing whatever influence he once had with Kane, which made my position even more precarious. Changing tactics, I leaned toward him slightly. "I couldn't help but overhear you and Kane arguing before I came in," I said carefully. "Is there anything I can do to help? You seemed pretty upset."

He hesitated, fingers tightening on the steering wheel until his knuckles blanched. "I'll explain everything on the drive back." The key slid into the ignition with a metallic scrape, and the engine came to life with a throaty purr that vibrated through the leather seats. Rain began to speckle the windshield as we pulled away from the gym, each drop catching the neon lights of the city.

We rode in silence for nearly ten minutes, the rhythmic swish of wipers marking time. Paul's jaw worked back and forth, like he was chewing through his thoughts before finally spitting them out.

"I'm sorry," he began, voice low and gravelly. "I've been trying to delay this fight that's why you haven't heard from me. I've called in every favour, pulled every string I could reach. But Kane..." He shook his head, the streetlights casting alternating shadows across his face. "Kane is adamant about getting you back in the arena. He's rejected three potential postponement dates already."

His voice carried the unmistakable weight of defeat. One hand left the wheel to rub at the stubble on his chin. "He's cutting corners everywhere—shortened medical clearances, bribing inspectors, rushing paperwork. He makes it seem like it's all about the money, about the betting pools, but there's something else happening here."

Paul took a sharp right turn, tires hissing on wet asphalt. "Every time I see him discussing your fight, there's this... hunger lurking behind his eyes. Not greed—something darker. And I'm certain he hasn't discovered our investigation." He gave a humourless laugh. "We'd both be dead if that were the case. No, it's almost like he's playing with his food, like a cat that's cornered something and is enjoying the terror before the kill."

My head spun with this new information, pieces clicking together like a jigsaw puzzle revealing a disturbing picture. The car slowed as we approached the safe house, tires crunching on the gravel driveway. The porch light flickered, a weak beacon in the growing storm.

Paul shifted into park but kept the engine running, turning to face me fully. Rain drummed on the roof as he fixed me with a gaze so intense I could feel it like physical pressure.

"Jess," he said, voice dropping to barely above a whisper, "I need you to be prepared for anything on the night of your fight. Kane's bringing in people I've never seen before. Security's been doubled. Whatever's happening goes beyond illegal fighting rings." His hand found my arm, fingers digging in with urgent pressure. "Stay alert. Trust no one but me."

He released me and I stepped out into the rain, watching as his taillights disappeared down the road. Standing there, water soaking through my clothes, I felt more confused and isolated than I had since this assignment began. The bruises on my body throbbed in time with a new, terrible certainty: there was much more at stake in this fight than just my survival.

CHAPTER 14

Fight Night Secrets

No one could dig up any information on my opponent. The night of the fight arrived with a sense of foreboding that settled in my stomach like lead. I sat in the dimly lit changing area with Paul and Walker, the concrete walls amplifying every small sound—the scratch of tape being wrapped around knuckles, the creak of the wooden bench beneath me, the distant roar of the crowd filtering through the corridor outside.

My thoughts kept drifting to Abby. She was out there alone, weaving through the crowd of bloodthirsty spectators, trying to gather intelligence for our investigation while I sat here, relatively safe.

"I really wish she wasn't out there alone," I muttered, wiping sweat from my palms onto my shorts for the third time in as many minutes.

Walker's hand landed on my shoulder—rough and calloused skin that had seen more fights than I'd had hot meals. The pressure was reassuring, anchoring me to the present moment when my mind wanted to spiral into worst-case scenarios.

"Don't worry, Kid," he said, his deep voice steady as a metronome. "You got this. Abby and I will be out there with you—watching your back every step of the way." His words were meant to be comforting, but they only served to remind me of the gravity of our situation. We weren't just fighting for sport or glory; we were infiltrating a dangerous underground operation with players who wouldn't hesitate to silence us permanently.

"Remember why we're doing this," Walker continued, his eyes locking with mine in the mirror across from us. "We need to get to the bottom of this and shut it down before it gets any worse. And don't hold back against your opponent as much as you did last time—we can't afford for you to do that."

I nodded silently, my mind racing with doubts and fears that threatened to overwhelm me. But I knew he was right. This wasn't a game or a test of strength—it was a mission with real consequences, lives at stake.

The locker room's familiar scent of antiseptic barely masked the underlying notes of sweat and adrenaline. It was a smell that both excited and terrified me. Excited because it meant action and a chance to make a difference. Terrified because it also meant facing unknown dangers and risking everything we'd worked for.

Paul paced behind us, checking his watch every few seconds. The nervous energy rolling off him wasn't helping my concentration.

We had no choice but to move forward. The greater good depended on us succeeding in this fight, on maintaining our cover long enough to gather the evidence we needed against the underground enhancement ring. I took a deep breath, filling my lungs completely before slowly releasing it, steeling myself for what lay ahead. The familiar pre-fight tension coiled in my stomach like a spring wound too tight.

I lifted my gaze to Walker, and what I saw surprised me. Genuine concern softened his usually granite expression, the harsh lines around his mouth relaxing for the first time since I'd known him. The fluorescent light caught the grey at his temples, making him look older, more vulnerable.

"Listen to me," he said, his calloused hand gripping my shoulder. "If your opponent is as dangerous as we suspect, forget the plan. Take them down. I don't care about losing a few matches to maintain our cover. We can always adjust our strategy if necessary." His fingers tightened. "But we can't replace you, kid."

The words hung between us, heavy with meaning. I'd never heard Walker speak with such raw emotion before. This man who'd barked orders at me for weeks, who'd pushed me until my muscles screamed and sweat poured from every inch of my body, was now looking at me like... like I mattered beyond the mission.

"I..." My voice caught. What could I possibly say? I nodded instead, the simple movement conveying what words couldn't.

As the minutes ticked down, my nerves frayed further. I focused on my breathing—in through the nose, out through the mouth—just as Abby had taught me during our training sessions. Paul's constant pacing didn't help, his shoes squeaking against the concrete floor as he muttered calculations and contingency plans under his breath.

I closed my eyes, blocking him out. Abby's voice echoed in my memory: "Composure is your weapon. When everything around you descends into chaos, your calm becomes your shield." She'd drilled this into me alongside the physical training—the proper way to take a hit, how to fall without breaking bones, the precise amount of resistance to show before "succumbing" to defeat.

Two weeks of the most intense preparation of my life, all leading to another planned loss. The irony wasn't lost on me. Every muscle in my body had been conditioned to fight, to win, to survive—only to deliberately surrender in the end. My knuckles still bore the scabs from countless hours on the punching bag, my ribs still tender from sparring sessions where Walker hadn't pulled his punches.

"Remember your cover story," Walker said, interrupting my thoughts. "You're just a desperate fighter looking for an edge. Nothing more."

I nodded again, the weight of our mission settling across my shoulders like a fighter's robe—heavy with expectation. Despite knowing I was meant to lose, a stubborn flame of determination burned in my chest. I would give them a show they wouldn't forget—right before I let them think they'd broken me.

The sound of a gym bag hitting the concrete floor with a thunderous BANG jolted me from my thoughts. My eyes snapped up to see Walker standing before me, a knowing smirk playing at the corner of his weathered mouth.

"Jesus Christ!" I hissed, my heart hammering against my ribs. "Are you trying to give me a heart attack or mess up my focus right before I go out there?"

Walker's smirk softened as he knelt down in front of me, his knees popping in protest. The fluorescent lights cast harsh shadows across the deep lines of his face as he reached for my hands.

"Sorry about that, kid," he said, his voice low and gravelly. "Just making sure you're still with us."

His calloused fingers worked methodically, wrapping the athletic tape around my knuckles with practiced precision. He pulled each strip with just enough tension—secure but not restricting. I watched his concentration, the way his brow furrowed slightly as he worked, treating this small act with the same intensity he brought to everything.

"Remember," he said without looking up, "I'll be right outside the ring the whole time, ready to step in if things get too rough." He finished the last wrap with a gentle pat on my wrist. "But I know you can handle it. You're ready."

The announcer's voice boomed through the corridor outside, calling my name with artificial enthusiasm that echoed off the concrete walls. My stomach tightened.

"Walker," I said, meeting his eyes directly, "I know you and Abby are both here for me. And I promise, you won't need to intervene this time." I swallowed hard against the lump forming in my throat. "I've learned from my mistakes. I'll put on the show they want, make them believe I'm desperate enough to seek enhancement, but I'll make sure to lose convincingly."

The words tasted bitter as they left my mouth. Every instinct in my body, honed through weeks of brutal training, screamed against the idea of deliberate defeat. All I wanted was to win, to see pride replace concern in Abby's eyes, to prove to Walker that his faith in me wasn't misplaced. But duty called with a voice louder than my pride. I would do what was necessary, even if it meant walking out of that ring as a calculated loser rather than the fighter I'd become.

***

The deafening roar of the arena crashed over me like a wave as the commentator announced my name, his voice booming through speakers that vibrated the very air. I left Walker and Paul standing at the entrance, their worried expressions etched in my mind like carvings in stone. Walker's final nod curt but laden with unspoken concern replayed in my thoughts as I walked the long corridor toward the fighting pit.

My mind kept drifting back to my match with Mal, that brutal encounter that had left me on deaths doorstep. The metallic taste of dried blood seemed to resurface on my tongue, a phantom reminder of the intense violence. Even now, I could feel the ghost of his weight pinning me down, see his eyes. pupils blown wide with the enhancement drug as he rained down blows that cracked my orbital bone and shattered my ribs.

The memory of bone breaking under Mal's relentless assault echoed in my ears, a sickening symphony of crunches and my own muffled screams. The thought of facing another enhanced fighter made my stomach twist into knots, acid rising in my throat. But I swallowed it down. Too much was riding on this performance. The entire operation depended on me appearing desperate enough to seek the enhancement drug myself.

The sand shifted beneath my bare feet as I stepped into the centre of the arena. The circular fighting pit stretched around me, surrounded by tiered seating filled with spectators hungry for violence. I forced myself to breathe slowly, methodically, blocking out the cacophony of shouting and betting that surrounded me. Focus. Assess. Survive.

In the opposite corner stood my opponent a lamia. The serpentine creature was not what I had expected; the underground fights usually featured humanoid combatants. This changed everything. She was at least seven feet long from head to tail tip, her upper body humanoid but covered in iridescent scales that caught the harsh arena lights. Battle scars marked her torso where scales had been torn away, revealing patches of vulnerable flesh beneath. Deep, jagged scars crisscrossed her muscular arms and serpentine lower half, telling stories of countless brutal encounters. Yet her amber eyes burned with undiminished pride—this was a warrior who had never truly been defeated, merely delayed.

I catalogued every detail as we circled each other: the way she balanced her weight primarily on the middle section of her tail, the slight favouring of her right arm, the calculating intelligence behind those reptilian eyes. Each movement revealed something the powerful coil of muscle beneath scale, the practiced fluidity of a predator. This was no amateur she had killed before and would not hesitate to do so again.

Despite the fear clawing at my insides, I maintained my composure. This wasn't just about surviving the next few minutes it was about infiltrating a criminal network that had already claimed dozens of lives through their experimental enhancement drugs. For my own sake, for Walker and Paul waiting anxiously outside, for the families of fighters who'd died horrible deaths from unstable compounds, I had to see this through.

As I made my way toward my designated corner, our paths inevitably crossed. She moved with surprising grace for her size, slithering across the sand without leaving more than shallow impressions. When we passed within arm's reach, she flicked out a forked tongue, tasting the air around me tasting my fear, my determination, my very essence. Her lips curled into what might have been a smile, revealing rows of needle-sharp teeth. It wasn't just a taunt it was a promise of what was to come.

The bell rang, a single clear tone that cut through the cacophony of the crowd. Before its echo had even faded, she was in motion, her powerful tail propelling her across the sand with frightening speed. The lamia's upper body remained eerily still as she closed the distance between us, amber eyes locked on mine with predatory focus. In that moment, I knew with absolute certainty that all our careful planning might not be enough to keep me alive.

With serpentine grace, she launched herself at me. I raised my arms in a defensive stance, but she was too quick. a blur of iridescent scales and coiled muscle. A powerful blow to my solar plexus forced the air from my lungs in an agonised gasp. Before I could recover, her tail whipped around and caught me across the ribs with a force that sent me flying toward the wall. I hit the barrier with a sickening thud, the impact reverberating through my bones as I crumpled to the sand.

These were the same tactics I'd seen Abby use in our training quick, overwhelming, designed to disorient. The lamia circled me as I struggled to my feet, her forked tongue flicking out to taste my fear in the air. The crowd's roar seemed distant now, muffled by the ringing in my ears and the thundering of my heart. But unlike my previous opponents, I wasn't going down so easily. I had a plan.

As she charged toward me again, I noticed a patch where scales were missing along her right flank a vulnerable spot of pink flesh amid the armoured exterior. If I could target that weakness, I might stand a chance. I feinted left, my feet sliding in the sand as I telegraphed my movement. The lamia adjusted her trajectory precisely as I'd hoped, closing the distance between us with predatory confidence.

At the last possible second, I pivoted back and drove my fist toward the unprotected area with every ounce of strength I possessed. Instead of connecting with soft tissue, my knuckles struck what felt like an invisible barrier. A blinding flash of blue energy erupted from the point of impact, crackling like lightning across my skin. The force flung me backward as if I'd been hit by a truck, my body helplessly airborne. Twenty feet above the arena floor, time seemed to slow. The crowd's roar dulled to a distant hum. I registered the shock on the lamia's face—she hadn't expected her trap to work quite so effectively. Her amber eyes widened, forked tongue flicking out in surprise.

As gravity reclaimed me and I began my descent toward the unforgiving sand below, one thought crystallised in my mind: this wasn't something training had prepared me for. Walker had warned me about enhanced fighters, about drugs and steroids, but magic? That changed everything.

Mid-air, instinct took over. I tucked my chin, pulled my limbs inward, trying desperately to control my fall. The arena lights blurred above me, spinning in nauseating circles. By some miracle, I managed to twist my body, positioning myself to land feet-first rather than on my back or head. The sand rushed up to meet me with brutal speed.

The impact shot through my legs like twin spears of fire. My knees buckled, absorbing what they could before I rolled, distributing the force across my shoulder and hip. Sand filled my mouth, gritty between my teeth. Every nerve ending screamed in protest as I tumbled to a stop, gasping for air that wouldn't come. My lungs had seized, diaphragm temporarily paralysed by the shock.

For several agonising seconds, I lay there, vision swimming with black spots. The crowd's noise swelled back to full volume, their bloodlust palpable. Slowly, painfully, I pushed myself onto hands and knees, then to my feet. My legs trembled beneath me, threatening to give way. Blood trickled from my nose, metallic on my tongue. Across the pit, the lamia stared, her expression a mixture of surprise and newfound respect most humans wouldn't have gotten up from that.

We stood frozen in mutual disbelief at the unexpected turn of events. The commentator's voice crackled through the arena speakers: "Ladies and gentlemen, this human refuses to stay down! Unprecedented resilience from our newcomer!" The crowd erupted, their bloodlust amplified by my survival. I tasted copper as blood trickled from my nose down my throat, and my legs trembled beneath me, threatening to buckle with each heartbeat.

There was no time for weakness. With deliberate slowness that masked my pain, I squared my shoulders and raised my fists once more, ignoring the grinding protest of what felt like fractured ribs. This setback wouldn't derail my mission. The enhancement dealers never approached losers who went down easily—they wanted fighters desperate enough to risk experimental compounds, fighters like me who showed potential but needed an edge. I needed to be noticed.

The lamia's scales glittered under the harsh lights as she slithered closer, her powerful tail leaving sinuous tracks in the sand. A hissing laugh escaped her lips, revealing rows of needle-sharp teeth stained with the blood of previous opponents.

"What the hell was that?" I spat, voice ragged but loud enough to carry. "Some kind of trick?"

Her amber eyes narrowed with amusement. "It's a common mistake," she said, her voice melodic despite its reptilian undertones. "Everyone goes for the obvious weak spot." She gestured to the patch of exposed flesh. "So I reinforced it with a defensive ward.

Most fighters fall for it... and never get back up." Her forked tongue flicked out, tasting my sweat and fear in the air. "You're different."

I circled her cautiously, each step sending shockwaves of pain through my battered body. My eyes darted across her form, searching for genuine vulnerabilities—not the obvious bait she'd laid before. The crowd's roar faded to white noise as I focused entirely on her movements, the subtle shift of weight, the almost imperceptible tensing of muscles before she struck.

When she charged, it was with frightening speed, her upper body remaining eerily still while her powerful tail propelled her forward. I pivoted at the last second, launching a desperate hook toward her jaw—her real weakness, not the false one she'd presented. For a heartbeat, I thought I'd connected, but she twisted with impossible grace, my fist grazing scales instead of flesh.

Her counterattack came in a blur—three rapid strikes to my torso, a sweeping tail that nearly took my legs from under me, and clawed hands that raked for my face. I blocked what I could, absorbed what I couldn't, each impact sending fresh waves of agony through my already battered frame. Blood and sweat stung my eyes as I fought to maintain distance.

"Our newcomer is putting up the fight of her life!" the commentator bellowed, his amplified voice barely penetrating my focus. "But the Serpent Queen is living up to her reputation as the most lethal fighter in the circuit!"

Minutes stretched like hours as we exchanged blows. My technique grew sloppier as exhaustion set in, lungs burning, muscles screaming for relief. The lamia showed no such fatigue, her movements as fluid and deadly as when we'd begun. I needed to end this—not with a victory, but with the right kind of loss.

With calculated recklessness, I deliberately lowered my guard on my right side, creating an opening no experienced fighter would miss. Her eyes widened slightly—surprise or suspicion, I couldn't tell—before she capitalised with a devastating combination that culminated in a tail strike to my exposed ribs. The impact lifted me off my feet, and I made no effort to break my fall as I crashed into the sand. To everyone watching, it appeared the Serpent Queen had finally broken me. In reality, I'd orchestrated my defeat perfectly—showing enough skill and determination to attract attention, but ultimately falling to a superior opponent.

Just as she delivered what seemed like a knockout punch, I deftly blocked in the wrong direction, making it seem like she had outmatched me. In reality, I had fainted from exhaustion and the excruciating pain coursing through my body. But thankfully, it looked like a believable defeat. As I lay unconscious on the ground, I couldn't help but wonder how much longer I would have to endure these staged fights before the dealers finally took notice of me.

I slowly regained consciousness to a pungent smell assaulting my nose and the looming figure of Walker peering down at me. "What the hell is that stuff? It feels like you're attempting to dissolve my face."

He offered me his hand with a steady grip and hauled me to my feet. "Well, at least that went better than last time," he said with a wry half-smile. Around us, the arena's lights cast flickering shadows over rough-hewn stone walls, and the roar of the bloodthirsty crowd battered my ears. The acrid scent of sweat and metal hung in the air, mixing with the dusty tang of old stone as I wobbled to find my balance on the sand-strewn floor.

My lamia opponent was already slipping away through the side gate, her scaled tail brushing the ground in sinuous waves. Halfway out, she paused, turned her head of coiling hair toward me, and gave a curt, respectful nod. In her knowing glance I detected relief she'd no doubt feared I might be badly hurt then she slipped quietly into the dim corridor beyond, leaving only the distant echo of her departure behind.

Walker, reached out and motioned for me to turn. I shifted my weight unsteadily and followed his finger to the crowd. There, framed in the gloom of the vaulted doorway, stood Abby. She should have blended in with the other spectators only silhouettes and murmurs around her but something about her posture betrayed her. Instead of cheering, her fists were clenched at her sides, and her eyes flashed with contained rage. I had assumed she was revelling in the spectacle like the rest, but the moment our gazes locked, I realised she was horrified by what she'd seen.

My heart sank. We needed to get out of there before her anger boiled over. I turned back to Walker and asked as we weaved through the departing crowd, "Walker, are you coming with us? Or will you meet us tomorrow?" My voice sounded harsh in the corridors of the arena.

He gave a calm nod. "I'll see you safely out first. Then I'll see you in the morning. It's probably best you and your vampire friend have some time alone to process what just happened." His tone was gentle but firm; I could hardly argue with him.

Together we navigated the maze of passageways, our shadows dancing along the walls. At the designated changing area fumbled with my gear. I peeled off layers as quickly as I could, trying not to waste a second while Walker secured the door behind us.

When I finally stepped outside into the cool night air, Abby was waiting at the curb, perched on the hood of her jeep. The street lamps cast pools of pale light over her, highlighting the tension in her shoulders. Her hair was slightly mussed, and though her jaw was clenched, relief flickered in her eyes as she saw me approaching.

Walker slipped away into the shadows without a word one moment he stood beside me, the next he was gone, like a wraith melting into the dark. I cleared my throat and called after him, but he didn't look back.

"Did I keep you waiting long?" I asked Abby, attempting a light tone that felt hollow in my chest.

She didn't hesitate. She climbed down from the jeep and wrapped her arms around me in a tight, trembling embrace. Her cheek pressed against my chest, and I felt the heat of her tears soaking through my shirt. "No," she whispered, voice thick with relief. "are You okay."

I froze for a heartbeat, surprised by the raw vulnerability in her grip. Then I slid my arm around her, pulling her closer. The cool night air swirled around us, but all I noticed was the rapid thump of her heartbeat against my ribs. The sounds of the city drifted past—distant traffic, the murmur of night guards—but in that moment, it was just the two of us, stripped of titles and duties. She clung to me as if I were the only anchor in a raging storm, and I held her back, determined to be exactly that. It was a rare and unguarded moment between us, a fragile connection that neither orders nor protocol could ever touch.

CHAPTER 15

The Call of the Council

Alex*

Reluctantly, I submitted to the summons of the council of watchers, a daunting responsibility that none could ignore, especially not someone of my station. I informed my colleagues at the Agency of my immediate absence, As I locked my office door and drew the blackout blinds, I mentally prepared for what was to come. The realm gate required blood activation. I pricked my thumb with the ceremonial silver needle kept in my desk's hidden compartment and pressed the crimson droplet against the wall's seemingly ordinary surface. As I reached out to grasp the shimmering doorknob that materialised, I steeled myself for the unique experience that awaited me. Unlike other portals that provided brief bursts of extreme temperature fluctuations, this particular gateway to the Watcher's Realm unleashed a searing heat that engulfed my body like an inferno, burning away the mortal world's physical limitations. The air around me twisted and shimmered in a dizzying dance, reality folding upon itself like origami in expert hands. My stomach lurched as gravity seemed to invert, my cells feeling simultaneously compressed and expanded. The familiar burning sensation intensified until it felt as though my very essence was being pulled through the eye of a needle. And then, with a sharp jolt that rattled my teeth and sent electric tingles cascading down my spine like lightning, I found myself standing on solid ground again - this time in the grand reception hall of the Watchers' Realm.

The vast chamber stretched before me, its vaulted ceiling disappearing into shadows that no mortal light could penetrate. Ethereal surfaces of polished obsidian and moonstone adorned every wall and column, constantly shifting and changing in an otherworldly sheen. These surfaces reflected impossible colours beyond the human spectrum colours I had learned to perceive only after centuries of exposure to the realm's unique properties. Motes of luminescent energy drifted through the air like fireflies, casting subtle patterns across the marble floor inlaid with ancient runes of protection and power.

As I slowly adjusted to the disorienting surroundings, my enhanced senses gradually returning to their full capacity, my eyes caught sight of Lyn. She leaned effortlessly against a crystalline pillar with a flicker of amusement lighting up her features, her posture betraying none of the discomfort most beings experienced when traveling between realms. Approaching me with graceful steps that barely made a sound on the polished floor, she moved with the fluid confidence that came from millennia of existence. Her tailored lilac business suit contrasted sharply with her vibrant Purple blouse - colours that subtly echoed her true draconic form's scales.

Her presence commanded attention not merely from her physical beauty, though that was undeniable, but from something ancient that radiated from within her very being. The subtle shimmer beneath her skin hinted at scales that could emerge at will, and her eyes held the wisdom of millennia. I bowed my head in the formal forty-five-degree angle, a gesture I had practiced countless times during my first century of service to the Council.

"Lyn, Dragon Queen of the Skies, it is truly an honour to stand in your presence," I said, my voice pitched precisely between the familiarity of our long acquaintance and the deference her station demanded. "May I inquire what brings you to the Hall of Watchers? The Council rarely summons those of draconic lineage unless matters are exceptionally grave."

She tilted her head slightly, the light catching the almost imperceptible purple scales at her temples. "I can only assume it's for the same reason as you, Alex," she replied, her sly smile revealing teeth just slightly too sharp to be human. "The summons arrived via phoenix flame this morning—most urgent. I was about to enter the council chamber when I sensed your portal opening and decided to wait." She reached forward, her fingers cool against my chin as she lifted my face. "Please stop bowing, old friend. After eight centuries, such formality between us seems rather ridiculous, doesn't it?"

"As you wish, Your Majesty," I said, straightening my posture while my lips curved into a small smile. "Shall we proceed to the chamber and discover what catastrophe requires our immediate attention this time?"

Lyn gracefully linked her arm through mine, the sleeve of her lilac suit brushing against my darker attire. We walked in perfect synchronicity down the corridor, our footsteps echoing against marble floors inlaid with prophetic runes that glowed faintly at our passing. The walls themselves seemed to pulse with ancient magic, gold and jewels embedded in patterns that told stories of creation and destruction to those who knew how to read them.

"Tell me, Alex," Lyn said casually as we passed a series of crystalline sculptures depicting the First War, her voice dropping to ensure privacy despite the seemingly empty hall, "how fares young Jessica? "

I hesitated, choosing my words with diplomatic precision. "She is well, according to the reports I've received from in the field."

Lyn's fingers tightened almost imperceptibly on my arm. "Reports? You haven't seen her yourself?" Her expression sharpened, the dragon beneath the human facade suddenly more apparent. "Where exactly is she, Alex?"

"She's currently engaged in a classified reconnaissance mission," I admitted, lowering my voice further and casting a quick spell of silence around us with a subtle gesture of my free hand. "I cannot reveal more, even to you, but I assure you the task force continues its work admirably in her absence. They've uncovered significant connections between Aldridge's financial network and Jeremiah's experimental facilities, and we've successfully interrogated seventeen surviving personnel from the raids."

Lyn's eyes narrowed, the pupils momentarily elongating into reptilian slits before returning to their human appearance.

Purple scales flickered beneath her skin like lightning beneath storm clouds. "And what of the children?" Her voice dropped to a dangerous whisper. "The ones who survived Aldrich's experiments? The Council swore to me they would be properly rehabilitated and protected."

"Our specialised medical team has established a comprehensive care protocol," I replied, choosing my words with precision. "We've created a sanctuary in the northern compound the one with the reinforced wards and healing gardens. until we are Abel to secure a suitable site for schooling. Families have been contacted where possible, though many remain orphaned by Aldrich's actions. Ogma has Benn overseeing everything with his usual military efficiency. Minerva has redirected her considerable empathic abilities to help the children process their trauma. She's particularly effective with the youngest ones, those who can't yet verbalise what was done to them."

Lyn's expression softened marginally as contemplated my words. Her fingertips, now tipped with the faintest suggestion of claws. "Ogma's reports are thorough but clinical. I appreciate your... more nuanced perspective."

As we approached the massive council chamber doors, ancient oak bound with metals not found in the mortal realm and inscribed with protective sigils that pulsed with ethereal light—I felt the weight of centuries pressing down upon us. The corridor itself seemed to constrict, the air growing thick with magical pressure that tested the resolve of those who sought entrance.

Lyn paused, her form shimmering like a heat mirage. In three heartbeats, her human appearance dissolved completely. Where the elegant businesswoman had stood now towered a magnificent dragon, scales shimmering in iridescent purples and violets, wings folded tightly against her serpentine body. Her transformation released a wave of ancient power that made the very foundations of the hall tremble.

With one taloned foreleg, she pushed open the immense doors that would have required four Watchers to budge. The ancient hinges groaned in protest as they swung inward, revealing the circular chamber beyond. Just as quickly as she had transformed, Lyn resumed her human form, the only evidence of her true nature now visible in the faint opalescent sheen of her skin and the vertical pupils that hadn't quite returned to normal.

"A necessary reminder of who they're dealing with," she murmured to me with a predator's smile.

We stepped through the doors and into the vaulted council chamber together. Above us, ribbed stone arches soared like the skeleton of some primeval beast, and flickering torches set the pale walls aglow, casting long shadows across the floor. Four figures sat in judgment at the far end of the hall, their tall ceremonial hoods pulled low, obscuring all but the sharp angles of their faces. Even at a distance, I could feel the weight of their attention an unspoken power humming in the cool air.

A cold dread settled in my stomach as we crossed the great mosaic of polished tiles underfoot. Each piece depicted a moment of cosmic birth—the forging of stars, the weaving of mortal souls, the first breath of dragons soaring above nascent realms. To walk upon such a tapestry was to tread upon the foundation of every world the Watchers cared for. Whatever crisis had summoned us here could not be small.

I glanced at Lyn's profile, her shoulders squared, her expression composed behind a mask of calm. I drew courage from her steadiness. "We stand ready to serve," I intoned, the traditional invocation feeling hollow in my throat as uncertainty coiled tighter in my chest. A Dragon Queen and I, summoned before the immortal Guardians of existence surely this augured calamity beyond any we had faced.

At our approach, the four figures inclined their heads. Penemue's voice rang out first, surprisingly warm and melodic, yet edged with ancient authority. She was said to have taught mortals to wield ink and quill, revealing to them the hidden language of the heavens. I dared to look fully at her then: her silver-threaded hair drifted over velvet robes, and her eyes glimmered with millennia of knowledge.

To her left sat Sariel, whose ethereal countenance reminded me of pale moonlight on still water. Legend credited him with unveiling the lunar cycles to early humanity. Baraqel lounged casually on a carved stone settee, long fingers drumming against his thigh he who had guided astrologers to chart the stars. And on the far right stood Armaros, tall as a forest sentinel, the Master of Enchantments, whose teachings bound magic to mortal will.

They gestured to a semicircle of plush, high-backed chairs woven with golden thread. One by one we seated ourselves, sinking into cushions that seemed alive, moulding to our forms. Tapestries on the walls depicted titanic battles: winged beasts clashing in crimson skies, armies of light against encroaching darkness. My heart hammered in my ears as I placed my hands on the armrests—honoured, humbled, yet wary of their inscrutable faces.

"Thank you for summoning us," I began, voice steady despite the tremor beneath. Lyn merely inclined her head, her gaze fixed on Penemue.

A hush fell over the chamber, the silence so profound I could hear the subtle crackle of the ethereal torches along the walls. Sariel leaned forward, moonlight pale fingers steepled beneath his chin. His voice, gentle as a lullaby yet weighted with ancient authority, broke the stillness.

"You must be curious why you have been called before us."

Lyn's hand twitched almost imperceptibly beside mine. Our eyes met in a fleeting exchange hers flashing with a dragon's wariness, mine tight with apprehension. We remained silent, a calculated response that acknowledged the Council's superior position while preserving our dignity.

Sariel's expression remained serene, but something shifted in his ageless eyes. "We have monitored your investigation with great interest," he continued, each word flowing like honey yet carrying an unmistakable venom. "much time has passed since the discovery of Aldriches betrayal and the experimental facilities. Yet those responsible remain free."

His gaze, silver as starlight and just as cold, settled on me with such intensity that I felt physically pinned to my seat. The air around me seemed to crystallise.

"Yes, Honoured Watcher," I managed, my voice steadier than I felt. "Progress has been methodical but slower than desired. The network is labyrinthine by design. We've mapped seventy percent of Aldrich's financial channels and identified eight potential locations that could lead to his current location."

Baraqel shifted in his ornate chair, the ancient wood creaking beneath him. Unlike Sariel's ethereal presence, Baraqel emanated raw power, his deep voice rumbling like distant thunder across a summer plain.

"We have intercepted disturbing reports of a new substance circulating among mortal society," he interjected, eyes flashing with celestial fire. "A compound that temporarily grants abilities beyond what the user can withstand. Our sources suggest a possible connection to your quarry."

I straightened, grateful for terrain I could navigate with confidence. "Your intelligence is accurate, Watcher Baraqel. We've documented seventeen definite cases so far. all have resulted in fatalities , all exhibiting the same crystalline residue in their neural pathways that we found in Aldriches laboratories. We're pursuing—»

"Yet you remain unable to determine who orchestrates this. we find it difficult to believe that Aldrich is the overall mastermind," Sariel cut in, his patience visibly thinning. "Perhaps more direct intervention is required. The Council could authorise measures that would—»

The massive doors exploded inward with such force that several ancient hinges shattered, fragments of metal older than human civilisation skittering across the mosaic floor. Arctic cold flooded the chamber, extinguishing half the torches and sending plumes of frost climbing up the stone columns.

Enlil stood at the threshold, his form nearly filling the doorway, radiating such primal power that the very air seemed to bow away from him. His eyes blazed like twin supernovas, and when he spoke, his voice resonated not just in my ears but through my entire body, rattling my bones and teeth.

"What is the meaning of this unauthorised tribunal?" he thundered, each syllable punctuated by a tremor that shook dust from the vaulted ceiling. "By whose authority do you summon representatives of the Dragon Conclave and the Agency like errant children?"

The temperature plummeted further as he advanced into the room, frost patterns blooming beneath each footstep. "These are emissaries of two of the most ancient and powerful factions in existence. I demand an explanation for this breach of protocol!"

Words abandoned me completely. I turned to Lyn and found her normally composed features frozen in an expression of genuine shock, her eyes wide, lips slightly parted. In all our years of partnership, I had never seen the Dragon Queen herself rendered speechless.

The Council members rose from their ornate chairs in unison, their ceremonial robes billowing around them like storm clouds. Sariel's silver eyes flashed with indignation, while Baraqel's massive frame tensed as if preparing for combat. Armaros remained perfectly still, only the slight narrowing of his ancient eyes betraying his displeasure.

"Enlil," Armaros's voice cut through the tension with deceptive softness, though I could detect the razor's edge beneath her words. "We meant no disrespect toward these representatives. we convened to discuss immediate actions regarding the breach. The situation grows more dire with each passing hour."

Enlil stood unwavering before them, his towering presence casting long shadows across the mosaic floor. Frost continued to spread from beneath his boots, crystallising in intricate patterns that crept toward the Council members. His face remained impassive, carved from stone, but power radiated from him in palpable waves that made the air shimmer.

"We will take no action beyond our mandate," he stated, each word falling like a gavel. "As you have sworn since the First Accord, we observe and record. Our influence can be no more than a guiding one. Have you forgotten your oaths?"

The accusation hung in the air like a physical thing. Sariel stepped forward, moonlight-pale hands emerging from his sleeves. "The balance shifts, Enlil. Surely you sense it. The old rules may no longer...»

A blinding flash of pure white light erupted between them, so intense it seared my retinas like molten silver. The sound that accompanied it wasn't quite thunder more like reality itself being torn apart at its cosmic seams and hastily stitched back together by some panicked celestial tailor. My ears popped painfully as pressure waves rippled through the chamber. When my vision finally cleared, iridescent spots still dancing across my field of view like drunken fireflies, I found the grand hall nearly empty. The ornate chairs where the Council members had sat moments before were vacant, cushions still bearing their impressions. Only Enlil, his towering frame now relaxed but vigilant, Penemue with her ancient eyes full of unspoken knowledge, Lyn with her dragon-queen composure slightly fractured, and I remained. The other Council members had vanished as completely as if they'd been erased from existence itself.

Enlil exhaled slowly a sound like mountain winds through ancient pines—and turned to face Penemue. His face, previously a mask of righteous fury, now settled into diplomatic neutrality. "Thank you for contacting me about this impromptu visit," he said in a measured tone that nonetheless carried the weight of millennia. "I will arrange a proper briefing with the entire council when relevant information is attained. Until then, I will personally keep you informed of any suspicious activity that warrants attention."

Penemue nodded respectfully, her movements fluid and precise as flowing water. She adjusted the folds of her shimmering robe before addressing Lyn and me with a warm smile that didn't quite reach her calculating eyes. "It was my pleasure to see you both today," she said graciously, her voice melodic yet somehow ancient. "But if you don't need me further, I'm sure I have other matters that require my immediate attention." With a graceful turn that left a faint trail of golden light in her wake, she simply vanished into thin air, the space where she stood collapsing in on itself with a subtle pop.

The atmosphere within the grand hall shifted once again after Penemue's abrupt departure. The temperature, which had been frigid during Enlil's entrance, now normalised, yet something intangible had changed. The air grew heavy with unspoken questions and mounting tension, as if a storm cloud had descended upon us, pregnant with lightning yet to strike. The mosaic floor, still frosted in places from Enlil's dramatic entrance, began to thaw, tiny rivulets of water tracing the intricate patterns beneath our feet.

I cleared my throat, the sound echoing unnaturally in the vast space. "Enlil," I began, measuring each word carefully, "would someone be kind enough to inform me why Lyn and I have been summoned here and why it felt distinctly like we were being interrogated rather than consulted?" I asked, struggling to maintain my diplomatic composure while posing the question as politely as possible. My hands, I noticed, were trembling slightly, and I clasped them behind my back. We were entirely at the mercy of Enlil now, our only potential source of information on what had just transpired.

Enlil's ancient eyes, eyes that had witnessed the rise and fall of civilisations studied me for a long moment before he replied. "Yes, I apologise for the confusion and the rather dramatic proceedings," he said calmly, though there was a tension in his shoulders that hadn't been there before. "I will explain everything in detail, but perhaps we could have this discussion back at the agency? It may be more comfortable for you both there, and I suspect these walls, though ancient, may have developed ears in recent times."

In tense silence, we walked back through the cavernous corridors of the Council chambers, our footsteps echoing against stone that predated human memory. The reception area, with its impossible geometry and shifting dimensions, seemed to contract around us as Enlil raised his hand and opened a gate directly to my office a swirling vortex of blue-white energy that hummed with power. Stepping through the portal felt like walking through a wall of static electricity, every hair on my body standing on end. When I emerged on the other side, a profound sense of familiarity and relief washed over me upon entering my own space, with its familiar scents of leather-bound books and coffee. The tension in my shoulders eased slightly as I gestured for Lyn and Enlil to take seats at the small mahogany coffee table in front of my desk, its surface reflecting the afternoon light streaming through the windows.

"Before we begin," I said at last, breaking the heavy silence, "let me have some refreshments brought in. A warm cup of tea might help steady our nerves." I turned to Lyn, offering a tentative smile, silently urging her to agree. In truth, I needed those few extra moments to pull myself together—to organise my thoughts and sketch out a plan of attack.

"That sounds perfect, Alex. Thank you," Lyn replied, her tension easing ever so slightly as a grateful smile curved her lips. "I could use a moment to collect my thoughts as well."

"Of course," I murmured, picking up the intercom handset on my desk. I pressed the button and addressed my assistant in clipped tones. "This is Alex. Send someone in with tea—black with a hint of bergamot—and biscuits. I'm not available for anything else right now. I have two guests with me and refreshments are urgent."

A crackle of static preceded my assistant's calm reply. "Understood, sir. Someone will be there shortly."I replaced the handset and rose from behind the mahogany desk, my legs unsteady beneath me. The weight of what had transpired at the Council chambers still pressed against my chest like a physical burden. As I unlocked the door, the faint click seemed impossibly loud in the quiet room. I retreated to one of the overstuffed armchairs near the window, sinking into its familiar embrace as afternoon sunlight cast long shadows across the Persian rug.

The leather creaked beneath me as I leaned forward, elbows on knees. I cleared my throat and squared my shoulders, trying to project a confidence I didn't feel. Turning to Enlil, whose ancient presence seemed to fill the room despite his perfectly still posture, I forced my voice to sound casual. "All right, then. Let's cut to the chase. What exactly happened out there? I've never seen the Council members behave like that, a"

Enlil's obsidian eyes met mine, centuries of wisdom and worry evident in their depths. A solemn gravity settled in his posture as he placed his palms flat against his knees. He inhaled slowly, the sound like wind through ancient caverns, as though bracing himself to deliver news he'd rather not share. "There has been an attempted breach of the realm gates," he said finally, his tone low and weighted with concern that made the hairs on my arms stand on end.

Just then came a polite knock, mercifully interrupting the moment before panic could fully take hold. My assistant's voice drifted in from the hallway, professional and measured. "Sir, I have your refreshments. The bergamot tea you requested and a selection of biscuits."

"Please leave them on the side table," I replied, softening my tone as much as I could while my mind raced with implications of Enlil's revelation. I gestured vaguely toward the antique table by the bookcase. "I'll be occupied for the rest of the day. You should take the afternoon off and perhaps tomorrow as well."

My assistant bowed slightly, set down a silver tray with steaming tea cups, biscuit tin, and a small plate of sandwiches, then withdrew, closing the door quietly behind her. The rich aroma of bergamot tea drifted through the room, but it did little to calm my racing heart.

Lyn was already leaning forward. Her steel grey eyes were fixed on Enlil, unwavering and expectant. The tense set of her jaw told me she'd heard enough preamble. "Please," she said crisply, "enlighten us. What kind of breach are we dealing with, and why have we been summoned here for questioning?"

Enlil exchanged a glance with me before settling back against the leather sofa. His fingers drummed against the armrest. "some on the Council believes this attack is connected to your ongoing investigation," he said, the cool veneer of professionalism slipping to reveal barely contained anger. "They're deeply dissatisfied with the pace of your progress in identifying those responsible for the initial disturbances. They suspect you may have overlooked critical evidence, evidence that could have prevented today's breach."

Silence fell for a heartbeat before Lyn spoke again, voice as resolute as ever. "Then tell us what you know. We need every detail when it happened, how the intruders gained access, and who they were targeting."

My own frustration boiled over, heat rising from my collar to my temples. I slammed my palm against the mahogany desk, rattling the untouched teacups. "What do you mean 'unsatisfied'? We have been working tirelessly day and night," I retorted, my voice rising with each word. "We've shut down seven facilities linked to these despicable experiments in the last month alone. We've rescued countless victims most of who are children, Enlil and we're establishing a comprehensive rehabilitation centre with round-the-clock magical and psychological support."

I paced to the window, then whirled back. "Jessica is currently deep undercover, risking her life daily to infiltrate this underground network. She's gathering leads on the new compound the one that's allowing ordinary humans to channel elemental magic. The same compound that's driving its users insane then killing them" My hands trembled as I leaned forward . "And yet, you're still not satisfied with our progress? You are the Watchers Council, supposedly the highest authority among all realms. If you truly find our efforts lacking, then perhaps it's time for you to actually take action instead of just sitting back and criticising from your ivory tower!"

My final words echoed against the soundproof walls of my office. Lyn sat frozen, her mouth slightly agape in shock, fingers tightening around the armrests of her chair. Enlil remained perfectly still, only the slight narrowing of his ancient eyes betraying any reaction.

After what felt like an eternity, Enlil raised a weathered hand. "You are right under the circumstances," he finally spoke, his tone grave, each word measured carefully. "You and your team are doing everything within your considerable power. The Council's dissatisfaction stems not from your efforts, but from their own growing fear." He paused, studying me with eyes that had witnessed millennia. "I am, in fact, deeply impressed you have uncovered as much as you have, given what we now understand."

My heart hammered against my ribs as I waited for him to continue. When he spoke again, his voice had dropped to barely above a whisper.

"As to your statement about the Council's involvement, we have tried to track those responsible, but something is actively blocking us," he admitted, the reluctance in his voice unmistakable. "We can still observe certain events and interfere as we always have in matters of cosmic balance. But something or someone is creating blind spots in our vision, specifically regarding anything connected to your agency's investigation."

Enlil's shoulders sagged beneath an invisible weight, the ancient lines of his face deepening. His obsidian eyes, which had witnessed the rise and fall of civilisations, now clouded with something I'd never seen in them before: uncertainty.

"We don't know how long this has been happening," he admitted, his voice barely above a whisper. "Months, perhaps years. The attempted breach of the realm gates three days ago was the first concrete evidence that our powers have been compromised. The wards we've maintained for millennia, wards that should be impenetrable showed signs of fracturing." He paused, fingers trembling slightly against the leather armrest. "It would seem that we have become lax in our duty to stand as guardians of the realms, and now we are paying the price for our complacency."

I exchanged a glance with Lyn, whose steel-grey eyes had narrowed to slits. The implications were staggering. The Watchers Council beings whose very existence predated written history were vulnerable. what did that mean for the delicate balance between realms?

"So what are the watchers planning now?" I asked, leaning forward in my chair, the untouched tea cooling beside me.

"As of this morning, the watchers are on complete lockdown," Enlil revealed, his voice heavy with concern. "All inter realm travel has been restricted to emergency situations only. They've recalled every available watcher from field assignments across all the realms. They are, as you say, circling the proverbial wagons, trying to assess the situation and formulate a response. The point of your summons today wasn't merely to inform you, it was an attempt by certain council members to place blame for their sudden seclusion."

"Why are you hiding away instead of mobilising those of us who could help?" I demanded, exasperation seeping into my voice. "And what exactly was this 'attempted breach' you speak of? What were they after?"

Enlil's gaze shifted to the window, where afternoon light cast long shadows across the Persian rug. When he turned back, his expression had hardened with resolve.

"It appears that someone has been systematically testing our defences, probing for weaknesses," he responded gravely. "Three days ago, they managed to penetrate the outer wards protecting our libraries and the dragon's archives." He nodded respectfully toward Lyn. "As you both know, this should be impossible. The combined magic of dragons and watchers has sealed those archives for ten thousand years. But somehow, they managed to create a hairline fracture in our wards, allowing them access to a specific tome the Grimoire of Ashur, filled with ancient spells and forbidden rituals from the Blood Wars."

My heart raced at the mention of that particular grimoire. Even I, with my limited knowledge of watcher history, knew of its reputation. The Blood Wars had nearly destroyed all nine realms before the watchers and dragons had formed their alliance to end the conflict.

"Do any of you know what specific secrets lie within this tome?" I asked, unable to keep the tremor from my voice. "What could they possibly be looking for that would be worth risking the wrath of both watchers and dragons?"

"I cannot say for certain," Enlil replied, voice trembling slightly. "But it has us on edge, knowing that someone could potentially wield such dangerous power." The atmosphere in the room grew heavier as we all realised the gravity of the situation and the potential consequences if this knowledge fell into the wrong hands.

CHAPTER 16

Brutal Encounters

Jessica*

My fifth fight had just ended, leaving my body a canvas of purple bruises and crimson streaks. The thing I'd faced in the arena, I hesitate to call it human, had moved with unnatural speed. Its pitch-black eyes had reflected nothing, not even the harsh overhead lights, and when it snarled, rows of razor-sharp teeth gleamed like broken glass. Even now, safely in the car, I could still feel its hot breath against my face.

My knuckles throbbed with each heartbeat, and my limbs felt like they were filled with cement as we drove away from the underground arena. I collapsed into the back seat, resting my head on Abigail's lap, wincing as my ribs protested.

"Abby," I whispered, tasting copper on my split lip, "are we even making progress, or am I just getting my ass kicked for no reason?" The smell of sweat and adrenaline clung to my skin, mixing with the metallic scent of blood and the leather upholstery. Through the tinted windows, I could still hear the distant roar of the crowd, their cheers and jeers fading as we pulled away.

For a moment, all I could see were disjointed flashes a blur of movement, the ceiling lights spinning above me, the creature's fist coming toward my face too fast to dodge. But now, in this brief moment of respite, reality crashed back in. Every bruise, every cut, every strained muscle announced itself with perfect clarity.

Abigail's fingers gently combed through my sweat-dampened hair, her touch cool against my scalp. The repetitive motion gradually eased the tension from my shoulders and slowed my racing heart. When she spoke, her voice was soft but unwavering, like steel wrapped in silk.

"Jess, what you're enduring is a sacrifice that's giving us invaluable intelligence," she said, her eyes meeting mine with fierce intensity. "I know it's far more brutal than any of us anticipated, but we're on the brink of shutting down this entire operation. Their network, their suppliers, everything." She paused, her fingers still moving through my hair. "How about we give you a break from training tomorrow morning? Let your body recover a bit."

A low, disapproving grumble emanated from the front of the car. Paul sat rigidly in the driver's seat, his knuckles white on the steering wheel, while Walker occupied the passenger seat, his broad shoulders tense beneath his jacket.My eyes flicked between them in the rearview mirror, catching fragments of their expressions— Paul's tightened jaw, Walker's furrowed brow. The tension in the car thickened like smoke as I waited for their response, knowing my battered body's fate rested entirely in their hands.

To my surprise, it was Paul who broke the silence, his voice clipped with barely concealed irritation. "Do you really think it's wise to give her a break from training? We can't afford any setbacks. Not with the way Kane is putting her in the arena at every available opportunity." His fingers drummed against the steering wheel, a nervous habit I'd noticed whenever he felt his control slipping.

Walker shifted in his seat, the leather creaking beneath his substantial frame. He turned just enough for me to see the scar that bisected his left eyebrow. "Paul," he said, his tone measured but firm, "how we train Jess is our decision to make. We don't need your input on this matter." His eyes, the colour of weathered steel, met mine briefly in the mirror. "And as for the fights, perhaps it's time we allow Jess to win a few matches. It may garner more interest if she's not constantly defeated. before the crowds get restless. they want a hero to root for, not just another victim."

A surge of gratitude washed over me, warm and unexpected. Walker had started out as just my trainer—a gruff, no-nonsense ex-military type who barked orders and pushed my limits without mercy. But after the disaster that was my first match, when I'd been carried out of the arena barely conscious with shattered ribs, a dislocated shoulder and a face that was reminiscent of ground beef. something in him had changed. He'd showed up on my doorstep that night, his weathered face etched with what I later recognised as guilt, he'd asked Abigail about the true nature of our operation, and by the time he left, he'd become an integral member of the investigation. Now, four brutal fights later, he wasn't just training me to survive he was actively protecting me, standing as a human shield between me and those who saw me only as a tool to be used and discarded once broken.

My eyelids grew heavy, each blink lasting longer than the one before. The exhaustion from the fight was catching up to me, my adrenaline finally depleting and leaving nothing but bone-deep weariness in its wake. I knew sleep would soon claim my body, dragging me under like a riptide. "That would be nice," I mumbled, my voice slurring as I fought against the pull. Every muscle in my body ached, begging for rest so they could begin repairing the damage I'd taken in the arena. The bruise blooming across my ribs pulsed with each laboured breath.

"Do you really think it's wise for me to start kicking some booty?" I managed to ask, my attempt at humour undermined by the way my words ran together. I could feel myself losing the battle to stay conscious, the heaviness in my limbs becoming impossible to resist.

A low, throaty chuckle rumbled from the driver's seat, followed by Walker's gravelly response. "Yeah, kid, I really do." His voice softened, a rare occurrence that I might have appreciated more if I weren't halfway to unconsciousness. "But for now, get some sleep. We'll discuss strategy tomorrow when you can actually remember the conversation."

"I wish we could give her a few days off to fully recover," Paul chimed in from the driver's seat, surprising me again with what sounded like genuine concern. His knuckles whitened as he gripped the wheel tighter. "But Kane won't listen. He just wants to keep throwing her into more matches, even though she's already bringing in more money than he knows what to do with." There was a hint of something in his tone disgust or jealousy, perhaps both that made my skin crawl. The car hit a pothole, jostling my bruised ribs, and I bit back a whimper.

As the words left Paul's mouth, they sliced through me like a knife. My stomach clenched painfully. Kane was profiting from my suffering—my blood and broken bones were just dollar signs to him. The bitter taste of bile rose in my throat, and I swallowed hard, trying not to vomit all over Abby's designer jeans. I could feel myself stiffen in her lap, muscles coiling tight despite the screaming protest from my injuries.

Abby sensed the change immediately. She pulled me closer, one arm sliding protectively around my shoulders while her other hand continued its gentle rhythm through my hair. The familiar scent of her perfume vanilla with hints of something spicy I could never identify wrapped around me like a security blanket.

"Don't worry, Jess," she whispered fiercely into my ear, her breath warm against my skin. "When this is all over, I'll make sure he knows what a real monster is capable of." Her voice dropped even lower, meant only for me. "And I'll enjoy every second of teaching him."

A chill ran down my spine that had nothing to do with pain or fear for myself. I'd seen Abigail in action before a memory I tried to suppress but couldn't quite manage to forget. During a warehouse assault, she'd moved with calculated precision, her eyes cold and detached as she systematically dismantled men twice her size who'd made the fatal mistake of underestimating her. Anyone who stood in her way regretted it. She'd stained the concrete with the blood of her enemies, methodical and terrifying. And in that moment, hearing her whisper her promise of retribution against Kane, I believed her with every fibre of my being.

The car jostled as it traveled down the dark, winding road, each pothole sending a fresh jolt of pain through my battered ribs. My left side felt like it was on fire, each breath a negotiation between necessity and agony. Streetlights flashed by in hypnotic succession, casting strange shadows across our faces illuminating Paul's tight jaw one moment, Walker's scarred profile the next, then plunging us back into darkness. The rhythmic pattern made me dizzy, or maybe that was the concussion. But Abby's promise lingered in the air between us, her words making me both comforted and terrified. Despite my fear or perhaps because of it a small, broken laugh escaped my lips.

"What's so funny?" Walker asked, his voice rumbling from the front seat.

"Just thinking about karma," I mumbled, my split lip making the words come out slurred. "Kane's going to get his eventually."

Abby's fingers continued their gentle rhythm through my hair, but I felt her other hand tighten protectively around my shoulder. The familiar scent of her perfume vanilla with that mysterious spicy undertone wrapped around me like armour.

As exhaustion finally claimed its victory, I surrendered to Abby's embrace. The rhythmic hum of the engine merged with the steady beat of her heart against my ear, the gentle swaying of the car becoming a lullaby that pulled me under. My last conscious thought was that I'd never felt safer than I did right now, broken and bloodied in the arms of a woman who could kill without blinking a strange comfort in a world that had stopped making sense long ago.

CHAPTER 17

Unleashing the Beast

Abigail*

I froze, my mind reeling with a mixture of confusion and amazement. The confession had tumbled from my lips without warning—that I would reveal my monstrous nature to Kane, the very man who had forced Jess into the brutal arena fights. My hands trembled slightly as I waited for her reaction, certain she would recoil with fear or lash out in anger. Instead, she laughed—a sound so pure and melodic that it seemed to pierce straight through my chest. The laugh started softly, then cascaded into something bright and uninhibited, echoing in the small space between us like wind chimes in a gentle breeze. It was the kind of laugh that belonged to someone unburdened by the horrors she had witnessed, someone who could still find lightness in the darkest corners of existence. This remarkable girl, with her scarred knuckles and fierce eyes, somehow remained unafraid of the shadows that lurked beneath my skin. As if sensing the storm of emotions raging within me, she shifted position, nestling her head more securely against my lap. The weight of her trust pressed against me as she drifted toward sleep. Her breathing changed, transforming from the measured rhythm of consciousness to something deeper and more primal. It wasn't the gentle exhale most people produced in slumber, but rather a rumbling snore that reminded me of a diesel engine struggling uphill—powerful, persistent, and strangely endearing. A small trail of drool escaped her slightly parted lips, glistening in the dim light as it traced a path along her chin. That tiny detail, that imperfection somehow made her fierce demeanour all the more precious to me. In sleep, the warrior who had faced down death countless times looked almost childlike, vulnerable in a way she would never allow herself to be while awake.

The heavy silence that had enveloped us during our drive melted away in her presence. This girl who saw beyond my darkness brought out something in me I thought long dead, something almost human. When we arrived at the safe house, I gathered her sleeping form into my arms, cradling her head against my shoulder to keep her from waking. Her body felt impossibly light against mine, as if the burdens she carried in consciousness had physically lifted from her in sleep.

Paul drove away without a backward glance, tires crunching on gravel. Walker stood waiting at the entrance, his weathered face betraying nothing as I carried Jess past him. The familiar scent of the safe house a strange comfort in our chaotic lives.

"Walker," I said quietly, pausing at the foot of the stairs, "tell Nixie and Lunette we made it back. No incidents." The unspoken rule hung between us. once our bedroom door closed, we weren't to be disturbed. Jess's night terrors were for me alone to witness and soothe.

I climbed the stairs carefully, each wooden step creaking slightly beneath our combined weight. The anticipation of our private sanctuary built with every step the one place where we could simply exist without pretence or danger. My arms tightened around her protectively as I reached the landing.

Inside our room, I nudged the door closed with my foot and laid Jess on our bed with deliberate gentleness. The moonlight filtering through half-drawn curtains cast blue-silver patterns across her skin, illuminating the violent constellation of bruises blooming along her collarbone and shoulders. Each mark told its own story, the purplish-black ones from today's fight, the faded ghosts of battles weeks past. With reverent hands, I examined each wound: the split knuckles where skin had given way against someone's teeth, the defensive cuts on her forearms from deflecting an attack, the angry red welt forming at her temple where she'd barely dodged a killing blow.

I retrieved the medical kit from beneath our bed the one I kept meticulously stocked with supplies . The antiseptic stung my nostrils as I uncapped it, knowing it would hurt her even in sleep. Despite understanding her supernatural healing abilities made my ministrations largely unnecessary, I couldn't help but try to ease her pain, to participate in her recovery in some tangible way.

My fingers worked with practiced precision, cleaning each abrasion with alcohol soaked cotton, applying antibiotic ointment to the deeper cuts, wrapping gauze around her knuckles with just enough pressure to protect without restricting movement. I'd become an expert in battlefield medicine without ever stepping onto a battlefield myself. The irony wasn't lost on me.

With a bowl of cool water and a soft cloth, I worked methodically to clean the dried blood from her hairline, the rust coloured flakes dissolving into pink swirls in the water. I wiped away dirt and debris from her wounds, watching her face for any sign of discomfort. Even unconscious, her features would sometimes tighten against pain, and I'd pause, waiting for her to settle before continuing.

As I carefully changed her into fresh clothes the oversized t-shirt she preferred to sleep in, soft from countless washings my heart ached at the sight of her broken form. The scars that mapped her body, some surgical and precise, others jagged and cruel, testified to a life of violence she never chose. It wasn't fair that someone who could laugh so freely, who could still find joy in small moments, had to suffer like this.

When the ritual was complete, I settled her under the warm covers of our bed. Without hesitation, I slid in beside her and wrapped my arms around her petite frame, careful to avoid pressing against her fresh injuries. Her body instinctively curled into mine, seeking the comfort and safety that had become our shared language. Her breath, warm against my collarbone, steadied into the familiar rhythm that told me she had fallen into deeper sleep.

Despite knowing that another night filled with nightmares awaited her—that soon her peaceful expression would contort with remembered pain in this moment, we were together in our sanctuary. I pressed my lips to her forehead, tasting the salt of her skin, breathing in the scent that was uniquely hers beneath the antiseptic and soap.

And as I held her close, my love for her overflowed and filled the room with a warmth that seemed almost tangible, like golden light spilling from my chest to envelop us both. I prayed to gods I didn't believe in that somehow, my presence and affection would bring relief to her troubled mind and offer a glimmer of light in the darkness of her pain. That tonight, just once, she might sleep without screaming.

The peace lasted exactly seventeen minutes. I know because I watched each minute tick by on the bedside clock, counting them like precious gems. Then her breathing changed—a subtle hitch, a quickening rhythm that I'd learned to recognise as the prelude to her nightmares. Her pale, porcelain face drained of what little colour it had, leaving behind a ghostly pallor that made the bruises stand out like violent constellations against a blank sky. The muscles in her jaw tightened first, followed by her shoulders, her body preparing for a battle that existed only in her mind.

"Jess," I whispered, brushing damp strands of hair from her forehead. "You're safe. I'm here."

Her once strong and resilient body now trembled beneath my touch, fine tremors escalating into violent shudders that shook the entire bed frame. Each whimper that escaped her lips weakened my resolve. I held her tighter, one arm cradling her head against my chest, the other wrapped protectively around her waist, careful to avoid the worst of her injuries. The heat of her skin burned through the thin cotton of her shirt, fever-hot against my palms.

"Please," I murmured against her temple, "come back to me."

But it was a fight I could not win for her. The nightmare had its claws in deep tonight. Her whimpers transformed into guttural sounds of terror, then into full-throated screams that tore through the quiet sanctuary of our room. Her eyes flew open, but I knew she wasn't seeing me she was seeing Jeremiah, the man who had broken her body but never her spirit, the monster who haunted her dreams with methodical cruelty.

"He's not here," I said firmly, holding her thrashing body as gently as I could. "Feel my hands, Jess. Feel where you are now."

She fought against me with surprising strength for someone so injured, her nails drawing blood from my forearms as she clawed to escape the phantom tormentor. I absorbed each blow without flinching, understanding that in her mind, she was fighting for her life. Tears streamed down her face, cutting clean trails through the remaining dirt I hadn't managed to wash away. My own tears fell freely, blending with hers where our cheeks pressed together.

"I've got you," I repeated, a mantra against the darkness. "I've got you. I've got you."

Gradually, agonisingly, recognition dawned in her wild eyes. The tension in her body released in waves, like a tide receding from shore. Her breathing slowed, hitching occasionally with residual sobs. She collapsed against me, boneless with exhaustion, her face pressed into the hollow of my throat.

"I'm sorry," she whispered, her voice raw from screaming.

I shook my head, pressing my lips to her damp forehead. "Never apologise for surviving."

We lay tangled together in the aftermath, the sheets twisted and damp with sweat and tears. I stroked her back in slow, rhythmic circles, counting her breaths as they evened out. This was our ritual, as familiar as the medical kit beneath the bed, as necessary as the locks on our doors. Two broken souls seeking solace in each other's embrace, piecing together something resembling peace from the fragments of our shattered lives.

"Tell me about the ocean," she mumbled against my skin, a request she made often after the worst of her nightmares.

So I described the Pacific at sunset, the way the water turned to liquid gold, how the salt spray felt against your face, the rhythm of waves that could lull you to sleep if you listened long enough. I painted pictures with words until her breathing deepened once more, until the furrow between her brows smoothed out, until sleep reclaimed her gentler this time, I hoped.

CHAPTER 18

Escaping Darkness

Jessica*

Waking up early as usual, I escaped from a nightmare that left me gasping for air and tangled in my sweat-soaked sheets. The cave walls had been closing in again, Jeremiah's cold laughter echoing off the damp stone as he tightened the restraints around my wrists until they cut into my skin. Even though I'd been rescued weeks ago, my subconscious refused to acknowledge my freedom. As my eyes adjusted to the dim golden light of dawn filtering through the thin curtains, I turned to find Abby sitting beside my bed, her familiar face wearing that signature toothy grin that somehow always made things better.

"Did you sleep well?" she asked softly, handing me a steaming cup of coffee in my favourite chipped blue mug. The rich aroma helped ground me in reality. She acted as though it was completely normal for me to wake up screaming and thrashing like a maniac, though the dark circles under her eyes suggested she'd been up most of the night watching over me.

"I slept as well as can be expected," I replied, my voice hoarse and strained from all the shouting. Wincing as I shifted position, I glanced down at my body and noticed fresh white bandages wrapped around my forearms and torso. "Did you bandage me up again?"

"Of course I did," Abby said, tucking a strand of her copper hair behind her ear. "If I left it to someone else, they would have just left you on the bed in your dirty clothes without treating your injuries."

Her tone was nonchalant, but the gentle way her fingers lingered on my bandaged wrist betrayed her concern.

I squirmed and wriggled, trying to break free from the soft, warm confines of my blanket that now felt suffocating. As I emerged, tangles of dark hair clung to my face and shoulders, damp with night sweat. My muscles ached with each movement, a painful reminder of yesterday's training session.

"I have to take a shower," I declared firmly, pushing myself upright despite the protest of sore muscles. My fingertips brushed against the edge of a bandage as I gestured toward the bathroom. "And then I want to catch up with everyone and see how our investigation is progressing." The case files were scattered across my desk in the corner, manila folders splayed open with photographs and notes spilling out, untouched since before the fight last night .

Abby gave me a stern look, her expression hardening as she crossed her arms over her chest. Her eyes, usually warm and playful like amber in sunlight, now reflected nothing but concern for my well-being.

"Alright," she said after a measured pause, "but remember today is meant for rest, not training. That means giving your mind a break from the investigation as well." She uncrossed her arms to tap the side of her head meaningfully. "It's probably taking a toll on both your mental and physical health. Those nightmares aren't coming from nowhere, Jess. So just get updates and then take some time for yourself. Maybe we could watch that terrible sci-fi movie you've been talking about."

I recognised the tone it meant No room for argument, just Abby knowing what was best before I did.

"Got it, boss. I'll be quick in the shower and meet you in the kitchen shortly." My words held a hint of playfulness, but deep down I knew she was right. Rest was just as important as action, and I needed to take care of myself if we were going to solve this case together. The last thing the team needed was me collapsing during a crucial moment.

Gathering my belongings hastily, clean clothes from the top drawer where I kept my softest t-shirts, the lavender soap Abby had given me last week saying it "complemented my natural scent," and a fresh towel from the neatly folded stack by the door I made a swift escape before she could add any more conditions to my day of supposed "rest." The thin cotton clothes I'd slept in clung uncomfortably to my sweat-dampened skin, the fabric catching on the edges of my bandages with every movement, sending tiny jolts of pain through my wounded body as I shuffled down the hallway. Once safely inside the bathroom with the door locked behind me, I finally had a moment to myself. I peeled off the damp clothes and took my first proper look in the full-length mirror for what felt like ages. The bruises and cuts from last night's fight had mostly healed already, leaving behind a mottled canvas of yellow and greenish hues across my ribs and shoulders where purple-black contusions should have still dominated. The deep gash above my collarbone that should have required at least twelve stitches and weeks to heal was now just an angry red line, already scabbed over and beginning to fade at the edges. I traced it with my fingertip, wincing not from pain, but from the absence of it. My wounds were healing at an alarmingly rapid pace twice, maybe three times faster than normal for me but strangely, that wasn't what was causing me the most concern.

It was the fact that I was getting stronger and faster with each passing day. Yesterday, during training, I'd managed to flip Walker over my shoulder all six foot four, two hundred plus pounds of him with barely any effort. The week before, I couldn't have done it with a lever and a prayer. Abigail and Walker's training should have been yielding small improvements, but instead, I found myself surpassing their expectations at an alarming rate. Last week, I'd completed the obstacle course in half the time of my previous record, leaving both of them staring at their stopwatches in disbelief.

Frustration gnawed at me as I realised I had to hold back more than ever during my fights. When sparring with Abby yesterday, I'd pulled a punch at the last second, sensing that my full force might have shattered her jaw rather than just bruised it. Even my body was changing muscles more defined, waist leaner, shoulders broader transformations that should have taken months of dedicated training appearing in mere weeks.

Glancing at my reflection in the mirror, I barely recognised the person staring back at me. The Jessica from before the cave had been athletic but soft around the edges. This new version looked dangerous, honed like a weapon. I flexed experimentally, watching unfamiliar muscles ripple beneath my skin.

Shaking off the momentary daze, I reminded myself that this was not the time to admire my own transformation. Whatever was happening to me wasn't natural, and that meant it couldn't be good. I turned on the shower, cranking the heat until steam billowed around me, and stepped under the scalding spray.

The water pounded against my skin, washing away the sweat and fear from the night before. I closed my eyes and let my body finally relax as the gentle pressure massaged my tense muscles. The warm droplets cascaded over me like tiny fingers, soothing away the constant ache and exhaustion that came with being in the arena. My mind wandered to Abby her unwavering support and love were what kept me going in this dark world. Without her, I don't know how I would survive the abuse and torture I endured, or the haunting memories of my time spent in the cave.

As I basked in the warmth of the shower, steam rose up around me, swirling and dancing like ghosts. The sound of water hitting tile echoed off the walls, creating a comforting rhythm that almost drowned out my racing thoughts about my changing body and abilities. After what felt like an eternity lost in contemplation, I slowly became aware that the once-scalding water had turned tepid, then cold. I reluctantly turned off the faucet, shivering as the cool air hit my wet skin. I quickly dried off, wincing as the towel caught on half-healed wounds, then dressed in the soft clothes I'd brought before heading to the kitchen.

The delightful aroma of freshly brewed coffee lingered in the cozy room, mingling with the comforting scent of fresh cinnamon rolls that Nixie must have baked this morning. we recently discovered she always stress-baked when worried . I took a seat at the cluttered counter, pushing aside a stack of manila folders that had migrated from my desk. My heart filled with unexpected gratitude for these individuals who had become more than just colleagues or friends, they were becoming family, the people who knew what I was dealing with and stayed anyway.

Walker lurked in the corner of the kitchen, his usual scowl deepened by exhaustion, sharp eyes alternating between watching the door and glaring at Argus the cat, who had somehow managed to shed an impressive amount of orange fur on his black tactical pants. The massive man looked comically uncomfortable perched on our smallest kitchen stool, his broad shoulders hunched forward as if trying to make himself smaller in the domestic space.

"Good morning, everyone," I greeted, my voice still rough from sleep and screaming nightmares.

Abigail slid a large mug of coffee towards me without a word, her warm brown eyes radiating concern beneath her practiced calm. The mug was my favourite chipped blue one and the coffee was prepared exactly how I liked it,

"Thank's, Abby. You're always so thoughtful," I said sincerely, noticing a faint blush creeping up her cheeks as she turned away to fuss with something on the counter.

"Walker, what brings you here so early?" I asked, turning to our gruff friend whose massive frame seemed to shrink the kitchen. His presence before noon usually meant trouble a new body, a fresh lead, or another paranormal crisis that couldn't wait. "Is there a new development in the case?"

Walker's eyes, bloodshot from what I suspected was another sleepless night, fixed on me with unusual intensity. "Nothing concrete," he rumbled, his voice like gravel being crushed underfoot. "Just figured since Abby's giving you a day off from training, we could compare notes. See if anything new shook loose overnight."

I nodded, wrapping my hands around the warm mug as I turned to address everyone gathered in our kitchen Walker hunched uncomfortably on the stool, Abby leaning against the counter, and Nixie and Lunette hovering near the doorway. "Has anyone managed to uncover anything about the drug? Distribution networks, low level dealers, suppliers? Even rumours at this point would be helpful." The tension in the air thickened like smoke, making it hard to breathe as I waited for someone to speak.

My gaze moved expectantly between Walker and Abby, our usual sources of intelligence. They'd been working their contacts for weeks now abby through her police connections and Walker through his network of fighters and trainers. But instead of the confident reports I'd grown accustomed to, they exchanged a look that sent a chill down my spine. Walker's jaw tightened. Abby suddenly became fascinated with the floor tiles.

It was Nixie who broke the silence, her voice so soft I had to lean forward to hear her. Beside her, Lunette shifted nervously from foot to foot, both of them wearing identical expressions of mingled guilt and apprehension.

"We've been... gathering information," Lunette finally stuttered, her gaze darting everywhere but at me. Her fingers twisted the silver rings she always wore, a nervous habit I'd noticed before. "Talking to travellers and settlers from various realms. People who wouldn't speak to humans or even to Walker's contacts." She swallowed hard before continuing. "And we've heard a lot of talk about a new drug that's been circulating. Something different. Something dangerous, even to paranormals."

My mind reeled at this unexpected revelation. I gripped my coffee mug tighter, the warmth seeping into my palms as I tried to process what I was hearing. The investigation had been at a standstill for weeks, and now this bombshell.

Before I could voice my thoughts, Nixie interjected, her delicate features tightening with concern. "Jess, please don't think we've been lurking in dark alleys or putting ourselves in unnecessary danger. We've been careful, methodical."

"How exactly did you get this information?" I asked, unable to keep the edge from my voice. Walker shifted on his stool, his massive frame tensing at my tone.

Nixie exchanged a glance with Lunette before continuing. "Do you have any knowledge about the drug trade in other realms?"

I paused, realising I had never really considered it before. "No, not really. Why is that relevant?"

"Because it's fundamentally different," Nixie explained, her voice gaining confidence. "In most paranormal realms, drugs aren't regulated like they are here because they don't need to be. Our bodies process substances differently—toxins that would kill humans might give a fae a mild buzz for an hour, or make a shifter's fur change colour temporarily."

Lunette nodded emphatically, her silver rings catching the light as she gestured. "Most recreational substances or medicines don't affect paranormal physiologies the way they do humans. Our metabolisms process toxins differently what might kill a human passes through our systems in hours. My cousin once drank an entire bottle of nightshade extract on a dare and just had hiccups that made flowers bloom from her ears for a day."

"And in the rare case something does go wrong," Nixie added, leaning against the counter, "there's always magical intervention. Any decent mage or druid can purge a system completely, no lasting damage." She leaned forward, her eyes intense beneath her copper-coloured bangs. "That's why paranormals who immigrate to this realm are genuinely bewildered by human drug laws. They think it's all a ridiculous overreaction to substances that, in their experience, are about as dangerous as drinking too much coffee."

I tried to imagine living without the fear that accompanied drug use in our world—no overdoses, no addiction, no destroyed lives just temporary effects easily remedied by one's own biology or a quick magical fix. The concept seemed so foreign, like imagining a world without gravity or oxygen.

My contemplation was interrupted when Nixie reached into her jacket pocket and extracted a small glass vial. The liquid inside was viscous and black, not the flat black of ink, but something deeper, almost three-dimensional, like staring into a miniature abyss. Tiny motes of purple light seemed to swim through it, appearing and disappearing like dying stars.

"This," she said quietly, "is what they're calling 'Eclipse.'"

She rolled the vial across the kitchen counter toward me. It moved sluggishly, as if the liquid inside was somehow heavier than it should be. I reached out but hesitated, my fingertips hovering centimetres away. Something about it felt wrong—a subtle wrongness that made the hair on my arms stand up.

"I promise we haven't taken any," Nixie reassured me, misinterpreting my hesitation. "We're not idiots. But this is definitely what you've been looking for. The dealer said it works on everyone human, fae, shifter, doesn't matter. One drop and you're experiencing 'transcendence beyond realms,' whatever that means." Her voice dropped lower. "He also said it's impossible to take just once."

I finally picked up the vial, surprised by its unnatural coldness against my skin. The glass itself seemed to pulse slightly, almost imperceptibly, as if the substance inside was alive and breathing. Even through the glass, I could feel something wrong about it—a kind of negative energy that made my fingertips tingle unpleasantly.

"And he just... gave this to you? For free?" I asked, unable to tear my eyes away from the swirling darkness inside.

"First taste is always free," Lunette said grimly, crossing her arms over her chest. "That's how they hook you. Classic dealer tactic, even in paranormal circles."

My eyes widened in shock as I looked at my housemates, unable to believe what they were telling me. "Holy shit, where did you get this exactly?" I exclaimed, my heart racing with a contradictory mixture of excitement and fear.

"It was at a meeting with other settlers," Nixie replied, her voice tinged with nervousness. She fidgeted with the hem of her shirt, avoiding my gaze. Her copper-coloured hair fell forward, partially obscuring her face. "We've been attending these gatherings for months now. It's supposed to be a place where we can share our experiences with each other, network, and just generally find a supportive and friendly atmosphere if you're feeling homesick for other realms."

"We used to go once a week just to connect with others like us," Lunette added, her piercing blue eyes glinting in the dim kitchen light. The silver rings on her fingers clinked softly as she gestured. "But ever since we agreed to help you with this investigation, we've been going multiple times a week and actively trying to build a network of informants."

"Paranormals love to gossip like old ladies at a church social," Nixie chimed in, her lips curling into a small smile that didn't quite reach her eyes. "So Lunette and one of the others set up a group chat and we have been monitoring it for anything strange or suspicious. Anything that might connect to what you've been looking for."

"But last night, when we were leaving the meet-up," Lunette continued, her voice growing more serious as she leaned forward against the counter, "we got approached by someone we'd never met before. A tall, thin man with eyes that seemed... wrong somehow. Too dark. Too empty."

My heart skipped a beat as I leaned forward, hanging onto every word. The vial seemed to grow colder in my palm, as if responding to the story.

"He asked if we wanted to try something new," Lunette paused, her expression turning grim as she exchanged a meaningful look with Nixie. "He promised it would take us to places beyond our wildest dreams. Said it would let us see between the realms, whatever that means. He guaranteed it would be the best trip of our lives and that we would keep going back for more once we had a taste. The way he said it wasn't like a sales pitch. It was like a threat."

As soon as she stopped speaking, I noticed both of them shudder involuntarily at the thought of the mysterious guy.

"I assume he was a real creep," I offered, my voice barely above a whisper.

Lunette was the first to reply, her voice dripping with disgust. "That would be the understatement of multiple lifetimes."

my mind raced as I processed the information. "So let me get this straight," I said, my brows furrowing in confusion. "He just gave this to you with no strings attached? And are we positive that this is what we've been looking for, and he isn't just some run of the mill drug dealer?" The weight of our potential discovery settled heavily on my shoulders, and I couldn't help but feel a mix of fear and trepidation at what this mysterious guy may have in store for us.

Nixie's voice was barely above a whisper as she spoke, her tone cautious and hesitant. Each word was carefully chosen, as if she feared someone would overhear us. Her eyes darted around the room nervously, her body tense as if any moment could bring danger.

she fidgeted with her shirt hem as she recounted the dangerous encounter at the secret meeting. Her hands trembled, still tense from the memory. Abby and I sat in our cozy kitchen, listening to her words, transported back to that ominous atmosphere. The room was heavy with tension and fear as Nixie's retelling only added to the weight on our shoulders. Abby tried to ease the mood by offering us warm mugs of chocolatey coffee, but my mind was already racing with thoughts of the danger we were all in. As I took a sip of the comforting drink, I knew we had to take action.

I cleared my throat, breaking the heavy silence that had fallen over our kitchen. The black vial sat between us like a bomb waiting to detonate.

"We need to change our approach," I said, measuring each word carefully. "Having all of us involved in this operation puts too many people at risk." Nixie's eyes widened slightly; Lunette's jaw tightened. Walker remained expressionless, but I could see the tension in his shoulders.

"If whoever gave you this Eclipse substance decides to track you down, or if the agency misinterprets our actions, the consequences could be catastrophic," I continued, glancing at the vial. Its purple motes seemed to pulse faster, as if responding to my anxiety. "I need you two to pack only what's essential change of clothes, identification, emergency cash and deliver this sample directly to Director Alexander at the agency headquarters. The lab there can determine if it's actually connected to this case or if it's something else entirely."

I turned to Walker, whose dark eyes met mine steadily. "You'll accompany them as security. Your combat training makes you the obvious choice for protection detail." His subtle nod confirmed his understanding.

"Everyone needs to understand," I said, looking at each of them in turn, "this could be the breakthrough we've been searching for. But it also makes us targets. Stay alert, maintain regular check ins, and for god's sake, don't let that vial out of your sight."

The weight of our situation pressed down on me like a physical force. We were stumbling through this investigation half-blind, and now we had a substance that could potentially kill people or worse sitting on our kitchen counter. My stomach knotted with dread. If we didn't move quickly, more people would die, more families would be destroyed. But rushing in unprepared could get us all killed.

Before I could say anything else, Walker's phone erupted with a shrill ring. He pulled it from his pocket in one fluid motion, glanced at the screen, and tapped the speaker button.

"It's the ass crack of dawn, Paul," Walker growled, his voice rough with fatigue. "What the hell do you want?"

"Good morning to you too," Paul responded . "Is she with you?"

I jumped in to answer his question before Walker could ask who 'she' was. "Yeah, I'm here. What's up?"

"Firstly, you left your phone in my car last night and I've been trying to contact you," Paul informed me. "Secondly, your few days off have been cancelled. You're fighting tonight."

My heart sank at the news. I thought I had a few more days until my next match, but apparently not anymore.

"I will pick you up from outside the gym at 19:00," Paul continued. "Do you have any questions?"

Confusion and frustration flooded through me as I processed this unexpected turn of events.

My heart raced as I protested, "What do you mean I'm fighting tonight? I thought I had more time."

Paul's voice was stoic as he replied cryptically, "You know as much as I do. If I hear anything else, what number should I call?"

Walker interjected confidently, "She will be using my number for the rest of the day."

Panic and nerves began to set in as the reality sunk in - I had little time to prepare for a fight that was seemingly sprung upon me.

"I haven't been informed of any location changes, but I will pass that information along if it should change," Paul reassured us.

"Okay, I will see you there," I said, trying to sound confident despite my racing thoughts.

"Paul, do you have anything else for us, or is that it?" Walker asked.

"No, that's everything. I will see you tonight," Paul responded before hanging up.

"Well, that changes things a little. So do you think you can act as a body bodyguard to get them to the agency and make it back to the arena by 19:00?" I asked Walker, although I was already sure of his answer.

He slumped in his chair, a look of determination on his face. "If I'm honest, I will be cutting it very close, but I will do everything in my power to get there on time."

CHAPTER 19

Anxious Anticipation at Dusk

As the clock struck 6:00, the sunset bled across the horizon in streaks of flamingo pink and tangerine. I checked my phone again—no texts, no calls. My heart hammered against my ribs as I paced the sidewalk, waiting for Walker to return from dropping Lunette and Nixie at the agency. I needed him here. Not just wanted—needed. The weight of tonight pressed down on my shoulders like a physical thing.

With trembling fingers, I texted him again: "Where are you? I'm heading to meet Paul now." No response.

Taking three deep breaths like Abby had taught me, I forced myself to walk toward the gym. Its concrete facade loomed ahead, fluorescent lights spilling onto the deserted street like toxic waste. The building seemed to pulse with an ominous energy that matched my racing pulse.

I got to the gym at 6:45. Every passing car made me jerk my head up, hoping to see Walker's familiar silhouette. By 7:00, the hollow feeling in my stomach had expanded into a cavern of dread. Something was wrong. Walker was never late, not for something this important. I drummed my fingers against the my leg, bit my lip until I tasted copper, checked my phone for the twentieth time.

"Focus," I whispered to myself. "Channel it."

Abby and I had spent hours perfecting our strategy. The dealers would be watching tonight, evaluating my potential. With Abby's and walkers training and my natural abilities, I could show them exactly what I was capable of. My muscles twitched with anticipation beneath my skin, coiled and ready. Despite my anxiety over Walker's absence, electricity hummed through my body—a current of adrenaline that sharpened my senses and steadied my resolve. My fingertips tingled with it, and each breath felt like drawing fire into my lungs. This was my opportunity to prove myself, to step out of the shadows and into the spotlight where I belonged. Beneath the fear and uncertainty, I couldn't deny the thrill that sparked in my chest at the thought of facing opponents who would truly test my limits—fighters who wouldn't hold back, who would force me to tap into every technique Abby and Walker had drilled into me over these past months.

Paul pulled up in his black sedan right on time as the clock struck 7:00. The headlights swept across me once before going dark. Without a word, I slipped into the silent embrace of the passenger seat, the leather cool against my skin. The drive to the arena stretched for twenty minutes but felt like hours, filled with a thick, tense silence that seemed to weigh down the air. Paul's knuckles were white on the steering wheel, his jaw clenched tight. It felt as though the entire world was holding its breath, waiting for what was to come.

The changing area was a concrete box with flickering fluorescent lights that cast everything in a sickly yellow glow. Without Walker by my side, it felt desolate and lonely—a void where his reassuring presence should have been. The silence weighed heavily on me as I nervously paced back and forth, my footsteps echoing against the bare walls. I tried counting tiles on the floor, stretching my muscles, anything to distract myself from the upcoming fight and Walker's unexplained absence. The only interactions I had since arriving were with Paul, who quickly wrapped my hands in white gauze before being called away by a man with a clipboard and a stern expression.

As I waited for my turn, every detail in the room seemed to heighten my nerves. The dented metal lockers loomed over me, casting long shadows across the dimly lit space. Someone had scratched "DEATH COMES" into one of them, the letters jagged and desperate. The air was thick and heavy with the stale, musky scent of sweat mixed with the unmistakable copper smell of blood that no amount of bleach could fully erase. It clung to the back of my throat, suffocating and overwhelming. To calm my racing heart, I closed my eyes and focused on my breathing—in for four counts, hold for four, out for four—the rhythm familiar from those endless hours trapped in the Caves with Lyn. Back then, the darkness had pressed against us like a living thing, the limestone walls contracting with each distant rumble until I could barely draw breath. But Lyn's steady voice had anchored me, counting each breath until my panic subsided. Even now, remembering her calm eyes brought a wave of tranquility washing over my frayed nerves.

As my muscles began to uncoil, another memory surfaced unbidden Abigail sitting cross-legged beside me on my narrow bed, moonlight spilling through the blinds and painting silver stripes across her concerned face. Her fingers had been intertwined with mine, thumb tracing small circles against my palm while I sobbed about the nightmares that wouldn't stop. "They're just echoes," she'd whispered, brushing tears from my cheeks with such tenderness that it almost broke me again. "They can't hurt you while I'm here." The memory of her perfume seemed to fill my nostrils, so vivid I could almost believe she was beside me now.

A sharp, searing pain sliced through my neck, hot and precise as a surgical blade. My eyes snapped open to a kaleidoscope of blurred movement, my body lurching upward before my mind could fully process what was happening. The fluorescent lights overhead swam in dizzying patterns as I tried to focus, to understand. A figure stepped backward, hands raised in a mockery of surrender, an empty syringe dangling between slender fingers. My hand flew to my neck, feeling the small, warm wetness there.

"Who are you?" The question tore from my throat, barely recognisable as my own voice hoarse and thin with fear. The room tilted sickeningly around me, concrete floor seeming to ripple like disturbed water. Cold sweat erupted across my forehead and down my spine, my heart thundering so violently I could see my shirt jumping with each beat.

The stranger's face slowly sharpened into focus angular features, clinical eyes the colour of tarnished pennies, lips curved in professional satisfaction. "I was worried that Kane was wrong about this working," he said, voice smooth and modulated like a radio announcer's, "but it seems he knows more about you than the rest of us." He checked his watch, making a small notation in a leather bound notebook he produced from his pocket.

"What did you give me?" I tried to stand but my legs betrayed me, trembling violently as the room continued its nauseating spin. My words emerged as a whisper, each syllable requiring monumental effort as something cold and heavy spread through my veins, radiating outward from the injection site.

He lifted the syringe to eye level, examining it with the pride of a craftsman. "Oh, this is something I've been working on for quite some time," he explained, turning the empty container so it caught the light. "A refined derivative of scopolamine—devil's breath, as it's colloquially known. Normally it simply renders the subject compliant, docile as a kitten." His eyes gleamed with intellectual excitement. "But this variant contains certain... enhancements of my own design. Magical accelerants that bypass the blood-brain barrier entirely."

The cruel smirk that spread across his face revealed teeth too white, too perfect—like a shark's mouth filled with polished porcelain. My vision blurred at the edges as he leaned closer, his cologne a nauseating mix of sandalwood and something medicinal.

"You'll find yourself unable to disobey direct commands within thirty seconds," he said, tapping his expensive watch. "The paralytic properties should be taking effect right about... now."

Fuelled by a surge of adrenaline cutting through the growing heaviness in my limbs, I lunged forward. My fingers grasped at his pristine lab coat, but my movements felt disconnected from my intentions—like trying to run through chest-deep water. He sidestepped with the practiced grace of a dancer, pivoting on his heel as I stumbled past.

"Fascinating response time," he murmured, jotting something in his leather notebook. "Most subjects are completely immobile by now."

Regaining my balance against the cold concrete wall, I turned to face him. The room tilted sickeningly, but I forced my eyes to focus on his smug expression.

"Why are you doing this?" I demanded, my voice emerging thicker than intended, consonants slurring together despite my efforts.

"Oh my dear," he chuckled, eyes lighting up like a child unwrapping presents. "That's simple. Kane has suspected for months there is something special about you, something hidden deep within your genetic makeup. Something worth the considerable expense of developing this particular formula." He tapped the empty syringe lovingly. "And with this little cocktail I've given you, we will finally get to see what you're truly capable of when those... inhibitions of yours are stripped away."

His words penetrated the growing fog in my mind, sending ice water cascading down my spine. My fingers and toes began to tingle with pins and needles as whatever he'd injected spread through my bloodstream. I tried to step forward again, but my knee buckled, betraying me.

"Now sit and stop talking," his voice commanded with a sharp edge that seemed to bypass my ears and strike directly at my brain stem. The compulsion was immediate and overwhelming—like a puppet's strings being yanked.

My body folded onto the bench behind me before I could even process the desire to resist. My jaw clamped shut with such force that pain radiated through my teeth. Trapped inside my increasingly unresponsive body, I watched him , my stomach churning with helpless dread. The storm wasn't coming—it was already here, and I was caught in its eye with no shelter in sight. My fingers twitched uselessly against my thighs, the last vestige of voluntary movement fading like a dying ember.

I tried to fight the effects of the devil's breath, focusing every ounce of my remaining willpower on simply lifting a hand, but it was useless. My limbs felt waterlogged, impossibly heavy, as if concrete had replaced my blood. I had become a mere passenger in my own flesh, watching through eyes I could no longer command to close. Even my breathing seemed to belong to someone else now— shallow and irregular, each inhale a struggle against the growing paralysis.

He approached with calculated steps, the fluorescent lights casting his shadow long across the floor. From a leather satchel at his side, he withdrew a wooden case lined with velvet. My heart slammed against my ribs as he unlatched it with a soft click that echoed in the silent room. Inside lay a collection of vials, each containing liquids of different viscosities and colours—amber, violet, and one that seemed to shift between deep crimson and black as it caught the light.

"These are quite special," he murmured, almost tenderly, selecting three vials and holding them up to examine their contents. "Compounds I've spent years perfecting." His fingers moved with the precision of a concert pianist as he filled three separate syringes, measuring each dose with obsessive care.

The first needle pierced the side of my neck, sliding beneath the skin with a burning sensation that spread like wildfire through my veins. The second and third followed in quick succession—one in the crook of my arm where the veins were most prominent, and the final one directly into my chest, just above my heart. Each puncture was deliberate, almost ceremonial, his eyes gleaming with scientific fascination as he watched the liquids disappear into my body.

Leaning over me, close enough that I could count the pores on his nose, his breath washed over my face. The stench emanating from him was incongruous with his clinical appearance—a putrid mixture of decay and chemical preservatives that reminded me of formaldehyde and rotting meat. Beneath that lay something else, something primal and wrong that made the hairs on my arms stand on end despite my paralysis. My stomach heaved involuntarily, acid burning the back of my throat as I fought the urge to vomit. If I did, I'd likely choke on it—another indignity in this nightmare I couldn't escape.

"I've never administered such a large or potent dose before," he said, voice dropping to a reverent whisper that somehow carried more menace than a shout. His eyes dilated with scientific ecstasy, pupils expanding like black holes. "I'm particularly eager to see what happens when the compound reaches your central nervous system. If Kane's theory about your genetic anomalies is correct, this will be extraordinary."

With the practiced precision of someone who'd done this countless times before, he depressed the plunger on each syringe in sequence. The liquid drugs disappeared into my bloodstream, and the effects were instantaneous and catastrophic. A warm sensation bloomed from each injection site like dye in water, spreading through my veins in tendrils that quickly transformed from warmth to scorching agony. My muscles seized and relaxed in violent spasms as though my body were trying to reject the foreign substance by force.

It felt like molten metal had replaced my blood, burning through tissue and dissolving me from within. Every nerve ending screamed in protest as my cells seemed to rupture and reform. Through the haze of pain, something else emerged—a white-hot rage that rose from some primal part of my brain, overwhelming even the physical torment. The air around me grew heavy with static electricity, making the fluorescent lights flicker and buzz. Tiny arcs of blue-white energy crackled between my fingertips and the metal bench beneath me.

A wide, childlike grin spread across his face as he clapped his hands with unrestrained joy. The sharp sound echoed through the room like gunshots, each clap stoking the inferno of my fury. But despite the tempest building inside me, I remained immobile, still bound by his earlier command—the devil's breath ensuring my compliance even as my consciousness rebelled.

"Now, Jessica," he murmured, leaning so close that I could count every blemish and pore on his skin, "listen very carefully." His tone dropped to a hoarse whisper, conspiratorial and dangerous, as if he were imparting the most precious secret in the world. My pulse hammered in my ears. I lifted my chin and met his gaze with all the contempt I could muster—an icicle stare I hoped would scorch right through him.

He chuckled low and slow, the sound vibrating in my chest. "Oh, I love that look," he purred. He straightened and surveyed me like a prize on display. "This is going to be a special show, indeed." He paused, letting the tension coil tight between us before he spoke again. "When you hear your name called, you'll step into the arena and wait for the bell. The instant it rings, you fight. Everything you have. Every. Single. Opponent. is your enemy. You must defeat them all."

His words landed like a judge's gavel, sealing the fate of whoever would face me next. My stomach turned over, dread curling icy fingers around my heart. I strained against the invisible shackles of his command, but I was as powerless as a marionette. My entire body trembled with a mixture of rage and fear.

"Do you understand?" His voice cut through me, sharp and unyielding.

A tight knot of emotion constricted my throat. My voice felt foreign, raw as gravel as I forced out a reply: "Yes... I understand." The admission felt like dropping an anchor inside my chest—it anchored me to this nightmare.

The man's lips curved into a triumphant smirk. His eyes glinted with predatory delight. "Good," he said softly. He tapped a finger against his palm, as though checking off a list. "There's just one more rule: under no circumstances are you to harm anyone in the spectator area. Clear?"

My heartbeat thundered; each pulse screamed rebellion. Yet my answer came in a brittle whisper: "Yes."

"Excellent." He turned away, brushing past me like I was already part of the scenery. In his wake, I felt hollowed out, as if he'd siphoned every ounce of agency I'd had. I remained frozen, a statue cast in dread. Time stretched infinitely, punctuated only by the distant hum of the crowd.

Moments later, the murmur swelled into raucous applause and rhythmic chants. The arena's gates loomed ahead, gaping like the maw of some feral beast. My breath hitched as anticipation rippled through the masses beyond the barrier.

A thunderous voice pierced the cacophony: "And now, for our final fighter, give it up for... Jessica!"

The crowd erupted in a deafening roar. It rolled over me like an ocean wave, rattling the ground and igniting raw adrenaline in my veins. The surge drowned out every whisper of doubt—until the man's parting command slithered into my mind, cold and insistent: "Go and show us everything you can do."

My chest feels as though it's being squeezed by iron bands. My shoulders hunch, and my fists clench so tightly that my nails bite into my palms, drawing thin ribbons of pain. There's no turning back now. I draw in a slow, trembling breath, counting each second as I steel myself. Behind me, the corridor lies cloaked in shadow—long, cold hallways lit only by distant, flickering torches—and with one final look over my shoulder, I step forward into the blinding light of the arena.

The deafening roar of the crowd slams into me like a wave. Dust swirls at my boots; the scent of sweat, blood, and scorched earth fills my nostrils. My body rebels, stiff and unresponsive at first, as if someone else is tugging the strings of my limbs. There's no willpower left to resist. I march automatically across the wide stone floor, each step pounding like a war drum. All around me, dozens of other fighters—at least fifty—fan out in every direction, eyes darting between one another and the scattered weapons arrayed across the arena's centre. Gleaming spears, jagged axes, ornate swords, and gleaming daggers lie ready for the taking, handles beckoning. Whoever reaches the weapons first will have the advantage.

I pause for a heartbeat at the very centre. From here I can see the elevated stands ringed by a shimmering teal barrier of crackling energy, designed—so they say—to keep onlookers safely removed from the carnage. The barrier hums softly, wavering with sparks, as though it knows what's coming. The audience leans forward in silence, their faces masked by the bright glare; I can almost sense the anticipation vibrating in the air.

My heart hammers against my ribs, and beneath the surface I can feel a quiet storm of anger swirling—pure, raw fury that thrums hotter with every passing second. I've never known a rage like this before, not even in my darkest moments. It claws at me, desperate to be released, yet I cling to the last remnants of my reason, searching for a way out, a crack in the barrier, a plea for mercy that might reach whoever's controlling this nightmare.

Then I spot her. Abby stands near the edge of the stands, her pale face illuminated in the harsh light. Her brow is furrowed, her lips parted in disbelief. Shock and worry flicker across her eyes, and guilt claws at my chest. I never wanted to drag her into this. I wanted to protect her. With every ounce of strength left, I manage to whisper her name, a tiny confession trembling on my lips: "I'm so sorry." I pray she hears me, that my apology can bridge the distance between us. But the roar of the crowd swells once more, drowning out my words.

A voice booms over the arena's loudspeakers—deep, relentless, commanding. "Fighters—no mercy!"then the bell rings The words strike me like a lightning bolt. In that instant, something primal within me snaps free. Every restraint shatters. The anger coalesces into a living thing, coiling inside my chest, demanding release.

I inhale sharply and let out a feral roar that echoes off the high stone walls. Pain, sorrow, rage—they all surge together, pushing through every vein in my body. My muscles tighten, then explode with newfound power. I feel a torrential current of energy rushing upward from my core, a furious river breaking through a dam. The ground beneath me trembles, tiny cracks spiderweb outward from my boots. A whirlwind of shimmering force swirls around me, whipping dust and grit into the air, setting the arena alight with its blazing intensity.

Despite the chaos—swords lifting themselves off the ground, spears quivering in mid-air, the barrier wavering like heat over asphalt—the fighters around me remain oblivious to the elemental storm I've become. Their focus is still on me, their expressions frozen between confusion and determination, too stunned to move as I stand at the eye of my own unleashed fury, power crackling at my fingertips.

The other fighters don't even attempt to hide their intentions—it's everyone against me. The excited murmurs rippling through the spectators confirm this is exactly what they've come to see: me, outnumbered and desperate. A gladiatorial sacrifice.

As the first four attackers close in, their weapons glinting under the harsh arena lights, I slip into a trance-like state. My movements become fluid and instinctual, as though someone else controls my limbs. With one swift strike, I catch my first opponent off guard—a burly man with a jagged scar across his left cheek. My foot connects with the side of his knee, and I hear the sickening pop of ligaments tearing. He crumples to the ground with a howl that's swallowed by the roaring crowd.

But before I can fully regain my footing, the other three are upon me—a woman wielding twin daggers, a mountain of a man with a spiked mace, and a lean fighter whose hands glow with unnatural blue energy. Their continuous attacks force me backward, keeping me constantly on edge, my breath coming in ragged gasps. With each blow landed against me, more energy crackles around my body, a corona of power intensifying with every passing second. My skin burns with it, my vision blurring at the edges as something primal claws its way up from deep inside me.

In a desperate attempt to protect myself, I unleash all of my energy in a fierce blast toward the blue-handed attacker. The force explodes from my fist as it collides with his shoulder, the impact sending a shockwave through the arena floor. His body flies backward with a sickening crunch, leaving a trail of crimson mist in the air.

For a moment, I'm too stunned to understand what has just happened. The arena falls eerily silent, as if the entire world has paused to witness the horror I've created. My ears ring in the sudden vacuum of sound. But then the rational part of my mind catches up to the scene before me: the enemy I just hit now lies on the floor, missing a huge chunk of his body. A gaping hole in his chest reveals the blown-away remains of his right side, including part of his abdomen and upper arm. Just a short distance away, his severed limb lies lifeless on the ground, fingers still twitching with residual nerve impulses. Blood pools beneath him, spreading across the arena floor in a widening circle that reflects the horrified faces of the crowd above.

The brutal scene threatens to make bile rise in my throat, the metallic scent of blood filling my nostrils and coating the back of my tongue like copper pennies. My stomach clenches and unclenches in violent waves. But even more unsettling is the realisation that this carnage is my own doing. My trembling hands are smeared with crimson stains that have already begun to dry and crack along my knuckles. The body of my opponent—a person who was breathing and fighting mere seconds ago—now lies lifeless at my feet, his remaining eye staring vacantly at the arena ceiling.

As I struggle to process this knowledge, time seems to snap back into motion. The rest of my adversaries quickly regain their composure, their momentary shock replaced by a calculated fury. They launch into a coordinated frenzy of attacks, clearly determined not to suffer the same fate as their fallen comrade.

A shifter—their body transformed into a fierce hybrid of human and wolf with elongated limbs and razor-sharp claws—materialises out of thin air three feet to my left. Before I can pivot to defend myself, they deliver a swift kick towards my legs. The force knocks me off balance, my ankles buckling beneath me, causing me to tumble to the ground with a jarring thud that rattles my teeth and sends shockwaves up my spine. The impact drives what little air I have from my lungs in a painful whoosh.

Before I can recover or even draw breath, another enemy—a burly woman with tribal markings etched across her forehead—lands a powerful blow to my ribcage that sends me skidding across the floor of the arena. My body carves a shallow furrow in the dirt as I slide ten, fifteen feet away from where I fell. The impact is so intense that I feel my ribs crack upon impact, the distinct sound of bone giving way beneath flesh unmistakable even amid the chaos. Yet my mind refuses to register the pain as adrenaline surges through my veins like liquid fire, setting every nerve ending alight. Desperately, I push myself back up, my palms leaving bloody imprints in the dust as I force my trembling legs to support my weight, determined to continue fighting despite the damage I've sustained.

Each opponent surrounding me is a fierce and deadly foe in their own right—some wielding elemental powers that crackle at their fingertips, others brandishing weapons that gleam menacingly under the arena lights. Their attacks come in rapid succession like a relentless storm, forcing me to react on pure instinct rather than conscious thought. Time seems to blur as the chaos and cacophony of battle consume me completely. The screams and grunts of combatants around me meld into a twisted symphony of violence, punctuated by the sickening sounds of weapons finding their marks and bodies hitting the ground.

Despite the overwhelming odds, I couldn't afford to be distracted by the alien sensations rippling through my body. Each strike and parry revealed new changes—muscles coiling with unnatural strength, reflexes sharpening beyond human capability, senses heightening until I could hear individual heartbeats from the fighters surrounding me. The transformation was happening faster now, accelerated by the violence and adrenaline.

My heart hammered against my ribs like a trapped animal as sweat beaded across my forehead, trickling into my eyes with stinging persistence. A tremor started in my fingertips, spreading up my arms until my entire body vibrated with barely contained energy. Then came the moment of horrifying metamorphosis—my fingernails split and peeled back as obsidian claws erupted from the beds, gleaming wetly under the arena lights. The skin along my forearms tightened, hardened, and then fractured into diamond-shaped patterns as iridescent scales pushed through the surface, each one catching the light with an opalescent shimmer. The pain was excruciating, yet somehow distant, as though happening to someone else.

A female fighter with ceremonial tattoos covering half her face lunged at me, a curved blade whistling through the air toward my throat. I pivoted instinctively, my newly transformed body moving with predatory grace. Something primal seized control of my vocal cords, and a guttural growl tore from my throat—not the sound of a human in distress, but the warning of an apex predator. The noise reverberated throughout the stadium, silencing the crowd momentarily before they erupted into frenzied cheers, mistaking my terror for bloodlust.

The tattooed woman hesitated for just a fraction of a second, her eyes widening at the inhuman sound. That momentary pause was all it took. My arm shot forward with impossible speed, claws sinking through flesh and cartilage as if they were butter. I felt the resistance of bone, then the sickening give as vertebrae separated. With strength I never knew I possessed, I wrenched upward, separating her head from her shoulders in one catastrophic motion. The severed head tumbled through the air, her expression frozen in eternal surprise, while a geyser of arterial spray erupted from the ragged stump of her neck, drenching my face and chest in hot crimson.

Horror flooded my consciousness as I stared at what remained of my opponent, bile rising in my throat. My hands—no longer recognisable as human—dripped with gore, yet they continued to move of their own accord, as though some other intelligence now piloted my transformed body. I wanted to scream, to collapse, to beg for this nightmare to end, but survival instinct overrode everything else as the remaining fighters regrouped.

They approached with newfound caution, forming a loose semicircle around me. Their weapons—serrated blades, spiked maces, and crackling energy gauntlets—glinted menacingly under the harsh arena lights. One fighter, a hulking man with runic script visible along his jawline, barked orders to the others. They began to coordinate their movements with military precision, each attack timed to exploit any opening I might leave.

Pain lanced through my side as a thrown dagger found its mark between my newly formed scales, but instead of weakening me, the injury only fuelled whatever transformation was consuming me. I could feel the wound already knitting itself closed as I whirled to face my attackers. My vision sharpened further, the world slowing around me as my perception accelerated. I could see the minute adjustments in their stances, the subtle tells before each strike. Their expressions shifted from determination to uncertainty, then to naked fear as they realised what they were truly facing wasn't human anymore.

Blood pounded in my ears like a war drum as I launched myself toward them, no longer fighting for victory but consumed by the primal need to survive this crucible of violence—whatever the cost to my humanity.

Their blows became more calculated, a choreographed dance of death. The hulking man with runic script along his jawline directed the others with subtle hand signals. A woman with a serrated blade targeted the soft junction between my neck and shoulder. A wiry fighter with mechanical augmentations aimed precise kicks at my knees. With each strike, I felt cartilage tear and bones fracture beneath my increasingly armoured skin. The cocktail of combat drugs Kanes had forced into my system before the match transformed agony into distant thunder, allowing me to fight through injuries that should have left me crumpled on the arena floor.

As minutes stretched like hours and my body absorbed punishment that would kill an ordinary human, something strange began to happen. The transformation accelerated, spreading from my arms to my entire body. My muscles and joints loosened and relaxed, sinews elongating, bones shifting beneath my skin with audible cracks. My movements became fluid and predatory, no longer human but something ancient and terrible. The arena lights dimmed around me as my pupils expanded, revealing opponents in stark relief against the darkness. I could smell their fear now

A fighter with ceremonial face paint lunged at me with twin daggers. Without conscious thought, I sidestepped and caught his wrist, feeling bones splinter beneath my grip. His scream cut short as my newly transformed arm now covered in scales whipped across his throat. The crowd's collective gasp washed over me as his body crumpled. Horror flooded my consciousness at what I'd become, at the ease with which I extinguished life. And yet, even as the crowd fell silent in shock at the brutal spectacle before them, I couldn't bring myself to stop. Kanes' underling had been explicit "Fight until you're the last one standing"

One by one, they fell before me some dead, others broken beyond recovery. The last fighter, a woman with glowing blue veins, backed away slowly, her weapon clattering to the ground in surrender. The primal thing I'd become didn't recognise the gesture. I lunged forward, my transformed body moving with impossible speed. she had just enough time to register fear before my claws found her heart.

As the dust settled in the arena, I stood alone in its centre, my body a roadmap of injuries that should have been fatal. Blood—

both mine and others'—formed rivulets down my scaled limbs, pooling at my feet in a growing crimson lake. My laboured breaths echoed throughout the silent space, each exhalation carrying a faint, inhuman growl. The screams of my opponents still rang in my ears, a constant reminder of the horrors I had just committed. the bodies lay scattered across the arena floor, their vacant eyes reflecting the harsh overhead lights.

Standing amidst the destruction, I fought to reclaim control of my transformed body, willing the scales to recede, the claws to retract. Guilt and self-loathing crashed over me in waves as the drug-induced battle haze began to lift. The announcer's voice cut through the silence, his tone stripped of all enthusiasm, replaced with poorly concealed fear. "What an upset. From the very start, it looked as though Jess was the underdog. Still, she has surprised us all and is the only fighter to remain standing." His words were met with a roar of applause that seemed to come from another world entirely. The crowd's cheers carried a new quality—no longer just bloodlust, but a morbid fascination tinged with terror as they gazed at me with twisted admiration, knowing they had witnessed something that defied explanation.

As soon as the match ended, Paul appeared at my side, his face drained of all colour. His voice trembled with strain as he pleaded with me, "Jess, look at me, please." I turned to meet his gaze, and the sight of me seemed to cause him pain, causing him to take a step back. "I need you to come with me, Jess. Do you understand?" I could only nod in response, feeling like a lifeless puppet being guided by someone else's strings. My body moved on its own as I followed Paul, my mind numb and distant. Every step felt heavy and foreign, like I was walking through a thick fog that refused to clear.

CHAPTER 20

Beneath the Surface

****Abigail****

My lungs refused to draw breath as Jess's fist connected with her opponent's jaw, the crack reverberating through the arena like a gunshot in an empty church. Blood sprayed in a crimson arc across the concrete floor, spattering against the barrier protecting the first row of spectators who howled with delight rather than disgust. This couldn't be my Jess the woman who cried during dog food adverts and couldn't bear to kill even the spiders that terrified her. But there she stood in the centre of this hellish pit, her once-delicate wrists now corded with sinew as she dodged a knife thrust with a fluidity that made my stomach clench. The blade whistled past her ear, close enough to slice a few strands of her hair, yet she didn't flinch instead, she countered with inhuman speed, driving her elbow into her attacker's sternum with a sickening crunch that I felt in my own bones. Each movement flowed into the next with terrifying precision, her body transformed into a weapon honed by something beyond the training we had put her through. The crowd's bloodthirsty roars faded to white noise in my ears as I watched blue-white sparks literally dance across her skin, crackling between her fingers like miniature lightning, leaving scorch marks on the concrete where her feet touched down. Her face—God, her face— had transformed, cheekbones suddenly sharp as blades beneath skin stretched tight over newfound angles, the soft curves I'd traced with my fingertips just days ago now hardened into something ancient and predatory. When she snarled at her next challenger, I glimpsed teeth too pointed for any human mouth, gleaming like polished ivory under the harsh arena lights. But it was her eyes that froze my blood and sent ice water cascading through my veins—pupils dilated until only a thin ring of amber remained, glowing with a hunger so primal and alien that I couldn't reconcile it with the woman who'd whispered "I love you" when she thought I couldn't hear. As I watched, paralysed with horror and fascination, actual talons erupted from her fingertips with a sound like knives being unsheathed, curved and gleaming, slicing through her opponent's flesh as easily as water, leaving ribbons of red in their wake that splashed across her face like war paint.

As the fight raged on, I witnessed Jess's metamorphosis with horrified fascination. Pearlescent scales erupted across her skin like frost forming on glass, starting at her fingertips and spreading upward along her arms in rippling waves. They caught the arena's harsh lights and refracted them into prismatic halos that danced around her body. The opalescent shimmer reminded me of Lyn's dragon form, but Jess's scales were more delicate, almost translucent at the edges beautiful in their terrible perfection.

My throat constricted as I watched her neck elongate slightly, the vertebrae shifting beneath her skin with audible pops that somehow carried to my ears above the crowd's roar. Her jawline sharpened, cheekbones rising higher as her face restructured itself into something both familiar and alien. The woman who would curl up against me at night to try and keep the nightmares at bay, who laughed at bad television, was transforming into a living weapon before my eyes.

I couldn't tear my gaze away even as my stomach heaved. This was Jess—my Jess—the woman whose heartbeat I'd memorised while she slept against my chest, now unrecognisable in her fury. Her once gentle hands now ended in curved talons that sliced through flesh with sickening ease. Blood spattered across her face in crimson constellations, yet somehow made her more beautiful in her savagery. Her eyes—God, her eyes—had changed to a molten gold, pupils narrowed to reptilian slits that tracked every movement with predatory precision.

The transformation wasn't just physical. Something fundamental had shifted in her essence. The Jess I knew approached conflict with reluctance and compassion was gone this creature revealed in combat with primal joy. Each blow she landed seemed to feed something inside her, some ravenous hunger that had lain dormant until now. Her movements flowed with hypnotic grace, each strike precise and devastating. She didn't just fight, she danced with death, and death followed her lead.

When her opponents rushed her three at once now my heart stuttered in my chest. But Jess merely smiled, a terrible baring of too sharp teeth. She moved like liquid lightning, flowing between their attacks with impossible speed. One man's arm snapped backward with a crack that echoed through the arena; another crumpled as her knee connected with his sternum. The third she lifted by his throat, scales glittering along her forearm as muscles I'd never seen before rippled beneath her skin.

The crowd's bloodthirsty cheers turned to gasps of awe and terror. Even these hardened spectators recognised something beyond their understanding had entered their midst. Some pressed back in their seats, others leaned forward, entranced. I understood both reactions because I felt them simultaneously repulsed yet magnetically drawn to this terrifying spectacle.

Blood streamed from a gash above Jess's eye, another across her shoulder, yet she seemed not to notice. Her breathing remained steady even as her opponents' numbers grew. Five now surrounded her, circling like wolves. .

The crowd around me bayed for blood like starving wolves, their faces contorted in ecstasy at each spray of crimson across the concrete. My knuckles turning white as I clench my fists tighter as I watched, bile rising in my throat. Though I despised them for their bloodlust, wasn't I just as complicit? Sitting here, My rage burned white-hot in my veins, threatening to consume me from within as I watched my beloved Jessica being degraded and twisted into this weapon. The scales rippling across her skin caught the harsh arena lights, throwing prismatic reflections across the crowd's rapturous faces. How could they find joy in such brutality? Each time her newly formed talons slashed through flesh, I felt the phantom pain of it across my own skin. All I wanted was to unleash my own monstrous fury upon this place to tear out Kanes throat with my teeth, to feel his pulse flutter and fade beneath my hands for what he'd done to her. But I couldn't risk revealing myself. i couldn't jeopardise Jessica's safety with a premature move. And so I remained hidden, muscles trembling with the effort of restraint, biding my time until I could rescue her from this savage spectacle.

My heart thundered against my ribs like a war drum as I watched the lifeless body of her final opponent fall, joining the pile of the defeated sprawled across the blood-slick arena floor. The metallic scent of spilled blood hung thick in the air, coating the back of my throat with each breath. My eyes narrowed at the sight of Paul that weasel of a man leading her away from the arena, his hand possessively gripping her elbow. Her eyes had dimmed now, her face a mask of exhaustion, the scales appearing to begin slowly receding beneath her skin. A burning anger took over, flooding my system with adrenaline as I slipped silently from my seat, my gaze fixated on Jess's retreating form until she disappeared through the exit door. Every fibre of my being vibrated with the need to follow, to find Paul and make him pay for whatever had happened. The crowd's roars faded to white noise as I moved with predatory focus, memorising the faces of every person I passed, accomplices, all of them. My determination drove me toward the nearest exit, muscles coiled tight as I pushed through the doors with frenzied urgency. The excited chatter of the other guests who had revealed in the gruesome spectacle crashed against me like a physical wave, their voices grating against my heightened senses.

The adrenaline rush coursing through the crowd's veins, their gleeful bloodlust as they watched Jessica transform would be nothing compared to the terror they'd feel when I unleashed my own monster upon them. They would learn what true fear tastes like, metallic and sharp, flooding the mouth like panic. They would understand regret in their final moments, when they realised their entertainment had summoned something far worse than what they'd witnessed in any arena.

Jessica's gentle touch ghosted across my memory, her fingertips tracing my collarbone in the darkness of our bedroom, her breath warm against my neck as she sleeps The contrast between that tenderness and what they had forced her to become tore something vital inside me. My vision tunnelled as I pushed through the exit doors, the cool night air hitting my feverish skin.

My heart hammered against my ribs as I reached the parking area, arriving just as Paul emerged dragging Jessica by her wrist. Her head hung forward, hair curtaining her face, shoulders slumped in defeat. Some of the scales had receded, leaving her skin raw and mottled with bruises blooming like violent flowers beneath the parking lot's harsh fluorescent lights.

A growl built in my chest, vibrating upward until it escaped between my clenched teeth. The familiar ache spread through my jaw as my fangs descended, piercing my bottom lip. I tasted my own blood, copper bright and electric. My transformation wasn't beautiful like Jess. it was ugly, brutal efficiency. My eyes burned as they shifted, the world suddenly awash in crimson gradients, Paul's racing heartbeat visible as a pulsing glow beneath his skin.

I stalked toward them, each footfall silent despite the rage thundering through me. Paul's scent changed abruptly fear sweat erupting across his skin, pupils dilating as he spotted me. His body went rigid, prey-still, as he realised what approached.

"Abby, please stop," he pleaded, voice cracking like thin ice. His arms trembled as he raised his hands. "I didn't know what was going on. I'm trying to get her out of here now." His eyes darted between me and the exit, calculating escape routes and finding none. "Please help me. Now that you're here, we have to leave."

The fury roiling inside me was no mere emotion, it was a creature, coiling and uncoiling in my chest, claws digging into my ribs, demanding blood. I could smell his terror on the night air, sweet and thick like spilled honey, and my fingertips tingled with the murderous urge to tear flesh from bone. Every fibre of my being itched for violence, for retribution. And yet, every rasp of Jessica's shallow breathing anchored me to the fragile thread of reason that still remained.

"Did you know?" I hissed, each syllable a blade. My voice had shifted with my transformation—now a cavernous growl, soaked through with rumbling subharmonics that made Paul recoil. "Did you have any inkling of what they planned for her? Did you deliver her to that slaughterhouse knowing the fate that awaited?"

Paul's face went pale. He stumbled backward, hands splayed. "No, no....I swear it!" he gasped, voice cracking. "I wrapped her hands up, taped the knuckles for the match, then I was pulled away. Next thing I know, the bell rings, and they're tearing into her. I didn't—I didn't know!"

I snapped, "Get in the car." The words were short, vicious. "We need to get her out of here. And once we're safe, you will explain everything. Every detail."

Without pausing, I scooped Jessica into my arms. Her weight was surprisingly light—her limbs limp as wet cloth. My heart hammered as I pressed her closer, inhaling the coppery tinge of blood mixed with sweat and fear. It soothed me, oddly, like a lullaby promising vengeance.

I laid her gently across the back seat of Paul's sedan and cradled her head on my thigh. The engine growled to life, its low rumble a heartbeat guiding us away from the carnage. Streetlights flashed by, casting elongated shadows across her pale face—skin slick with blood and dried sweat, eyes closed as if sleep might whisk her pain away.

I ran trembling fingers through her damp hair, brushing stray strands from her forehead. Every inch of her trembling form sent a new spike of guilt through me. I should have saved her sooner. I should have known better. Protect her. that was my promise, and I'd failed in the most horrific way. But there was no time for remorse now only the drive ahead, and the fragile pulse against my leg that told me she was still alive.

Tears pooled in my eyes as I smoothed my hand against her temple, trying to will calm back into her battered body. Each tear that escaped was an apology, a vow I mouthed in silence. I will keep you safe. I will not let this end in blood.

I looked back at Paul through the rearview mirror—his face twisted in guilt and fear. "Paul," I said, voice low but unyielding, "you're taking us straight to the agency headquarters. You will drive faster than you ever have in your life. If you hesitate, if you wobble, I swear I will make sure your death is slow, excruciating, and unforgettable. Understand?"

He swallowed hard, hands trembling on the wheel. "Yes," he whispered. "I understand." He slammed his foot on the accelerator, tires screeching as we tore away into the night—and I leaned over Jessica, determined that this drive would not be in vain.

The weight of my words hung between us like a physical presence. Beads of sweat formed on Paul's forehead, trickling down his temples in rivulets that caught the harsh glow of passing streetlights. His knuckles whitened as he gripped the steering wheel, the tendons in his hands standing out like taut wires. The threat of what I would do if he failed us, if he failed her, radiated from my body in waves he could surely feel.

Paul slammed his foot onto the gas pedal with such force that the car lurched forward, throwing me back against the seat. Jessica's head jolted in my lap, a soft moan escaping her cracked lips. The speedometer needle climbed rapidly—70, 80, 90—as buildings blurred into streaks of neon and shadow outside the windows. My phone felt slick in my trembling hands as I fumbled to dial Alex, my fingertips leaving smears of Jessica's blood across the screen.

"Hello?" Alex's voice crackled through the speaker, tight with concern.

"It's me," I said, my voice raw and unrecognisable even to my own ears. "They've done something to Jess—something monstrous. We're coming in hot. I need a full medical team at the south entrance, trauma kit ready, and security lockdown protocols initiated the moment we're inside. And Alex" I swallowed against the burning in my throat, " prepare for the worst. I don't know if she's going to make it."

The car swerved violently around a corner, tires screaming against asphalt. My body instinctively curled protectively around Jessica as we were thrown sideways. Paul muttered desperate apologies, his eyes wild in the rearview mirror as he navigated the labyrinthine streets at breakneck speed. Each second stretched into an eternity, each mile a desperate battle against the clock ticking away Jessica's life.

I ended the call without waiting for Alex's response, dropping the phone to cradle Jessica's face between my palms. Her skin felt clammy, unnaturally cool against my feverish hands. Without warning, her body went rigid, back arching at an impossible angle as convulsions ripped through her. A strangled sound tore from my throat—half sob, half scream as I fought against my instinct to restrain her.

"No, no, no," I chanted, gently turning her onto her side as her limbs jerked and spasmed. Frothy saliva tinged with blood bubbled at the corners of her mouth. I brushed matted hair from her face with shaking fingers, leaning close to her ear. "Stay with me, Jess. Please. We're almost there. Just hold on a little longer."

Her eyelids fluttered, revealing slivers of white as her eyes rolled back. Each rattling breath she took sounded more laboured than the last, her chest rising and falling in an erratic rhythm that made my own lungs ache in sympathy. The metallic scent of blood mixed with the acrid tang of fear filled the car's interior, making my fangs throb painfully against my gums.

"Faster," I snarled at Paul, not caring how inhuman I sounded.

The car shot forward, engine screaming in protest as we careened down the empty pre-dawn streets. Jessica's convulsions gradually subsided, leaving her limp and unnaturally still in my arms. I pressed my fingers to her throat, relief flooding through me at the faint but present flutter of her pulse beneath my fingertips.

When the gleaming glass facade of the agency headquarters finally came into view, its security lights cutting through the darkness like beacons, I felt something inside me crack open. A single, hot tear traced a path down my cheek as I gathered Jessica closer, her head lolling against my shoulder.

"We're here," I whispered against her hair, allowing myself one moment of desperate hope as Paul screeched to a halt before the entrance where figures were already rushing toward us. "We made it, Jess. Now fight. Fight to stay with me."

CHAPTER 21

Guilt in Free Fall

Alex

The abrupt sound of the disconnect signal pierced my ear like a shard of ice. My stomach lurched violently, acid rising in my throat as the phone slipped from my trembling fingers. The ground seemed to open beneath me, plunging me into a free fall of dread and panic. Jessica I thought. she's just a child, and was in danger because of me. The realisation crushed against my chest with physical force, making it hard to breathe. Guilt consumed me like wildfire, scorching away all rational thought. but I had put this innocent girl in danger it was the only choice.nevertheless Her blood would be on my hands. But I couldn't collapse now, not when seconds could mean the difference between life and death.

I bolted towards office Jessicas team had been using, my heart hammering against my ribs like a caged animal desperate for escape. The fluorescent lights overhead blurred into streaks as I ran, my footsteps echoing in the empty corridor. Sweat beaded on my forehead, trickling down my temple. I reached the door, my hand slick with perspiration as I gripped the handle and swung it open with such force that it slammed against the wall with a resounding crack.

Every head in the room snapped toward me. eyes wide with surprise, locked onto my face. I could see my own terror reflected in their expressions as they registered my disheveled appearance.

"Abigail is on her way with Jessica," I gasped, the words tumbling out between ragged breaths. "We need a medical team at the front entrance immediately. She's in critical condition." My voice cracked on the last word, betraying the fragile control I was desperately maintaining.

The team transformed before my eyes, shifting from startled colleagues to a precision unit. No questions, no hesitation just immediate, coordinated action. . Within seconds, they had evacuated the room, their footsteps fading down the hallway as they called out to each other in the clipped, efficient language of professionals in crisis.

I stood alone in the sudden silence, the empty chairs and abandoned coffee mugs stark reminders of how quickly everything had changed. My hands were shaking uncontrollably now, and I clenched them into fists to stop the tremors.

Not wanting to impede their well-rehearsed emergency protocol, I forced myself to move, navigating the familiar corridors to the medical wing. The antiseptic smell hit me as I pushed through the double doors, finding three healers already preparing for incoming trauma.

"Front entrance," I instructed, my voice steadier than I felt. "Abigail's bringing her in. It's Jessica. She's—" I couldn't finish the sentence, the words sticking in my throat like thorns.

They nodded grimly, gathering their equipment with practiced efficiency before rushing past me, leaving behind the faint scent of herbs and healing magic.

With trembling fingers, I pulled out my phone and made two brief calls—first to Lyn, then to Enlil. I kept the explanations terse, my voice mechanical as I relayed the bare facts, hanging up before they could hear the emotion threatening to overwhelm me.

Feeling utterly helpless yet unable to remain still, I made my way to the entrance, each step heavier than the last. The waiting area was eerily quiet, the usual bustle of activity suspended in anticipation of the emergency. I paced the length of the room, each turn bringing me face to face with the large glass doors through which Jessica would arrive—if she arrived at all. The thought sent a fresh wave of nausea through me.

Tick. Tock. Tick. Tock. The wall clock's mechanical heartbeat seemed to grow louder with each passing second. Minutes stretched into small eternities, each one a torturous cycle of fear and desperate hope. My mind conjured horrific images of Jessica's condition, each scenario worse than the last. I bit my lip until I tasted blood, trying to anchor myself to reality. The medical team stood at attention, their faces masks of professional calm that couldn't quite hide the tension in their shoulders. We all jumped at the sudden screech of tires that cut through the silence like a knife. The roar of an overworked engine followed, growing louder until it culminated in a desperate mechanical wail as a car skidded to a violent stop directly in front of the entrance.

Our collective intake of breath was audible as time seemed to freeze for one crystalline moment. Then the nightmare truly began.

Without hesitation, the team of medical professionals exploded into action. The head physician barked orders as two nurses rushed forward, their scrubs a blur of pale blue against the stark white of the entrance. The emergency team flung open the car door with such force that the hinges groaned in protest. My heart hammered against my ribcage as I caught my first glimpse of Jessica.

God, no. Please, no.

It was Jessica, but not Jessica. Her body was contorted, limbs bent and flailing at unnatural angles as if something inside her was trying to break free. Her skin, once smooth and olive-toned, now stretched taut over bulging veins that pulsed an unnatural purple-black beneath the surface. Patches of her flesh had mottled into a sickening grey, cracking in places to reveal raw, weeping tissue underneath. But worst of all were her eyes—still Jessica's eyes—wide with terror and recognition, silently pleading for help from within a face that was becoming less human by the second.

I staggered backward, bile rising in my throat, my vision tunnelling until all I could see was her transformed body. This was my fault. My choices, my actions had reduced this vibrant young woman to this... this aberration. The weight of my guilt crushed down on me like a physical force, making it hard to breathe, hard to think.

The medics worked with choreographed precision, their movements belying the horror of what they were witnessing. With gloved hands that never hesitated, they carefully transferred Jessica onto a stretcher, securing straps across her writhing form. The head physician was already inserting an IV, his voice steady as he called out vital signs that made no sense to my shock-addled brain.

Abigail and Paul stumbled out of the car after her, their clothes splattered with what I prayed wasn't Jessica's blood. Abigail's face was a mask of fury and despair, her usual composure shattered. Paul looked shell-shocked, his complexion ashen, eyes darting nervously between Jessica and the exit as if calculating his chances of escape.

"What happened to her?" I managed to choke out, but my question was lost in the cacophony of urgent medical instructions as they wheeled Jessica through the doors. The stretcher's wheels squeaked against the polished floor, the sound obscenely mundane against the backdrop of this horror.

I watched, paralysed, as they disappeared down the corridor. The smell of antiseptic mixed with the metallic tang of blood hung in the air, a sickening reminder that this wasn't just a nightmare I could wake from. This was real, and Jessica, innocent, trusting Jessica, was paying the price for my choice.

***

With a leaden heart and trembling hands, I herded everyone into the conference room like a shepherd gathering frightened sheep. The fluorescent lights hummed overhead, casting harsh shadows across drawn faces as the heavy door clicked shut behind us. The air instantly thickened with unspoken accusations and fear I could almost taste the metallic tang of it on my tongue.

"I need someone to explain what happened," I said, my voice cracking like thin ice beneath too much weight. My guilt was a physical presence crushing my chest, making each breath a struggle. "Please."

The sudden scrape of chair legs against hardwood floor shattered my spiral of self loathing. Abigail rose with deliberate slowness, her slender frame vibrating with barely contained rage. The temperature in the room seemed to drop several degrees as her lips pulled back to reveal elongated canines not metaphorical fangs, but actual, gleaming points designed for tearing flesh.

In one fluid, inhuman movement, she was across the table. Paul's feet dangled inches above the carpet, his face rapidly purpling as Abigail's pale fingers constricted around his throat. His eyes bulged, bloodshot and terrified.

"Tell me everything you know, Paul," Abigail growled, her voice no longer human but something ancient and predatory. A thin line of saliva hung from one exposed fang. "Every. Single. Detail. Or I swear by all that is unholy, I will make you beg for death as a mercy."

My body moved on instinct, lunging forward to intervene, but Gudmundur's massive hand clamped down on my shoulder with bruising force. The Viking-like man towered beside me, his weathered face grim in the harsh lighting.

"Don't," he whispered, his breath hot against my ear, voice like gravel. "This might be exactly what we need. Some men only speak truth when facing their mortality."

Abigail released her grip just enough for Paul to draw a desperate, wheezing breath. Her eyes normally a warm now glowed with an unearthly crimson light that reflected in the tears streaming down Paul's cheeks.

"I've told you everything I know, Abigail," Paul gasped, hands clawing uselessly at her iron grip. "I swear it on my life, on my mother's grave please!"

The lie hung in the air between them. Even without my abilities, it would have been obvious but with them, I could see the deception swirling in his aura like oil on water, dark and slick with fear. Abigail saw it too, her nostrils flared as if she could smell the falsehood on him.

She raised her free hand, fingers slowly curling into a white-knuckled fist. The fluorescent lights flickered ominously, casting momentary shadows across her face that made her appear skull-like, death personified.

"Last chance, Paul," she hissed, each word dripping with venom and promise. "The truth. Now. Or what comes next will make you nostalgic for the simple days when all I did was choke you."

Paul's desperate eyes darted around the conference room like trapped animals, seeking any ally, any escape. The faces that stared back were stone some averted their gaze, unable to watch but unwilling to intervene. Everyone in that room had seen what had happened to Jessica; everyone knew the stakes. And every single one of them loved Jess with fierce loyalty.

No one would stand against Abigail's wrath to protect the man who might have helped orchestrate Jessica's suffering.

The silence stretched, punctuated only by Paul's ragged breathing and the soft tick-tick-tick of the wall clock counting down his options. His face contorted with the internal war loyalty to Kane versus fear of the very real monster before him. Sweat beaded on his forehead, running in rivulets down his temples despite the room's chill.

Something like pity stirred in my chest as I watched him squirm under Abigail's merciless scrutiny. He was pathetic, yes, but also human flawed, frightened, and facing something beyond human understanding. The pity, however, was quickly washed away by the tide of urgency rising within me. Jessica was fighting for her life down the hall, her body rebelling against her, her humanity slipping away with each passing minute.

We needed answers. We needed them now. And if Abigail's methods were the fastest route to those answers, then God help me, I would let her proceed. My stomach twisted with the moral compromise, but Jessica's contorted face flashed before me, those pleading eyes trapped in a body turning against itself.

Finally, after what felt like an eternity suspended between heartbeats, Paul's resolve shattered like thin glass.

"Fine, I'll tell you everything. Just—please—let me go," he pleaded, voice cracking on the last word.

Abigail's response was immediate and merciless. She hurled him against the wall with such force that the framed motivational poster beside him cracked, sending a spiderweb of fractures across its glass. Paul crumpled to the floor, gasping, a thin trickle of blood running from his nostril down to his quivering upper lip. Abigail returned to her seat with predatory grace, her eyes—still glowing that unnatural crimson—never leaving Paul's trembling figure. The message was clear to everyone in the room: his intentions and reasons were no longer relevant. He was a condemned man. Abigail had already sealed his fate.

Paul pulled himself up to a sitting position, back pressed against the wall as if trying to melt into it. His breath came in ragged gasps that seemed to scrape against the silence.

"Soon after she started attending the gym, just before her debut fight," he began, each word carefully measured, "Kane approached me privately. He's always been perceptive when it comes to these matters—almost supernaturally so. I could tell immediately he had caught onto something about her."

Paul swallowed hard, Adam's apple bobbing painfully in his throat. "I reassured him that Jessica was the only one from the agency, carefully avoiding any mention of you. All he wanted, he said, was for me to keep an eye on her and report back any noteworthy activities."

His fingers twitched nervously against the carpet. "So I did. I would casually mention her part-time job, her training schedule, other mundane details to appease his curiosity. But that's all I ever divulged to him, I swear it."

He paused, taking a moment to collect his thoughts. The conference room felt like a pressure chamber, the air growing heavier with each passing second. I could hear the soft wheezing of Gudmundur's breath behind me, feel the collective tension of everyone present pressing against my skin like static electricity.

"He sent me a message this morning," Paul continued, his voice dropping to barely above a whisper. The words stuttered out of him like reluctant confessions. "The text just said to make sure she was alone in the prep room. So I did as I was told. After I carefully wrapped her hands in cloth,God, her hands!"

His voice broke, and for a moment I thought I saw genuine remorse flash across his features. "I made some excuse and left to meet Kane at the designated time. And then…»

Sweat beaded on his forehead, gathering until a single drop traced a path down his temple like a tear. "And then he told me what he had planned. The giving her the drug. about The fighters waiting in the ring to ambush her. All of it."

Paul's words trailed off, the weight of guilt visibly pressing down on his shoulders until he seemed to physically shrink before our eyes. His gaze dropped to the floor, unable to meet the accusatory stares surrounding him.

"It wasn't supposed to end the way it did," he finally admitted, the words hollow and pathetic in the charged air. His eyes darted frantically around the room, searching for a sympathetic face, an escape route, divine intervention—anything. "She was just supposed to show enhanced abilities, not become... that." His voice cracked. "Not hurt so many people. Not hurt herself."

Paul's shoulders hunched forward as if carrying an invisible weight. A thin sheen of sweat glistened on his forehead under the harsh fluorescent lights.

"She shouldn't have been able to beat that many, and he kept sending more fighters in," he added, desperation creeping into his voice. His hands trembled as he gestured vaguely toward some unseen horror. "They were all hardened mercenaries and fighters—men twice her size with years of combat experience. But she tore through them like paper dolls."

The tension in the room thickened until it felt difficult to breathe. Every pair of eyes fixed on Paul with predatory focus, a collective killing intent locked onto his trembling form. If this man somehow managed to evade Abigail's wrath, there wasn't a person in this room who would let him leave unscathed. Not after what happened to Jessica.

I leaned forward in my chair, the metal legs scraping against the floor in the silence. The sound made Paul flinch. His face was a canvas of fear and exhaustion—dark circles beneath bloodshot eyes, skin pale and clammy. But I couldn't let him stop now. We needed everything.

"What happened during the match exactly?" I asked, keeping my voice deliberately calm, a counterpoint to the murderous energy surrounding us. "How did you manage to escape, and where is Kane now?"

Paul's fingers drummed nervously on the arm of his chair, a frantic rhythm betraying his inner turmoil. He took a deep, shuddering breath before answering.

"At first, Kane was ecstatic," he recounted, bitterness seeping into every syllable. "I've never seen him like that before. He was practically vibrating with excitement, whispering about finally perfecting the drug, about changing the future of combat sports forever." Paul's eyes took on a haunted quality. "But then Jess started... God, she started literally tearing apart the other fighters. Limbs. Blood everywhere. Screaming that wouldn't stop."

He swallowed hard, Adam's apple bobbing painfully. "That's when Kane's excitement turned to anger. His face went completely cold. And that's when this doctor—this thin man in wire-rimmed glasses I'd never seen before—appeared in the VIP area and announced to Kane that he had tripled the dose to test its limits. Said something about 'pushing the boundaries of human potential.'"

My stomach churned violently at the thought of someone so callous, so twisted, conducting dangerous experiments on Jessica— on any human—for their own scientific curiosity. The room seemed to tilt slightly as rage pulsed behind my eyes.

"What happened next?" I pressed, my knuckles white as I gripped the edge of the table.

"After the fourth set of reinforcements had been sent in—and after Jessica had..." Paul's voice faltered, his face contorting as though physically unable to articulate the horror he'd witnessed. His hands trembled violently against his thighs. "Kane grabbed the doctor by his pristine white lab coat and fled through the emergency exit. The coward didn't even look back at what he'd created."

Paul's eyes grew distant, glazed with the reflection of memories no human should carry. "Blood on the walls. On the ceiling. Spattering across the VIP glass like crimson rain. The sounds—" his voice cracked, "—God, the sounds were worse than the sights. Bones snapping like kindling. Men screaming until their voices gave out. And Jessica... laughing."

His jaw set with unexpected determination, a flicker of resolve cutting through his terror. "That's when I made my way down to the exit of the arena, past security guards who were too paralysed with fear to stop me. I waited there for Jessica's rampage to end, clutching her gym bag like some pathetic offering of atonement. I thought maybe I could get her out safely, make up for what I'd done. Guide her back to herself somehow." His eyes welled with tears. "But by then it was too late. When she finally emerged, covered in—" he swallowed hard, "—she wasn't Jess anymore. Her eyes were empty. Like looking at a stranger wearing her skin."

I lunged for my phone, fingers fumbling across the screen as adrenaline surged through my veins. The medical wing answered on the second ring, and my voice trembled with an urgency that surprised even me.

"Listen carefully," I commanded, pressing the phone so hard against my ear it hurt. "Whatever they gave Jessica is a highly potent derivative of the compound you've been studying. It's at least three times stronger than anything we've encountered. Her system is drowning in it." My free hand clenched into a white-knuckled fist. "My recommendation is to keep her heavily sedated—maximum dose—and do everything possible to obtain a clean blood sample before you flush her system. We need to know exactly what we're dealing with."

Ending the call, I rounded on Paul with such ferocity that he shrank back against the wall. The room seemed to darken around us as my patience finally snapped. My voice emerged as a low, dangerous growl that barely resembled my own.

"Do you have any idea where they could be producing this vile crap?" I demanded, each word dripping with contempt. "Where is Kane taking his pet scientist? Where would they go to ground?" The questions came in a rapid-fire burst, my composure crumbling in the face of Jessica's suffering. "If there's even a shred of humanity left in you, you'll tell me everything."

Paul's response came hesitantly, his gaze darting between me and Abigail as though calculating which of us presented the lesser threat. "I think—I'm almost certain it's down by the old shipping docks, the abandoned warehouse district. Building 17." He licked his dry lips. "But that's all I know, I swear. Kane never trusted anyone with the full picture."

Drawing myself up to my full height, I turned to Gudmundur, who stood ready by the door, his massive frame tense with anticipation. When I spoke, my voice carried the weight of absolute authority, leaving no room for misinterpretation.

"Listen to me carefully. I want you and your team to find this facility and conduct a raid immediately. You have full tactical authority to use Osaki and Danielle's specialised teams—all resources at your disposal." My eyes narrowed, emphasising the gravity of what came next. "Our top priority is retrieving Kane and this doctor alive for questioning. They are the only ones who can tell us how to help Jessica. Secure any samples, any research, any scrap of information about what they've created." I stepped closer, my voice dropping to a deadly whisper. "Do I make myself absolutely clear? This isn't just a mission. This is personal." My voice cracked slightly on the last word, betraying the storm of emotions churning beneath my professional veneer.

Gudmundur's face tightened, a muscle jumping in his jaw as he nodded solemnly. His eyes cold and typically unreadable flashed with something I rarely saw there, raw hatred. "We will head out now," he replied, his Icelandic accent thickening with emotion. "We'll find them."

"Keith," I called, spotting another team member preparing to follow Gudmundur. The fluorescent lights caught the sheen of sweat on his forehead as he turned.

"Yes, sir," he answered, standing straighter, the leather of his tactical holster creaking with the movement.

I crossed to him, lowering my voice to ensure Paul couldn't overhear from where he sat trembling. "I have a different assignment for you." My fingers tapped against my thigh, a nervous habit I'd never managed to break. "I need you to extract everything from Paul—names, addresses, shell companies, offshore accounts—every person who's touched these fights or profited from them. I want them all brought in for questioning." I glanced toward the door where Jessica was being treated. "also organise a forensic team to dissect Kane's business operations. Every email, every transaction, every phone call. Leave no stone unturned."

Keith's eyes darkened with understanding. "Consider it done," he replied, voice steady despite the gravity of what we faced. With practiced efficiency, he crossed to Paul, gripped his upper arm, and guided him toward an interrogation room. Paul's shoulders hunched forward as if already anticipating what awaited him.

Suddenly, Abigail bolted from her chair with such force it toppled backward, clattering against the floor. Her eyes, red-rimmed and wild, fixed on Paul's retreating back with predatory intensity. The look on her face sent ice through my veins; it was the expression of someone beyond reason, beyond restraint.

My heart hammered against my ribs as I lunged forward, blocking her path. "Abigail, stop!" I hissed, grabbing her wrist. Her pulse raced beneath my fingers. "You can't have him. Not yet. He may hold vital information we haven't uncovered."

She wrenched her arm free, her breath coming in short, sharp bursts. Grief and rage warred across her features, transforming her usually composed face into something almost unrecognisable. For a moment, I thought she might strike me.

"I know," she finally managed through clenched teeth, each word precise and brittle. "But time is running out for him. Can't you understand that?" The unspoken threat hung between us, what she would do to Paul when we no longer needed him.

She attempted to push past me, the scent of her shampoo—something floral and incongruously gentle—momentarily filling my senses as her shoulder brushed mine. I planted my feet firmly, becoming an immovable barrier.

"Where are you going?" I demanded, my voice cracking with desperation, the words escaping sharper than I'd intended. The fluorescent lights overhead cast harsh shadows across her face, highlighting the hollows beneath her cheekbones. I needed her expertise, her uncanny insight. We couldn't afford for her to lose control now not when everything balanced on a knife's edge.

"To sit with Jess," she answered, her voice breaking like thin ice underfoot. "She shouldn't be alone right now, and I need to be there for her." Her chin lifted defiantly, a familiar gesture that spoke volumes about the steel beneath her gentle exterior. "Don't even think about trying to separate us now."

The raw emotion in her voice hit me like a physical blow. I'd seen her face down armed mercenaries without flinching, but this naked vulnerability was somehow more devastating. My arguments died in my throat, dissolving like smoke.

Defeated by her unwavering determination, I slumped my shoulders. "I understand," I conceded with a heavy sigh that seemed to empty my lungs completely. The weight of responsibility pressed down on me like a concrete slab. "I'll join you there shortly. Right now, I need to get things underway."

As she turned and walked away, her footsteps echoing against the polished floor, I caught a glimpse of unshed tears glistening in her eyes diamonds of grief that refracted the harsh institutional lighting. Her shoulders were rigid with tension, spine straight as a blade as she disappeared through the doorway, leaving me alone in the suddenly cavernous conference room.

The silence engulfed me like a physical weight, broken only by the distant mechanical hum of the ventilation system and the sound of my own ragged breathing echoing in my ears. I made my way back toward my chair, each step leaden as though I were wading through quicksand. The leather creaked in protest as I collapsed into it, my body suddenly feeling twice as heavy, drained by the adrenaline crash that followed Abigail's departure.

With a heart that felt like a stone in my chest, I stared at the empty doorway where she had disappeared. Jessica's life hung in the balance, and the weight of that responsibility threatened to crush me. My fingers trembled as I reached for my phone, the cool metal case slipping against my sweat-dampened palm. I dialled the extension for an onsite dorm room, holding my breath with each number pressed. The electronic tones seemed to stretch into eternity, each one feeling like another precious second ticking away from Jessica's chances of recovery.

After what felt like an agonising eternity but was only a single ring, a gruff voice answered. "Hello?" The familiar rasp of Walker's voice sent a surge of desperate hope through me.

"Walker, it's me," I said, unable to keep the raw emotion from my voice. "I need your help. it's about Jessica's . Please come to my office right away."

The line abruptly disconnected without another word. I pulled the phone away from my ear and stared at it, momentarily paralysed by uncertainty. Had he hung up on me? No Walker wasn't the type for pleasantries. The abrupt disconnection was his way of saying he was already on his way.

I let out a frustrated grumble and pushed myself up from my seat, joints protesting after the tension of the last few hours. A glimmer of hope flickered in my chest as I made my way to my office. If anyone could help us navigate this nightmare, it was Walker. His extensive contacts in the paranormal underground might just pull us from the fire.

As I walked down the dimly lit hallway, fluorescent lights flickering intermittently overhead, shadows seemed to dance along the sterile walls. They stretched and contracted with each step, creating an eerie atmosphere that mirrored the darkness spreading through my thoughts. What if we were already too late? What if Jessica was beyond saving? The questions clawed at my mind, each one sharper than the last, as my footsteps echoed hollowly against the polished floor.

***

In the dimly lit office, I sat across from Walker—the man who had been assisting Abigail in Jessica's training. The harsh fluorescent light above cast deep shadows across his weathered face, highlighting the jagged scar that ran from his left temple to his jaw. His hands were clasped so tightly together on the mahogany desk that his knuckles had turned bone-white, the veins in his forearms standing out like blue rivers against tanned skin. He'd brought Jessica's two housemates in earlier that day at Abigail's direct order, and my team had been debriefing all three of them for hours now, extracting every fragment of information they possessed about Kane's operation.

I drew a slow, deliberate breath, feeling my lungs expand painfully against my ribs. The weight of Jessica's condition pressed down on me like a physical burden. When I finally spoke, my voice emerged cold and detached carefully constructed facade that barely contained the hurricane of rage and fear churning inside me.

"Do you grasp the gravity of our current situation, Walker?" I asked, my fingers unconsciously tracing the edge of the case file before me. "we failed to anticipate Kane's next move."

His jaw clenched so tight I could see a muscle twitching beneath the stubble. Though he maintained his professional demeanour, the slight flaring of his nostrils betrayed his own concern. "All I've been told is that it's an emergency and we are to intervene only if explicitly requested." A flash of frustration darkened his eyes momentarily before he regained his composure, squaring his broad shoulders beneath his tactical jacket. "Do you have a specific task in mind for me to assist with, sir?" he inquired, his deep voice resonating in the confined space.

I leaned forward, the chair creaking beneath my weight, and locked eyes with Walker. His weathered face remained impassive, but I could see the pulse quickening at his temple. "I need detailed information on the realm gates housed within Kane's gym," I said, my voice dropping to barely above a whisper. The fluorescent light flickered once, casting momentary shadows across the room that seemed to dance like the otherworldly entities we both knew lurked beyond those gates. My stomach clenched as memories of the briefing flashed through my mind. My mouth went desert-dry, tongue sticking to the roof as I swallowed hard. "I need to know exactly how many gates exist, where each one leads" My voice cracked betraying the panic I was desperately trying to contain.

Walker's jaw tightened. "I've already shared what I know about the gates with your Agent's ," he said, leaning back and crossing his arms defensively. "We're only allowed access to certain ones. The others..." He paused, eyes darkening with what looked like remembered horror. "The others from what I was told can potentially lead to death—or worse. Realms where time moves differently, where the mind unravels, where what enters rarely returns intact."

I pressed my palms flat against the desk to hide their trembling. "I understand the risks. But can you guide a team to these gates?

Identify which ones are safe and which are off-limits?" The desperation in my chest was a living thing now, clawing at my ribs. Jessica's face pale, vulnerable flashed before my eyes.

Something shifted in his expression recognition of the raw fear I couldn't fully conceal. "I would be more than happy to assist," he replied, though confusion creased his brow. He leaned forward, his shirt stretching across his broad shoulders. " Kane's security isn't just human there are things guarding those gates that..." He trailed off, the concern in his voice unmistakable, his loyalty to my team evident in the tight lines around his eyes. I spoke firmly, my tone brooking no argument as I conveyed the urgency of our situation. "My team understand the danger, but with each passing moment, Kane grow closer to destroying any evidence that could incriminate him."

"fine but before that I want to know what's happened?" The man opposite me demanded.

"They discovered Jess's true identity and she is currently being treated in the medical ward. she was injected with the drug we have been investigating and set her loose in the arena filled with mercenaries."

His face visibly paled at this information. "Take me to her, then we will proceed with your operation." he demanded, I nodded, leading the way as we hurried towards the med ward.

CHAPTER 22

Awakening in Pain

****Jessica****

The sharp sting of pain jolted through my body, and I welcomed it eagerly. It was a reassuring reminder that I was still alive. As I slowly regained consciousness, the first thing that registered in my mind was the constant beep of hospital equipment, filling the sterile room with its monotonous rhythm. The smell of cleaning chemicals lingered in the air, mingling with the faint scent of antiseptic. Despite the starkness of my surroundings, I found solace in these familiar scents and sounds. They were proof that I was somewhere safe.

But even as I clung to this thought, I couldn't bring myself to open my eyes. If I kept them closed, maybe I could deny the reality of what had happened. Maybe it was all just a nightmare, or perhaps someone else had committed those horrible acts. I couldn't have been responsible for such unspeakable deeds.

But deep down, I knew the truth. I remembered everything, every moment of agony and despair that drove me to inflict harm on others. And as these thoughts swirled in my head, overwhelming me with guilt and regret, a choked sob escaped from my throat. In that moment of vulnerability, someone's warm hand gently squeezed mine, a silent gesture of comfort and understanding.

Despite the fear bubbling in my chest, I forced my eyes to remain closed. The consequences of my actions loomed over me like a dark cloud and I couldn't bear to face them. So I stubbornly kept my eyes shut, hoping to stay lost in the darkness and avoid the harsh reality waiting for me when I opened them again.

But then, a familiar voice cut through the stillness. "I know it's hard, Jess, but I need you to open your eyes now for me, baby girl," Abby's voice was gentle yet firm. "Don't let this beat you. Please face this, and I will stand by your side and help you." She had stayed with me. She had been here all along. My heart swelled with gratitude and love for her.

Slowly, cautiously, I opened my eyes. The bright lights stung at first, making me squint and shield my gaze. As my vision adjusted, I saw IV tubes poking out from beneath the white blankets covering my arms. And then, I saw Abigail's hands wrapped tightly around mine.

My throat felt dry and scratchy as I tried to speak, but no words would come out. Panic set in as I searched frantically for something to drink. But before I could even signal for help, Abby was already there with a cup of water and a little bent straw. "Small sip," she instructed gently. "You've been heavily sedated for a few days, so you might be feeling disoriented."

As I took a sip of the cool water, relief flooded through my body like a wave. Abby's presence beside me was a soothing balm, reassuring me that I was not alone in whatever lay beyond these sterile hospital walls.

My voice was raw and raspy as I forced out the question that had been haunting me. "What happened?" Every word felt like it took all of my strength to utter, but I needed to know the truth.

Abby placed the glass gently on the side table and sat down on the edge of my bed with a grave expression. She seemed hesitant to answer, her eyes filled with concern. "Are you sure you want to know?" Her words were gentle, but held an underlying weight. "I would understand if you wanted to take some time to recover before facing the news."

But I couldn't wait any longer. My heart raced in my chest, begging for answers to the questions that had been haunting me so I simply nodded when Abigail asked if I wanted to know what had transpired.

"Do you remember what happened in the arena?" At her question, a lone tear slid down my cheek as memories flooded back, causing me to flinch away. But I was restrained, tied down to the bed by unknown restraints. Panic rose in my chest as I screamed, my eyes wide with shock and fear.

"Jess, you need to calm down," Abby's voice cut through my panicked screams. "We had to restrain you. They gave you a variant of the drug, and as it worked through your system, you became dangerous. As soon as the healers return, I will have them release you, but you need to calm down."

I struggled against the restraints, trying to control my breathing and calm myself down. But being tied down like this brought back memories of Jeremiah and the torture he put me through in those caves. The fear and helplessness threatened to consume me once again. And then Abby's words sank in, I had hurt someone while under the influence of the drug. Guilt and shame washed over me as images of the fight in the arena flashed through my mind.

Abby seemed to sense my thoughts and leaned in close, giving me an awkward hug despite being strapped down. "Jess, it wasn't you," she whispered fiercely into my ear. "Please remember that everything that happened was out of your control." Despite her comforting words, I couldn't shake off the feeling of being a monster.

She held me for a few more moments before pulling away and starting to fill me in on everything that had happened, the fight and subsequent events. My heart and mind were in turmoil, struggling to come to terms with what had transpired.

She tried to skim over the events at the arena as much as possible, but I could tell that they had taken a toll on her as well.

"After the fight ended, Paul rushed you out of the arena. My main concern was finding you. Fortunately, I caught up with Paul as he was trying to get you into his car. Without hesitation, we drove straight here. You were in bad shape when we arrived. They had injected you with a stronger variant of the compound than anything we have seen before. They also gave you something to make you compliant; our healers are still trying to determine the full effects." She shot me an anxious glance and continued her explanation.

"Once we finally managed to get you into the capable hands of the healers, Alex swiftly gathered everyone together and delivered a thorough briefing on our current situation. With Gudmundur's tracking abilities, we were able to pinpoint Kane's whereabouts, along with his accomplice, the alchemist. And from what I've heard, they didn't stand a chance against us. Kieth has been placed in charge of apprehending anyone who was even remotely connected to Kane or the arena fights. As a result, we now have a number of prisoners being held in various facilities run by multiple factions. Even the dragons have joined forces with us, keeping a watchful eye on the fighters and making sure they don't cause any more trouble. To further bolster our efforts, I personally convinced the vampire council to lend their assistance, so they are currently detaining the mages and those responsible for concocting the drugs we have been tracking"

"Do they know what it was that was getting put in the drug? What was its purpose?" I asked not sure if I really wanted to know.

"Jess, darling, you shouldn't be concerning yourself with such things right now. Your focus should be on recovering." Abby gently tried to reassure me .

My determination burned like a raging inferno, fuelled by an unrelenting fire within me. "No, I won't give up," I declared fiercely, refusing to let myself falter in the face of adversity. "I need to see this through." The weight of my words hung heavy in the air, echoing off the walls and reverberating through my bones.

Suddenly, a loud knock thundered through the room, followed by Abby's frustrated groan. Without hesitation, the door burst open and Alex and Lyn stormed into the room. My eyes widened in surprise as I saw them standing before me, their expressions a mix of concern and annoyance.

"Well, well, well," Lyn scolded, her voice stern but tinged with worry. Her brows furrowed and her lips pursed in disappointment. "What am I going to do with you, little one?" She placed a gentle hand on my shoulder, her touch comforting yet chiding at the same time. "Every time I turn around, you end up back in a hospital bed." Her voice softened as she let out a heavy sigh. "You promised me you would be careful." She shook her head in exasperation, knowing that her words were falling on deaf ears yet again.

My head hung low in shame, my body trembling with exhaustion and guilt. I had failed in my mission, and needed to be rescued like a helpless pup. But what was even worse was the knowledge that it was my own body that had committed those terrible acts in the ring. Even though I wasn't in control, it was still me. "Lyn, I'm so sorry," I began, feeling tears prick at the corners of my eyes. "I didn't mean to disappoint you. I'll do better next time, I promise."

But before I could finish my apology, she silenced me with a gentle shushing sound and placed a finger over my lips. "Why would you ever think I'm disappointed in you?" she asked, her voice laced with concern but also pride. "You did an amazing job out there. Abigail has filled me in on everything, and so have your new friend's," she added,

An overwhelming wave of emotions pulsed through my body like a storm, crashing against the walls of my heart. Relief flooded me at her forgiveness, but confusion and uncertainty still lingered like clouds on a stormy day. I lay there in a state of shock, unable to form words or comprehend what was happening.

"Do you truly forgive me for what happened in the arena?" I finally managed to whisper, my voice trembling with emotion. As I spoke, my eyes scanned over my body and I was completely covered by a thick blanket. It was so heavy that it obscured any view of my restrained body, making me feel powerless and vulnerable.

"Now that everyone is present and it's clear that I am acting rationally, could we perhaps remove these restraints? Please," I asked tentatively, my voice barely audible as I mustered up the courage to add a soft plea at the end. The sound of chains rattling echoed in the silence as I waited anxiously for a response, hoping for some semblance of control over my own body again.

Alex spoke first, his voice trembling with a mix of fear and concern. "We need to show you something before we remove the restraints," he said, taking a tentative step forward. "And before you react, keep in mind we have everyone available trying to figure out what happened and how to reverse it."

My heart raced as I tried to process his words. They were keeping me restrained because something was wrong with me?

Panic threatened to consume me, but I took a deep breath and forced myself to remain calm.

With shaking hands, Alex pulled back the blanket covering my body, revealing the shocking truth underneath. My nails had elongated into sharp points, reminding me of their deadly purpose in the arena. As I took in the rest of my body, I noticed I was dressed in a horrid blue and white hospital gown and my arms and legs were bound tightly in thick steel restraints. But that wasn't what caught my attention.

All over my exposed skin in patches were delicate scales of shimmering iridescence.they reminded me of Lyns when she was in her dragon form. they were beautiful, but the realisation of what it meant caused tears to prick at my eyes. Looking up at those gathered around me, their expressions filled with pity and worry, I couldn't hold back any longer and began to cry.

My heart was pounding with a frantic rhythm, each beat echoing in my chest as I tried to make sense of the chaos that had enveloped me. My head swirled with a thousand thoughts and questions, none of which seemed to have an answer. "What's happening to me?" I whispered in a trembling voice, barely audible over the rushing waves of fear and confusion. My hands shook violently as I fought against the restraints, desperate to free myself from this nightmare. But with every futile struggle, the fear only grew stronger, threatening to consume me entirely.

I could feel Alex's worried gaze on me, his hands gentle as he tried to calm me down. I took a deep breath, trying to push away the panic that threatened to overwhelm me. Lyn and Abby stood nearby, their expressions filled with concern and uncertainty.

"We honestly don't know what has happened," Lyn began, her voice strained with emotion. "It could be delayed effects of what Jeremiah did to you in the caves." The mere mention of the caves, where my life had changed forever, sent shivers down my spine.

As I struggled to make sense of it all, Alex caught my attention and gently released my restraints. His eyes were full of worry and compassion. as the last of the restraints got removed Lyn voice began to cut through the chaos again.

"All I can say for sure is that you are still beautiful and I love you like my own daughter," she said, placing a reassuring hand on my shoulder. "So please believe me when I say that we will do everything in our power to figure this out." Her promise lifted some of the weight off my shoulders, but deep down I knew that this was only the start of a long and uncertain journey ahead.

Alexander's voice cut through the sterile silence of the hospital room, his tongue clicking against the roof of his mouth in a show of nerves. "Jess, I want you to try and get some rest," he said softly, concern etched deep into the lines of his face. The harsh light from the overhead fixtures cast shadows across his features, making him appear almost skeletal. "We'll figure everything out. But for now, I will be taking over your team until you are given the all-clear by the healers."

My body jolted upright at his words, a surge of adrenaline coursing through my veins. "No!" I exclaimed, my voice coming out louder than intended. I sounded like a petulant child throwing a tantrum, but I couldn't let Alexander take me off this investigation. This case was personal to me, and I had to be a part of it. My determination burned within me, mirrored by the surge of energy radiating through my body.

"I will see to it that these bastards are apprehended and spend the rest of their miserable lives rotting in Tartarus." As I spoke, an intense current began to pulsate from my body. It surged up the wires and over the cold metal bed frame, causing the electrical equipment I was attached to to go haywire.

"Shit!" I yelled, As Sparks and bolts of white-hot energy leapt from my body and the machines surrounding me, weaving a pulsating web of power that crackled through the air. I felt a surge of fierce determination and anger flowing through my veins. The power within me grew stronger with each passing moment, fuelling my resolve to stay on the case. The crackling energy enveloped me, creating a flowing web of power. "What the fuck is happening?" I screamed, my voice barely audible over the chaos, but my determination remained unshaken.

The sudden burst of bright lights and chaotic energy caused Alex to jump back, desperately trying to avoid being hit by the wild web of electricity crackling through the air. Lyn and Abby immediately wrapped me in their arms, their touch a comforting embrace amidst the chaos. "Jess, baby girl, calm down," Abby whispered urgently through gritted teeth. "We need you to stay focused if we want to solve this case. Take deep breaths and centre yourself." As I fought to regain control over my racing thoughts and panicked body, I remembered the breathing techniques that Abby and Walker had taught me. Slowly but surely, the room around me began to quiet down until all I could hear were the steady inhales and exhales of the four of us.

Lyn's voice rang out, a hint of amusement laced within her words. "That's better now. Let's discuss what's going to happen next, Alex." She gestured for him to come closer, a sly grin on her face as she watched him grumble and reluctantly make his way back to the hospital bed where Lyn and Abby sat, with me nestled between them.

Lyn's posture was rigid and her voice carried a weight of gravity as she began, "As I'm sure you have been told, a clean-up operation is currently underway. All factions, regardless of their allegiances, are cooperating to bring an end to these illegal fights. Our holding facilities are rapidly reaching maximum capacity as we detain anyone who has been documented participating in or associated with these events."

As Lyn spoke, her eyes darted over to Alex, who sat at the bottom of the bed with a tense expression on his face. He kept a wary distance from us, as if he feared our reactions.

"Furthermore," Alex interjected nervously, "we have also apprehended Kane and the alchemist responsible for creating the drug used." At the mention of the alchemist, my instincts kicked in and I let out a low growl that surprised even myself.

Alex's voice was strained as he continued, "Despite our tireless efforts, we have yet to extract any useful information regarding this case." The tension in the room was almost suffocating as they all anxiously waited for My reaction to this news.

"However," Alex quickly added, "our investigations have led to some surprising leads in other cases. So that's a small victory." Before he could say more, I interjected with a pressing question.

"What about Kane and his alchemist? Have they not provided us with anything?" I demanded, convinced that their expertise must have yielded some valuable information.

"Not yet," Alex admitted with a sigh, "but I'm sure that will change once they realise you are still among the living. They both seemed certain that you wouldn't survive what they did to you." A chill ran down my spine at his words. "Once you are feeling up to it, I would like for you to personally interview them. Perhaps you will be able to get more out of them than we have."

The words echoed in surround sound as Abby and Lyn made their demand simultaneously, their voices reverberating off the walls of the small room. I had to stifle a laugh at the synchronised nature of it all, if not for the shock and embarrassment etched on their faces.

"Of course, ladies, I have no intention of putting Jess in harm's way, but I must remind you that you are not permitted to interview any of the detainees," Alex stated firmly, his tone brooking no argument. My eyes first landed on Abby, her pouty expression giving away her disappointment at being denied access. But when I turned to Lyn, I was met with a blazing fury that radiated from every inch of her body. "How dare you presume to dictate who I can and cannot speak with, elf?" Her voice dripped with authority and disdain, making even Alex seem small in comparison. Despite myself, I couldn't help but feel a twinge of admiration for her boldness and confidence in challenging his authority.

Lyn's jaw tightened as she stared at Alex, her frustration mounting. "I will remind you, Lyn, that I am here to enforce law and order," he said firmly, not backing down despite the tension in the room. "Having you interrogate the people responsible for harming your adopted daughter is just stupid." They held each other's gaze for longer than was comfortable, sparks flying between them as they both refused to back down. Finally, Lyn released an exasperated breath and conceded defeat. "OK, you win," she said through gritted teeth. "Still, I would like to be apprised of everything going forward. I refuse to leave Jessica's side until I'm satisfied she is safe." Her tone held a hint of threat, and Alex couldn't help but feel a pang of guilt deep in his chest. He knew that Lyn held him accountable for what happened to Jessica, and no matter what else transpired, she would never forget that he was the one who put her in harm's way. As he looked into her determined eyes, he knew he had a long road ahead in earning back her trust.

My heart ached with worry as I asked about the well-being of my friends, Walker, Nixie, and Lunette. Had they made it here safely? I couldn't bear the thought of something happening to them because of my actions.

"They arrived unharmed," replied Alex, his voice heavy with relief. "The sample they delivered has been crucial in your recovery. Without it, I fear we wouldn't have been able to save you. And Mr. Walker has been instrumental in helping us locate Kane's other facilities. It turns out he had more than just one gym or fighting arena. He also showed us the realm corridor."

My mind whirled with questions at this new information. What else had Kane been hiding? What other horrors awaited us?

"Our tactical team and some skilled mages accompanied Mr. Walker as we ventured into the realm corridor," continued Alex, his tone grave. "After breaking through the wards on the doors, we were met with truly terrifying sights." A shiver raced down my spine, sending a chill through my body. Dread crept into my thoughts as I imagined what they might have found behind those doors.

Despite my fear, a tiny spark of curiosity burned within me, yearning to know the truth and validate all the struggles I had endured. But as I trembled with both anticipation and trepidation, I knew deep in my heart that no answers could ever justify the pain and suffering I had endured.

"We discovered some doors that led to hostels filled with emaciated junkies, driven mad by the drug, Others seemed to be holding areas for fighters who were addicted and still useful. And we even stumbled upon the alchemist's lab." Alex paused, catching their breath before continuing. "We're still investigating every door to make sure we haven't missed anything, but this find would not have been possible without your help."

Before anyone else could speak, a stern-looking healer approached us. "That's enough for now," they said firmly. "She needs rest, and you can all come back later if she is well enough."

This sparked a heated argument between Lyn, Abby, and the healer as they refused to leave my side. They declared that if anyone tried to remove them, it would take an army to succeed. The fierce loyalty and protectiveness of my friends warmed my heart even in such a dire situation.

CHAPTER 23

Confronting the Paranormal Council

Three long days had passed since I was jolted awake in the sterile, white walls of the medical centre. Now, here I sat in Alex's office, facing four powerful individuals from the paranormal community. Three of them wore stern expressions, their anger palpable in the air, while the fourth, and perhaps most influential, sported a smug smirk on his face.

Sitting at the head of the table was Enlil, a prominent figure known for his calm demeanour and wise counsel. His deep voice carried a tone of patience, as if he were humouring a child before delivering a firm no.

"Please explain to us why you believe it is necessary for you to interview Kane," Enlil asked pointedly, his steely gaze fixed on me.

I took a deep breath before responding, knowing that my words needed to be carefully chosen. "He's not talking, and we need information. We can't afford to let these two question him." I gestured towards Lyn and Abby, who sat beside me with tense postures and glints of malice in their eyes. "If you do not trust me to refrain from harming him, then send someone in with me or use magic to prevent me from doing so. Also, Alex promised that once I was healed enough he would allow me back on the case. That includes letting me interview Kane and his alchemist."

As my words hung in the air, the room fell into a heavy silence. The tension was palpable, like a thick fog that filled every corner of the space. I held my breath, hoping against hope that my plea would sway them to grant me access to Kane. But each passing second only added to the doubts and fears swirling in my mind. Would they continue to deny me the chance to gather crucial information?

Sensing my hesitation, Enlil spoke again, his voice irritatingly calm. "What makes you think he will speak to you when he has been unwilling to talk to Alex and myself?"

I turned to look at Alex, who had remained silent throughout this exchange. I wondered if he had an opinion on the matter. "He knows me," I replied earnestly. "In his eyes, I was just a tool to be used and discarded. And then I ended up being the one responsible for his world falling apart and turning into chaos. If I were in his position, I would want to speak with the person responsible."

I paused, searching for the right words to convince them. "I may not get any useful information from him. But on the other hand, my presence alone could push him over the edge and cause him to slip up.after all he expects me to be dead not changed" I gestured towards my appearance which had continued shifting and changing as I continued to recover from my injuries.

"I believe there is merit in my plan," I concluded, hoping they would see the potential in my risky strategy.

As their eyes scanned over me, I felt like a specimen under a microscope. It was as if they were seeing me for the first time, noticing every intricate detail of my appearance. The once dull locks that hung from my head had transformed into a vibrant shade of purple, shimmering and reflecting the light like precious gems. My eyes, once round and human-like, now bore slitted pupils like those of a cat, giving me an otherworldly aura. And worst of all, scales covered parts of my body like a strange, iridescent armour. They glinted in the light, adorning my arms and legs with their intricate patterns and designs. The sharp claws that extended from my fingertips were now a permanent fixture, a reminder of the fantastical transformation I had undergone.

But it wasn't just my appearance that had changed. Along with it came newfound abilities and instincts, but also unexpected challenges. Every movement was accompanied by the sound of ripping fabric as my clothes struggled to contain my new strength and sharpness. Abby's disapproval radiated off her as she sat cross-legged, her arms tightly folded against her chest. She believed I hadn't given myself enough time to heal and adjust to these changes.

The words came from Lyn like a gentle breeze, her voice carrying a hint of apprehension. "I am inclined to agree with Abigail. It is too soon for you to take an active role in the investigation."

"If you two had your way, I would be locked in the medical centre for the foreseeable future." They didn't even try to deny it, so I turned my attention to Alex and Enlil, trying to gauge their thoughts through their expressions.

"And what do you both think about my suggestion?" I asked

Enlil's lips curled into a mischievous smile, his eyes sparkling with amusement at the scene unfolding before him. His carefree demeanour didn't surprise me, given the little I've learned about him. He was a creature of impulse, following his whims without regard for anyone else's understanding. On the other hand, Alex was more pragmatic, always considering what was best for the agency as a whole. And it was his opinion that concerned me the most.

"I hate to admit it, but I think you have a point," Alex finally spoke up after a moment of contemplation. "If you went in as you are now, it might just unsettle him enough to say something."

Enlil nodded sagely and gracefully rose from his seat, a glint of determination in his eyes. The atmosphere between us crackled with unspoken tension and eager anticipation.

"It seems you have everything under control for the moment," he stated, his voice laced with authority, "so unless there is anything else, I must be off. There are matters that require my immediate attention." With a single swift movement, he vanished before anyone could even think to respond, leaving us all stunned and speechless.

Finally,

Summoning all of my courage, I finally broke the suffocating silence. "So...does that mean we're moving forward with my plan?" My heart raced as I turned to face my companions, searching for any signs of approval or disapproval.

To my relief, they all nodded in unison. "In that case, should we go now? The sooner we get answers, the better," I said eagerly, determined not to let this opportunity slip away from me.

But before we could head to the interview room, Alex spoke up with a nervous edge to his voice. "Before we move forward, there's something important I need to discuss with all of you." His words filled me with unease. "Jess, there is something I want you to do once you have completed the interviews. And I must warn you, it may not be something you'll like. But it is necessary and all I ask is that you listen to me before reacting."

My stomach churned with anxiety as I waited for him to continue. "Jess, we can't ignore what has happened to you. It's essential that we start seeking explanations sooner rather than later." Deep down, I knew he was right. As much as I wanted to focus on this case and bring justice to the victims, I couldn't deny the fact that my own appearance would hinder our progress.

Despite understanding his reasoning, the thought of abandoning this case felt like a painful stab to my gut. But if it meant finding answers and possibly reversing whatever had happened to me, I knew I had to trust Alex's judgment.

My heart raced as i stood in front of Alex, trying to make sense of the unexpected turn of events.

"I'm not taking you off the case. If anything, I'm expanding its scope," Alex explained, his voice low and intense.

Lyn's eyes widened in surprise, her emerald green irises reflecting the light. "Alex, this isn't what we discussed," she interjected, her tone almost pleading as she looked at him with a mix of concern and disappointment.

"You're right. It isn't," Alex responded with a heavy sigh, his normally confident demeanour faltering for a moment. He ran his hand through his hair in frustration, the strands catching the light and casting shadows on his face.

Caught off guard by the sudden change in plans, I couldn't help but feel bewildered. My mind raced to catch up with the conversation, trying to make sense of what was happening. "Would someone like to inform me as to what's going on because I'm completely lost right now?" I asked, my voice tinged with confusion.

Taking a deep breath, Alex turned to face me directly, his gaze locking onto mine. "I need you to accompany Lyn back to the dragon realm. Your current appearance won't raise any suspicions there," he explained, gesturing to my changed appearance. "And apart from the elves, they are our best chance at figuring out what's happening with you." His words hung heavily in the air, each one laced with worry and determination.

My thoughts raced like a wildfire, consumed by questions and concerns. "But how am I supposed to continue my investigation if I'm stuck in a different realm?" I asked hesitantly, unsure of what was to come next.

The air was thick with tension and uncertainty as I waited for an answer. My Alex's gaze was steely and focused, his face lined with worry and determination.

"While you were undercover, I received troubling news from the watcher council that both the dragon archive and watchers library have experienced breaches, their most guarded secrets exposed. And the culprit has obtained information and forbidden spells from the ancient blood wars," he explained, his voice low and grave.

I felt a knot form in my stomach as he continued. "The watchers have retreated into seclusion, with only Enlil willing to leave their personal realm to assist us. It is my belief that the same individuals responsible for the abductions, experimentations and even the fights are also behind these break-ins."

His intense gaze bore into mine, searching for any hesitation before he continued. "That is why I ask of you to delve into the dragon archives. This task serves a dual purpose: to gather any clues that may lead us to those responsible and to find a way to aid you in your current predicament."

My mind whirled at the enormity of the request. "But how am I supposed to do this alone? Lyn will have her own responsibilities and I have no idea where to even begin," I confessed, feeling overwhelmed by the weight of the task.

But Alex's unwavering faith in me gave me a glimmer of hope. "You are a resourceful and skilled individual, Jessica. Have confidence in yourself, and you will find a way, But You're right, you will have a lot on your plate. The breach is not yet public knowledge, but it has caused turmoil within the council. That is why Abigail will be joining you on this journey."

"I'm sure Abby has other obligations," I said with a tinge of sadness. "She can't always be stuck by my side while I recover and investigate."

A sudden scraping noise brought my attention back to the present. I found myself face-to-face with a stern-looking vampire, her aura exuding authority. The room fell silent as if everyone was holding their breath.

"Let me make one thing clear so there are no further misunderstandings," she began in a firm tone. "I did not witness everything you went through for mere entertainment. When Lyn first asked me to keep an eye on you, it was out of gratitude for someone who had helped me greatly. But after witnessing how you conquered challenge after challenge that would break most individuals, I developed a deep admiration for you. And now, Jessica, I say this with the weight of my centuries of existence: I love you with every fibre of my being and it would be an honour to accompany you to the dragon realm."

My mind was blank, unable to find the right words to say. I could feel Abby's concern and care emanating from her presence, but I couldn't figure out how to handle this situation. Suddenly, a warm wetness on my cheek made me aware of my own tears, and before I knew it, I was enveloped in Abby's comforting embrace as my tears flowed freely.

"It's alright, Jess. You don't have to feel the same way. I just want you to know that I will always be here for you. You don't have to go through this alone," she whispered soothingly into my hair, her gentle touch easing my sobs.

I had been so oblivious to her deep feelings for me. How could she possibly love someone who was so oblivious to her?

"Alright, let's not get too caught up in emotions. We still need to question Kane," Abby spoke up, breaking the moment. Everyone nodded in agreement and we made our way towards the interrogation room with heavy hearts and conflicted minds

CHAPTER 24

Watching Kane's Arrival

I stood on the observation side of the thick, reinforced glass, my fingers pressed against its cool surface as I watched them bring Kane into the interrogation room. Each passing second felt like a ticking time bomb in my chest, counting down to an inevitable explosion. My stomach twisted into knots, acid burning at the back of my throat as fear and adrenaline coursed through my veins. The fluorescent lights overhead cast harsh shadows across Kane's face, highlighting the cruel set of his jaw and the calculating gleam in his eyes. Beside me, Abby's entire body tensed visibly her shoulders hunched forward, jaw clenched tight, muscles coiled like a spring ready to snap. Her breathing had become shallow and quick, and I could practically feel the hatred radiating off her in waves. Without thinking, I reached out and took her trembling hand in mine, squeezing it gently, trying to project a strength and calmness I didn't feel. My own heart hammered against my ribs, threatening to burst through my chest. "You'll be right here," I repeated for what felt like the hundredth time, my voice strained with forced confidence that sounded hollow even to my own ears. "And if anything goes wrong, anything at all you and Lyn can come in and help me faster than anyone else." As I spoke those words, I stole a glance at Lyn, who stood rigid on Abby's other side. Her face was carved from stone, jaw clenched so tight I could see the muscle twitching beneath her skin. Though her arms hung loose at her sides, her fingers kept curling into fists, then relaxing, then curling again. Her eyes never left Kane's figure, tracking his every movement like a predator. The hatred radiating from her was almost a living, breathing thing between us. She despised the idea of me going in there alone, and I knew she was fighting every instinct to burst through that door and tear Kane apart herself.

The thought of letting either Lyn or Abby into that room with Kane sent icy shivers cascading down my spine. Their restraint now was nothing short of miraculous. They gave me silent nods when I caught their eyes, a wordless promise to stick to our plan and stay under control at least for now. The tension in the observation room was so thick it felt like breathing through wet cotton, and I found myself offering silent prayers to whatever gods might be listening that everything would go according to plan.

My eyes narrowed as I studied Kane through the one-way glass. He stood tall and imposing in the interrogation room, his broad shoulders pulled back, arms crossed over his chest in a display of arrogant confidence that made my stomach turn. The bright orange jumpsuit that adorned his muscular frame seemed almost mocking in contrast to the gravity of his situation, multiple counts of murder, torture, trafficking. Yet he wore the prison garb like an expensive suit, somehow managing to look untouchable even in custody. His eyes, cold and calculating, scanned the room methodically, lingering on the mirror behind which we stood. Though he couldn't see us, I felt exposed under that gaze, as if he knew exactly where I was standing.

With a shaky breath that I couldn't quite control, I squeezed Abby's hand one last time before leaving the relative safety of the observation area. The short walk to the steel door felt like crossing a minefield. My heart hammered against my ribs with such force I was certain the others could hear it. As I reached for the handle, my palms were so slick with nervous sweat that my fingers slipped on the cold metal. Fear and dread consumed me from the inside out, a gnawing sensation that threatened to hollow me completely. I couldn't let it show not to my team watching behind the glass, and certainly not to Kane.

I closed my eyes and took several deep, measured breaths, counting slowly in my head. One, two, three in. Hold. One, two, three out. The trembling in my hands subsided slightly, though adrenaline still coursed through my veins like electricity. I straightened my spine, squared my shoulders, and arranged my features into what I hoped was a mask of professional detachment. Whatever happened in that room, I couldn't afford to let Kane see my fear. He fed on fear like a vampire fed on blood, drawing power from others' weakness.

Stepping into the interrogation room felt like crossing a boundary between two worlds, the safe ordered reality of law enforcement on one side and the chaotic underworld Kane represented on the other. The fluorescent lights buzzed overhead, casting harsh shadows across the institutional green walls. Kane sat at the metal table somehow still managing to look like he owned the room. His calculating gaze, cold and unrelenting, bore into me the moment I entered. Those eyes utterly devoid of empathy tracked my movement as I crossed to the chair opposite him. A chill ran down my spine despite my preparation. This was no longer just a routine assignment. it had become deeply, irrevocably personal. The memory of what he'd been doing to those fighters, what he'd done to me, burned in my mind like acid.

"I'm glad to see you survived, Jessica. If that is indeed your real name," Kane said, his voice smooth as oil on water. His words caught me off guard. I hadn't expected him to speak first, to take control of the conversation before I'd even settled in my chair.

I met his gaze directly, refusing to flinch. "Yes, Kane, it's my real name."

His lips curled into something approximating a smile, though it never reached his eyes. "I must say, I do like the new look. Is this your natural form?" He gestured vaguely at my now changed body . "If it is, I can understand how you were able to tear through your opponents in the last match." The delight in his voice made my stomach turn. His eyes gleamed with the same predatory excitement I'd seen in the arena spectators, pupils dilated, a slight flush creeping up his neck. He actually enjoyed watching the carnage unfold, the suffering he'd orchestrated like some twisted puppet master. His tongue darted out to wet his lower lip before he spoke again.

"And if you've been capable of that level of brutality all along," he continued, leaning forward until his forearms pressed against the metal table, chains clinking softly, "it must have been absolute torture for you to let those pathetic weaklings beat on you in your earlier matches." His voice dropped to a conspiratorial whisper. "Tell me, Jessica, did you enjoy finally letting loose? Finally showing what you're truly capable of? The way you tore through your opponents in the ambush" he made a ripping gesture with his hands, "was magnificent. I've never seen someone fight with such... primal instinct."

The fluorescent lights buzzed overhead as Kane spoke, casting sickly shadows across his face. His words hung between us, poisonous and provocative, referring to the other fighters who had faced me. The air in the room felt thick with his satisfaction, his complete lack of remorse for the lives he'd destroyed.

I refused to let him get under my skin, though my stomach churned with revulsion. Sitting across from him, I met his gaze with a steady one of my own, keeping my breathing measured despite the rage building inside me. My hands remained flat on the table, deliberately relaxed.

"That's none of your concern, Kane," I stated firmly, my voice low and controlled. "I'm not here to talk about me or what happened in that arena. I'm here to learn more about you and your operation." I leaned forward slightly, mirroring his posture. "This whole thing, the fighters, the drugs, the underground matches. it must have taken someone with real cunning and influence to put together." I paused, letting my next words land with precision. "And we both know you're more of a bottom feeder. So who's really pulling your strings?"

Kane's carefully constructed facade cracked. His nostrils flared and a muscle twitched violently in his jaw as anger flashed across his face. The veins in his neck bulged.

Kane's face contorted with rage. "Fuck you, bitch," he spat, saliva flying across the metal table in glistening droplets. "I'm better connected than a piece of shit like you can imagine. My contacts go all the way to the top, government officials who owe me favours, beings from other realms who'd tear you apart for sport." His lips curled into a cruel smile that revealed yellowing teeth. "Just wait until all of this is over. When I get out, and I will get out, I'll make you my little whore. From what I heard, Jeremiah had you well trained before his capture. Said you'd cry so pretty when he'd....»

Before he could finish, I lunged across the table. In a blur of movement that surprised even me, my clawed hand wrapped around his thick throat, talons digging into the soft flesh beneath his jaw. he instinctively tried to defend himself, but my supernatural strength rendered his struggles useless. His eyes bulged in sudden terror as he realised his mistake.

"Now, let me clarify something for you," I growled, my voice dropping to a dangerous register I barely recognised. I leaned closer until our faces were inches apart, close enough to smell the fear sweat beading on his skin. "You are not in charge here, and I don't give a damn about your connections or what you think they can do for you." With each word, I incrementally tightened my grip around his neck, feeling his pulse hammer frantically against my palm. "At this exact moment, I quite literally hold your life in my hands, and I will not be disrespected."

To emphasise my point, I squeezed harder, completely cutting off his airflow, and drawing blood. His face turned a mottled purple as he clawed desperately at my arm. Behind the one way glass, I knew my team was probably scrambling, debating whether to intervene. But I needed Kane to understand the power dynamic between us with absolute clarity.

When his eyelids began to flutter, I released him abruptly. He collapsed back into his chair, and he clutched at his throat, drawing in ragged, desperate breaths. Fear radiated from him in palpable waves, and I couldn't help but feel a dark satisfaction. He deserved to be scared after what he'd done to countless victims, after what he'd done to do to me.

I calmly returned to my seat, smoothing my jacket as if nothing had happened. "Now," I said, my voice returning to a professional coolness that contrasted sharply with my violent outburst, "are you ready to speak with me in a civilised manner?"

Kane nodded jerkily, one hand still massaging his throat where my claws had cut in. Four crescent-shaped wounds oozed blood between his fingers. His earlier bravado had evaporated, replaced by the wary caution of a predator who'd just discovered he was actually prey.

"Good. I want to know everything about your operation. I'm aware it involves more than just testing this drug and organising blood sports." I leaned forward slightly, maintaining eye contact. "Let's begin with who provided you with the drug and how they trained your alchemist to produce it. Leave nothing out, Kane. Your continued ability to breathe depends on it."

Kane swallowed hard, his Adam's apple bobbing painfully against the fresh wounds. "Aldrich," he rasped, voice hoarse from my grip. "Aldrich was the one who approached me first."

"Tell me everything about him," I demanded, not letting my gaze waver.

Kane shifted in his seat. "Aldrich was the guy I turned to whenever I needed to stay out of prison.head of the agency's London branch with connections everywhere. He helped me avoid serious jail time three times before, and in return, I became his go-to person for anything outside the law." A flicker of pride crossed Kane's face despite his predicament. "Started small—acquiring restricted magic artefacts, rare potions, things normal people couldn't get their hands on. But Aldrich saw potential in me."

Kane's breathing steadied as he continued. "Within two years, I was smuggling people between realms. Runaway's, criminals, anyone willing to pay. The money was incredible, and I told myself it wasn't my business what happened to them after delivery. I was just transportation."

His eyes darted to the one way glass before returning to mine. "About ten years ago, everything changed. Aldrich started asking me to find specific types homeless Paranormals, drifters, addicts. people nobody would miss. I'd collect them and ship them to different locations. Some went to facilities around the world, others through realm gates. I didn't ask questions."

Kane leaned forward, lowering his voice to a conspiratorial whisper. "As time passed, Aldrich cared less about discretion and more about numbers. Quantity became the priority. He'd send me lists—specific types he wanted. Young ones with untapped abilities. Older ones with rare gifts. he also wanted tones of normal humans.his one rule though was only take people who wouldn't be missed."

He licked his dry lips before continuing. "Then, three years ago, he introduced me to Jeremiah. That sadistic bastard had medical training and an obsession with paranormal physiology. That's when I started arranging the fights. They weren't just entertainment, they were methodical testing grounds for Aldrich's experimental compounds and Jeremiah's surgical modifications."

Kane's eyes took on a distant look. "The subjects that survived the initial treatments became the main attractions. You should have seen what they could do, enhanced strength like you wouldn't believe, accelerated healing, some even developed abilities they weren't born with. The crowds paid fortunes to watch them rip each other apart while hopped up on whatever new compound they were testing that week. Rich humans and paranormals alike, betting millions on which modified fighter would survive."

The weight of Kane's words settled in the interrogation room like a physical presence. My colleagues behind the one-way glass would be frantically recording every detail. This operation had been going on for far longer than we had realised, and on a scale we hadn't imagined.

"What else do you know?" I asked, my voice betraying my growing anger despite my efforts to remain professional. "Who funded these operations beyond the gambling?"

"Aldrich never asked for a cut of my profits," Kane continued with a shrug that made my skin crawl. "And let me tell you, I was clearing eight figures annually by the end. Private boxes alone went for fifty grand a night." He actually smiled at the memory. "Aldrich only wanted detailed reports on the outcomes, which modifications worked, which compounds produced the most dramatic effects, survival rates, combat effectiveness. All very clinical."

He tapped his fingers on the table. "Sometimes he'd have me ship the winners to other facilities. The losers who survived went to Jeremiah's lab for... salvage operations." He said this last part with such casual detachment that made me feel physically ill.

As Kane spoke without a hint of remorse, I knew with absolute certainty that we couldn't release him back into society. His actions were too despicable, his moral compass too broken. There was no telling how many more innocent lives he would destroy serving clients with the same ruthless dedication.

The words flew out of my mouth, dripping with venom. "So let me get this straight. You knowingly put people who had been tortured and experimented on into an arena to fight for their lives, all while you profited from their suffering? And you have the audacity to sit there and act like you didn't do anything wrong?"

I couldn't help but bare my new fangs at him, feeling them extend fully for the first time since my transformation, it was like a physical manifestation of the disgust and rage boiling inside me toward this monster sitting across the table.

Kane's eyes widened at the sight of my fangs. He shifted uncomfortably in his chair, finally showing a semblance of shame as he averted his gaze. "I didn't have a choice," he said weakly. "Aldrich would have killed me if I refused. And most of them didn't last more than one or two fights anyway. compared to what Jeremiah would have done to them it was merciful."

I could feel my blood boiling at his callous attitude. "And what happened to the ones who survived?" I asked, afraid of the answer but needing to know.

"They were drudged and shipped off through one of the realm gates," he replied casually, as if discussing mundane tasks. "After that, I don't know what happened to them. They were no longer my responsibility."

It took every ounce of self-control to prevent myself from reaching over and ending this monster's life then and there. The thought of all those innocent lives being discarded like trash made me sick to my stomach.

But I managed to hold back, my emotions roiling like a tempestuous sea. What about the drug? How did you get your hands on it?"

A few years ago, before he lost his position and everything that went with it, he met with me in secret. In a dimly lit room, he spilled all of his secrets about Jeremiah and his plans for other facilities to conduct his research. That's when he introduced me to the alchemist, a dark figure cloaked in mystery and power. Together, we worked tirelessly to develop the drug one that was meant to give its users a berserker like rage while also making their minds malleable and easily controlled. The added bonus was that it would provide a euphoric high, ensuring they wouldn't remember the horrific acts they committed while under its influence.

We experimented with countless combinations, but nothing seemed to produce the desired effect. Frustrated and desperate, we turned to testing on humans - but the results were catastrophic. They simply went berserk, often dying in the process.

My stomach churned at the thought of the innocent lives sacrificed for our failed experiments. "I'm done with you," I spat, my voice dripping with disgust. "But make no mistake, you will answer every question posed to you from this moment on, or else I will hand you over to a vampire council enforcer and a powerful dragon queen who have both claimed me as theirs. And they are eager to have some alone time with you." My words carried a weight of warning as I stared into his fear-filled eyes. "Do I make myself clear?"

The colour drained from his once smug face, leaving it a pale and ghostly white. The realisation that his life hung in the balance hit him like a ton of bricks. His voice shook with fear as he asked, hopefully "should I assume that i'm to be sent to Tartarus?"

I couldn't bring myself to look at him as I answered, "No, not yet. You will remain here for the foreseeable future. Until we are sure you have no further use."

As I got up and walked towards the door, I could feel his desperate gaze following me. Before leaving, I turned to face him one last time. "How does it feel to be at the mercy of another?" My words broke him completely, and as I closed the heavy metal door behind me, I could still hear his cries of anguish echoing through the empty halls.

I took a deep breath and tried to shake off the weight of what had just transpired. I didn't want to think about how vulnerable and helpless he must have felt in that moment. Instead, I focused on the blessed silence that enveloped me as I stood outside the observation room.

But my peace didn't last long. Soon enough, the door opened and I was greeted by Lyn, Abby, and Alex. Before I could say anything, Lyn pulled me into a warm embrace while Abby held onto my hand.

"Child, I never knew you had such power," Lyn chuckled. "You were truly terrifying."

Abby said nothing but her tight grip on my hand spoke volumes.

"I'm sorry for using you both as leverage against him," I admitted, feeling guilty for putting them in harm's way. "But I had to try something. And Alex, if possible, I recommend keeping him here or transferring him to a different holding facility. He seems too eager to be sent to Tartarus. Keeping him off balance may prove useful in extracting more information from him. I wanted to continue interrogating him, but the mere thought of his actions made me feel physically ill."

My stomach churned and my hands trembled as I apologised to my colleagues.

I couldn't bear to meet their gaze.

"Jessica, you did an incredible job in there. You obtained more information than I could have imagined. Now we have leads for your team to follow and a potential gold mine of information. Although it's not quite a closed case yet, we are one step closer to uncovering the mastermind behind all of this." As he spoke, the weight of the case seemed to lift just slightly, giving us a glimmer of hope in a sea of darkness and despair.

CHAPTER 25

Awaiting Command

Aldrich

My heart pounded against my ribcage as I stood before the imposing oak doors, their ancient wood scarred with symbols I recognised from grimoires forbidden to all but the highest echelons of paranormal society. My escort—a seven-foot tall monstrosity whose face remained hidden beneath a cowl of impenetrable darkness, finally removed my hood, allowing me to take in my surroundings. a dimly lit corridor of cold stone that predated modern civilisation, illuminated by torches whose flames burned an unnatural blue-green.

"Wait here until summoned," My escort commanded his voice like gravel scraping metal. and gestured toward a bench carved from a single black wood bench,

I sat, wincing as the preternatural coldness seeped through my expensive suit. Dampness clung to everything here, carrying the metallic scent of old blood beneath the mustiness. The darkness felt alive, watching, assessing. For someone who controlled a network of supernatural and human informants from across various realm, this forced subservience rankled. Yet I remained still. In the hierarchy of the collective, I was merely a mid-level operator. Important enough to be summoned rather than eliminated, but expendable nonetheless.

My last clear memory was news that the Council of Devils required my immediate presence. then I felt the sting of the injection its effects almost instantaneous the disorientation that followed was still in effect. I'd awakened in transit, blindfolded and bound, the vehicle's movement suggesting we'd left conventional roads far behind.

For years I'd served the collective, orchestrating the acquisition of artefacts and "resources" both human and otherwise. I'd heard whispers of the Devils—the ancient beings who formed our ruling council, but never dared hope for direct contact. Their existence predated recorded history. some claimed they were the original templates from which humanity derived its concepts of demons across all cultures and religions. Their true forms and names remained their most guarded secrets.

My palms slicked with sweat as I considered the possibilities. Direct summons typically meant one of two things: extraordinary promotion or immediate execution. The collective tolerated neither failure nor excessive ambition.

The silence shattered without warning.

With a thunderous groan that vibrated through the stone floor, the massive doors began to swing inward, releasing a gust of air that carried the scent of ozone and ancient power. Beyond the threshold, darkness waited, punctuated by twelve pairs of gleaming eyes arranged in a perfect semicircle—watching, evaluating, judging.

My heart hammered against my ribs as I stepped into the chamber. The ceiling soared impossibly high, disappearing into shadows where occasional flickers of movement suggested things better left unseen. Columns of obsidian rose like petrified titans, each carved with hieroglyphs that seemed to writhe and shift when viewed from the corner of my eye. Between them stood braziers of hammered bronze, their flames casting an unnatural violet light that did little to dispel the gloom.

A masked servant materialised before me, his appearance so sudden I nearly stumbled backward. His attire was unmistakably Victorian—a crisp white shirt with elaborate ruffles cascading down his chest, beneath a tailcoat of midnight black velvet that pooled around his feet like liquid shadow. The mask itself was porcelain white, featureless save for two narrow slits where eyes should be, revealing nothing but darkness within.

"My masters will see you now," he intoned, his voice resonating with unnatural depth, as though multiple throats spoke in perfect unison. "Please follow me."

I trailed behind him across a floor inlaid with precious metals that formed intricate patterns—wards and bindings, I realised, designed to contain whatever power resided here. The chamber's vastness became more apparent as we walked, revealing alcoves housing artefacts of obvious antiquity and terrible purpose. Glass cases contained withered organs floating in amber fluid. Weapons of bone and metal hung suspended in air without visible support. A crystal sphere the size of a human head pulsed with internal light, within which shadowy figures appeared to scream silently.

At the centre of this museum of horrors sat a single wooden chair, unadorned and painfully ordinary. The servant gestured toward it with a white-gloved hand.

"Please take a seat, and I will announce your arrival." The simplicity of the chair stood in stark contrast to the opulence surrounding it—a deliberate statement. Here sat the supplicant, the lesser being, while the trappings of true power encircled them. I lowered myself onto it, feeling the wood creak beneath my weight. It was uncomfortable by design, forcing me to sit straight, alert, vulnerable.

The servant glided to a position before the semicircle of watching eyes and bowed so deeply his porcelain mask nearly touched the obsidian floor. I remained perfectly still, muscles locked in place, acutely aware that even the slightest unauthorised movement in this ancient chamber could trigger my execution. My breath came in shallow, controlled measures. Whatever these Devils wanted from me, I would provide without hesitation—fifteen years of service to the Collective had honed my survival instinct to a razor's edge. I'd learned precisely when to assert myself and when to submit. This moment demanded nothing less than absolute submission.

The chamber stretched before me, its dimensions seeming to shift in the violet light. As my eyes adjusted to the gloom, I noticed that most of the thirteen ornate thrones surrounding the raised dais remained empty—all but three. These occupied seats held cloaked figures whose very stillness suggested predators watching prey. Their masked faces angled toward me with unmistakable authority, the weight of millennia behind their gaze.

The masked servant rose from his bow and stood with unnatural stiffness beside me. When he spoke, his voice filled the chamber with resonant power that belied his slender frame.

"My illustrious masters—Lord Azazel, Grand Duke Balaam, and Her Eminence, Lady Mania," he intoned with ceremonial precision. "I present to you operative Aldrich." He prostrated himself fully before them, his form becoming a dark puddle against the floor, then swept one gloved hand toward me in a gesture that clearly commanded the same obeisance.

I dropped immediately to my knees, then bent forward until my forehead pressed against the cold stone. The position was deliberately humiliating—designed to remind me of my insignificance before these ancient powers. Questions raced through my mind . What transgression had warranted this tribunal?and why where only 3 present My heart hammered against my chest as I awaited their judgment.

"Rise, Aldrich." The command came as a sharp, almost amused feminine voice that echoed through the chamber's vast expanse. I lifted my head cautiously, gaze drawn to the central figure—Mania. Even in the chamber's perpetual twilight, her presence dominated the space. Power emanated from her in palpable waves that raised the hair on my arms and neck. As my eyes adjusted further, I discerned a distinctly feminine silhouette beneath her heavy cloak of midnight silk embroidered with silver sigils that occasionally sparked with their own inner light. The mask adorning her face was a masterwork of ivory and platinum, its intricate design featuring delicate curves and feminine features that somehow enhanced rather than concealed the menace behind it. Two eyes like polished obsidian gleamed from within its confines.

"Aldrich," she continued, her voice dripping with aristocratic disdain. "You have been summoned before this tribunal to account for a series of catastrophic failings that threaten centuries of careful planning." Each precisely enunciated word cut through me like a ceremonial blade, the weight of her displeasure pressing down until breathing became difficult.

The chamber fell deathly silent as Lady Mania leaned forward upon her obsidian throne, the ancient stone seeming to absorb rather than reflect the violet light. The platinum filigree of her mask caught the torchlight as she tilted her head, studying me with predatory intensity.

"Because of your staggering ineptitude," she hissed, voice low and venomous, each syllable precisely enunciated, "we have squandered resources that took decades, not years, Aldrich, decades to amass." Her long, pale fingers drummed a deliberate rhythm on the armrest, each tap echoing like a death knell through the cavernous hall. "The entire London network lies in ruins. Seventeen human operatives are currently under interrogation by the Agency's fortunately they are only pawns and know nothing of importance."

She paused, allowing this revelation to sink in. My blood ran cold at the implication.

"And now," her tone dropped to a steel-edged whisper that nonetheless carried to every far corner of the vaulted hall, "we are forced into more direct actions to salvage what remains of our objectives, methods that expose us to unwanted scrutiny from both the agency and the paranormal council." I felt the words settle around me like toxic gas, my stomach knotting with genuine panic. In the Collective, failure was never met with mercy, and I had failed spectacularly.

"Your shoddy oversight led directly to Jeremiah's capture in Ireland," she accused, voice sharpened to a blade's edge. "This initial failure cascaded into the loss of not only a prime test subject but also our source of invaluable dragon components, fresh dragon materials are notoriously difficult to obtain and your failure lead to our dragon captive to escape ." Each syllable struck me like a hammer blow, and I could feel my ribs constrict as if caught in an invisible vice. I searched fruitlessly for a defence but found none.

She straightened, her fury building visibly as the sigils embroidered on her cloak began to pulse with silver light. "Then you further proceeded to lose not one but four research facilities across London," she continued, counting off my failures with elegant, accusatory gestures. "You failed utterly in your attempt to recapture Jeremiah's escaped experiment, who, need I remind you, carries within her genetic material worth more than everything else we've lost combined. And on top of all that," her voice rose sharply, "you botched the underground fights you were supposed to supervise that operation was perfect for testing our experiments ." Her disappointment manifested as a palpable force pressing down on my shoulders, crushing any thought of justification before it even formed.

A cold wind seemed to sweep through the room as she rose to her full height. "Explain to us how this latest catastrophe unfolded," she demanded, voice laced with aristocratic contempt. The torch flames reflected in her obsidian eyes danced wildly as she descended the three steps from her throne, advancing toward me with deliberate, measured steps. The hem of her midnight cloak whispered against the stone floor, leaving momentary trails of shadow that seemed to move independently.

"Jeremiah's test subject was alone, wounded, cornered in the arena. The compliance drug running through her system should have guaranteed her cooperation within minutes, so where is she?" She paused mere feet away, close enough that I could see the fine cracks in her ivory mask, ancient fractures sealed with what appeared to be gold. Her nostrils flared beneath the mask's apertures, as if she could literally smell my fear. "And now you've bled us of still more assets: the fighting arenas, Kane's training facilities, every affiliate business in a fifty-mile radius is under Agency scrutiny because of your blunders."

Mania's fury crescendoed into a roar that rattled dust from the vaulted ceiling far above. "Tell me, Aldrich," she demanded, leaning so close I could feel the unnatural cold radiating from her form, "has anything anything at all you've touched in the past six months gone according to plan?"

My throat constricted, a thousand unsaid apologies coiled in my chest. I sat rigid beneath Mania's unrelenting glare, aware that no excuse, no mitigation or explanation, could shield me from the reckoning I so clearly deserved. Each silent second stretched into an eternity as her wrath bore down on me like a physical weight.

I could feel the truth burning in my bones. On paper, my failures in London looked catastrophic, operations I'd overseen had collapsed in ruin, allies lost, strategies blown to ruin . And though I had no direct hand in the Ireland fiasco, I knew they would not concern themselves with technicalities. I knew that the next time Mania spoke, it would be to pronounce my death sentence.

Before Mania could unfurl her verdict, a low, velvety voice cut through the tension. The speaker was Balaam, tall impeccably dressed in silken robes that caught the torchlight, his presence commanding yet measured. His words slid into the room like warm oil, smoothing the edges of hostility with subtle persuasion. I felt a shiver race down my spine as he addressed Mania.

"Now, my dear Mania," Balaam intoned, each syllable deliberate, almost caressing. "Let us not be hasty. The mandate we all agreed on was not to condemn, but to reassign. Am I correct?" He swept a graceful hand toward the empty seats circling us—each seat bore the insignia of one council member, all conspicuously unoccupied.

Mania's lips pressed into a thin line, but she said nothing. I seized a breath. "Wait... I'm not being punished?" My voice cracked, betraying how desperate I was for any reprieve.

Balaam's eyes—dark as oil—rested on me. He shrugged, as if dismissing a trivial point. "Not at this moment," he replied softly. "Yet heed this well: the Council's mercy is not infinite. Should you fail again, there will be no second chances. Your past service, your victories, your innovations, have earned you this single reprieve. Do not squander it."

His words settled over me like a shroud. I swallowed, the pressure in my throat easing just enough to think again. The silhouettes of unseen councillors seemed to lean closer, hungry for my reaction.

Balaam's voice cut through my thoughts. "This is your final opportunity to prove your worth," he said, each word resonating through the chamber like a tolling bell. The air itself seemed to constrict around me, every breath a labor. Time slowed until I felt rooted in place, as if the world had paused to watch my answer.

"I understand," I managed, my voice barely more than a rasp.

Balaam nodded. "Good. As for your next assignment… it is time for Tartarus to fall."

His declaration reverberated in my bones. Tartarus an impregnable fortress of legends, said to harbour the most depraved criminals throughout all the realm.the prison stood like an eternal sentinel at the crossroads between realms. To bring it down would require every ounce of cunning, every ally I could muster. Yet I knew the stakes, succeed and I might salvage my honour, fail and death would be the kindest sentence.

Printed in Dunstable, United Kingdom